$\mathcal{D}$ EATH ^{AND} _{THE} MAIDEN

J. I. RADKE

DREAMSPINNER PRESS

Published by
DREAMSPINNER PRESS

5032 Capital Circle SW, Suite 2, PMB# 279, Tallahassee, FL 32305-7886 USA
http://www.dreamspinnerpress.com/

ISBN: 978-1-63476-498-8
Digital ISBN: 978-1-63476-499-5
Library of Congress Control Number: 2015942827
First Edition September 2015

Printed in the United States of America
∞
This paper meets the requirements of
ANSI/NISO Z39.48-1992 (Permanence of Paper).

To all those who are still afraid of the dark, who never give up on forever, and who still smile about what they love.

ACKNOWLEDGMENTS

For you who never turned away during the wee hours, for the world you helped me build, the rants and tangents you patiently endured (more than once, I'm sure), the faith you never lose, and the support that never fails, for the inspiration you never cease to spark in me—thank you. I couldn't do anything without you.

There are more things in heaven and earth, Horatio, than are dreamt of in your philosophy.
Hamlet (1.5.167-8)

PART ONE
LITTLE LAMB, STAINED IN RED
LONDON, 1888

If this will satisfy thy mind, thy whim I'll gratify, howe'er absurd.
"Blood is a juice of very special kind...."
    Goethe, *Faust*

CHAPTER ONE

AUGUST ESCAPED.

Out the window and onto the attic roof while his little maid stepped away to empty the chamber pot.

It was only a handful of minutes, but it was short-lived eternity to August. He was sick; he knew he was sick. The fever raged in his veins. He could have lost his footing and fallen off the roof, surely, but it was blissful, momentary *freedom.*

The little maid returned to an attic full of cold air and smoking candles, leaded northern window shoved open as far as it could go, and August gone from his bed.

"Help!" she stammered, all panic and soft black plaits under her lace cap. "*Help!*"

August clung to a blackened chimney stack as the nighttime wind tried to pry him away like an ember from a hearth. This was a dream, surely. The air kissed his hot face cool, and the bruises too, and the clots on his throat and neck. The roof tiles scraped his bare toes. Vertigo rattled him with delicious chills. London sprawled out around the rooftop.

London.

He knew this area; he knew that square with its plane trees and Munro statue. Beyond, not too far beyond, was the West End, in all its nocturnal glory, and the shadows of Westminster clawing for the sky.

Inside the attic, the little maid still shrieked for help. August swallowed a deep gulp of fresh night air, hugging the chimney stack and closing his eyes. "Scream all you want…," he hummed to himself, and he didn't mean it out of cruelty. Maybe out of apology. He'd escaped. He could make his way across the roof to other roofs and monkey down on the vines of a house. He'd never done something like that before but he could probably manage it, and then he could run—find someone who could help him, a constable or some good stranger—that is, if the feverish wooziness went away—

"*August!*"

August opened his eyes in a flutter of lashes. A shiver twisted down to his bones and his grin of triumph crumbled away. Mouth hanging open, he looked around to the attic window.

Two faces beckoned him from the open casement. There was the little maid, her big gray eyes close to shattering into tears, and beside her one of *them*—the monsters, the kidnappers, the torturers.

One of the *vampires*.

The vampire had called his name.

August's heart fell. "Go away!" he croaked. He didn't want to think about how the vampire knew his name. Had he told any of them? The urgency to escape, to keep going and get away, slithered under his skin—but he couldn't move.

The vampire in the window had caught his gaze. The vampire's eyes were green, a sharp and charming green. They cut through August. They stirred him up inside. They made him blush.

"I know you," August whispered, and the vampire's expression twitched. But it was a curious thing, saying "I know you." It was like talking while sleeping and waking up to one's own words, the meaning and origin of which remained undefinable. The understanding was there and then gone again, like a bat in the night.

August felt stupid, suddenly, sick and stupid because of course he knew the vampire.

The vampire lived in the house.

The vampire fed on him like all the rest of the vampires in the house fed on him and had been for the last few nights.

"Come back inside," the vampire in the attic window called sweetly, tenderly, this vampire with the green eyes and the finger-combed hair and the silver-damasked high-collared waistcoat. He didn't seem all that proud of begging the house's human to come back inside, rather than the opposite as myth and folklore decreed, but he also seemed markedly distressed, reaching out for August, imploring August with all his undead charm to come back to the window, back inside.

The desire to flee faded away.

August stared. The wind buffered him, tugged at him. Suddenly escape couldn't hold a candle to being back in the attic room with the vampire and the maid, back in bed safe and warm and ready to sleep.

August sighed. It sounded more like a defeated moan than it felt. He was so tired. He was shaking. He needed to lie down. He was ill, remember? He was ill.

August edged back toward the window, clutching the chimney stack. He lost his footing but he didn't fall. His nightshirt fluttered about his knees and he laughed at his brief loss of balance because it made his heart leap and his head spin, which was a delightfully ticklish sensation. Like a night well spent with the green fairy, or Turkish cigarettes.

The vampire was not so amused. He was impatient. In one smooth, decisive motion, he climbed up across the windowsill and out onto the roof with August. The maid cried out in horror. But the vampire navigated the Collyweston roof with a bold finesse, and drew August in against his chest without an ounce of resistance.

The vampire closed his arm around August's waist. Like a dance partner, he hoisted August up ho-hum with that one elbow, enough that August didn't have to stand on his own anymore. It was definitely a feat. August wasn't all that much smaller than the vampire. The night sky was thick with smog and smoke beyond the vampire's scowl.

And August thought that maybe this green-eyed vampire would be the only one of them that he liked.

This vampire smelled like wine and sweet candles. He stormed out with a ferocious slam of the attic door as soon as he'd deposited August back safely in bed, but August didn't mind one bit.

The vampire had saved him. Surely the vampire was his friend.

The little maid cried into her pinafore for a few moments, leaning against the closed window with shaking knees. August covered his head with the pillow and wished the room would stop spinning. He shivered. When the maid finally approached him, bitterly, he put down the pillow and said, "Sorry for scaring you...."

The maid glared and shoved a rather healthy dose of Daffey's at him. August fell asleep quickly.

AUGUST KNEW nothing but the attic, the sunset, and his feverish, memoryless existence. It was as good as being dead.

All right, *memoryless* was a lie.

August remembered. A little bit at least—some things, important things, enough to piece together that they had taken him.

The *vampires*.

From some other place, some other time, some other life, some other *him*, they'd taken him, and those other details he couldn't remember, but he was theirs and they kept him in the attic until they needed him.

And now the windows were nailed shut.

August knew a total of seven things for sure, if only because they were the immediate present.

One—his name was August Quincy Prescott, and he was a fresh young bachelor at twenty-three years of age.

Two—they'd come for him in the night because they were vampires. Logically it couldn't be; realistically it *was*.

Three—he was there for the vampires to feed upon.

Whoever had started the rumor that vampires wasted a human in one deadly embrace was either quite the storyteller or had not met vampires like the ones in this house. These vampires had rules, it seemed, and some manner of regulation, and one of those rules or regulations was that the vampires did not sink their fangs in to kill once and for all. These strangely sophisticated creatures were like the men and women of some upside-down London, where monsters looked and spoke and dressed like everyone else but took turns drinking tiny sips of blood from the throat and wrist and sometimes even the fingertip of a young man they kept in the attic. *Him*.

Four—the world was not what August thought it was, but he couldn't for the life of him remember details about the world as he'd known it before. This conundrum exhausted him. It was terrifying to be so suddenly empty of self—cold, hollow present divided quite manifestly from a past that felt close, felt multidimensional and important, but that held no shapes or names or colors to unfold.

And yet maybe it was also sort of freeing.

The other things August knew for sure because somehow they were flashes in the memorylessness that connected the empty, inhospitable *before* with the shocking reality of *now*, fleeting but indisputable, like shapes and shadows burned into his eyelids after staring at the sun. Enough for him to understand, but not enough for him to know more.

He remembered the hook-nosed vampire who'd snatched him out from amongst the finely dressed London crowds he knew so well, away from whomever his friends and family were. The hook-nosed vampire was not one of the vampires in the house. He'd been a mess of flashy rags and a beardless face. Never mind thieves and beggars; in all the hypnotizing colors and sounds of the West End on a damp autumn night, with fingers like claws and a flurry of thrashing limbs, it was this monster who dragged August right into the nearest alley and knocked him out with one hard blow to the back of his head.

August also remembered being cold, very cold, and dizzy, and confused. He didn't know where the hook-nosed vampire had taken him, but wherever it was, there were more like him. They gripped him with their strange hands, and their sharp teeth pierced his throat and his wrists like vicious little love bites. They lapped up sips of his blood and laughed when he screamed and wrestled. They were boisterous and rough like seedy men in a pub; they smelled strongly of dirt and something strangely metallic. Up became down and down became up and it was a blur of blood-stained strangers pawing at his hair and his clothes as he stumbled and swam amongst them, foggy and frantic as a drunk. Hell. He was in hell. They were not trying to kill him, he realized. They played with him as a cat played with a mouse, as if they were *testing* him, and then there was the cluster of narrow, filthy cells under the church.

What church, August didn't know now, and he hadn't known then. *Vampires. They're vampires. They've kidnapped me and they're vampires.* Kidnapped, yes, for ransom. His father had surely made some poor gamble or another—August was in trouble and it wasn't even his fault, or something. That made sense. That suspicion felt clear and instinctual. The rest was a mystery. The sound of church bells drifted down through the earth like thunder, down into the almost-dungeon, as torches in ancient sconces cast long shadows across the bitter chill and disconsolation of dank stone and loose, dirt-covered ground.

There were others—young men; older men; pretty, crying ladies. Rationality receded and August gave in to cold, witless panic. Witless? Could a man even be witless if he hadn't a clue who he was and from whence he came? His head ached; his joints were stiff. Every muscle sang sore songs and every movement was punctuated by the sharp, inhospitable clack and rattle of iron from the rusty shackle biting at his ankle, and a surge of irrational courage sent August charging for the iron bars of the cell only once, to shout hoarsely, "What's going on?

Where am I? Who are you? Where are you? My father's going to bring the authorities, don't you doubt for—"

He remembered the chain at his ankle jerking him backward roughly; he tumbled down in a knot of elbows and knees and it knocked the wind out of him with the interrupted words, a frantic moan of uncertainty. Others in neighboring cells hissed at him to hush up. Some begged to know whether it was true about his father. A boy in a dark corner of August's cell hummed to himself as he impaled spiders with the pointed end of a pin from his shirt.

August believed in God and the devil, of course.

He believed in spiritualists even though they said not to. They said it wasn't virtuous or enlightened. They—who? His father. His older brothers. Maybe. He was guessing now. Trying to summon names or faces was an uncomfortable tickle in his head, reaching, stretching, groping around with weak fingers for anything but finding nothing in the place of his identity. Never mind that; every man and woman on God's green earth had fallen irreconcilably in love with darkness of various flavors—ghost conjuring, fortunetelling, tragedy, creatures of oddity and ghastly curiosity.

But oh, what would they all say if they knew the beloved fairy-tale monsters of penny dreadfuls were *real*? They were real. They were very real, and they'd taken August away—

He and the other humans were held hostage as prizes for an auction. August remembered that with stunning clarity.

In the moonlit dark, the vampire auctioneer had stood atop a vast hexagonal mausoleum of Portland stone and flint, the names of its inhabitants carved above granite angels, urns, and columns. Wandering past the graves and up the long hill, gathering under the mausoleum as if attending some great Season affair, was a large flock of strangers. *More vampires.* But they looked perfectly normal, nothing like drawings or books said. They were a horribly misleading bunch— ladies and gentlemen in furs and overcoats and dancing mufflers, pretty hats, bowler caps, glittering attentive eyes. They nodded, they winked, they whispered behind gloved hands together. Sharp little fangs flashed in their smiles. Hills rolled off into the distance from the churchyard, dotted by gnarled trees and broken fences. Little homes far away spilled warm light from their windows, strangers within utterly unaware of the auction in the country cemetery.

August remembered exactly the way the auctioneer had stood atop the mausoleum and made the sign of the cross upside-down across his chest, the way the vampires below emulated the gesture, and as if reciting a prayer or a hymn, or a pledge to royalty, the auctioneer's voice had filled the cemetery, chillingly festive:

"My brothers and sisters, pay heed! 'For the life of the flesh is in the blood: and I have given it to you upon the altar to make an atonement for your souls, for it is the blood that maketh an atonement for the soul!'"

The crowd murmured a resounding elegy:

"To he who has been elected according to the choice of Christ, the Most Holy Lamb, blessed and sanctified by the blood of the Spirit—in sacrament and in honor, for salvation through sin, in the name of the Lord, the dead teach the living. In nomine Domini, mortui vivos docent!"

One by one, all the way down the rows of shivering, bruised, and bitten prisoners, the humans were auctioned off, hoisted high into the air with unnatural strength by a boorish dark vampire with silver and gold rings in his ears, then announced gaily by the auctioneer with his long coattails and ribbon-cinched hair. Tears and prayers and terrified shouts were one with the murmuring chorus of the vampires gathered for the sale.

August peered down from the top of the mausoleum at the milling crowd, unsure whether he should really be afraid or not. How could curiosity be so bold? He wanted to observe; he wanted to know what was going on. There in the auctioneer's strong hand, ripped mercilessly and without cause or explanation from a life he couldn't remember—a life meaningless and irretrievable—

August remembered feeling strangely empty of hopelessness.

Maybe it had to do with the absence of memories. Whatever it was, it was a little more comforting somehow. It was easier to know nothing. He guessed knowing something would have made it all unbearable. But everything beyond that moment seemed otherworldly and dreamlike as voices rippled and the wind tugged and clawed at him, and by the auctioneer's proclamation he was reduced to a set of apparently appealing features.

"Tender age of twenty-three! Blond hair! Brown eyes! Fine in stature, strong constitution, immense pranic energy! *First offer!*"

An offer was made, confirmed, and finalized into a purchase, and the auctioneer pushed August over the high edge of the mausoleum.

A vampire caught him but August was still panic-stricken from the drop. He remembered thunder in the dark. It made him jump. He remembered very clearly that in the shadows of the church on the hill, he wobbled before the vampire who bought him. The vampire's smile was cordial, softening the angular face of a veritable gentleman; his sharp penetrating eyes glinted in the darkness. A few threads of gray accented his neatly clipped honey-colored hair. Nothing about him screamed monster but for the flash of tiny fangs behind his full, normal-looking lips.

"I am the Alpha," this vampire gentleman said, his voice deep and placatory, grosgrain. "And I own you now."

THESE WERE the things August remembered. With the few hazy things he knew, what he remembered did not seem to make sense, but maybe that was because he had no idea how much time had passed since. Either way he did not want to forget. He thought them over and over like memorizing a poem, trying to carve them into his mind lest they go flitting away like family, friends, childhood, and the rest of him.

After the auction, there had been a dark, musty tunnel, the smell of dirt again, water dripping somewhere. Consciousness drifted in and out like a candle in the night. A set of broad, richly carved doors opened up before him and the Alpha with an old, inanimate yawn. Blinding white, white everywhere, cool air and white everywhere, and candles, the heady scent of blood and incense. Somebody touched August, took his wrist. The room spun, spun, spun.

The Alpha sank his teeth into August's throat at some point, and August's wrist throbbed, so maybe he'd been bitten there too. *Testing. Tasting.* Everything ached. He was soaking wet, he was cold, and he was confused. The Alpha brought him through a new place: coffered ceiling, cobwebbed chandeliers, giltwood angel faces. Lamplight shadows slithered on the Alpha's face, around every smooth angle and contour.

It was the vestibule of a luxurious Georgian townhouse passing by then, candelabras ablaze, the shadows of dark furniture floating dimly above the floor. Up a set of splendid stairs, into the womb of the house they went. Carpeted halls and rosewood-paneled walls. Vases and urns and painted roses, thick dusty drapes with golden chains and tassels. A young lady peeked out of a doorway, watching curiously.

She couldn't have been very old at all, mint-colored tea gown dusting her toes and Caesar-inspired leaves perched in her blonde hair.

She caught August's half-conscious stare and smiled cattily before she slipped without a sound back into the room.

The world moved around him and August felt as if he were falling for a moment, falling into a bed of cool sheets in an attic room—oh, he *was*—and it was bliss.

Here in this attic room, it was bliss until it was failed escape.

But the green-eyed vampire saved him from falling off the roof, and August knew that for sure.

"HE'S *GORGEOUS*, though," Anastasia purred, which seemed only natural for the catlike expressions she wore so well.

She meant the sacrifice. *August Prescott*, Alistair had said his name was when he returned with him from the Buckinghamshire auction. And he was special, according to the Lamb.

God, Theo couldn't wait until the adjustment period was through. He wanted to taste the new sacrifice again so badly. He wanted August Prescott's blood blooming on the tip of his tongue; he wanted the shiver of August Prescott's life under his fingertips as he had had it on the roof that reckless night last week, when the feverish sacrifice almost *got away*—

"But who left the window unlocked?" Laurel asked, sitting with a thumb pressed to one of his fangs, a habit recycled from nail-biting, and Theo tried to look as if he'd been listening the whole time.

Like a pleasant family or cozy colleagues, the vampires gathered in the lounge with hearth ablaze and candles dancing, lying about on fine upholstered seats, drinking the Baron's Remedy.

It was always the Baron's Remedy until the adjustment period was over—rationed blood on the nights the sacrifice was not brought to the Sanctuary. Thick, dark rationed blood from a jug supplied by a Blood Baron, fresh enough, of course, but far from the luxury of a regular coven sacrifice. As soon as this August Prescott was well enough, once his fever and delirium broke, yes, the adjustment period would be over and there would be no more wincing through quickly souring blood, wondering just from whence it came and how long it had already been in the jug before being delivered to the coven's

Berkeley Square townhouse. There would be blood every other night from a warm, sweet-tasting throat. There would be a heartbeat on the tongue. Not the occasional blood clot to spit out like a fruit pit.

Theo almost gagged on a long mouthful of the Baron's Remedy. He'd spoiled himself pining for August Prescott even for just a moment. *Stop, stop imagining it.* He'd go mad.

August.... Soft, wavy blond hair, even softer skin, with that vitality about him that was so sweet, so taut and supple, so typical of young men whose youth clung to their edges well into practical adulthood. He was strong but narrow, grown but tender still. Breaking through that flesh was like closing his mouth on a fresh peach. They had fed on him four times already, only four times in the past fortnight, and it was a sweet, sweet torture. Tiny sips, adhering to ritual so as not to destroy the man. Tiny, tormenting swallows that tasted like the sacrifice's fear—no. Not fear.

Theo had tasted *hatred* and *curiosity* at once, and it took all his strength of will not to grab August Prescott by the back of the neck and kiss him hard when he was in Theo's arms in the Sanctuary. Theo couldn't say why. He blamed the hunger. The time between the last sacrifice and this new one had been too long, too long for certain. It made quite the desperate fatalist out of an Undead gentleman.

"I'm sure that damn girl did it," Ishmael grumbled. They were still on the topic of the window, apparently. A wine glass of rationed blood hung daintily from Ishmael's pale fingers. His face was too aglow with undying youth for his no-nonsense scowl; it was more like a contemptuous pout. "Correct me if I'm wrong, but didn't she want to air the room out after Twenty-Eight died?"

"She did," Owen confirmed with a nod.

Alistair, with his neatly combed hair and somber dark suit, reassured his coven, "She's been punished. Adequately, I assure you. I've had the maids lock every casement in the house and turn in their window keys to me. The problem's been fixed, simple as that."

"It's only the third time it's happened in seventy years, Ishmael," Pearle reminded him. Ishmael wasn't comforted. He sat unmoving and unmoved. Anastasia giggled from where she perched atop the piano, wanting bosom very obvious at the rather racy neckline of her dress, an old gauzy Empire silhouette.

Alistair shrugged, raising his brows. "I find it quite amusing, actually. The sacrifice, escaping to the roof.... What a feisty one we've got! Thankfully our hero Theo acted calmly enough."

"Theo? Calm? Ha!"

"Oh, our savior! Saint Theo!"

"We'll nail the window shut, then. Satisfied?"

"Why haven't we done that before?" Owen snapped.

"Well, I like to believe we're a little more humane than that, Owen...."

Laughter rolled between them like thunder from one corner of the room to the other—simpering there, sneering here, Pearle's sentimental chuckles and Alistair's questionable smile. Yes, from one to the other, all of them, fine-looking gentlemen and their one lady, sharing their Baron's Remedy ration of blood like coffee and sweets after dinner in the smoking room.

Our hero Theo, except not. Theo was just a miserable starving vampire who knew better than to let the coven's transitioning sacrifice escape across the goddamn roof.

Gorgeous, Anastasia had said about the new sacrifice. Theo had thought so too, immediately. Alistair went to Buckinghamshire as the Lamb proposed; he'd returned with a bleary-eyed and bumbling new coven sacrifice properly marked and recorded, and Theo had watched from the music room with Anastasia, watched as Alistair half carried, half guided the bruised and bloodied sacrifice up to the attic where his maid would nurse him back to a healthy enough state.

It was a law, after all. For every ten vampires in a coven, there was one sacrificial lamb to feed upon. Feeding on any mortal outside the coven was grave criminality. Thus the Baron's Remedy during adjustments and transitions between sacrifices.

Theo avoided the glances of the others, each quick and pointed but none cast his way at the same time. Surely none of them really thought him a hero; the word felt cruel and mocking, and Theo scowled down into his ruddied wine glass.

Pearle motioned for Alphonse to strike up the violin. Theo's insides ached with the hunger. Alas, on the Baron's Remedy it was never satisfied.

Owen leaned to Alistair and offered obligingly, "I'll talk to that undertaker on Fleet Street. I'm sure he's got some coffin nails to spare for the attic windows."

CHAPTER TWO

AUGUST WASN'T dead, just in a foreign place—with a deep throbbing ache in his neck and crawling up his wrist. He was sticky with sweat and squirming in the sheets, and there it was again, the mantra, the prayer, inconsistent and desperate.

They've kidnapped me. They're going to eat me, they're going to hurt me, and oh God, they've kidnapped me.

No.

They're vampires, they're vampires, they've kidnapped me and they're vampires.

August tossed and turned in the bed, fitful and feverish. That little maid came with a tray of food.

"You need to eat," she told him. "You belong to them now," she tried to explain, among other things. "They're vampires, the 'Undead'—not dead, but not alive. They're really just like you and me, except they dine on blood instead of food or drink, and they don't age, nor do they procreate." She stopped for a moment. Then she said, more like an order than a promise, "You're going to live."

August couldn't remember what cruel words he flung at her as she tried to feed him, and he begged her to leave him alone if she wasn't going to break him out, because how dare she, clearly a human, help keep him hostage here.

Not that he honestly wanted to *break out* anymore.

Really he just wanted to talk to the green-eyed vampire who had saved him.

He was scared of the shadows in the plain, empty attic room, and he was scared of the bright sunlight spilling in through the curtainless windows, and he was scared when the sound of the door opening woke him up—but it was mostly just the maid who came to feed him, to bathe him, to check on him and swim in his vision for a while. Then it was the Alpha, the one who bought him, come to take him downstairs for the feeding.

The dark halls were lit by fat candles and reeked of mold beyond the decorative flowers. August was embarrassed of the way his head cocked back so easily at the vampires' touch. He was too tired to fight their sharp teeth, hungry mouths masquerading as kisses. He was terrified of himself for wanting to understand what was going on. And then he was back upstairs in the attic, tingling with exhaustion.

Faces and voices swirled. "The Sanctuary" the vampires called the room where they passed August from arm to arm like some rented lover. His blood stained their lips red like rouge.

But they were careful with him. They needed him apparently. He was special to them somehow.

"Not too much, he's already ill—"

"Finally a sacrifice!"

"I want a clean entry…." August was nodding off, dizzy, but then one of them sank his teeth into his shoulder and he growled in defiance and swung a few fists. That was just crossing the line.

This happened every three nights.

The little maid cleaned and bandaged all the bites, up in the attic. She brought syrups to soothe his cough, his fever, opiate remedies and elixirs that made the room spin. She left him to toss and turn and dream and weep. Surely he had known freedom before; surely there was some other place and time to which he belonged, not this servitude and isolation.

August woke up one late afternoon to the maid unwrapping the bandage on his wrist. Underneath there was a scar, still pink and soft. It was obviously a branding—a little *l o n* carved just below the cleft of his palm.

Once, he stirred awake to the Alpha standing across the attic room, hands clasped behind his back as he stared at him in deep contemplation. August hid under the covers, but when he peeked out, the Alpha was gone again. Maybe he'd never been there in the first place.

At some point the maid peeled off his striped nightshirt and cotton shorts. She sponged him down while he shivered and mumbled about modesty and decency. She didn't listen. Maybe she could tell he didn't have the strength to pretend to mind those things. Maybe it was just the moral division of the working and middle class. She tended to his wounds and tucked him back into bed and locked the attic door after leaving.

Memory made a person.

August remembered almost nothing.

There was nothing but *them*, the vampires, drinking his blood in the Sanctuary. Nothing but the feverish tossing and turning, the recital of the things he knew and the things he remembered, the echo of life beyond the locked attic door all night long.

God knew how many nights it was after he tried to escape and the green-eyed vampire saved him that the fever finally broke and August rolled over to fix his eyes on his little maid.

She was small—surely no older than him—and with the dark wool of her livery and her darker hair and the dark circles under her eyes, her soft pale face was like the moon peeking through a cloudy night.

She lit the candles in the attic with an old taper. August watched. He licked his dry lips and said huskily, "What's your name?"

"Hazel." She didn't look at him; she moved across to the foot of the bed, where she replaced the hot water bottle at his feet.

August was satisfied. It was good to place a name with the face of the girl who had been taking care of him. She even bathed him, after all.

August looked out the northern window. He could watch the colors change as the sky deepened beyond dusk and into the heavy blue of night, stars choked by the usual smog and fog.

Hazel stopped, arms crossed. She studied August silently, owl eyed and grave. Finally she observed, "You look very awake."

August offered a noncommittal grunt in response. Hazel squinted at him from the foot of the bed. He didn't want to meet her eyes. He wasn't angry at *her*, anyway.

Still he demanded, "Why haven't I died yet?"

Hazel rolled her eyes. Without missing a beat, she replied, "Because you're not going to." There was nothing cheery about it, nothing grim. It was stuck somewhere between the two where there was no room for unnecessary drama.

"Why?" August croaked next, brow knotting.

The look on Hazel's face shifted, maybe a little injured by his sharp glance. August tried to mend it, sitting up on one elbow and imploring her with a gentle frown. The flames danced on the candles in their baroque silver sticks.

"I've read the books," August pressed stubbornly, even though instinct told him it wasn't so. "I know what *they* do. They are going to slowly drain me until I die. They're vampires."

With plenty of disregard for the virtue of deference or ladylike decorum, Hazel snorted. She parried curtly, "You don't believe that, and you know it."

"Why wouldn't I?" August fired back. "Why *shouldn't* I?"

"Because you don't. You know you don't." Hazel cast him a glance of reproof, mouth tight and eyes hooded. She straightened the blankets at the foot of his bed as if she needed somewhere to channel the impatience. "You'll find that they are very different from word of mouth and literature," she explained thinly.

And then suddenly everything about her changed. Her dark eyes challenged him still, but her cold frown was much more sympathetic. She gripped her pinafore in little handfuls at her sides.

She said, "You're the sacrifice to vampires now. They are your masters and your mistress, and you are their lamb. They feed on you to prevent the terrorizing of random Londoners. Yes, think about it that way—thanks to you they're not out on the streets stalking innocent strangers. You'd better get over yourself, sir, and quick, because your life has changed."

August gawked mutely.

He was angry and he felt sick because he was quite aware of what use he served to the vampires. To have Hazel thrust it in his face was something else entirely. He wanted to contest it. But her argument rang all sorts of truthful chords, and he looked away lest she see the helpless frustration sour his face.

"How long have I been here?" August mumbled.

"A little over a fortnight," Hazel said. Her voice was light and impersonal again as she drifted over to the door. Her fingers cradled the crystal knob as she waited, as if wanting August to say something more before she left. Her eyes were sad. August wanted to believe it was because she hated having to deliver such ghastly news. Barely a fortnight, really? He would have sworn it had been longer, but fevers had a way of playing with time.

Sacrifice.

The memorylessness was good for one thing, August supposed. It saved him the trouble of having to untangle and reweave the entire tapestry of the world. He was free of obligation, free of prescribed probity, free of troublesome convictions, free to adapt.

And maybe that was not so bad.

"My name is August," he said after a moment of wracking his mind for something appropriate to say in the uncertain silence. Just speaking it aloud made him feel real. He relaxed without knowing he'd been tense.

Hazel stared at him. For a moment in the glow of candlelight, she didn't look tired and strained. She actually looked a little beautiful.

"I'll be back with your breakfast," she announced as she opened the attic door to leave. She paused in the threshold, adding over her shoulder, "The name 'August' doesn't suit you, by the by. You're a small, bitter little gentleman."

AUGUST.

It meant "great" or "powerful," even "magnificent." August was memoryless, not uneducated.

But Hazel was right. He didn't feel great, or powerful, or magnificent either.

He decided he should have been absolutely terrified, but now that he was awake and aware, he couldn't bring himself to truly be afraid.

A house of vampires….

By definition vampires were supposed to be dead. At least halfway, according to fiction. They were immortal except under the rays of the sun and they drank the blood of humans to sustain themselves.

But the vampires who kept him seemed very much alive and well.

They made August think of *Carmilla* or Polidori's Ruthven—full of social graces and tricking their victims into believing they were beautiful, even honorable, before their handsome faces opened gaunt and wide upon sharp fangs, an inescapable mistake. Oh God, they were *real*.

Time was a confusing element in the dark.

August learned the schedule as his sleep cycles shifted. He decided he would start praying when he woke up at dusk and when he went to sleep at dawn, no matter how miserably exhausted he was and how much more inclined to tumble into dreams than kneel reverently at his bedside.

The feeding hour was every three nights, at midnight.

The Alpha arrived and stood in the attic doorway, holding his hand outstretched. There were other servants in the house, it seemed. A maid August had never seen before made the sign of the cross as they passed her in the hall. August wanted to stop and look at the cases of pinned butterflies and the old oil paintings, the ornate clocks and other glinting Victorian decorations.

"Hurry up," the Alpha said over his shoulder. "You're feeling better, aren't you?"

Hidden behind french paneling in the drawing room was the Sanctuary. The other vampires lounged on old tight seats and couches, elaborately twisted oak and stately silk, velvet, leather.

They waited with ashen faces and bags beneath their eyes, and the quiet rang with their anticipation. They were like wolves tailing a kill; they were like socialites waiting for evening tea. There were eight of them.

Flames crackled beneath an old mantle flanked by marble gargoyles. *Vampires.* August was fascinated. He could not pretend he wasn't. Somehow the dread and the terror went away in the Sanctuary. August had a feeling it came from them, some black magic supernatural persuasion, perhaps, that warped all the fear into a twisted acquiescence. He wanted to be angry about it. But more than that, he just wanted to understand what had become of him.

That was the physical horror of it, yes, not to mention petting hands or utter negligence. August wasn't sure which he preferred, a vampire who personalized the act or who dragged and shoved him like a prop. As if in some Bacchanalian orgy, their bewitching smiles promised pleasure and their open mouths promised death. Their eyeteeth extended into fangs as they craned toward his throat. How was it possible for something to be monstrous and human at the same time? A questionably intimate embrace became the penetration of skin by two jabbing teeth, his blood rolling back on a vampire's cool tongue.

The Alpha's smile scared August. The tap into his blood was a sickening pinch; it burned through his veins and knotted his stomach.

They fed in an order he recognized but couldn't justify. He had to differentiate between them somehow, though. The Alpha was Number One, then, and Number Two had faint scratchy stubble and scars that puckered his face. He always seemed apologetic. Number Three sipped from August's finger, no eye contact, no comfort. Four sneered, "I want a clean entry," and drove his fangs into the slope between August's neck and shoulder.

"*Ishmael*," the Alpha spat, and the fire popped and August shuddered as the pain made him gag.

Five was the only girl, the girl in taffeta and muslin from the doorway that first night. She broke the skin on August's inner wrist to drink. Her eyes were icy blue; her fingers ran through his hair as a mother's might have.

Six was the green-eyed vampire.

Six made August blush.

Six made the whole event quite bearable. Six had that loose, messy brown hair, finger-combed and breaking into soft almost-curls where it fell out from behind his ears. Six reached for August, pulled him from the girl. Blood ran down into August's palm but he didn't think about it. Every nerve in his body was alive with pain, but it kept him focused.

He liked it, the closeness with Six as their hearts beat in time and the pain wove together with the pleasure like some completely new idea altogether—why did he like it? It was torment, but torment of what kind? It broke down his morals. What morals? He groaned, yielding to Six's touch. Six had brought him in from the roof. Six made him feel safe. Six was his only friend.

Six suddenly fisted his fingers in August's hair and caught his mouth in a kiss, and August went stiff with panic.

Chords of alarm rang through him. Deviant, wayward, unvirtuous, wicked—guiltily *thrilling*—men didn't kiss men—and strangers certainly didn't kiss strangers—that's what they said—not the vampires, *they* from before, *they* whom August couldn't remember—the same *they* who told him he was too romantic, too dreamy, too obsessed with books and music and art to be a practical, respectable gentleman—

August's eyes fluttered shut. His wrist throbbed and his throat throbbed and the room spun from the blood loss, but he tilted his head back to part his lips and give in to Six's curious tongue.

Their mouths moved together, ripe with desire. Six's teeth grazed his lower lip. The teasing scrape of fangs was far from threatening. It was alluring. August shuddered. Lust sparked under his skin. What was wrong with him? He forgot to worry about getting blood from his wrist on Six's clothes as he clung tight. Men didn't kiss men, no, but August was very sure he'd done this before. It was familiar and comforting, and Six, the green-eyed one, the one who'd gotten him off the roof, Six felt more human than any of them. Really August deserved a little bit of selfishness in all this nightmare, didn't he? Nobody would know. Oh God, if Six kept this up, August would give way completely, he could feel it. He was vulnerable and lonely and empty of meaning, and if Six wanted to break every rule of propriety, if Six wanted to take him as a lover right then and there, August wouldn't hesitate for an instant—

"Enough already!"

"Oh, *Theo*—"

"Christ, here he goes...."

The others jeered and scoffed like drunken friends. They *were* drunk; they were drunk on his blood. August moaned. This was utterly depraved. This was irrational. This was *fascinating*.

Six drank. His mouth kneaded on August's throat. He shared the others' same puncture wounds, drinking August's blood in tiny, controlled swallows. August was in a daze. He was love-struck. It was as if they knew each other. *Enthousiasmos*, one with the god, a deep dreamlike pleasure. Their hearts beat to the same tempo, and he knew Six and then suddenly he didn't and it was just a desperate, one-sided embrace, August clutching for purchase as the blood trickled down into his shirt and Seven pulled him into his lap next.

Six stared as if *August* were the terrifying unknown, not the other way around.

Seven, and then Eight, and then the ritual was done for the night.

How had a smart young man like himself fallen into such a nightmare—snatched by monsters and helpless to their whims? Sacrifice. Sacrificial lamb. August had heard those words before, coming from the vampires' mouths, but it had never sunk in with such vitality until now. How utterly sacrilegious, how macabre.

They fed on him. He was their source of blood, their sustenance. He was the vampires' ward and sacrifice. He would never have his own life back, whatever life that had been. The thought was grave and hopeless, but perfectly clear: he was their slave. Not a servant, but a slave. He belonged to them.

You'll find that they're very different..., Hazel had said.

You'd better get over yourself, because your life has changed....

Right, this was a new world now, one of dark skies and candlelight and blood, and August felt that, like Alice, he'd fallen down a rabbit hole into a spectral Wonderland nobody would ever find.

He was a prisoner—an intimate and desecrated prisoner of vampires, and a few months ago, they had been nothing but works of the imagination. Now he was their lifeline and their victim, and he knew nothing about them. He knew nothing about himself. What the hell was he supposed to do with that?

Did the vampires think he could just accept that? He wouldn't. He *couldn't*.

But he wasn't sure how he could hate this life when he couldn't remember the life that had come before it.

The passionate kiss from dark-haired Six had burned its ghost into his mouth. With a rebellious little glee, August couldn't shake it away.

THEO WAITED for Alphonse in the music room, alone with the old rococo designs on the walls and regal green drapes on the window. The glow of the lamps flickered.

He felt good.

His heartbeat was strong and steady. His skin was warm. He felt light on his feet, sharp of mind. His limbs and joints were revitalized; the lethargy from three nights of the Baron's Remedy was no more.

August Prescott's blood was inside him.

He had drunk it, and it had by the black magic of the vampiric covenant diffused into his own blood, the blood of any others he'd ever swallowed, the blood of the Baron's Remedy. If asked, he could not explain how this worked. It just was and always had been. When a mortal man was turned to the Undead, the blood inside him changed, and like some ancient offering to fickle gods, like some alchemy of white silver and mercury in his veins, it blended with any blood he drank—purified it, turned it Undead too. The more a vampire drank, the fresher the blood a vampire took, the better off he was.

And these were the shackles of a sacrifice system that made civilized, moderated creatures out of them all. *Mēdén ágan*—"Nothing in excess," or so said one of the Seven Sages of antiquity.

It was all right, though. Theo had known no other way, only heard histories and tales of glory days, along with the occasional, mild plaint. The sacrifice system seemed only right.

Alone in the music room, Theo pressed his fingers to his lips.

He could still feel the passion charged there like the center of a flame, a heat his fingertips could not catch but one that gave the rest of him delicious shivers.

He could see August in the Sanctuary, over and over, as he remembered seeing images on his eyelids after staring at the sun too long. He clung to experiences like that. He never wanted to forget them, even after fifty-seven years with no sun.

He could see August slipping away from him. Falling into Laurel's arms panting as if he should have been flushed from pleasure, although he was pale from bloodletting. And as he drifted from Theo's hands, pulled by Laurel's arm around his waist, he met Theo's eyes directly and his face shone with a smile.

Never before had a sacrifice looked at Theo with such wide, enchanted eyes. As if he'd actually *see* Theo. As if he *knew* Theo. No, Theo was so accustomed to being the monster, the tormentor, the Undead master. But as broken blood vessels flowered around the bites on August's throat, he had looked at Theo with no hate in his eyes, and that had never happened before. Never, never. He did not look at a monster. He looked at *Theo*.

The trust still tingled on the tip of Theo's tongue.

He could taste it, vaguely, however that worked. Like he could taste bits and pieces of who August was—headstrong, perceptive, secretly curious, privately tortured. A comfortable childhood, the guilt of a free spirit, kisses with a man named *Lucius* and tears, streaming tears, heartache just before the night auction pimps had stolen him for sale. All of those things shivered behind Theo's mind's eye when August Prescott's blood rolled back on his tongue, down his throat, into his soul. That was it. No, he didn't *know* August Prescott; he knew vague things about him like overhearing a whisper, like skimming a page in a book. Rebellion, a lover, innocent pain. What Theo did know, however, was there was something about this sacrifice that refused to *break*.

Theo could taste August Prescott's wonder, cold and dark as it was. It was important to him. So, so important.

For a moment in the Sanctuary, Theo had forgotten the others were there.

And from the way August had kissed him back, apparently so had he.

"Theo."

Theo turned, dropping his hand from his mouth.

Ishmael was in the doorway of the music room, peeking in like the boy he hadn't been for a very, very long time.

"Ugh," Ishmael sighed with a dainty frown of disgust, "you like him, don't you?"

Theo's mouth twisted in a bitter smile; Ishmael was painfully transparent to him. Ishmael with the ash blond hair and the fast, distrusting eyes. Ishmael, small in stature and smaller even in integrity. His face was flushed and lively from the fresh blood of the night. In the lamplight he was a sprite of contention. Perhaps he was even pouting.

"Don't you?" Ishmael echoed himself with a little impatient flick of one brow.

"What does it matter if any one of us *likes* our sacrifice?" Theo argued carefully. He shrugged and crossed his arms, leaning casually against the back of a love seat. "Whether or not we like him doesn't change the fact that he's our—"

"Don't you remember?" Ishmael interrupted, his jaw tight. He inclined his chin, studying Theo judgmentally down his nose. "Having a soft spot for the sacrifice is heartache and nothing more, Theo."

"That didn't stop *you*, now did it?" Theo fired back coolly, watching Ishmael without lifting his head.

Ishmael did not rear back, but the surprised flinch was obvious in the flicker of his face from spiteful to stony—with a faint flash of vulnerability there in between.

Alphonse arrived then, tousled but ready. He came in behind Ishmael with a bright smile on his face, his eyes wide and attentive. It wouldn't last; it was the blood that sharpened his focus. He'd be back to his distracted, daydreaming self by the next evening.

"Are you going out with us?" he asked excitedly, fastening the buttons on his sleeves and pinning Ishmael with that contented grin.

"You're insufferable," Ishmael muttered through his teeth. It was meant for Theo. He ignored Alphonse altogether. "Don't say I didn't warn you."

With a scrape of his heel on the floorboards, Ishmael was gone again.

"Did I interrupt something?" Alphonse chirped, smile faltering.

"No. Come on, then." Theo sighed curtly, striding strong past Alphonse but catching him by the elbow to guide him along. "We're meeting the Oxfords at the Gaiety, aren't we?"

"Yes, we are!"

"Is Anastasia coming?"

"She is!"

Ishmael wanted to put Theo ill at ease; Theo knew that. It was not all that hard to shake it off. Ishmael was a hypocrite if he believed Theo would fall for such mind games. It was Ishmael who had suffered heartache by falling for a sacrifice, anyway, and it was all his own fault, no one else's.

Theo would not be so weak of mind and spirit. He was just so pleased to have a sacrifice in the coven again.

THE VAMPIRES kept him, and August was lonely.

He woke up in the attic as Hazel lit candles and the sun went down. Hazel brought him breakfast at eight o'clock sharp, supper at about three in the morning. The meals were simple and rich in protein, sometimes with coffee instead of tea. The attic room was plain, wanting for decoration and distraction. August looked forward to Hazel's visits, even if they were a little tense. But when she came, he wasn't alone, and otherwise he was just stowed away there with no explanation to put rationality at ease.

In the attic, shadows danced. Wind whistled across the peaked rooftops. The sunset started taking on the hues of late autumn. A dirty black portion of the stove stack ran through the room, but it was still quite cold. Hazel brought two more coverlets for August's bed.

She tried to teach him post and pair one evening, with little smudged and dog-eared playing cards. They gambled pieces of August's breakfast. Hazel settled down at the foot of his bed with the deck of cards she'd pulled from her pinafore, and August asked, quite innocently, "Don't you have tasks to do? You're a maid."

Hazel's face soured. She shot him a cross gaze with her gray-blue eyes, brow knotted. "I'm the keeper of the sacrifice," she corrected very slowly, and August noticed for the first time the slight lilt of a Northern accent in her words. "Taking care of you, making sure you're well—these are my tasks." She paused, fiddling with the playing cards. "Sometimes I do lend a hand to the others as well," she added, as if to save her reputation.

August found it bitterly amusing he was pampered in such a way—nonetheless his apparent worth to the vampires was still mildly unnerving.

They abandoned post and pair for a game of patience instead, the air between them a bit grim, but comfortable enough. August nibbled at the pieces of breakfast they'd betted.

"I had a dream I was on the roof," he said, finally breaking the silence.

"It wasn't a dream." Hazel moved a card for him.

August knew it wasn't a dream. He wanted to know what Hazel thought about the event, but he didn't want her to be angry with him. But maybe he also wasn't sure whether the cold, volatile urge to escape was even still there anymore.

"Oh," August breathed. He flipped a card out of the deck.

"You gave us quite the scare," Hazel murmured tersely. It almost felt like a lecture, but she wasn't quite invested enough. "The window's nailed shut now, I'm sure you've noticed."

"Who was it?"

Hazel looked up quizzically, card in hand.

"I mean what's his name?" August asked a different way. A strange sense of muted nostalgia loomed at the back of his mind like panic. "The green-eyed one, the one who got me back in the house that night. Who is he?"

"Theo," Hazel replied impatiently. Then realization dawned and she looked up again sharply. "But you're still to call every one of them 'master' or 'mistress,' because that's the way it is. You understand?"

Master or mistress. August had nothing else to call them, anyway, other than the numbers he'd given them in place of their names.

Theo.

"Why do you need his name?" Hazel asked quietly. She was far better at patience than August. Her eyes flickered up without her chin lifting; in a hard, intense way, she dared him to answer honestly.

August didn't really have an answer, though.

"You're warming up to them," Hazel mused aloud, almost gleefully, as if to spite his freedom of will. "It's all right. Don't pretend it won't happen, because it will."

August was curious. He wanted to know. But he needed to be careful. Someone once said, "Your obsession with ethical understanding is the most unethical thing about you." Wait, but *who*? God damn it, he wanted to remember. The words were there; he could hear them spoken to him. But he didn't know by whom. "You're such a contradiction of yourself: you're logical to a fault, you're sensible out of dangerous naiveté, and yet you are rebellious by nature and you thirst for the world while fearing its rejection...."

Who, who had said that? They had meant something to him, obviously, whoever they were. But they'd been ripped out of him somehow. There was a void there, a hollow space with a shadow and that was it. A brother? A friend? His father? A lover?

A familiar pang thrummed deep in August's chest, a wistful, nostalgic heartache like long-ago childhood summers that were bright and warm and full of innocence. Ah, perhaps he'd hit a truthful chord there. *Lover.* His face burned. He hated not remembering. He couldn't even judge himself because he couldn't remember. The feel of Theo's kiss in the Sanctuary tingled in his memory.

Stubbornly, grumpily, August avoided Hazel's waiting smirk. He moved a four and a five up to their matching ace card and tucked the name *Theo* into the back of his mind, to be remembered.

Regardless, he'd sworn that night on the roof that Theo would be the only vampire he'd like.

CHAPTER THREE

"COULD I walk around?"

Hazel stared at August from the foot of his bed, hot water bottle in hand.

"How are you feeling?" she snapped back, resuming motion and smoothing the bedding down. August thought about this.

"I feel well," he replied. "Almost very well."

It was the truth. The wounds from the vampires' mouths ached and itched as they healed, but they didn't throb constantly. He was afraid they wouldn't completely heal with the feeding hour every third night, but they were not troublesome, and he actually did feel almost very well. He implored Hazel with the most hopeful frown he could muster, raising his brows.

Hazel moved around the room, trying to find a distraction. Her eyes were clouded in thought. Finally she heaved a sigh.

"Yes," she conceded. She squinted at him from over her shoulder. Her firm, reproachful frowns always made her seem so old and impatient, like a contentious old governess or a brother's persnickety wife. "You're allowed to walk around."

August lit up. He kicked the blankets back and slid out of bed. He was a little light-headed but it was all right. He was getting out of the attic room!

Hazel smiled thinly. "August, wait...."

August stopped at the door. For the first time, he realized just how tiny and dark Hazel was, like a little mouse—a strict, feisty mouse. She made him feel tall. Or maybe it was just that he hadn't done a lot of standing lately, all pale and fragile in his nightshirt, hair uncombed and a childlike fervor about him he blamed mostly on the memorylessness. Unless he was always like that. He was still trying to figure it out.

Hazel shrugged, drooping in concern. "Be good. Don't open a closed door, don't snoop on the second floor, and for the love of God, just don't cause a scene."

The hinges of the attic door creaked and the shadows danced in the glow of the candles as August leaned into the darkness of the stairs.

He hesitated at first, frowning. Getting out of the attic room meant wandering about amidst vampires. *His captors.* Was it really a good idea to explore on his own? August glanced back. Hazel was making his bed.

He slipped down the dark, narrow stairs into the third-floor hallway.

This was not about escape. This was about *knowing*.

The hall seemed empty and cold. He could see over the balcony, all the way down into the checker-floored vestibule.

August stayed close to the wall as he made his way forward, palm brushing the wallpaper and toes curling on the edge of the carpet. Goose bumps prickled him head to toe. For all the fires lit, the house was still chilly.

Rosewood paneling and dark red wallpaper lined the hall, dancing with black velvet damasks and fleur-de-lis patterns. Amongst stylishly painted urns and vases were gas sconces and candelabras, busts with austere stone expressions, and little bundles of flowers on upholstered cabinets and sideboards. Sweet scents tickled his nose of incense and age, of rouged silver and candles drowned in their own wax.

Where did the money for all this come from? Did the vampires steal? Did the city know they lived here? Dear God, did they *work*? Or were they like nobles, lost somewhere in the question of the new market world?

August trailed his fingers along the giltwood edge of an oil painting. It was Ruisdael, a *Bentheim Castle*. It evoked the old stories of vampires he'd once believed, the leisure literature, the fiction, the romantic and fantastic serials read aloud in the dark before a crackling fire while ladies gasped and clung tight to their gallant men. All that Oriental and savage folklore that appalled London society, ghost stories told before going to sleep at night.

The Ruisdael painting was beautiful.

There were more. August recognized Waterhouse, Fuseli. Paintings of boats and castles and beautiful open land, skies and seas and trees, and the occasional scene from old mythology.

The house felt empty. It left August puzzled. It was as if the vampires hid themselves away—or spirited around like ghosts in the night, there one moment and gone the next. Even the servants seemed to have vanished. At the corner, August turned left into the west hall, glancing over his shoulder uneasily. "Empty" was the wrong word. The house was quiet and still, but certainly it was far from vacant.

A spacious washroom there was themed in every different shade of blue. Its vanity was sparsely decorated. August passed by slowly. A real bath sounded divine.

The second door in the west hall was slightly ajar. August peeked in, nervous but nosy. It was just a little room with thick curtains drawn tight and no candles lit. Sheet-covered furniture sat scattered about on the bare floorboards, abandoned and unused. There was no fire beneath the dusty elaborate mantle, no artwork on the walls. It was plain and chilly and obviously unused.

August turned from the neglected room and—pale white in his periphery, *the girl* was at the corner of the hall.

"Ah!" August choked on a breath, eyes widening. Immediately he assumed apology, bowing his head and moving back demurely to the wall.

He was alone with one of them for the first time, essentially, and the fear and the curiosity were at war in his gut like nervous little butterflies.

Number Five. The girl vampire had appeared without a sound, seemingly as immaterial as a ghost. She looked no older than twenty, a thin muslin gown showing quite a lot of swanlike throat and chest. She was beautiful in a cold, porcelain way, blonde curls pinned up loosely and her long neck bare of jewels. Her gown was a light, light blue and so were her eyes, glinting in the low light of the hallway.

She squinted at August like a cat happening upon a mouse. "Pardon me," August mumbled, suddenly noticing the way the girl vampire's nipples poked at the muslin of her dress. He blushed hotly, glancing away. "Pardon me, *Mistress*," he hastened to correct himself. It was strange to say. He wasn't sure how he liked it. He bowed his head. "I just wanted to walk around," he explained. And it was practically the most he'd spoken to any one of them. At least, that he was aware of.

"You're allowed."

The girl's smile was disarmingly sweet, her voice a fine treble. August fought the urge to show resentment for the contradictory way she liked to drag him to her by the ankle in the Sanctuary when it was her turn to feed on him.

"I see you found my fainting room," she announced on a sigh. Her gown danced delicately about her legs as she wandered nearer.

August tensed. He didn't trust her. She was beguiling in a daunting way, and before he could really think it through, he skirted wide past her and hurried back around the corner into the other hall.

She laughed as he rounded the corner. It was like ice crackling on a cold window.

August scurried down to the second floor. The wallpapering in the dark vestibule needed replacing. The checked tile floor was dull and scuffed. Shadows danced in the soft light and dated furniture sat under empty chandeliers—Flemish designs, velvet upholstery, long tapestries of suns and moons and other archaic symbols on the walls. Under an old painting sat some lamb's ears, recognizable by shape but old and faded in the night.

August lingered against the balcony, clutching the thick walnut balustrade. He waited, shifting from foot to foot, listening to the sounds of the house around him. The creak of wind outside, the pop of melting wax and burning wicks, the drip of water off the eaves of the house. Somewhere in this front hall, a clock ticked. But there was no sign of other movement, no presence in the vestibule that August could discern.

He was alone.

He was breaking Hazel's rules, but he was alone again. Supposedly. What did it hurt?

August wandered into the almost medieval vestibule. The drawing room was here on this floor. August knew that room well enough, gold embossments on the white walls that matched the golden tassels on the drapes, the gold threads in the Chinese carpet and fauteuil chairs. August crossed through the low, bouncing shadows of the front room. An open archway led into a dining room. There sat a walnut table covered in a rather simple but beautiful design—petals and crystal, fine china, unlit candles, and dishes of incense framed by ribbon and lace. There was a beautiful fireplace against the wall, thick ornate columns and grate with a delf-case to the left. A dining room for vampires. It seemed a sad joke.

A maid passed by the back doorway of the dining room. She didn't notice August.

There were voices, he realized. Whispers, so quiet he hadn't thought about them until he stood still and quiet. The voices were muffled but close.

They came from the drawing room.

He shouldn't; he was blatantly snooping now. But the fusion of fear and curiosity made him bold. He wanted to know. August held his breath and moved quietly back around to the drawing room.

The door was not open but it was not closed. It sat just an inch or so from the jamb, a sliver of lamplight escaping in a small slant across the floor.

August moved out of sight against the wall. He listened.

Someone in the room laughed. August recognized the sound. It was the Alpha's chuckle, and it gave him a quick shudder. It was a laugh of secrets and schemes, parading from his throat in the guise of amiability. Or so August felt.

"...not at all," the Alpha was saying as August tuned in, the end of some thought. "Why do you ask?"

"I just know that for some of us, the adjustment period is always rather difficult...."

This was a stranger's voice. August had never heard it before, but it seemed of the same beguiling ilk as the Alpha's.

The Alpha replied, "I think it's most difficult for those of us who remember a time of freedom."

There was something significant about this conversation. August didn't understand what they spoke of, but he felt the import. It made the quiet tense and brittle.

"That's true," the stranger said.

"James, I do hope that dissatisfied sigh of yours isn't a sign of noncompliance...."

"Of course not! You can't blame me for feeling nostalgic, though."

"Ah, but you've got me there."

"So—Alistair—this new lamb of yours, what is he like?"

Alistair.

The Alpha's name was *Alistair.*

And they were talking about August now.

August stood stiff and wide-eyed in the dark just outside the drawing room, mouth bitten into a nervous line.

Alistair laughed, another one of his deliberate and charming chuckles. "I don't want to make you jealous now, James."

"Never! I enjoy my own lamb."

"He's delicious, this man. And in the moonlight he's like a little Ganymede. He's deep and brooding one moment, hateful, just hateful, then the next he's full of awe. And I bought him on a whim too!"

The Alpha—*Alistair*—spoke of August so casually, so possessively. *Brooding, hateful, full of awe.* Blast, so his conflicted curiosity didn't go unnoticed. August felt freshly violated. *Ganymede. Delicious.* His self-image scrambled to adjust to remarks like that. Was it wrong to also feel a little proud?

"He's not the most powerfully built," Alistair lowered his voice, "and we were afraid he wouldn't last—but his pranic energy is worth it. The Lamb assured me he was special. I still don't know why. Luckily he's quite nonresistant. James... have you ever been so hungry that you've just stood at your sacrifice's bedside and watched the lamb sleep? Have you ever just wanted to crawl into bed with the lamb and drink their blood while they dreamed, pressed up against your chest?"

"Alistair! My friend, you are truly a *fiend*—"

It was not an insult. The guest named James said it with resounding frivolity; the words dissolved into shared laughter and then more easygoing chitchat, but August didn't stay to listen.

He ran. He ran immediately. He tried to be quiet, but his bare feet slapped on the tile as he bolted across the vestibule and back up the stairs. His breath tore hot and urgent from his chest and his heart felt near to exploding, it was pounding so hard.

The Alpha *had* watched him while he slept.

The memory came back as cold as the panic in his veins, of waking up to Alistair standing across the attic room in dim light, and August had hidden beneath the blankets like a child—

Have you ever just wanted to crawl into bed with the lamb and drink their blood while they dreamed, pressed up against your chest?

Bastard!

There was a newly opened doorway on the third floor. August hurried by without stopping, dizzied and ready to dive back into bed. Familiar vampires lay about in what appeared to be a music room—but that was it. Vampires lounging around casually. *Imagine!*

August looked forward again, only to see the front of someone's waistcoat as he slammed right into it.

"Christ!" he sputtered, staggering back. He almost lost his balance, but the body in the waistcoat hardly swayed. Strange, unnatural grace of the Undead, the cool, very specific smell of cold skin and a vague whiff of metal, and the vampire in the waistcoat caught August at the small of the back before August could rear away, a gentle touch like they were dancing.

August caught his breath and gawked up into the face of Six.

Number Six, the one who kissed him in the Sanctuary like nobody was looking, the one who pulled him back in from the roof.

Theo, the green-eyed vampire he'd sworn respect.

August flushed bright red in embarrassment. He opened and closed his mouth as he searched for words, but he was breathless from the run and from his shock, and Theo's intense eyes silenced him. They pierced into him, penetrated his skin, and hovered over his soul. His hand was a comforting pressure at the dip of August's spine. August wanted to melt into it.

"Pardon me, Master—"

The reverent title fell easily from August's lips now. He blushed hotter to realize that.

Theo peered down at him, in all his queer glory—fine brown hair, combed out of his face but coming loose about his temple and ears; high-collared waistcoat studded with ornate buttons; tapered trousers reminiscent of eras past, which only served to showcase his long, strong legs and trim waist. *Theo*. He had the finely contoured faced of an Adonis, a beautiful beardless man, the fascinating fusion of intelligence and youth, but he studied August with wide, childish eyes. Those eyes had been much sharper from the window of the attic that night long ago, reaching for August to come back inside. Those eyes were darker and terrifyingly focused during the feeding hour, in the Sanctuary, darker and maddened like the raw part of love.

August was rendered speechless with all the flustered worship of a schoolboy. Where was the exhaustion from running? All right, if Theo moved his hand from his back, August would surely go tumbling. But that wasn't from weakness. It was from utterly yielding to Theo's support.

"So you're up and about now, eh?" Theo asked.

"How is this?" August sputtered. "What *are* you, all of you?"

Theo shook his head, quizzically. "Vampires," he replied in a soft, dubious way, as if he didn't know how August didn't understand.

"Yes, I've noticed that," August spat, and he really didn't mean to be so short, but he was shaken from overhearing Alistair's conversation with James and he didn't have the energy to suppress the panic. "But what *are* you?"

Theo's receptive smile faded into a grave, conspiratorial stare. His eyes darted to the stairs, around the hall, but they were safely alone. He righted August steadily on his feet again and then dug his fingers like claws into August's arm. He dragged him into the shadows behind a sideboard.

"*Vampir*," he whispered, eyes wide and full of honest intent. The word was foreign, lyrical and exotic. "We are not the walking dead. We are alive, but not human. We are the Undead. We drink the blood of the living to exist."

"But why?" August snapped, yielding to Theo's bruising touch. "How—"

"Life is in the blood. Like the child-devourer Lamia, or Greek ghosts come up from the underworld, like Tiresias and the others summoned in the afterlife, we require blood for the exchange of life in it."

"So it's a curse," August blurted, aghast. He couldn't stop the words. They crowded their way out of his mouth, and this was Six, this was Theo, he wanted nothing more than to be around Theo, but his voice came out shocked and offended as he grasped for some semblance of sensible truth in this house. "You're damned in this existence, then, more than dead but less than alive, forever compensating for your inferiority by stealing life from others in their blood?"

Theo snorted. The pale face of a well-bred gentleman was briefly replaced by a sarcastic, cunning smirk of displeasure. His fangs were nowhere to be seen. His green eyes sparked. "And who has ever confirmed for you that yours is the superior species? Enlightened leaders and philosophers?"

"Species" divided them like man and animal. August was dumbstruck. The nervous taste of metal rose on his teeth.

"Ah, there it is," Theo sighed, softening a little again, as if he were working on control of his temper. It was almost patronizing. "There's the understanding. You get it now, don't you? Tell me: what is it that animates a body? The soul? But what is the soul? And who says you, and all the rest of you presumptuous, *educated*, rational mortal men"—each of the words seemed like fearless mockery—"are not still missing pivotal parts of the larger picture? Ours is an ancient, unholy covenant. And just as the soul makes you alive, the blood makes me alive now, and that's as much as I can explain the magic. No more than you could explain the magic of science or God."

For a moment all August could hear was his heart thudding steadily in his ears. He gawked up at Theo.

But very slowly, but very surely, the panic drained out of him.

There was an impasse here between them, a truce. Perhaps it had something to do with Theo being the only one August trusted, or maybe it had something to do with Theo's mystifying speech making sense, glittering threads woven into the tapestry of all things.

It seemed so simple and obvious in the terms Theo illuminated. August almost felt ashamed for having not understood the fundamentality before. It seemed like something revolutionary and dark and romantic, which were things that felt right to him. Wasn't all that Theo explained rational enough?

"I'm sorry, sir," August said huskily, voice barely there under his nervous breath. He was distracted now by Theo's hand still on his arm. It summoned the desperate craving for the green-eyed vampire August was trying to keep restricted to nights in the Sanctuary, where it didn't leave him feeling so lonely. "I was only looking around. I wasn't trying to escape again—"

Theo finally let him go, gently. "Looking around, hmm? Well, I'm sorry to say it, but I don't think you'll find the best company around here."

August shrugged roughly. "It's not as if I have a choice, Theo."

Theo stared. It seemed vacant at first, confused. And then August realized he'd called the vampire by name.

Laughter echoed from the open room down the hall. August stood rigid and wide-eyed, wondering whether Theo would reprimand him— hit him, condemn him? What happened when he broke the rules, the rules he did not really know?

But Theo didn't say anything. He lifted his hand and August drew back instinctively. Theo just reached down and touched August's face, cool palm on his cheek. August went stiff, heart jumping. For a moment, a breath or two, there was something intimate about it. Something trusting, something meaningful. There it was again, that shiver of closeness between them, like moments in the Sanctuary when Theo's fangs were in his skin and his mouth worked the blood from his throat and their hearts fluttered together and August wanted to curl his fingers in Theo's hair, press closer, tangle the two of them together, make the rape something worthwhile.

Theo patted August on the shoulder, a lingering touch, then brushed past him. He slipped his hand into his pocket and moved off toward the open room, where other vampires sprawled, and August ran again.

The warmth left with Theo.

August didn't mean to, but he slammed the attic door when he got upstairs. He hit his shin on the bedframe as he tumbled into the blankets. He jumped when Hazel came through the door a little while later with tea.

"Oh Lord, you look white," she commented offhandedly. "I knew walking around would be too much for you. I just knew it."

August didn't argue. He drank the tea she brought and wished he hadn't acted like a fool in front of Theo.

CHAPTER FOUR

AUGUST TRIED to walk around the attic room every night.

He pulled the wingback chair over in front of the window and sat bundled snug in two coverlets, feet drawn up and toes curled on the edge of the seat. He watched the rooks as they flitted by the rooftops. He could hear their cawing outside the house. He saw the familiar pasty gray of the sky as it faded past twilight into dark, and it was pale and foreboding as it always was in the winter.

He wished he could walk around outside.

He felt isolated. He knew the vampires kept it that way on purpose. But he'd be damned if he wouldn't make the most out of it.

The attic was cold and it felt like a haunted house, but it was his. The floorboards were dingy and faded from years of sunlight. They cracked and popped under his feet. The pale walls were dusty below peeling wallpaper. One wall was completely stripped of paper altogether, revealing stained and scratched and patchy plaster. Besides the two long windows, a mullioned skylight poured moonlight down into the attic. If *time* had a particular scent, the attic was filled with it. And this—the attic—was home.

August stretched his legs at the window, peering longingly out through the dark and wondering just how far he was from whatever home whence he'd come.

The skies were growing ever grayer, the advent of a London winter, and August didn't know how much longer he could bear to be cooped up all alone.

"I can wash myself, you know," he told Hazel one evening.

Hazel's eyes widened. She blushed, glancing away. She sat in the chair by the window, fingers laced in her lap. She looked sad in the soft light of the lamp.

August turned his back on her to wash up in the corner with lukewarm water and a little rag, and a shining razor blade, though he didn't need it very often. His brothers had teased him endlessly about that, about his blondness, about his hairlessness, and his father had said, "He's just twenty-three. By twenty-five he'll have a handsome mustache and surely a wife," and his brothers had mocked that too....

Right? That had happened? It wasn't his imagination trying to fill in the blanks, to create for himself a history, fleshing out actors and dialogue, giving meaning to the seemingly arbitrary patterns of himself as a person? There were no names, no faces still. The characters no longer felt part of the present. They were long gone, consigned to some vast, ravenous *past*.

"Could I use the washroom?" August ventured.

"Not by yourself," Hazel replied curtly. It was her humble way of saying no because, although both had conceded to her sponging him off, that was a completely different thing from her sitting in the washroom while he consciously stripped down and bathed. August sighed. He rolled his wrist over and peered at the scar there, just below his palm: *l o n.*

August wasn't sure where the question came from; it was just there suddenly, burning on the tip of his tongue. He looked up, waiting for Hazel to meet his eyes. He demanded, "Why did they choose me?"

Hazel frowned in that taciturn way of hers.

"I know he bought me," August said. "The Alpha. Alistair."

"Your master," Hazel corrected. She chewed on the question. She conceded bitterly, "He must have liked you."

"I overheard him," August said in a flat voice. He didn't mean to sound so bleak about it. "When I was walking around the other night, I overheard him. He said that he bought me on a whim."

There was a small hush, awkward and powerless. Hazel heaved a sigh, discarding her maid's formalities and flopping back into the wings of the chair with all the grace of a tired little girl. She closed her eyes and waited as if she knew August had more questions.

August did. He turned around, sitting cross-legged on the floor half-naked and mid-sponge bath, imploring her with a furrowed brow.

"What do you know about them?" he asked. "Hazel, I can't stand not knowing anything about them. See, I've read stories—I know that they drink blood and that they sleep during the day, that they're essentially dead, that they can hypnotize and charm, but they're so... *normal*. They're normal, Hazel! I mean, they're not and yet they are, like a different race."

"Oh, they're the Undead," Hazel whispered. There was the echo of caution in her voice, a shadow of vigilance in her eyes. "I told you before, you'll find them very different from the vampires of stories and fairy tales, August. And you'd better stop comparing them right now."

"You didn't even answer my question." August squinted at her through the low lamplight, agitated. "Don't you struggle around them? Don't you feel torn, as if you could accidentally love them—"

Hazel's eyes grew dark. Sharply she interrupted, "August, I've found that the world outside this house is one of horrible hypocrisies. Men and women are just children, and the more privileged they are, the worse they behave. They like to pretend they're moral and just, but it's a dangerous sham. That's what I've come to learn. So of course I love the vampires, and not accidentally either. I admire them. They're not pretending to be anything more than what they are, and they behave the way they do for the safety of the balance of the world, not for greed or selfishness. Think about it that way. You're just scared, August. That's all that it is."

"Are you making a parable out of supernatural creatures?" August scoffed.

Hazel sighed again, exasperated. She looked old suddenly. Incredibly old and wise and wearied, and August wondered where she'd grown up—what her life was like before she became his maid—how old she actually was in spirit, not in age. He hated how guilty she made him feel, hunched over the porcelain washbasin, guilty of these hypocrisies she spoke of, and he didn't know why. They were both at the disposal of vampires, for Christ's sake. This was some fantasy. How could she so easily appropriate them into the regular world of daylight and society, humanize them like any other stranger on the street? Because it was true?

"It's not a parable," Hazel said coarsely. "It just *is*."

She was right.

August understood what she was saying.

Seeing was believing, wasn't it?

"GOOD MORNING," Theo greeted from the attic doorway, but his lack of smile sort of undermined the gesture.

"It's not morning." August gawked at Theo from the bed.

Theo stared back pensively, like he needed to figure out what August meant.

There was a moment there, a bated breath of significance as they stared at each other, the vampire in the doorway and the sacrifice in the bed—and then there was just emptiness again as Theo kept his preternatural charm in check.

August waited. He cleared his throat and prompted, "Why are you here? Have I done something wrong?"

"No, not at all." Theo closed the attic door and drifted over to stand between the window and the chair. "You said not too long ago that you were bored, so I thought you might enjoy some company," he confessed, squinting down at August. "Say, don't you comb your hair at all?"

"What? Why?" August clutched at his hair, mortified. He knew it was unruly and full of stubborn cowlicks. He'd seen his reflection in the washbasin, in a mirror or two when he'd walked around the house. But it wasn't as if he had anyone to look nice for anymore. He was in bed all day.

Theo shook his head, eyes wide as he tried to play off the unintentional offense, but he looked as if he were stifling laughter. God, but he was like a big child, hiding behind decorum. August squinted at him for a moment, trying to figure him out. He couldn't. It was either the dark, dreamy nature of the Undead, or it was just Theo's pretenses.

"You can keep me company," August invited.

How strange it was, befriending a vampire.

Theo's eyes burned into him. Chills zipped along August's spine. It simply wasn't natural, the way Theo made him feel. He was hypnotizing, innately or by way of a vampire's magnetism, like black magic on the air, and if August wasn't mistaken, sometimes it felt as if Theo really were already his friend.

"I'd be honored, August," Theo said.

August stopped, cutting Theo a quick look. Had he ever spoken his name to Theo—or any of them at all besides Hazel, for that matter? Wasn't too important, he decided.

Maybe they could taste it in his blood.

"I BROUGHT these for you."

The next night, Theo dumped a stack of books at the foot of the bed. August pulled his feet up, frowning. "Don't throw them!" he

scolded, chancing a glance at Hazel where she stood in the corner, face
all pinched up and eyes narrowed at Theo.

Theo waved a hand at her. "Hey there, Witch Hazel, don't be so
crabby."

Hazel blushed, but she drew a sharp impatient breath through her
nose at that, squinting harder at the vampire. *Witch Hazel*. It was
apparently a nickname. Theo's dry, recalcitrant sense of humor made
August smile. He was a little embarrassed by how much he admired
Theo; he blamed the loneliness. He reached down and sifted through
the pile of books Theo had brought, organizing them into two stacks
from biggest to smallest.

"Good evening, sir," Hazel curtly replied as she bobbed in a little
curtsey.

"He's right," August volunteered, lifting *The Masque of the Red
Death* from the pile of books and running his fingers over the old
cover. "You're crabby."

Hazel's impatient eyes jumped to August now, almost like a
warning. She gave him a daring once-over, and August looked away so
she didn't see him blush. She knew; she knew exactly how he felt about
Theo, Number Six, Theo the green-eyed, blood-drinking gentleman.

Because that was what he was, wasn't it? It was that simple. He
was a blood-drinking gentleman.

Or August was just scrambling for reasons to forgive Theo for all
he was guilty of, as a vampire and one of August's captors.

No, August was not that fickle.

Theo flopped down in the chair by the window with the gauche
grace of a tipsy bachelor, already making himself at home in the attic
room. He said, "Are you happy?"

August opened a newer book, with glittering lettering across the
face that read *Philologie: Die Natur auf Virtue*. There was a page
bookmarked. Someone had underlined verses from a Homeric hymn.
Vandalizing the footnotes in pencil was an English translation:

"Your hair is nice and long, not like a wrestler's, but curling
sexily beside your chin. Your skin—peaches and cream, untouched by
sunburn, but pale from hunting love in amorous shadows."

August was stricken by the quote. It felt secret and personal,
addressed to him. With a knotted brow, he sought Theo's eyes. But
Theo was not watching him.

Hazel gathered up the brass tray of August's half-eaten breakfast. Theo sat up straight. "Witch Hazel," he said, "you don't have to leave."

"Of course not, sir," Hazel returned with another little nod of the head. "I thought I'd just take this down to the kitchen and be back, sir."

She slipped out of the attic, fine Saint-Cloud china rattling delicately on the breakfast tray. August cleared his throat.

"Thank you for the books," he said, pulling out *The Sketch Book* and thumbing through idly. He glanced at Theo. Theo shrugged, legs crossed and candlelight dancing on the planes of his face. There was a small hush. August noticed for the first time the nearly inaudible ticking of Theo's pocket watch, muffled beneath his waistcoat.

Theo licked his lips, and August watched his tongue. It made his stomach knot, made him think of nights in the Sanctuary. He shivered. He wasn't sure whether he was more comforted or amused by the gifted books; there was something awkward and endearing about it, as if Theo was trying very hard to make him feel at ease but had no idea how. As if they were estranged lovers, or adoptive families. As if he'd forgotten some parts about being human.

Unless the books and stories lied about that too, and vampires were never human to begin with. Where did they come from, then? August wanted to ask. He didn't ask.

"You'll read them?" Theo pressed.

"I'll read them all," August promised.

SOMETIMES AUGUST woke up feeling the vampires' tongues on his neck and their hands down his shorts, but when he opened his eyes, he was not in the Sanctuary. He was still all alone in the attic room.

He didn't have trouble sleeping during the day, even with curtainless windows. The house's nocturnal rhythm had become more comfortable.

When Hazel wasn't around, he read. He smelled the pages of the books and he read, wondering whether the books were Theo's or whether there was a whole library somewhere in the house that he could explore. He and Hazel played card games. Sometimes August read aloud to her. Theo brought him an oversized smoking jacket because the nights were getting chillier. August slept with his nose buried in it.

Sometimes music floated up into the attic from somewhere else in the house—strings, pianoforte, now and again accompanying each other but usually solo. August sat curled in blankets against the locked attic door with the candlelight flickering and his head tipped to one side, listening to the sweet melodies as they slithered their way up through the house.

Theo started visiting the attic room regularly.

"I'm twenty-three," August told him, mainly to feel real, to keep his identity straight when there wasn't much to prove it. "I believe in God and the devil, and spiritualism, and vampires now, obviously. I think I'm the youngest of my brothers—but don't ask me what their names are. I can't remember if I was employed anywhere. I do remember feeling like this is somehow my father's fault. I think he has a gambling problem. Theo—*Master*—I know I'm still in London, you know. That's Berkeley Square, out the window."

Immediately August realized the poor phrasing divorced his existence from the house and its inhabitants, which seemed insolent, unsympathetic and selfish. Theo and Hazel exchanged looks of shock, like no other sacrifice had sleuthed the house's exact location before.

"How do you know that?" Hazel urged, for the first time seeming truly vulnerable as a frantic uncertainty pinched her face.

August shrugged, frowning at Hazel and then at Theo. "Because I'm from London," he explained. "Aren't you two?"

Their confidence in his resignation faltered. August hastened to patch it up, miserably. "Don't worry," he insisted. "I can't remember anything about… *before* all of this. So even if I somehow got out, I'd have no idea where to go, who to see. I don't *want* to get out. Not right now at least. I'm too afraid of not knowing anything, and this is all that I know presently."

He didn't mean for such an intimate confession to come out, but it did. And after that he didn't want to talk anymore. There was no more moral tug-of-war because there was no reason to hold on to it. He'd given in.

Perhaps there was a small, shocking bit of pride in that.

He tried not to feel insignificant on the nights without the feeding hour. But now Theo visited him.

Theo carried himself with an almost oppressed kind of poise, a dignity and ease but an air of bored curiosity. Every now and then, as the soft light illuminated his face, the layers beneath his mask flickered by in the open and his intense eyes were hard to hold. He looked clever, so clever, but young and full of hope at the same time. He was captivating. He was like fire.

August adored him for all his hidden fragments. One of them was his kindness. It was as if he tried to bury it, and all the other softer parts of him, below an exterior of irony and elegance. But August saw it. He saw it in a short-lived burst of feeling, tangible on the air as he was finding so many of the vampires' immediate emotions were. He saw it when Theo visited him one night and gestured promptly for Hazel to take a seat in the wingback chair.

"You look tired," Theo told her. "Rest."

Hazel was just as stunned as August. She obeyed, sitting down—and surely enough she was as tired as she looked. She was asleep soon after, dozing as Theo and August played chess. Theo had brought an old set of fine walnut and elephant ivory, and the pieces made delightful clinking sounds when they were moved.

August played lazily which meant Theo won twice in a row, but after the second time, Theo looked at him pointedly.

"You aren't trying," Theo said.

"Sorry!" August sputtered, eyes widening. Theo just laughed, setting up the pieces for another round. When Theo laughed it was all too easy to forget he was Undead—that was the word Hazel had used, wasn't it? Yes, the candlelight hit the planes of Theo's face just perfectly, giving vibrant life to his green eyes and filling his pale skin with handsome, manly magic. Everything was softer in candlelight, and Theo looked extraordinarily human.

"You go first," Theo demanded, sending a stern glance in August's direction. August jumped a little. He tried to laugh off his foolish staring, but Theo had definitely noticed.

August moved his queen's pawn two spaces forward.

"Ah, the French Defense," Theo whispered as he mimicked the move on his side of the board, and the game began again.

CHAPTER FIVE

HAZEL SAID it was October, but August wasn't keeping track of the days. He slept through them.

"Can you leave the door unlocked?" August ventured, offering Hazel the most gentlemanly smile he could muster. She squinted at him with a critical frown.

"You're a man, but you're wily as a *boy*," she mumbled in reproof.

She held his eyes as she left the door unlocked and slipped the key into the pocket of her pinafore.

August waited. Nobody came back to lock the door after her. He threw on the smoking jacket Theo had given him and slipped down to explore the house again, peeking out around the corner at the bottom of the stairwell to make sure the hallway was empty. There was no more fear. Ruthless curiosity had finally won.

There was an open doorway down the hall. August trotted down warily, but he was alone. He peeked between the hinges.

It was a music room. The curtains were tied open to let in the moonlight. A pianoforte sat between both windows, before the wide hearth. It was a striking contrast to the fainting room, all smooth polished spruce, knots of winding, braided elm carved into the frames of tight seats and sofas. Scattered across the floor was a carpet of sheet music.

August passed the black-keyed pianoforte and the harp, the big gilded cello case slumped against the wall. He stooped to his haunches and started to sort the mess of papers out, opus numbers and concertos, pages ripped from binding, ink smudged in the corners. He gathered the music sheets into piles and stood, holding the ruffled stack to his chest—and then a set of eyes met his from the shadows near the drapes.

Someone was there, lurking.

"*Christ!*" August cried in surprise, dropping all the papers.

They rained down and scattered across the floor again. August recognized the vampire near the drapes. The warm glow of lamplight danced on one half of him. Pupils dilated, hazel eyes wide, the vampire watched him passively.

It was Number Eight. His loose dirty-blond curls were tucked behind his ears, combed neatly along his neck and out of his eyes. Sleeves rolled up and waistcoat unfastened, he stood idly holding a violin at his side. The bow dangled from the other hand.

"I'm sorry," August choked out, trying again to gather the music sheets. His heart pounded in his ears. His stomach was in knots. He just didn't trust any of them alone as he trusted Theo.

Number Eight held out the violin bow to stop him, pointing it right in August's face like the threat of a switch.

"I'll pick it all up," Number Eight said in a flat, even voice.

August looked up at him warily. The vampire gestured with the bow. He looked younger than August by a few years at least. And it was sort of unsettling to feel so below someone so much softer and smaller.

Number Eight said, "My name is Alphonse, but I believe it's better you still call me 'Master' as you're supposed to." He reached out, dragging music sheets back to him with the tip of his bow. He smiled cordially. "I just supposed you'd like to know my name," he explained.

Number Eight was *Alphonse*, then. He was young, yes, but his gaze was distant and dazed. August swallowed hard on a catch in his throat.

Alphonse didn't seem to notice anything else, concentrated on gathering his music sheets slowly, fishing them forward with the end of his bow. August stood awkwardly. He gave a quick tip of the head in obeisance, then hurried back out to the hall. He didn't announce his departure. He watched Alphonse between the hinges of the door, safe in the hall, queer blond-curled vampire just staring at the music at his feet. He wasn't even playing.

Was it Alphonse who played the melodies he heard from the attic, then?

August hurried back down the hall, heart still pounding. He passed a maid on the stairs down to the first floor.

He knew he wasn't supposed to, but he opened a door to the west of the stairs. It opened on another hall, and directly across from him was a library.

"Yes!" August breathed in victory.

It was cramped, dark but welcoming with its leather chairs and ornate wooden mantle. August was thrilled. He pined for the books. He wanted to gather a greedy mountain of them and sit before the blazing fire and rip through them. He'd already read most of the books from Theo.

Behind him in the vestibule, the front door opened. August froze.

It was the Alpha and that snot Ishmael, coming inside in the midst of what seemed an intense conversation.

August hurried away. He dashed all the way back up to the attic room, and he tried not to think about the way he'd felt their eyes follow him as he left.

The bolt of the attic door snapped back to locked from the outside a few hours later.

"LAUNDRY," A little maid who was not Hazel declared, and August tumbled from his bed as she snatched up his blankets and then went for the sheets. He hit the floor staggering and hopped over to the chair beneath the window, curling up there and covering a wide yawn as the strange maid stripped the bed and he tried to rub the sleep from his eyes.

"You could have woken me up more pleasantly," August mumbled. "Where's Hazel?"

"Many apologies," the maid grunted below her breath, gathering up the bedding. She didn't mean it. She wasn't sorry at all. Her Irish accent was thick and didn't help her case any. "Here," she said, tossing him a quilt. "I'll leave this one with you so you don't freeze all alone. Hazel's gone with Meredith to the market."

"Oh. Thank you." August took the quilt. "Miss…?"

The maid stopped at the door with a rough swish of skirts and bedding. She shot him a stony look, tart mouth and reproachful eyes. August fidgeted.

"Why do you work here?" he asked.

The maid bristled. August watched the pain flicker across her face. He knew he'd asked a difficult question. He didn't regret it. He wanted to know. The maid's hand twitched on the door and she looked around quickly, then opened the door farther and made to leave.

"I don't have time for games," she grumbled, but she halted halfway out the door and stared at her feet in deep contemplation. She cleared her throat after a moment, lifted her shoulders, and spoke more to the laundry than to August.

"You're the twenty-ninth they've had in over seventy years," she remarked, voice jagged. "My son was the twenty-fourth. I've been working here since he became their sacrifice."

The words rushed out of her. Loudly she left the room before hardly a second had passed beyond her last breath, and she shut the door hard.

August listened to her stomp down the attic stairs. He sat, dumbfounded, in the chair below the window. He stared at his bare bed. He stared out the southern window. He stared at his hands and then at his knees as he felt around the scarred, bruised places of his throat and neck. *Twenty-ninth*. He was the vampires' twenty-ninth sacrifice in seventy years. Her *son* had belonged to them, and she'd given her life up to them to be around him—

"What's got you all in a mood?" Theo asked when he came to visit, spinning the attic key on one finger as he kicked the door shut behind him.

August scowled at him from the chair under the window, curled up in a blanket. "I'm trying to piece everything together."

"What's there to piece together?" Theo grunted.

"I want a pen and paper," August said next, deciding it was futile or perhaps just bad taste to complain to Theo about the injustice of house rules he didn't know and a system no one would explain to him. He understood his ignorance meant more power for them. But he didn't exactly think his curiosity posed much threat.

Theo's lip curled, an inquisitive look creasing his brow. "Why?"

"I want to write."

"You write?" Theo popped his pocket watch open and closed idly, standing tall and regal with his hair swept out of his eyes, untamed as ever. August nodded mutely.

"What do you write?" Theo probed, turning to lean against the wall. He replaced his watch in its proper pocket and crossed his arms.

August shrugged. "Poetry."

"That's right," Theo murmured as if he'd just remembered it too. August shot him a look, vexed. Theo avoided his gaze. Finally he heaved a sigh and met August's eyes again, explaining flatly, "The taste of blood tells many stories, August."

"So you can read my mind," August surmised, a little uncomfortably but more skeptically. With a heavy thud of the heart and a twist of the stomach, he remembered Theo knew his name even before he introduced himself. But that wasn't exactly the same; Hazel could easily have told them as much, once she learned his name. Except Theo had even known it the night August got onto the roof too.

"That's not what I said." Theo drummed his fingers absently on his elbow. He seemed genuinely frustrated. "We're not telepathic. I can't read your mind just by looking at you, but if you feel strongly about something—or when I drink from you—I can taste things, I can feel pieces of what you're feeling, what you've felt...." He shrugged and turned back to the window as if he expected August to disdain him.

August didn't. He felt a little violated, of course. He was angry they could invade his soul like that. He wasn't so sure it was appropriate he didn't mind Theo knowing things about him without his speaking them aloud. That intimacy was terrifying and yet so much simpler than having to put forth effort.

"Do you know who I am, then?" August blurted before he could measure the words.

Theo's brow knotted; he curled his lip. "What?" he said.

The words crowded their way out of August's mouth. "The things I can't remember. Can you taste them in my blood?"

Theo stared at him. He didn't answer—not out of secret keeping, it seemed, but out of helplessness. He either didn't know what August meant, or he didn't know what to say. Finally he cleared his throat and husked, "I'll bring you pen and paper." And that was the end of it.

He indeed brought pen and paper the next night. He left afterward, respectfully, and August wrapped himself in blankets and moved over to sit beneath the window. In the pale moon and the dance of candlelight, the blank stationary gawked up at him. He traced what looked like a family crest in opposite corners of the page, little arabesques and bars that framed the area to write, and he felt the words, the thoughts, the urge to be creative or at least smart.

But nothing came. It distressed him.

He abandoned the paper and pen beneath the window and crawled back into bed. Instead of writing, he read, and the stationery was neglected with just one meager line scratched at the top.

A bird in a cage

That was all.

CHAPTER SIX

"I WANT a real bath," August insisted.

Hazel stared, disheartened. She stood near the candles, wringing her hands, lace cap a little crooked atop her head. She looked nervous, as if she didn't know what to say.

Theo glanced between the sacrifice and the maid, hands propped on his hips.

August shrugged, leaning with his face pressed to the cool glass of the northern window. "Hazel says I can't take one alone," he explained.

"So take him down to the washroom and sit there with him," Theo concluded, casting a staid glance at Hazel. He spoke matter-of-factly; August's wishes should have been granted already. The indecency of a female maid chaperoning a male sacrifice's bath, which Theo was sure was the issue at hand here, was preposterous.

"I won't go with her," August cut in quickly, as if he wanted to protect Hazel's reputation. Theo's gaze veered back to him now, perplexed and mildly impatient with this impasse. "It's not proper," August tried to explain further. He turned back to the window, meeting the reflection of Theo's eyes there. Hazel stood fidgeting in the opposite corner, her reflection a little glimmer of black and white.

Finally it dawned on Theo. He deduced, "You want *me* to take you."

August nodded. Hazel nodded. Theo frowned deeply, one hand on his hip and the other raking back his wavy hair over and over. It was a laughable situation. And yet it wasn't unusual. The sacrifice was getting comfortable. The sacrifice deserved comfort too. Other sacrifices had sought normalcy in the same way before. Theo heaved an inconvenienced sigh that was mostly dramatics.

"Fine," he conceded brusquely.

This clearly excited August. He hurried over to grab the smoking jacket from the foot of the bed.

"Thank you, sir," Hazel peeped from the corner. Her face was white, as if she'd been afraid of the verdict. August smiled at her lovingly. He touched her shoulder as he moved to the attic door. Theo expected her to scowl. But she just watched August follow Theo out with a sad dimple in her brow.

Theo led the way. Downstairs he nudged open the washroom door. "Do you need my help?" he grunted. He didn't quite know what to do or how to handle the situation. He'd never escorted a sacrifice to a bath before.

August eased the washroom door open all the way, shaking his head.

"Well," Theo said decidedly, "I'll just wait out here, then, and make sure you don't drown."

August laughed. It infected Theo with such a pleasant feeling. "If it's because you want to respect my privacy," he said, slipping into the washroom and closing the door most of the way; he peeked at Theo from the sliver of open space there, "then just say so. I'm content with that."

Theo nodded curtly but he didn't say anything. *Privacy* seemed a joke for a coven sacrifice.

The door closed. Theo waited to hear the water drawn. He really hoped nobody happened upon him standing guard at the washroom like some watchdog or butler. He wasn't entirely sure what he'd say if asked what he was doing. *I'm giving the sacrifice a bath.* That was just pathetic. And entirely suspicious.

The washroom door suddenly swung open again. August stood half-dressed in the soft lamplight, frowning.

"Just come in," he said, and Theo had to bite back laughter at how disappointed August sounded that he hadn't followed him in on his own already.

The washroom was tidy because it was rarely used. The walls were papered in periwinkle, floor dressed in a lavish imported rug. A small sofa sat against one wall, an ornately carved trunk against the other, and August swayed as if to some unheard tune as he ran the water and began to undress.

Theo would have bet money on just what August was thinking: a bath, a regular bath, with real, new *plumbing*. Was there any luxury higher than this, any sweeter retreat that could more quickly reduce a grown man from tense hostage to hopping around in delight?

Theo cleared his throat as August plucked at the buttons of his nightshirt. "Should I look away?"

August shrugged. The striped nightshirt hit the floor at his ankles. He stood idly beside the running bath, facing Theo, and raised his brows very slowly.

"I don't know," he murmured, lips barely moving on the words. His gaze drifted away; he looked around the washroom but seemed only to tend to private thoughts. He turned away to peel off his drawers, clinging at least to that small measure of decency. It was provocative only in that August really didn't seem to care that Theo's eyes were drawn instantly to the dip at the base of his spine, the dimples in his smooth buttocks as he lifted one leg and climbed into the bath.

The hunger coiled and snapped inside Theo like a whip—once, twice. That was it. He was in control of himself.

He smiled, watching from the closed washroom door.

On a stand beside the tub was a wide variety of soaps. August settled for a cream-colored one. He hummed softly, and Theo wasn't sure what he hummed, but it sounded pleased.

Around them the house was quiet. Eerie, lonely. Maybe there was the echo of life from outside, but this was an old, sturdily built house, and the rest of the world if heard at all was muffled and faraway. There was nothing but the chime of the tall clock out in the hall and the slap of water as August washed himself. Quiet as the dead—or the Undead.

"Why did you want me in here?" Theo ventured.

August looked over quickly, almost fearfully. He slipped the cream-colored soap from hand to hand before offering a nervous smile. He could make no excuses about being a sacrifice and needing a chaperone; he did, after all, wander around the house on his own, contradictory as that was. The truth was all that was left.

"I didn't want to be alone," August said, still smiling that tiny, distant smile and looking down at the bath water through his lashes.

His eyes looked empty, dazed, tired. He looked sick, Theo decided. Did coven sacrifices always look this sick? He could have traced the blue of August's veins up the insides of his arms. His hair was getting long. It was curling out at his ears and the nape of his neck.

August was looking at his reflection in the bathwater now, it seemed. Hesitantly he touched the cluster of bruises on his neck. The actual bite marks themselves were considerably faded. Normal wounds didn't heal that fast; there was something in the saliva of the vampire that accelerated the recovery.

August frowned, turning over his hand to view the puckered scar there below his palm. *L o n.* Theo bristled. He held his breath, loath to answer any questions August might have about what the branding meant and why he had it, who had given it to him and how. Not that Theo didn't know. He just really did not want to talk about it right now.

"I'm not very good company," Theo mumbled in apology. "There's not even any conversation."

"Just you being here is enough," August whispered back, quite unafraid of honesty. But perhaps it was more that he didn't realize how much he said, focused on tracing a thumbnail along the branding on his inner wrist. *L o n.*

Theo watched him.

The flicker of his muscles under pale skin, the thoughtless grace of his steepled fingers as he dragged damp hair out of his face, the smooth slither of his naked shoulder blades, and throat, and middle. His nipples were a warm pink, standing out in the cool air. The details caught by the vampire's eyes were merciless.

If Theo listened closely enough, he could hear the steady thumping of August's heart.

Rush of blood.

His ears rang; his attention sharpened. He had a hunch August had not asked him in just because he feared being alone.

It was because of the kiss in the Sanctuary.

Theo sighed through clenched teeth, crossing the washroom in a few short purposeful strides. He snatched a towel from the nearby stand and held it out, signaling for August to stand, to take it.

"That's enough," he said, nodding curtly. "Come on, then."

It was not punishment. August had done nothing wrong. It was just that if this moment spun out any longer, Theo was sure he himself would do something… *wrong.*

Did he really feel it was wrong, though? The things he wanted to do to August?

No. He really did not. As long as there was no blood spilled, he was not breaking rules.

Having a soft spot for the sacrifice is heartache and nothing more.

August did not protest. He climbed from the bath and took the towel Theo offered. Theo struggled not to let his eyes wander before August could cover his nakedness. There was nothing spectacularly forbidden about it to Theo; the line drawn between mortal and immortal eliminated that concern. But August did indeed appreciate nods to decency, so Theo tried.

A silence fell—heavy, meaningful. Theo could feel it, something there in the quiet between them. It was not the sacrifice's deference to a vampire's presence either. It was a natural, peaceful quiet that didn't require any words, but....

"What's the matter?" Theo whispered.

"Aren't you going to kiss me?" August asked, raising his brows.

Theo reared back, shocked. A look of innocent confusion flashed across August's face, followed by a defensive frown. "What?" Theo demanded.

August frowned back. "You kissed me in the Sanctuary. Remember?"

Yes. Yes, I remember.

"And you want me to kiss you again now?" Theo pressed.

Yes. Yes, let me kiss you again now, let me gather you up against me and feel your body pressed tight to mine, let me drink in your love and swallow it whole, let me kiss you until my mouth goes numb, let me.

"Well, normally when a man kisses a woman—or another man—er, *anyone*—like that—he plans on kissing them again." August was blushing. His face twisted in uncertainty. He reworded in a tentative grumble, "A *respectable* man, at least."

Theo threw his head back and forced a laugh. He still felt the pinched look on his face, however. He moved to the vanity across the room, digging around for a comb. He met August's eyes in the mirror and smiled faintly. It was, perhaps, the first time he had left his smile utterly unguarded around August. Passing the comb from hand to hand, he said without turning around, "'Respectable.' You really think any of us are respectable, August? Never mind. You don't know any of us yet. Listen, I was very hungry when I kissed you. I apologize."

I was very hungry when I kissed you.

Why? Why did he deflect like that? Why did he make excuses? Was it because a sacrifice had never cut right through him to the very core before, had never been so perceptive of his secret self no matter how Theo struggled to hide it away? Would August even understand what it meant, the connection of hunger and kisses?

Heartache.

"Apology accepted," August mumbled.

God, but Theo couldn't resist.

The beast in him wanted that heat again, the press of August's body. It wanted the *blood*. But blood outside the feeding hour was against the rules, and so he hungered for the vitality in the man's *sex*. It was a weaker energy than was found in the red wine of his veins, of course, but it was ambrosia and nectar in his release. The creature in Theo yearned. The gentleman in him longed more for the sweet taste of August's lips. He wanted the tickle of his breath, the twist of his tongue, the moan purring in the back of his throat and those wide eyes following him.

He wanted that acceptance.

Theo passed August the comb. August reached for it—but Theo thought twice and pulled it back again, out of August's reach, so he could catch his mouth in a kiss instead and let his free hand move to cradle the back of August's head.

August tensed; Theo felt it. And then August yielded completely, softening under Theo's arm as Theo gathered him close, pulling at the towel, pressing their bodies tight together. August's eyes fluttered shut, lashes tickling Theo's nose.

It was nothing like the kiss in the Sanctuary.

It was either penitence, or clemency, or a promise of feelings far less desperate and reckless than those in the heat of the feeding hour. Theo was neither willing nor ready to explain which it was. It was just sweet, and tender, and innocent. And it burned away all of Theo's flowery objections. They could not stand a chance against August's mouth.

August broke away with a tiny, startled breath as if he'd shocked himself by giving in to the gesture. Blushing hot like any proper man, he snatched the comb from Theo and started to brush his dripping hair, trying to turn away, clearing his throat and biting his mouth into a thin line.

"Isn't that what you wanted?" Theo murmured, his voice barely a whisper.

August stared dumbly. Finally he whispered, "Yes."

THE ATTIC door unlocked and opened with a small rattle. August lit up, expecting to see Theo—but it was Alistair, the Alpha, climbing the last step up into the attic room and gently closing the door behind himself.

August stiffened, sitting up straight and rigid, trying to restrain any look of uncertainty or distrust. Alistair's presence brought all the intimidation of an angry father, broad, thick shoulders and all, but his smile was somehow beguiling.

Alistair approached the foot of the bed. August's thoughts raced. Had he done something wrong? Did Alistair know he'd eavesdropped on him and that stranger James? Did he know about the kiss in the washroom? Had it broken some rule? He really needed to ask what the rules were because some of them just seemed plain contradictory—

"You must have found the library," Alistair commented, voice cutting through the dark. The candlelight shivered as he swept an arm out, gesturing to the books in the room.

August shook his head mutely. He closed *Philologie* and wished he didn't feel like such a weak, spineless thing before the Alpha. "They're Theo's."

Alistair was still for a painfully long moment, studying August. "I see," he finally said. His smile was soft and warm, but it seemed dishonest. It made August uneasy. "You and Theo read together, then?" Alistair pressed.

"Sometimes."

"Does he spend quite a lot of time with you?"

"Not a lot."

Alistair moved off to peek out the southern window at something unimportant before retracing his steps to the center of the room.

He announced, "The schedule has changed. You're doing well, which means the adjustment period is over. We require more sustenance, you see, to live healthily and normally—so the feeding hour now occurs every other night, strictly."

Alistair's eyes fixed on August, piercing into him. August's skin crawled. He really didn't want to be alone with Alistair, especially after what he'd overheard from the drawing room two weeks before. "Yes, sir," August whispered, not quite sure what else he should say.

Alistair nodded. "You see, August, we have a system here. We depend on you, just as you depend on us. Do you understand that?"

August almost asked how Alistair knew his name, but he remembered Theo saying they could taste things in his blood. Servants probably talked. Theo probably talked. August simply nodded in reply. He wanted to ask next why whomever Alistair had mentioned down in the drawing room said he was special. The questions burned on the tip of his tongue.

He didn't ask.

The Alpha bid him adieu and turned to leave. The door closed and August felt cold, gripping the blankets beside him.

He had questions. He had so many questions. Why did Alistair buy him? Why was there a mark on his wrist? Who did it? Why did they only feed on him? Was this what vampires were really like? Why did they have a set of rosary beads on a beaufet in the hallway if the cross repelled their kind? Where did they come from?

With a sick turn of the stomach and a frustrated scowl, August wished he'd asked at least something.

THE OXFORD coven visited London quite often, playing human with the metropolitan Undead. Ronald, Irene, Oliver, Angelique, and Daphne. The ladies cleaved instantly to Anastasia, snickering and gossiping behind lace fans with their hair swept up in fashionable knots and ringlets dangling down before their ears as the men threw back goblet after goblet of wine, waistcoats embroidered with metallic thread sparkling in the lamplight. Ronald and Alphonse could have been twins, walking arm-in-arm, dancing, laughing; Theo and Oliver sat together on the fringes of chophouses and dance halls, discussing the politics of the living and watching unknowing strangers in the nighttime crowds.

They saw plays and operas together. They visited museums and parks. They politely declined absinthe and opium-laced cigarettes in all the most popular clubs, and at séances and other spiritualist galas, they listened carefully out of kindred curiosity. If scientists were cataloguing ghosts and demons now, why, how long would it take for them to publish new reports on vampires that wouldn't be consigned to the era of witches and faith-based paranoia?

It was only natural, especially during the transition period between coven sacrifices, for a vampire to lust after faces in the city crowd.

"What about her?" Oliver purred confidentially, leaning close to Theo where they sat at a table overlooking the rest of the dance hall. They'd abandoned the card games earlier. The burlesque shows were starting. Oliver pointed to a young woman in a luscious silvery-blue gown, laughing at something an obvious suitor said as if she were well-practiced at pretending boring conversation pleased her.

Theo focused in on the woman, gaze roaming her over head to toe. If he focused he could pick up on her heartbeat. He could smell her perfume. If it were a few weeks later, he might have caught a strong thought or two from her even this far away, just from the energy she put off. But as it was, his vampire's acuity was weak.

"We only just returned to regular feeding hours," Theo explained.

"You must be going mad out here, then!" A look of pained sympathy twisted Oliver's face. "Mad with all this temptation—"

"No." Theo shook his head, drawing a long swallow of smoky red wine. He licked his lips, pressed them into a thin line, and cleared his throat. His teeth ached as he fought the tingling yawn-like urge to slip his eyeteeth out into fangs. "No, actually. Not quite."

"Really?" Oliver's face softened into friendly doubt. "You aren't lusting for blood?"

Theo shook his head another time, avoiding Oliver's eyes. He threw his gaze out elsewhere, observing the club around them but not really looking at anything. He *was* lusting. But not for anyone in London's crepuscular world, no. Not tonight. Not for the past few nights.

He saw all the beautiful men and women, so many prime specimens with sweet, healthy blood pumping through them, but all he could think about was August Prescott.

August, the twenty-ninth sacrifice of the London coven, back in the attic of the house in Berkeley Square. August, precious August, and the way his blood sparked on Theo's tongue like his utterly compliant kisses.

A young lady in red and darker red flirted at him with her eyes from across the balcony.

Theo smiled faintly, nodded her way in dismissal before looking elsewhere.

He was angry suddenly—it was like a tight knot in his chest. This setting suffocated him tonight, the swirl of people, the colors and sounds of the world, the vast everything that left him anonymous and shadowy. Most of the time he loved it. It was comforting, promising, freeing.

Tonight he could not stop thinking about that bastard Lucius who had wronged August.

He could taste the bitterness as if he were swallowing it from August's throat again now, the muffled pain and injustice. August himself did not remember. It was a fleeting feeling Theo caught from him. But it was enough to understand that Lucius, whoever he was, had been important to August, and Lucius had hurt August, and it was a strong enough feeling that the pain was surely fresh. The fact that it sparked a mild flame of jealousy worried Theo a little.

He wanted to mend the deep, cold ache left by Lucius in August's murky memories.

And while all the others, his coven brothers and sister, all of them, flirted with temptation tonight out with unknowing mortals, August was nothing but blood to them.

It was not so to Theo. It was not so at all.

Damn. He was in trouble, wasn't he?

"Well, thank God your adjustment period is over," Oliver said, clearly hoping to lighten the mood. He lifted his drink, smirking softly over his patterned solitaire necktie.

Theo met Oliver's drink with his own. "I'll toast to that," he muttered.

"YOUR HAIR is getting long," Hazel announced. She spoke like an older sister. She set the rosewood dinner tray down at the foot of the bed, turning to study August where he sat below the attic window with pen and paper.

August frowned, squinting, trying to see his reflection in the window in the glow of the candles. Yes, his hair was certainly getting long. It waved in unruly layers on his neck, tousled by sleep and otherwise ignored.

"Your food will get cold," Hazel said.

"I talked to the Alpha," August announced, dragging his blanket like a royal cloak as he abandoned the paper and crossed the attic, climbing onto the bed to eat his dinner. *"Alistair,"* he corrected himself. Hazel's eyes burned into him. She said nothing. August cleared his throat and poked at the chops on his plate. He added, "He told me that the feeding hour will happen every other night, now."

"Yes," Hazel murmured, as if she knew this.

August frowned. "I wanted to ask him questions, questions about the vampires and the rules and this way of life, but…." He shrugged, scowling now. "I couldn't."

"That's all right," Hazel whispered, looking lovingly down at one of the books stacked near the bed. August almost offered it to her, but he wasn't sure how well she could read. He needed to read it to her aloud sometime, then. He glanced up as he ate, studying Hazel's face—the soft girlish features, the incredible maturity on such young cheeks, the way a few curls fell loose from the plaits about her ears.

"How old are you?" August asked.

"I'm eighteen," Hazel said. August thought that maybe, if they had met under different circumstances, he might have fallen in love at first sight. She had such a solemn beauty. But as it was, he loved her in a respectful, thankful way. She was his friend. And he was finding that presently he was much more inclined toward the same sex. It was a lot easier to admit that to himself here, alone, memoryless, without all the world breathing down his neck.

"One of the maids said she worked here because her son was a sacrifice," August ventured next. His dinner sat for the most part forgotten in front of him. "Why do you work here, Hazel?"

Hazel flopped down in the wingback chair and glared at him. "You're talkative tonight," she mumbled.

"Why do you work here—"

"I heard you." Hazel sighed, lacing her fingers in her lap. "I decided it was much better than joining a ladies' boarding house."

August was momentarily taken aback by her bitter humor. She stared at him as if challenging him to inquire further. He did.

"But were you really driven to that choice?"

"I started housekeeping as a scullery maid," Hazel confessed finally. "I moved to a different house when I was thirteen and I governed these lovely children in a huge country home. I miss them sometimes. It was only a short while that I was there, because the family left for the Continent and I was let go because I wanted to stay in England. My only choice then was between Madame Felicity's on Fleet Street and an ad for a household many servants gossiped about." She paused, nodding decisively. "I chose the ad."

August was silent, watching her. She showed not the slightest twitch of nostalgia or regret on her face, and although he felt as if she might have been intentionally vague with her story, he didn't blame her. August had heard about Madame Felicity's Fleet Street *maison de joie*, Madame Felicity the voluptuous crimson-clad mistress who "never aged." Rumor said that like women were hired every few years to keep the hoax alive. Wasn't that ironic? He—

He *remembered that*.

Heart jumping to his throat, August offered Hazel his tea. She politely declined, smiling wistfully.

"I'm glad you chose the ad," August said, desperate for distraction suddenly. "I don't think I could have wished for a better maid."

Hazel blushed. For the first time ever, it seemed she was plagued by humility. She smiled primly, lashes lowered. She didn't say anything.

August wasn't done, though. "But why did you choose here? What did you think of them? The *vampires*?"

"I didn't know at first." Hazel shrugged idly.

"I'm sorry," August commiserated. "I wish I could tell you about me, but I don't remember. I can't really remember, not a thing before that place below the church—"

"What place?" Hazel whispered.

"With the vampires. The place that smelled like dirt," August mumbled.

Hazel stared at him sadly, but she didn't pry any further. Her sadness curdled; she was closing up again. August watched her, and something occurred to him with a bitter little chill of insight.

Hazel knew everything. She knew everything about the vampires, and she wouldn't tell him.

That irritated him. It alarmed him. But more than that, it troubled him.

It troubled him greatly.

CHAPTER SEVEN

HAZEL LEFT the attic door unlocked, waving at August from the stairs as she dropped the key into her pocket. It was the second night she'd done as much in a row. She smiled quickly, tightly, and then she was gone.

August put on the smoking jacket from Theo and slipped out and down to the third floor.

The vampires were downstairs. He could hear the echo of voices and assembly, like friends gathered for a casual evening of leisure.

There was the *click* of a latch and the sigh of a door opening down the hall. August looked over quickly, startled.

From the door next to the music room, warm light spilled out into the hallway. There was a flash of color near the hinges as whoever had opened the door moved into the room, and then nothing. The door stayed open.

August didn't think twice.

He strolled down the hall toward the open door. He could hear movement. It wasn't a maid; he knew that much for sure. It was one of the bedrooms.

It was Theo's room.

August stood in the open doorway, fiddling with the long sleeves of the smoking jacket. Theo looked up from the cabinet in the corner of the room and met August's eyes immediately.

There was a small, shy silence between them, empty-eyed vampire and inquisitive coven sacrifice.

"I see my robe's come in handy," Theo announced.

August nodded.

"Come in," Theo invited, sounding impatient. He turned away again, throwing down his frock coat and rolling up his sleeves. His braces hung off his shoulders, casually. August glimpsed in a flash of pale skin a familiar-looking scar on Theo's left wrist.

L o n.

So the vampires had it too. Or at least Theo did.

Theo's bedroom was as perplexing as its owner. August pushed the sleeves of the smoking jacket up to his elbows, wandering into the jumbled room with curiosity buzzing in his fingertips. The bedroom was typical enough, drapery drawn on the windows to let in the moonlight, a few candles lit around the room, a sturdy oak bed with a high headboard and hand-carved posts. Weren't vampires supposed to sleep in coffins? Stripes of blue danced down the wallpaper, and there was an imported rug somewhere on the smooth floorboards August couldn't see for the zoo of odd furniture stuffed in the room. There was hardly even space to walk.

Theo dragged a velvet wingback armchair out of the corner. He situated it before the fire and sat down with an idle sigh, while behind him August stood dumbly amongst an army of other chairs marching about the room. Two curricle chairs, a bergère chair, walnut stools, a thick old Elizabethan oak chair. Against the far wall was a day bed of different-colored stripes, a few mismatching pillows tossed along its cushions.

Littered amongst the collection of chairs was an even wider collection of chessboards and clocks: a games table, the ivory-and-walnut set August recognized, tiny delineated figures of queens and kings and knights and bishops, next to broad, thick sets with fat marble pieces. Theo had them set up and ready to play, waiting around the room untouched. There was a satinwood bracket clock, a white-and-blue French clock, and a giltwood ebonized clock that matched the mirror above it.

Next to Theo's bed was a detailed side cabinet with fabric-paneled doors of a delightful cream color, flanked by shelves of books. A bottle of wine and stained glasses sat abandoned atop it. Somewhere in the middle of the army of chairs stood a revolving bookstand full of more books. August caught the title of one: *Fantasmagoriana*.

August wandered around the room, touching all the old chairs that Theo had collected and carefully arranged, the spines of the books on all the shelves. He moved with as much caution as he could, so as not to knock over any chess pieces as he examined them. He touched all the faces of the clocks. It was warm and it smelled like old book pages and the rich fruitiness of wine. All the clocks ticked away, a chorus of background noise.

The room was in perfect chaos, disorderly and quaint, and Theo sat contentedly before the fire like a proud man before all his tenure.

"Where did you get all these things?" August probed.

Theo shrugged.

"Why?" August asked next, touching the edge of *Fantasmagoriana* with a timid fingertip and a pining in his chest. And all around it were books in other languages, books he recognized, fantastic literature of all the different gothic, tragic spectrums he enjoyed. Maybe *Philologie* had come from these shelves.

"Because I like these things," Theo confessed quietly, as if he were afraid to be open about it.

"Theo…," August said, running his hand down the arm of the red chair Theo sat in. He smiled when Theo glanced at him, and the heat from the fire was warm, but as he realized that Theo looked at him as if he was something important, the flame that swelled in his chest was much hotter. August motioned to a nearby setup of untouched chess. "Shall we play?"

Theo was silent. For a moment he looked very much like the vampire August often forgot he was—pale, tired, the glow of the dim light bouncing on the narrow ashen features of his face. But then his mouth twitched into an acquiescent smile, and the clever-eyed gentleman was back. Maybe a little sick, a little alluring, but human enough.

They played chess on three of Theo's seven sets, rearranged the chairs together, smiled and talked like old companions.

"I got this chair from Moscow, and this from Venice."

"You did?"

"I took these books from a library in Paris."

"Theo, you're a thief!"

Theo delivered August back to the attic room just before midnight, but they came together again when August fell into his lap halfway through the feeding in the Sanctuary, bloodied and breathless and begging for more of that delicious connection, that vampiric magic that welled up inside him and calmed him down when they drank from him. Theo held him close and August could feel his wizened heartbeat as a fluttering echo between their chests.

Hazel brought dinner at three o'clock, when the world outside the attic seemed frighteningly dead. Theo followed her up. He brought *Fantasmagoriana*.

AUGUST DREAMED he was in the forest.

He didn't know what forest, but he was deep in it, turning circles in the filtered light. Pine needles made a cool green carpet underfoot, between his naked toes, fresh on bare skin like mint on the tongue. The breeze combed its fingers through his hair and swirled whisper-soft kisses on his face, threading through his fingers as he held his hands out and turned round and round.

He stepped carefully over fairy circles, aware somewhere in the back of his mind he was making wish after wish, but he couldn't hold on to them long enough to know what it was that he wished for. There was an echo on the wind, a humming voice, a singing voice, a low and bubbling hymn that swam through the clearing and tickled his ears. It made his hair stand on end, his heart pound, his blood rush.

Someone approached just outside the clearing. August didn't know who it was. Just as the shadow came close enough to be a form in the leaves, with the easy subtlety of dreams the scene changed.

Thunder growled somewhere above. A darkness fell, swallowing up all the green and leaving nothing but fog. August looked around. Creeping mist rippled away from his elbows and knees. The carpet of pine needles and grass turned to the cold hard-packed dirt of a land too bitter for crops. August searched for the line of trees, for the place where he'd seen the shadow, but it was gone. Thunder clapped again and there was one flash of lightning, right before the fog began to thin and August realized with a flinch of surprise he stood in the middle of a funeral.

He knew the voice on the air now. It was the requiem of grief-laden men and women, shivering along as the dream took a turn for the lachrymose.

August watched as they passed him, rendered speechless and disoriented. The people moved with sluggish purpose, some watching their feet and some looking up into the thundering sky, all of them singing, singing. They ran into him, jostled him. The people were shadows. He could make out their presence and outlines, but the fog was still too deep; they stumbled along, encumbered and grieving.

And then there was the casket.

The shadow people laid the flower-covered casket at his feet like a sacrifice to a god. The wails of the funeral procession echoed. There were no lyrics, just ghostly hums, stretched-out whispers tickling his ears and running down his spine like a cold sweat. The casket overflowed with hawthorn and wild roses, rosary beads fixed among the blossoms, the velvet, the moldering lace. August's breath tasted like the fog, like death and rain. He knew—he had to know—exactly what hid beneath the ornamentations, and when the lid of the casket began to move and the doleful singing wavered on the air above the scratching of nails and the grind of wood upon wood, his ears began to ring and he watched in horror as the corpse began to rise from the casket—

And suddenly August was in a dark bedroom, surrounded by dancing clocks and chess pieces and chairs, and in the middle, arms open for him, lapels the same stunning claret as the blood staining his lips, was a vampire.

August woke up with a start to the little attic room.

It was cold and the sun was still setting. He tumbled out of bed, scampering to the corner where the stationary and quill pen Theo brought him had been lying for nights. The images and sensations from his dreams whirled in his head, a tempest of a vision he yearned to put into words.

The last enemy to be defeated is death joined *A bird in a cage.*

That was it.

He wasn't satisfied with it.

He tried to read the book Theo had brought, but some of the words were beyond his humble knowledge of French. That upset him more.

Hazel came by. She removed the bloody bandage from his neck and washed the bite marks, which seemed to heal faster than they should have. August knew she could sense his bad mood. He was thankful she didn't pry.

HAZEL WAS actually quite the little rebel, apparently.

She stopped locking the attic door at all, smiling and waving at August when she left, dropping the key into her pocket with an innocent purse of the lips as if to say, "Oops, how did that get in there before I locked up?"

August tiptoed down to Theo's room, but the door was closed and there were no sounds of movement within.

He tried again the next evening, bringing *Fantasmagoriana*. All the rooms save one were open, but empty. He passed Alphonse in the hall and offered him a humble smile. Alphonse stared at him as if he didn't recognize him, chin moving over his shoulder as his blank eyes followed August—but then suddenly recognition bloomed in them and he lit up, offering a wink in greeting.

Theo was in his room this time, sitting cross-legged on his bed. He was picking through the cogs of a little clock that had broken down. Gone were the traces of the pale-faced, encumbered vampire. In their place was a handsome man—smooth jaw, perfect straight nose, almond eyes full of concentration.

Theo didn't notice August in the doorway, so obsessed was he with the infrastructure of the little clock, but then he spoke as if he'd known August was there the entire time, beckoning "Come in."

August shuffled through the chorus of *clicks* and *clanks* as Theo fumbled with the timepiece on the bed. French clocks, German clocks, Italian clocks, Russian clocks; there were clocks from decades ago and clocks that didn't work anymore, a grandfather clock, a pile of discolored pocket watches, clocks set to railway time, clocks stuck at midnight, and a singular one ticking away at a totally wrong time while a few others were just a couple minutes off.

August stopped below the black-and-gold giltwood clock in the corner of the room. He looked up into the mirror above it. He could see Theo over his shoulder, hunched down fastidiously on the bed still.

Maybe it wasn't just Alphonse who was strange. Maybe all vampires were a little peculiar, tarnished by the passing of time. Vampires didn't age. What did that do to a soul, anyway? August couldn't imagine going on forever and ever. Then again, he hadn't really tried to imagine it, either.

Theo's smoking jacket dragged the collar of his nightshirt low on one shoulder and August was caught for a moment by the pallor of his skin, the bruises, the spidery violet broken blood vessels and sickeningly livid bite marks.

"The bites heal faster than scrapes," August commented.

"We're vampires," Theo said quickly, as if it would explain everything.

The wine glasses atop Theo's cabinet had been cleaned up from the other night and a new bottle of wine sat among them. August wandered around the chairs to the revolving bookstand, easing down to sit on the little stool there. He studied the titles of the books, one by one.

"What do you read?" August asked.

"Whatever I want," Theo returned curtly. August frowned at him over his shoulder, but he knew Theo's apathy wasn't meant to be spiteful. "You can see my collection. I have some ghost stories. I particularly enjoy vampire stories. They amuse me."

Theo liked vampire literature. That was laughable in the same sense that it was somewhat melancholy. August was suddenly a little cowed as he watched Theo fiddle away with the clock. The stealthy longing for the touch of the vampire stirred in his chest. God, it was dangerous, the black magic of the Undead. But wasn't it only natural to be so fiercely fascinated with that which one feared?

Theo returned the backing to the timepiece with a triumphant little gasp, not quite a word yet but an adequate vessel for his excitement. The clock started to tick away, joining the chatter of all the others.

August cleared his throat, finally gathering the courage to ask what he meant to ask. "Would you read to me, Theo...?"

Theo stared blankly at August as if he hadn't realized he was there despite talking to him. He looked down at the clock he'd fixed, then back to August. He blinked a few times and focus returned to his piercing green eyes.

August held up *Fantasmagoriana*. "I've tried, but I can't read this very well...."

Theo reached for the book. August stood, handing it to him. Theo squinted at it, stroking his thumbs over the old cover. "Yes," he conceded. "Why not? Should I read it in French or in English?"

"English," August said, taking a seat in a chair near the bed. "Do you speak French, Theo?"

"I speak whatever language I want to," Theo replied.

"Because you're a vampire?" August surmised dryly.

"Because I'm a vampire," Theo confirmed without noticing August's sarcasm. It seemed to be the answer for whatever question August might ask. It made sense, though it was a clear injustice. August could forgive it. He wanted to know everything.

Theo drew a breath, and as he prepared to read, he looked perfectly soft and human. August smiled.

The Family Portraits began in Theo's silky tenor. The story opened, unfolding in August's mind as Theo read, upon a stagecoach making its way through the old Holy Roman Empire just after dusk, as Ferdinand Meltheim returned home to accept his father's inheritance....

STANDING TOGETHER at the southern window, looking out at the London plane trees in Berkeley Square, August told Hazel, "I think I'm beginning to understand them."

Hazel shot him such a touched expression that August blushed, glancing away. She whispered, "Pardon my audacity," and clutched his hand tight. Her fingers were warm. They were reassuring after endless nights of the cool fingers of vampires, and August closed his eyes, leaning against the window, fingers laced with Hazel's.

"I wish we could have met under different circumstances," he admitted aloud. He watched her reflection in the window shift and shiver in the candlelight. Her dark feathery hair, her oval-shaped face, her gray owl eyes. Hazel gawked at him as if appalled. Maybe if they had been a boy and girl meeting formally at a drawing room party, she would have blushed. But as it stood, they both worked for vampires, her lace cap was crooked, and she smiled wryly as all her cynical nature called for.

"You're a romantic little thing," she scorned kindly, as if she were the elder of them both. "Well, I'll tell you, August, I like it better this way. You're my only good friend." She gave his hand a gentle squeeze. "And that aside we both know who you'd rather kiss."

Embarrassed, August cast her a look of guilty shock, mouth open. But there was nothing to protest. She wouldn't let go of his hand.

"Enough of that," he mumbled. "I can read to you, if you'd like? I have *The Sketch Book*, which we have yet to finish...."

CHAPTER EIGHT

HAZEL BROUGHT him hot cider instead of tea.

"It's All Hallows Eve," she justified.

The thought made August shiver once—and then the shiver returned, this time with enthusiasm in its touch. Outside the northern window, dead leaves danced, and in the candles Hazel lit they cast their shadows around the attic. It was the night of spooks and spectaculars, of inexplicable childhood fears and bobbing for apples.

He shared hot cider with Hazel. They both jumped at every creak of the house and whisper of the wind as he recounted tales from *Fantasmagoriana* (from Theo's translation, of course) and she spun wild ghost stories out from her memory, told to her during childhood or eerie nights working in a country manor.

It was when Hazel took the dirty dishes back down to the kitchen that August heard it. Floating up the stairs, leaking into the attic from beneath the door—*music*.

A single violin, the soul-stirring whine of a number August felt as if he recognized but could not give a name.

He slid out of bed, wrapped in his blanket. He opened the door just a crack, peering down the dark stairs. The glow from a well-lit hallway filled the landing, and as the wind of an early winter scattered leaves against the roof, August neatly folded his blanket at the foot of his bed and trotted down the stairs. He peeked around the corner to see if the hall was clear. It was.

The heart-wrenching voice of the violin shivered between feeble *piano* notes and powerful, vibrating echoes, filling the hall. It came from the music room, without a doubt. It sounded a little like a funeral's Requiem Mass, but it seemed as if whoever played it played by memory, taking the liberty to bounce through the different movements at will as the only instrument involved, skipping from *Lacrimosa dies illa* to *Dies irae* to *Lux aeterna* and back.

It was Alphonse.

The door to the music room was open and all the flames of all the candles danced as if to the mournful melody. August was enchanted by the magic Alphonse could create when he actually lifted the bow to the violin—awkward, sometimes-a-bit-off-key magic, but it drew August in like a siren song.

Alphonse met his stare from across the music room, head bowed over his instrument and body swaying to the tune. His hazel eyes glinted, pierced into August with the strength of words. They beckoned him in, and August was not afraid.

Maybe it was the mystery of All Hallows and the magic of Alphonse's clumsy playing, but August was excited. He wanted to make Alphonse laugh. He bowed as if he were in a hall full of people, and then into the music room he swayed.

He danced with an imaginary lady, whispering the steps to himself that he'd tried so hard to memorize in some distant life before. He waltzed slowly about the room between piano and harp, stepping carefully over more scattered music sheets and not worried about stepping on his invisible partner's skirts.

The music whirled around them and Alphonse cheered, pleased apparently to not be playing for an audience of candles tonight. August felt ridiculous—a grown man dancing alone like a fool. And yet he didn't care. He laughed too, and their laughter was the choir.

Alphonse closed with a smooth *ritardando*, fingers quivering on the strings. August froze in another bow, winded, flushed, grinning at Alphonse. Alphonse returned the gesture, and for the first time Alphonse seemed actually lucid.

August applauded. Alphonse took another bow.

A second round of applause sounded from the doorway, and both Alphonse and August looked over sharply in surprise to find Theo there near the hall.

August bristled, eyes wide. "Theo!" he snapped indignantly, a little embarrassed Theo had watched unannounced. Alphonse watched as if the dynamics at play piqued his curiosity.

Theo smirked. He wore a black waistcoat with collar near to his jawline, ornamented with vertical stripes of a dark red. He shrugged, crossed his arms, moved into the room, and leaned against the pianoforte.

"Are these the festivities for tonight?" he prompted.

Alphonse gasped. "Tonight is—! Oh, are there any masquerades we could go to? Oh please, Theo, say there are!"

Theo shrugged another time. Alphonse wilted. Theo gestured with his usual casual grace. "Play again, would you, Alphonse? Schubert, please. His String Quartet number fourteen, *andante con moto*."

Theo held out a hand.

August stared at it.

Slowly he reached out to acquiesce. For a moment he considered a teasing comment about who would be dancing the man's part—but then he let Theo take his palm and move out into the open floor of the music room, away from the chairs and the piano and the harp. August didn't mind following Theo's lead. He didn't know what dance they'd be dancing, anyway.

Alphonse played the Schubert piece. Together August and Theo danced, and the candlelight seemed to dance with them, the shadows of their fellow ladies and gentlemen swirling about an imaginary ballroom.

And August believed in All Hallows Eve again. He believed in it beyond the ghost stories, the tradition, the excuse for upright and strict-natured men and women to have a party. He believed in it with all the irrational faith of a child, eyes wide as he gawked up at Theo, and they danced.

August understood.

The world belonged not just to the living, but to the Undead.

There were no lines to cross; their worlds did not parallel. It was but one realm, and the living, the dead, and the immortal all shared it.

August trembled as this finally sank into him, and he trembled because he could feel the magic working beneath his skin—that unsympathetic charm of the vampire, stirring delicious warmth and desire in the pit of his chest. It just wasn't fair. He couldn't even be afraid.

Theo danced without a flaw, and Alphonse played music about doom as August dipped along with Theo, heart racing. He could not get rid of his breathless smile. He was lost in the motions and the music, and *this*—this ironic, macabre, alluring scene in the music room as the lamb danced with the lion—*this* was what All Hallows Eve was about, surely.

One of the vampires whose name August did not know—Number Three in the inventory he observed, with dark hair and deep, intelligent eyes—appeared in the doorway. August stopped short. Theo looked offended. But August was unsure of whether or not they were about to be reprimanded; he was still intimidated by the colder and more impersonal masters of the house.

But Theo just laughed. "Come on, then!" he coaxed Number Three, and the dancing became merrier all of a sudden.

Alphonse skipped to the *presto* of Schubert's piece, however coarse as the only violin. August stumbled through the steps with Theo. Theo was still laughing. Number Seven of the vampires showed up next to Number Three, his young man's mask of impartiality lifting for a moment as a smile broke across his face and he clapped to the beat. Number Three finally joined him, chuckling.

The eeriness dissipated, leaving nothing but a handful of carefree men dancing with each other like fools. No one cared about the right moves or steps; the room was full of laughter and music as its occupants were reduced to playful children. It was freeing. It was comforting. It was—

Familiar.

August had been here before. No, he had felt this before, this blurring of the line between play and work. With close friends and loved ones before all of this. Bachelors. Cousins. Brothers. Dancing in a gentlemen's club, screaming, laughing, popping champagne bottles in someone's drawing room, smoking endless chains of cigarettes, hair loose, waistcoats undone, wild drunken liberation of the senses, and—*Lucius*.

A name.

Oh God, he remembered a name. Lucius.

And kissing. Wandering hands. Hot, excited, illicit embraces, a popular rebellion against society's stuffy demands. With Lucius or someone else?

August shoved away from Theo to dance arm in arm with Number Seven, frantic for distraction.

He didn't want to remember.

Not right now at least.

Remembering would threaten everything his world had become, and to be honest, in this moment, on this night, in this room with Theo and Alphonse and Seven and Three—he was *happy*.

With a strange, lonesome throb in his chest, August realized the vampires were much more human than he accredited them. These in the

Berkeley Square coven were most certainly more elegant than the ones who had auctioned him off. They weren't kind, but they weren't beasts until the feeding hour. With their mystery and chilling charm, they were monsters, but in their own way, each one of them was still so very human.

Hazel had told him the vampires fed on him so that they didn't terrorize innocent humans. He'd wrongfully equated them with murderers. He'd thought of them as killers, monsters and blood-drinking fiends, and yet—they fed on nobody but him. He thought of Hazel's words, so many uncomplicated statements, and of the vampires' obvious mercy on mankind, their grisly, cursed sophistication.

How was he to hate them for that? It would be a selfish thing.

Number Seven's fingers were smooth like satin. Number Three danced as if he'd studied gypsies. August ducked under Theo's arm, spinning behind him. He saw the girl vampire, blonde curls and ribbons, standing with Ishmael near the door. She grinned. Ishmael was not so entertained. He turned and stormed away as the girl skipped in to join the party. August danced with her. He didn't know the last time he'd danced with a girl. They tripped and stumbled, neither of them being very practiced. But tonight the girl did not scare him. She grabbed his face with both hands and planted a kiss on his mouth, and Seven cheered. They circled each other palm to palm, mocking prudence, and as August passed, Theo locked eyes with him.

August's heart jumped. His smile fell. Theo's eyes burned into him. There was no smile on Theo's face. There was something dazed and strange, a little threatening. Like the way he'd looked at him before he kissed him. Not in the washroom, but so many nights ago in the Sanctuary.

August was out of breath and caught victim by Theo's endless eyes, so intense in their Undead sway—

The music stopped with a horrible shriek of bow on violin strings. The vampires fell absolutely still. August followed suit, eyes wide, but with a little less grace as he stumbled over a footstool.

In the doorway was Alistair. Behind him was Ishmael, and there might have been the despicable gleam of a spoiled child in his eyes.

Like a candle being snuffed out, the innocent fun was gone. The Alpha's presence seemed to sap it all out, leaving nothing but a cold, capricious tension in its place. There was nothing but the crackle and hiss of burning candlewicks and August's nervous breath.

Ah, right; these were his vampire masters, not his friends.

Alistair surveyed the inhabitants of the room with hands clasped behind his back. He wasn't upset, no. But he looked a little perplexed.

Behind him Ishmael's narrowed eyes sparked.

"What exactly is this?" Alistair asked, voice cutting through the silence. He glanced from vampire to vampire, to human sacrifice, to vampire. He didn't wait for a response. "We must remember the rules now, brothers and sister, and the rules may easily be forgotten in such a scene as this."

"It's a festive night," Alphonse insisted, looking like a puppy left out in the rain. "Alistair, we were just having fun—"

"Sometimes fun leads to intemperance, and intemperance often leads to mistakes." Alistair spoke as if teaching virtue and decency. It was annoying to August. It was a new thing to be annoyed by Alistair. He wasn't sure it was good.

"Alistair," Number Three prompted gently, meeting Alistair's eyes. "It's All Hallows Eve," he reminded, but he must have said something else in his glance because the expression changed on the Alpha's face. There was a long, heavy hush—and then suddenly Alistair was across the room and standing before August.

August recoiled, startled. Alistair did not smile; his eyes were distant.

He held his hand out as if asking for a dance.

The silence rang in August's ears and all their powerful stares crawled on his skin.

August looked to Theo, uncertain. Theo's eyes ushered him on sharply. August didn't really like it. It felt as if he were being thrown to the wolves as some sort of sacrifice—*oh*. Well, that made sense, didn't it?

August took the Alpha's hand in consent, and suddenly wild, imaginative scenes flooded his mind as if Alistair's touch passed them on through some Undead sorcery.

They were foreign images; August did not think them up on his own. He heard music, beautiful music, a quartet with the correct instruments and a vast ballroom with the buzzing presence of many vampires swirling about in resplendent dress, sharing kisses and blood, and in the middle of them all was a beautiful boy with the eyes of an old soul who looked up at Alistair and said something, something awful and unsympathetic, and then the beautiful boy disappeared into the crowd. The heady scent of blood and flesh bloomed around him, and August gagged, drowning in the preternatural caress of the vision Alistair shared with him somehow—

August blinked and the scene was gone as quickly as he'd felt it, and he realized with a start that he was dancing around the cluttered music room with the Alpha.

It was a waltz again, but this time Alphonse played the correct music, though anxiously. The other vampires in the room stared. Alistair led August around between piano and harp and sofas, drifting on the smooth graceful squares of the Waltz. August was tense. Alistair's hands were cool and firm. He was power, authority, darkness, death—

Yes, August felt a little bit as if he were dancing with Death itself. But Alistair's smile was also… *tender*.

Obvious hatred burned in Ishmael's stare from the doorway. All the others watched them as if watching royalty. August was dumbfounded. The Alpha was actually a handsome man, middle-aged maybe when he had become what he was. August remembered seeing him in the crowd below the mausoleum when he was auctioned off. He remembered the way it had felt when Alistair's teeth plunged into his virgin neck.

Alistair spun him out, and then back in.

"Oh my God," August breathed, looking up at the Alpha. "You're not evil, you're just *sad*, aren't you?"

Alistair dipped him back and the waltz ended. August panted in the Alpha's strong hands, dizzy, suspended above the floor. The blood pounded in his ears. His skin was hot. Without thinking, he fisted his fingers in Alistair's lapels and cocked his head back, offering his throat. He waited. He waited for the sharp, burning pinch of needle-like teeth slipping through his skin. He waited for the almost erotic pull of blood from his throat. He—

Alistair dropped him.

August tumbled to the floor in a mess of elbows and knees. "Ouch!" he cried, everything rushing back into focus, a pinpoint of painful clarity as Alistair turned and swept out of the music room, Ishmael close on his heels. He cast a glance back at August. It seemed a protective threat.

"Bravo!" The girl vampire laughed, highly entertained. She clapped. It shattered the silence. "Bravo!" She hastened toward August, crying, "My turn!"

Theo shoved her back, snatching August up by the elbow. He dragged him out of the music room, and August was still wide-eyed and mute with shock.

AUGUST'S ELBOWS hurt from hitting the music room floor.

Theo sat with his back to him in a dusty satin-lined chair, a crystal glass of vintage wine in his hand.

The silence was volatile. August didn't know what had happened. Had he done something? Had he forgotten something? Where was the quick young man with the cat-eyed smile who had been playing with him earlier? Was Theo angry with him, or angry with Alistair?

What came out instead of any of those questions was, candid and meek, "You can drink wine?"

"Transubstantiation," Theo hissed. He gestured to the bottle, wine swirling in his glass. "Pour yourself some, why don't you?"

August obeyed, pouring a glass of wine. He sat down again in a chair off to Theo's left. The wine was thick and sharp on the tongue, burning gloriously in his chest as he swallowed.

"Theo," August ventured, "what just happened in the music room?"

"You need to be more careful," Theo snapped, avoiding the real question altogether. "If you tempt us too much, one of us might break the rules, and the rules are very important."

"If I *tempt you* too much?" August echoed, appalled and mildly offended by such blaming of the victim. "I'm your *pet*."

Theo shot him a look that made August flinch back, holding his breath. As if struggling to keep his fury in check, Theo finished off his wine in one long swallow and then refilled his glass.

"I'm sorry," he whispered. "I'm just hungry." It was pitiful and frightening at once for exactly what it was, almost misery. Theo's eyes were honest and his face ashen.

"The feeding hour was only last night," August insisted.

"That doesn't mean I feel satisfied," Theo countered almost combatively.

"And you can't feed otherwise—?"

"It's against the rules."

"Does wine help?"

"I told you, *transubstantiation*, August."

"I don't understand."

Theo laughed. It was a little cruel. There was an aggrieved tension in every line of his body, from his crossed ankles to his rigid shoulders to his narrowed green eyes. "The 'blood of Christ,' August. If I were to eat or drink anything else, my body would reject it within minutes. But the blood of Christ—*wine*—somehow our unholy nature is granted one precious commodity like that. And yes, it helps. A little."

Theo's eyes were sharp and wild. It was the same Theo, the same cultured, handsome Theo, but it was a part of him he had hidden well from August until then. It was a part of him that seemed to struggle with self-control, as if all his resolve and strength trembled as string after string connecting them to his will snapped. He looked a frightening mess, ashamed and scared and furious, and it intensified the inhuman glint in his eyes. August didn't like it. He wanted Theo to be calm and well-behaved again. He wanted Theo to be a curious, very human monster again. They could read *Fantasmagoriana* and drink wine together, and—

"Vampires," Theo said through his teeth, voice raw and ragged, "do not feed because they want to. We feed because we have to. It's our *nature*, a need and a hunger—and it cramps tight in the chest, and won't let go until satisfied. Adjustment periods between sacrifices are difficult. When we go back to feeding every other night, my self-control falters. It's a shameful thing. I despise it. I'm sorry you have to see it. God damn it, August, I was doing so well. So well! But seeing you, being around you, that close to you and with such formalities stripped away—I wanted you. *I want you*, August."

August stared. His heart thundered in his chest. His fingers were cold suddenly.

And yet some secret, haunting part of him whispered greedily, *Yes, finally.*

"I'm hungry," Theo said, as if it were August's fault. His words almost quavered. His narrowed eyes were glassy. He craned over from his chair, jaw tight. "I want to feel you and taste you, and I want your blood and your love. I want you to offer yourself, and I want you to look at me with eyes full of worship. How selfish is that? I was controlling myself, August. I was stifling it. I had control over this damned hunger, this cold, empty need, and then tonight...."

Theo shook his head. He stood swiftly, tossing back another mouthful of wine. God, there was something very wrong with August's moral sense if he found even Theo's volatile side this attractive, in a harsh, lissome way. *Passion*. It was fierce, violent, natural passion.

Theo set both hands on the arms of August's chair. He loomed down over him. August's eyes widened. He could smell the wine on Theo's breath, and something rotten. He was paralyzed below Theo's burning eyes, the eyes of a trapped man. They bored into August as if seeking to burrow into his very soul. He felt guilt. He was driving Theo to this point, after all. Theo, sophisticated and profound, was this affected by him. He was losing grip on himself. He had been the whole time they'd been in the music room, and here August had thought it was simple gallivanting for all of them.

"Tonight, when Alistair had you," Theo seethed, caging August in on the upholstered chair, "when he moved with you and the *feeling*, oh, it was so palpable on the air, in your eyes, and I was so angry! I was jealous! I was possessive all of a sudden, I wanted you in my hands, I wanted to steal you away from him because I don't want anybody to have what I can't. Christ, August, yes, I was distinctly possessive of you, and I don't know why it was so... so formidable—"

August's nails scraped the fabric as he clutched the arms of the chair, enchanted and aghast at the same time. His heart pounded as he feared the impending feeding, Theo losing control and breaking the vampire's rules. He didn't fear for himself, though. God no. He should have, maybe, being so objectified. But he feared for Theo's sake.

"There's a love between a vampire and its sacrifice, you know," Theo edged out, quietly. "It's different from any love you've ever known. Are you frightened?"

August opened his mouth. Nothing came out. He closed his mouth again.

"Yes?" Theo answered for him. "You should be, because this is the reality. You think I am your friend, but I am a monster, and my desire for your friendship springs from that crucial fact."

August was stunned. He was confounded. He was furious because he couldn't find the words to reply. He felt as if he should have been terrified of the vampire looming over him—and on some level he was—but—sin, what sin? What was immorality? And was any love comparable to this, this delicious hedonistic warmth throbbing in his chest as August abandoned his wine and threw his arms around Theo's shoulders, succumbing completely to the vampire's noxious desire?

He missed the table. His glass of wine crashed to the floor with a splash of deep, vibrant burgundy on the carpet as he clawed close and craned up into a desperate kiss.

Theo's mouth was cool, sweet from the drink, otherwise tasteless but smooth and pliant. He moved his hands, one slipping to the back of August's neck, the other gathering him roughly, frantically, up into the crook of his arm. He dragged August off the chair with him. He did not care about the spilled wine.

Theo threw August to his bed and August immediately offered his throat. Theo was hungry. August was too much temptation. He deserved this. He owed Theo this. Theo was breaking a rule and risking punishment, but oh God, he was letting the vampire in.

Theo followed him down. There was the foreboding graze of his teeth, still humanlike for the time being. With a rustle of clothes, Theo pulled him closer, closer. August's heart raced. He was lost in the haze of the wine and ensnared, enchanted by the vampire on top of him. The anticipation had him writhing, waiting for Theo to sink his teeth in, to drink his blood then and there and make that connection between them that seemed far greater than any intimacy he could ever have found in bed or in church or in a friend or anywhere else—

"Do it, Theo," August moaned, because the passion was stronger than the guilt. "Do it...."

Maybe Theo wasn't lying. Maybe Theo only loved him because he was a young man full of blood, and maybe their friendship was like atonement for the brutality of that fact. But Theo was the one August trusted, Theo was his favorite, Theo was his friend, and if Theo wanted blood, August would give it to him.

"No—"

"Theo, it's okay."

"It's against the rules to feed outside the Sanctuary—"

"Theo, I'm not afraid!"

"It's against the rules when it's not the feeding hour—"

"*Theo*—"

In the room of little clocks and chairs and chess sets, Theo ravished August with covetous hands. Groping, pawing, squeezing, exploring every inch of his body with the same meticulous obsession he'd bestowed upon the broken clock nights before.

He raked his fingers through August's tousled hair; he traced August's nose with a thumb and his jaw with kisses. He gripped his side, his thigh, his bare foot, ran his lips along his satiny eyelids and the edges of his eyelashes.

August squirmed beneath him in enthusiastic horror, the kind of horror that knotted his stomach and crawled in delighted shivers under his skin. His breath wavered on his lips. He didn't know what to expect next. His toes curled; his knees twitched. The pleasure was rushing between his legs already, stiffening there, hot and sensitive. Ah, he was depraved. And he didn't even care. Maybe he would later. In the moment it was far from a deterrent. He trusted Theo. He wanted Theo. He owed Theo.

Theo grabbed him by both wrists and rolled over, hoisting August to straddle him from above. August shuddered. The feel of Theo beneath his lap was sweet torment. He rolled his hips. It had been so long since he'd made love to anyone, he was sure. It had been—how long? He hadn't even touched himself in the past two months out of curiosity, or loneliness, or rebellion against moral codes of conduct that were utterly repressive and moronic—not his words, Lucius's words. There was that name again. Forget Lucius. He was grinding down against Theo's hips now.

Theo moved his hands up August's arms to his shoulders, clutching him lovingly by the throat. He pulled him lower. He looked tortured, impatient, maddened and impassioned. He said, with all the raw power of a kiss, "If you don't distract me, I will break and I will drink your blood right here, I'll spill it on my sheets and then I'll have to sleep in it...."

It was low and full of lust, jagged, strained. Like a growl, a guttural moan. And something in August snapped.

He fumbled with the rich silver buttons of Theo's waistcoat, ripped the braces off his shoulders and went for his cotton shirt next. He yanked it out from Theo's trousers. He ran his hands greedily up and down Theo's bare chest, savoring the feel of soft skin—ah, connection! A little bit of physical comfort when he was so isolated, so lonely, so lost for meaning. Raw need, primal seduction, the black magic of Aphrodite and her little Eros that rewrote the way feelings pumped through love-struck veins.

August dropped kisses down Theo's neck and chest, emboldened. He wrestled with the front of his trousers but Theo made it difficult, clawing for August's nightshirt at the same time. He stripped him down. The nightshirt fell off the side of the bed. Theo's fingers pinched and played with his nipples and August gasped, dismayed but delighted, rocking his body down against Theo's. He was throbbing now; he was throbbing with lust.

Once again Theo flipped him, to the bed instead. August grabbed at the sheets, at the blankets, hands shaking. He was so dizzy. He was breathless. Theo's mouth closed on his sex and August let out a brittle moan, back arching up off the bed. Funny how this sensation was so like the feel of feeding—the tongue, the teeth, the cool, wet tightness and slithering pressure—and yet it was so, so very different. Theo gripped at his leg, and August wanted him to leave bruises like fingerprints.

"Theo—*nngh, Theo!*"

"Shh.... Sh-shh...."

Theo toyed with him as if this were some sort of experiment. He worked him with his mouth and with his fingers. August trembled. The pleasure choked him up. He couldn't keep still; he was afraid of thrusting too deeply into Theo's mouth, but Theo didn't seem troubled at all. He took every roll of August's body with a grunt and a low satisfied groan that vibrated up through August's hips, and August saw stars.

Theo didn't stop when August begged him to.

Well, he didn't want Theo to *stop*, he just didn't want Theo to *swallow*.

Theo swallowed. He swallowed him whole, drank the pleasure right out of him, even licked up what he missed, what had oozed onto his thumb as August lay wrecked and winded on his bed, buzzing with blushing disbelief.

"You're shaking," Theo whispered from between his knees.

August's voice cracked as he breathed a slow, soft moan of exhaustion.

"Why are you shaking?" Theo pressed, very concerned, apparently.

The room spun. "Because," August said, mouth dry. "Because you're a filthy depraved animal and I *love it*—"

Theo rolled away and stood up. He paced the room. He marched to the cabinet for the bottle of wine, drinking straight from its neck with one hand propped on a hip. He looked worn out and guilty, hair mussed and sleeves rolled up. August watched from his bed, in a daze.

"Come on, then," August entreated, rolling up onto his elbow. "Come on, and I'll do the same for you...."

Theo squinted at him quizzically, cocking a brow. He shook his head and shrugged at the same time. "August," he croaked, "you can't."

August sat up too quickly; the room spun harder. "What?" he spat, vigilant and doubtful. "You can't make love?"

Theo took another swig of wine before handing the bottle to August. He smiled as if August's guess was just so endearing. He watched August drink from the bottle of wine as if it were some special erotica, something for his viewing pleasure. He also looked remarkably more like his usual self than before their impromptu affair.

"I *can*," Theo corrected quietly. "But I'm afraid to say I'd be rather limp and useless if I made love to you right at this moment. The wine helps, your release helps, but...."

August choked on a mouthful of wine, eyes widening. *Release.* Theo meant all that sticky mess he'd swallowed. There was something about saying it aloud that made it quite a lot less sensual and attractive than it was unspoken.

Theo didn't seem to notice the way he'd scandalized August. "We vampires can make love in a rather human fashion, you know, but really only with fresh blood in us. If not it makes me fatigued, and I itch to replenish it all afterward, and nothing ever seems to satiate the hunger—"

"Replenish *what*?" August pried.

"The blood lost," Theo explained as if August should have known the answer already. "Does that make sense?"

No; no, it did not. Why would Theo lose blood during sex? August nodded without trying to actually make sense of it. He reached for his nightshirt. Theo retrieved it for him. The grandfather clock in the corner of the bedroom announced the midnight hour.

Theo checked the hall and then ushered a flustered, redressed August out with a chuckle. August clutched Theo's wrist behind the open door, still in the safety of the bedroom. He lifted his chin; Theo met him in the middle, kissing him softly, tenderly. There was a small *pop* of their mouths as he pulled away. August didn't want to go. He wanted to sleep in Theo's big bed with him. He wanted Theo's touch, Theo's body.

"I'm not frightened of you," August challenged boldly, holding Theo's eyes. They were dulled by the wine and the new type of feeding.

Theo heaved an impatient sigh. He tried to argue, "You should be—"

August shook his head. "There's a love that a sacrifice has for the vampire." He echoed Theo's earlier threat. "It's unlike any love you've ever felt before, I'm sure."

Theo squinted at him doubtfully. He scoffed. He said, "What the hell do you mean?"

August wilted in defeat. "I don't know," he mumbled, leaning against the door. "I thought it was clever and meaningful."

"Go," Theo murmured with a smile on the same mouth that had milked moans and quivering gasps out of August. "Back to the attic, *go*."

August went.

They'd know. *The others.* He was certain of it. If he looked any one of the others in the eye at the moment, they'd know what he'd done.

It was thrilling, this secret.

August stared wide-eyed at Hazel, wondering whether she might be able to read the secret on his face too. She didn't; not that she showed, anyway. She knew he'd spent time with the vampires, but she didn't ask.

She brought him dinner and told him more ghost stories.

CHAPTER NINE

DRURY LANE had Letty Lind on loan from the Gaiety tonight, and it was sure to be a night of uproarious fun—excited talk said she'd be burlesquing with some Cleveland Street and Chelsea boys, and the Oxfords were coming down again from up north. What man could resist a night like that, living or Undead?

"You're using him," Ishmael sneered.

Theo heaved a weary sigh, casting Ishmael an impatient glance over his shoulder.

Outside Covent Garden the blustery autumn night swarmed with crowds in the best imported fashions and behaviors. Shadows swam like puddles between the buildings of Bridges Street as Theo shoved his hands in the pockets of his coat and turned to face Ishmael fully. "What's all this about now?" he prompted dryly. "Who am I using?"

"The lamb," Ishmael muttered. "The sacrifice. Our human. You're using him to keep from facing your own loneliness. We're all alone in the end."

"And why is that?"

"Our days aren't numbered like theirs."

"For a man who loves his solitude, you are really very bitter about things, aren't you?"

"*Man*," Ishmael scoffed, as if the word were laughably inappropriate. Perhaps it was to an extent. But it hadn't been once. "I do love my solitude."

"Immortality has made you afraid," Theo insisted gently.

"And immortality has made *you* rash," Ishmael countered.

"Do not speak to me as if you know me." It wasn't entirely a threat so much as it was a protective measure on Theo's end, but its power was almost swallowed by the noise of a coach rattling by on the uneven pavement.

Ishmael's eyes did not waver from Theo's face as the shadows slithered over them, cast by the passing coach. "I did once," he said very quietly.

There was a brittle impasse there, a heavy pause that swirled between them, ripe with unspoken memories and unvoiced pains. Theo sighed between his teeth, scrubbing a hand tiredly over his face. "You're impossible," he whispered. "Absolutely impossible."

The crowds were really getting lively now; they needed to get inside and find seats. Alphonse was perhaps already in with the Oxfords, in some box watching the musicians in that strange, fanatic way of his while Oliver and Ronald and the ladies laughed and spoke together and flirted with unknowing mortal strangers. Alphonse was nothing but an accessory to them sometimes. It upset Theo.

I did once.

Indeed Ishmael had known Theo once—as Theo had known Ishmael. And how sad and glum was it that such a statement made perfect sense. Did they not know each other now? Not in the sense that Ishmael meant. Not in the way Theo had said it. This was not the Ishmael he'd known half a century ago.

And he was not entirely displeased by that.

"What do you have against me?" Theo demanded, taking the conversation to the shadows out of the way of passersby. "Is it your new game for eternity, to make me miserable?"

"I'm concerned," Ishmael replied flatly. He would not look Theo in the eye. Typical. He held his chin high and watched the crowds moving into Drury Lane with a distant, cavalier look on his young face. *Young.* Ishmael was older than Theo, technically. It was a shame, such youth and handsomeness rotten at the core like a bad fruit.

"Concerned?" Theo echoed, knowing full well he had to goad the sentiment out of Ishmael.

"For the coven." Ishmael bristled like an alley cat—a small, elegant, well-dressed alley cat. Perhaps it was not all too far from the truth, somewhere deep in his personal history. His narrow eyes were bright with a cold, defensive light as he held them on Theo. Ah, Theo knew that look too well. Ishmael had a vendetta. "I'm concerned for the safety of the coven should you break any rules with the new sacrifice. You're young in this world. You're not strong enough to resist.

"I'm not strong enough to resist?" Theo laughed cruelly. "Are you saying you don't trust me to control myself?"

"I'm saying if you fawn too much over a sacrifice, temptation might surprise you. It'll weaken you. It will soften you. You know what happens if rules are broken. It's not good for any of us. And it's not fair either. You know how Alistair feels about the Lamb and if you did something that brought the Lamb to our coven halls—well, that would be a disaster."

Ishmael spoke sense in that. It plucked a nerve for Theo. He tensed, jaw tightening against a fierce scowl. Ah yes, the Lamb, the vampire sovereign who had designed the current coven system and enforced it quite arbitrarily. But how dare Ishmael play the hypocrite again? How dare he pry into Theo's private thoughts and feelings? Better yet, how dare he try to force Theo into spilling intimate things with such twisted words? Ishmael wanted to catch Theo in an accidental confession. He wanted Theo to think he knew everything when in fact he did not. But Theo had done nothing wrong. He had not broken a single rule. He did not intend to break any rules. *No spill of blood outside the feeding hour. No spill of blood outside the Sanctuary. No feeding on anyone but the coven sacrifice.*

He was hungry. So goddamn hungry all the time now. All Hallows Eve had almost been a disaster because of it. That was why he was out tonight, to flirt, to play, to find a bold, pretty girl or a lively young man with rebellion in his eyes, and he would just have to hope it wouldn't be like the other night, when everything and everyone had absolutely failed to distract from the flame burning in him for August Prescott. He had to *hope—*

"Perhaps you should take your concerns to Alistair," Theo spat. "You've always been his favorite, as he's always been yours."

Father, friend, lover, master—no one quite knew just what Alistair was to Ishmael, just that Ishmael was the only one to ever see the inside of Alistair's rooms alone. That Ishmael was the only one to follow Alistair around like a puppy, to play games of secrets, spinning webs of contention and distrust with him and the Alpha at the center. Ishmael was the only one Alistair spoke to in confidence, and— seemingly—vice versa. Ishmael would do anything at Alistair's command, anything, at his every beck and call.

Listen to them, bickering like jilted lovers.

Why did Ishmael show only Theo this crestfallen side? Theo couldn't stand it. He didn't want the responsibility of it; he didn't want to care. He would not be the place for Ishmael to put his weaknesses for safekeeping. Ishmael did not deserve that security from him unless he was to be honest, and Ishmael and honesty were not well acquainted. Theo was not going to be ruled by Ishmael's unhappiness or his suspicions. But he did not want to appear suspicious either, and if Ishmael found him suspicious, what did the others think? Dear God, could they tell what he'd done with August? He was granted nothing sacred, was he? Not when the taste of a man's blood could say so much.... He knew better than that.

"You know nothing about me," Theo whispered thinly.

Ishmael shrugged. He did not agree or disagree. "I know that you're selfish," he said with disdain. He brushed past Theo and headed across the street, to the Theatre Royal. His coattails danced about his knees. What a handsome little bachelor he seemed, handsome and lovable and utterly useless.

Theo had done nothing wrong. He had not broken a single rule. And he would not fall victim to the popular vampire custom of cynicism and indifference either.

If anything his selfishness would be his resilience.

He needed to distance himself to be safe, though. He would survive because he was selfish, but he would destroy himself with hope if he did not keep it tightly in check. Hope still needed to be reasonable.

A man watched him from the shadows of a jumbled, narrow alley at the back of Drury Lane.

Theo bristled. His ears rang. He could tell by the glint in the stranger's eyes, by the energy he gave off, that it was no mortal man. Hooked nose, dirty old leather coat, ratty fisherman's sweater. He was a vampire. He smiled darkly, issuing a subtle nod Theo's way in the greeting of unspoken Undead brotherhood. Theo did not recognize him from any nearby covens. A wanderer, perhaps—well, it was asking for trouble trotting around London unaffiliated. The Lamb was not known for his consistency in disciplinary force.

Hooked nose. Dirt. Wizened skin. No, Theo knew him. Not from a coven, but from a flash of memory that was not his own—something he'd tasted.

The hook-nosed brute who'd kidnapped August for the Buckinghamshire auction.

Fury flared briefly in Theo's chest, pumped hot and hard from head to toe before dying away again into little embers. He was gritting his teeth; his fingers had flown to fists. But why? What had the hook-nosed stranger ever done to him?

The embers of hatred sizzled. Theo stared numbly at the vampire in the dirty coat as he turned and disappeared into the alley.

Dear God, Theo was lost.

He was loath to consider it, but perhaps Ishmael had a right to be concerned.

Theo had sworn he would never break himself on anyone—mortal or immortal—as Ishmael had broken himself on *him*, but here he was pining and angry and unfocused, and he felt broken.

"THEY LEAVE the house?" August asked begrudgingly when Hazel told him Theo was out.

"What," Hazel mumbled, gathering up his breakfast dishes in the dip and swell of candlelight, "you thought they stayed hidden away like you?"

No, that wasn't practical; it was just surprising how much he felt rather abandoned and ignorant. And maybe he was a little jealous.

Theo returned, however, an hour before feeding. August joined him in the peaceful shadows of his bedroom. Theo's satin waistcoat was unbuttoned, his frock coat on with cuffs turned up once. He sat with his feet up in front of the small mantle, firelight dancing across his face. Sickly—he looked sickly, just a bit ashen and frail, eyes sunken in faint circles, but he always looked that way in the advent of the feeding hour. They all did. They pushed themselves to their limits, it seemed, like religious fasting or some other spiritual journey.

Had Theo gone out because August's presence bothered him now? Because he couldn't control himself, or because he was perturbed?

"Where did you go?" August demanded.

"Drury Lane and the Strand with the Oxfords." Theo didn't miss a beat.

"The Oxfords?" August echoed.

"Another coven," Theo replied plainly enough.

August's heart gave a little nervous jump. "There are more of you?"

Theo shot him a look of contempt, but he spoke with an offhanded lilt. "Yes," he affirmed. "From Dublin to St. Petersburg to the Orient, all over the world."

"Do you always go out to playhouses?" August pressed, careful not to seem too jealous. He wasn't sure he'd be able to quash the feeling of abandonment if Theo left him alone in the house to indulge in sacrifice-free leisure.

"Yes," Theo said. "Most of us do. Theatres, clubs, operas, the ballet, dances and parties...."

"You have friends, then," August concluded skeptically. It was almost a scoff. It was altogether too easy to imagine them enjoying the night as he used to—shows, playhouses, clubs and dances, gallivanting with all the other nocturnal men and women of London. Did crepuscular crowds notice their pale skin and sharp eyes, did they fall victim to vampire charm, or were they utterly ignorant? The realm of moonlight was a wholly different world from that of the sunlight, this underbelly of a world he'd thought he'd known, woven into the shadows stealthy and seductive.

"Yes." Theo nodded. "We do."

The vampires went out on the town, to performance halls and clubhouses. They had *friends*. It was strange to think about, these ghastly beings who seemed to spirit around the house, forgotten by the human world—and then August remembered the night in the cemetery somewhere outside London, where an auction was held and all the vampires gathered as if it were a party—

"Well, aren't you so very *human* still?" August snapped, in moody disbelief.

Theo scrutinized him, startled. The shadows moved on his face and he laced his hands on his lap. He smiled a little bitterly, a little awkwardly. August met his eyes in a sidelong glance, frowning darkly.

"Yes," Theo concurred, "we are."

SO VERY human.

Yes, until the plunge of fangs into his neck, the clutch of hungry hands, the subtle kisses, and the flow of blood from mortal heartbeat to Undead tongue, and then August squirmed. He bucked. He clung to them, each of them, under the coffered ceiling of the Sanctuary. He hissed and moaned because it hurt—it always hurt—but once or twice he gasped because he *liked it*.

What did that say about his humanity, then?

HAZEL AND August huddled together in a blanket under the northern window to watch a storm brewing black and murky over the rooftops of London. Hazel told him about when she first answered the ad for the position she now held so faithfully.

"I remember it being stormy like tonight, though I don't know whether it truly was," she said. She looked out into the shadows of the evening beyond the attic window as if she read the memories in them. "The ad said to call at eight o'clock sharp, and I remember that I thought, 'Oh, they must be busy people to have a day so tightly scheduled, they aren't free until eight.'

"I wore my best dress and I had my friend Elizabeth Temperance curl my hair because this wasn't just any house; it was in Westminster and I needed to look more than acceptable. Elizabeth... I miss her. August, she was like a sister to me. People told us all the time we looked like sisters.

"It was cold. I came upon the house, and for a while I was distracted by the light in all the windows, all the vines and moss, and then the door opened like they'd known I was there all along.

"Alistair welcomed me inside. We sat down in the drawing room and he and Pearle interviewed me. It was all sorts of creepy, with this sense of farce. I remember thinking to myself that they were rather quaint, and it was as if the whole household were just pretending to be normal. I never expected to be right.

"Anyway they asked me questions like 'If this happened, what would you do?' or 'If an accident like such were to occur, how would you react?' They made sure that I was okay with working all night and sleeping all day. Then they asked me where I had been raised, what my heritage was, and what superstitions I believed in. They asked whether I had any immediate family. They wanted to make sure that if I were to cut myself off from the outside world, there wouldn't be any difficulty."

Hazel fell quiet, eyes clouding. "Yes," she added, "that part wasn't a problem at all. Though I do miss Elizabeth Temperance."

"When did you realize what they were?" August probed, lifting his head and watching her through his lashes.

"Oh God, the first night I worked here." Hazel laughed. "They made me sign the contract first, adhering to their rules and promising the outlined years of servitude, and I'd signed enough of those to not really care, so I didn't read it. I moved into my new bed, and the whole place was like a dream. I couldn't help but think about all the girls I'd ever known who'd fallen prey to some lunatic in the alleys here and how lucky I was now, and I laughed about it and I told one of the other maids about my fears that a murderer ran the household. I hadn't seen them in all their bloody glory yet, you see. It was only the first few hours, and the hair was upright on the back of my neck the whole time. I constantly felt like someone was watching me, and I was afraid of the dark.

"Paula looked at me, all stunned, but she didn't say anything. She just shook her head and clucked her tongue. I was her assistant, after all, and I went with her with a meal up to the attic and I realized what they kept up here—"

Hazel shot August a wide-eyed look as if that might offend him, as if she'd forgotten he was the one in the attic now. She said, as if they both didn't already know, "They kept a young man, neck bruised and bandaged, and... Well, somehow that was all I needed to see to understand. I didn't even ask for an explanation. It felt like I'd known it all along, anyway.

"When they realized that I finally got it, the Alpha took me into the drawing room again and had me swear an oath to keep their secrets. He told me their rules. He told me their history. He told me all my duties and the most relevant secrets of their nature and their kind. He told me if I broke any of the rules, or my oath, or if I told anyone, I would be killed. And since then—" Hazel shrugged, as if to punctuate. "—I've been the keeper of the sacrifice. Paula trained me before she resigned."

August stared at her, letting all of this sink in. He almost asked her what she knew about them. He didn't. *Resigned.*

"Did they kill her? Paula?" August whispered.

"I don't know." Hazel glanced at him pointedly. "But what I do know is that those of us who work here.... There's no life for us to return to outside the house, so what's the difference? You either renew your contract with the vampires, or you *resign.* The vampires' existence is a fragile one, August. They can't trust just any human servants with their protection, can they?"

"You talk like you're one of them," August said flatly.

Hazel smiled, shaking her head. Something passed in her eyes—a memory, maybe? A thought of a secret she kept of her own, one that tempted August, but one that he respected. He wasn't sure he wanted to know. There was just so much to Hazel that seemed sad and secret.

Hazel hummed. "Can I comb your hair, August?"

August uttered a sound of dismay, somewhere between a scoff and a sigh. "Is my hair really that awful? You and Theo, I swear...."

ISHMAEL WAS not *trying* to get Theo in trouble, in all honesty. Though it would be a convenient complement, should it happen that way.

He waited in the library adjoined to Alistair's office, listening very carefully from the corner closest to the connecting door as Alistair spoke to Theo. There was no fire under the mantle tonight, no candles lit, no lamps up. In almost complete darkness, Ishmael idly ran his fingers along the edge of a bookshelf and listened.

"Did *he* tell you I'm having trouble controlling myself?" That was Theo, full of cornered spite. He spoke of Ishmael. Ishmael knew by that indignant tone of voice. It was only typical.

"He brought me concerns," Alistair answered, so judicious and regal. There was something about that rich baritone that never failed to give Ishmael chills. It was like thunder—that natural, that awe-inspiring, that fearsome. Ishmael waited for him to scold Theo for speaking so ill of him. Alistair didn't. "He said that they were your concerns, that you begged he bring them to me."

"Alistair...." Theo almost sounded admonishing; Ishmael was offended.

"Now listen," Alistair said firmly. "I am not your father. I am not Ishmael's father. And I am not your king either. I won't play games of diplomacy with you two. I told you that—how long ago? Be honest with me, Theo. Are you pushing yourself to the limit?"

"It's difficult not to! We just ended an adjustment period, and everyone's hungry all the time! It won't go back to normal for a while. You know that!"

Ishmael scowled, jaw tight. He drummed a finger on the bookshelf, then pulled his hand back fast, worried the sound might give away his presence. Of course Theo would have some gallant argument to milk sympathy and romantic pity out of Alistair. Alistair was so vulnerable when it came to the angst of their kind. Theo was shameless. Or perhaps he and Alistair just shared something common there between them—*no*. Ishmael knew Alistair better than any other soul. Of course he did.

In the other room, Alistair asked Theo, "Have you slept with the sacrifice?"

There was a long pause. Ishmael was quietly flustered by glee. Yes, confess all to Alistair! Let the Alpha know just how close Theo was to breaking a rule!

Theo's voice sounded next, uncomfortable and low, muffled by the closed door: "Yes, sir. Has it—has it become against the rules?"

"No...."

There was the creak of a chair; Ishmael could just picture Alistair shifting in it, crossing one leg over the other, leaning back to appraise Theo with his chin propped in his long, manly fingers. Ishmael hoped Theo was suffering under that incisive stare. He hoped he was panicking, guilty, fidgeting—

"How was he?"

Ishmael's jaw dropped and he surveyed the dark library as if there were someone or something to share in his shock. *How was he?* Was Alistair really asking Theo how sleeping with the sacrifice had been?

Theo chuckled. Ishmael wanted to swear aloud and swing his fists. Then again, maybe the chuckle was part of Theo's pretense. Perhaps he was trying to appear unaffected by Alistair's judgment. If Alistair was judging him at all.

"It was delicious," Ishmael heard Theo say in a tender, deferential tone. "Though it was also private. If you can respect that, sir."

"You fed on him without spilling blood, didn't you?"

"Alistair...."

"You act as though I've never done the same myself. Or anyone else for that matter."

"Alistair—"

"I don't care what you do with the sacrifice. Hate him, love him, honestly I do not *care*. And I never have, have I? But you must remember: just because you might want him all for yourself does not mean he is yours. He still belongs to the rest of us as much as he does you. Don't expect anything less. And the moment you break a rule or get possessive, you answer to me. You break a rule a second time, you answer to the Lamb. Is that understood?"

"Yes, Alistair."

"He's something, though, isn't he?"

"He… Yes, he is."

"Something's changed. Since All Hallows."

"I agree."

"He's really part of the coven now, is what I mean."

"I would say the same—"

"Perhaps more thanks to your little initiation."

"Alistair!" Here Theo laughed and it raised Ishmael's hackles. "Please, no—not any more than thanks to you—and that dance—" He was kissing Alistair's rings, metaphorically. Paying court to stay on the Alpha's good side. It made Ishmael sick.

He stared dully into the dark, empty library, feeling the rage encase him like a silvery chrysalis. He shook his head in disbelief. He shoved a chair out of his way and stormed from the library. He didn't want to remember the way Alistair had looked at the sacrifice in the music room on All Hallows. He did not want to think about the way the sacrifice had looked back at Alistair, right in the eye, so intimately. He didn't want to wonder whether Alistair wanted to sleep with the sacrifice too, or whether—whether—God, Ishmael hated when the coven lambs were lovable because it proved such a pain in his ass. Why couldn't the line between mortal and immortal just stay where it was, dividing them like black and white, day and night?

Loving a sacrifice. *Please!*

APPARENTLY AFTER the All Hallows Eve scene in the music room, the vampires started to think of him as more than just "the sacrifice."

August felt it, the subtle change in the air, the way their glances warmed to a more personal, probing intensity. Alistair's glances were even more befuddling than before, and Ishmael never failed to linger with a glare in the periphery, but all the others seemed suddenly interested in August's time and presence. Not one of them seemed to pay heed to the fact that the attic door was being left unlocked; nobody seemed to have a problem with August exploring the house, awake and alert. If any of them knew about his and Theo's wayward collision in Theo's bed, they didn't say a word.

These rules everyone spoke of were not very properly enforced, or they were much more convoluted than August initially thought.

He'd had enough, though.

It wasn't fair. He was tired of everyone around him having answers and not sharing them. He was determined to ask.

In two old upholstered chairs pulled up by the fire, the games table between them, he played chess with Theo.

"Ah," Theo breathed, hunched over August's first move, "the Queen's Pawn Game. A rather unusual opening move, as if defying the popularity of moving the king's pawn first. And I think I'll continue it with the Dutch Defense."

The little pieces clinked as they moved them, fire warming the bedroom as the night settled outside. November was upon them in all its rainy glory. It would become snow soon, blanketing London at first before turning to gritty slush and muck.

Theo's sleeves were rolled up again, offering glimpses of his scarred white wrist like a taunt. August watched his hand for a moment. The pale flesh peeked from an open cuff as Theo moved and then gestured wildly, stumbling into a tangent about the mechanics of the Dutch Defense.

August shot out his hand. He caught Theo by the forearm, deliberately not meeting Theo's sharp green eyes because if he did, he'd lose all his resolve and just want to kiss him. Maybe like memorylessness there was a similar peace in not knowing, though. Maybe ignorance was not so bad. But no, he wanted to *know*—

August pushed Theo's sleeve up, revealing the smooth white of his arm. Theo was silent, watching, calculating the moment with his eyes. It was almost as if he knew what was happening and going to happen thereafter. As if he'd just been waiting for it to take place, tedious and predictable.

August rolled Theo's wrist over in his hand and stared at the scar there, pale puckered skin in the shapes of letters. *L o n*, and below it the Roman numeral for six. A flash of panic shot through him, hot, sinking in his gut as he touched the scar.

"How did you get this?" His words tasted bad suddenly.

"The same way that you did," Theo replied, stubborn and cryptic.

August scowled at him, flopping back in the chair. "Well," he said flatly, because he knew the game he'd have to play now if he wanted answers, "I can't really *remember* how I got it. I just remember the vampires snatching me off the street and selling me to Alistair, and after that everything is really a fog. Unless, of course, when you said you could taste memories and feelings in blood, it means all of you probably know everything about me already. More than even I know about myself. And that's not very fair, is it?"

Theo glared at the chess pieces as if they'd done him some wrong in failing to distract August. He heaved an inconvenienced sigh, then threw August a new look.

"The Lamb," he divulged. "The Lamb gave it to you, and he gave it to me, and he gave it to each one of us and every other coven member there is. When a human receives the mark, it is done with a blade. When a vampire receives the mark, it's burned into the skin."

August shuddered. He stared at Theo, aghast. "How horrible," he muttered. "But—wait, what lamb? I thought I was your lamb. Your sacrifice."

"You are." Theo shifted, getting more comfortable in his chair. He leaned back, folding his hands on the edge of the games table. He was quiet for a moment, staring at August, and it felt as if he was picking through him in his mind. He probably was.

"This Lamb is our ruler," Theo finally confirmed.

August licked his lips. "Your ruler," he validated, slightly skeptical.

"Yes," Theo said curtly. "He is the one who approved of and marked you."

A silence fell as thoughts raced through August's mind, connections being made. "He *approved* of me," he echoed. "And yet he's a lamb too, like me."

"No. He's *the* Lamb," Theo corrected.

"*The* Lamb," August amended. He stared down at their paused game of chess, suddenly feeling a little cold. He glanced up at Theo. "He's in charge, then?"

Theo nodded.

"What do you mean he *approved* of me?"

Theo was wordless at first, staring blankly as if his own thoughts were too much to ignore. Then he broke the silence, voice brisk and smooth:

"There is a system, August. The Lamb is our king. Under his law all vampires reside in covens, in certain jurisdictions. Each coven has a unique mark and all its members must bear it. We are allowed one sacrificial lamb for every ten members, and we cannot feed on anyone else. Do you understand? Does that make sense?"

August leaned back, fiddling with the upholstery of the chair. He was a little stunned. Theo's eyes were sharp but not vindictive. August thought about this—about Hazel telling him that they only fed on him, not innocent humans, that the world was full of horrible hypocrisies and the vampires were admirable to seek a balance in the world when they could so simply wreak havoc instead. *Law. King.* God, there was so much he didn't know. There were only eight vampires in all of London? What about the hook-nosed one who'd stolen him? Unless he did not belong to a coven?

The Lamb. August stiffened. That was who Alistair had mentioned before, when August eavesdropped. Yes, Alistair had mentioned "the Lamb."

It chilled August right down to the core.

"I understand," he whispered. "Theo, I want to know more."

Theo smiled, but his eyes were stormy. He pushed the games table to the side, leaving the chess pieces set up so they could resume later. They sat in front of the fire like old men, watching each other in the dance of its shadows and the circle of its heat.

For a long moment, Theo looked as if he might not go on. But then he ran his fingers through his wild hair and began to speak.

There hadn't always been a system, Theo explained, but he hadn't been a vampire at that time. He claimed to be a rather young and naïve member of the Undead, to which August profusely objected, and Theo chuckled softly. It left August blushing and stubbornly flustered.

Theo said the sacrificial system had been implemented decades ago, in the Year Without a Summer. The system called for a balance between humans and vampires. The rules were simple: apart from the basic rules of the vampire, one could not feed on humans other than the sacrifice unless the Lamb approved; one could not feed on the sacrifice outside of the feeding hour; one could not turn a sacrifice or *keep* a sacrifice without the Lamb's approval; there was to be no murder of the sacrifice, and monthly coven records had to be forwarded to the Lamb through the jurisdiction's elected representative—which apparently wasn't Alistair, but a vampire closer to the Lamb.

"Why won't anyone tell me these rules?" August grumbled.

Theo shrugged, cocking a brow. "You're the sacrifice. Why would we want our human to know all our weaknesses? Don't ask about the rules, August."

Apparently August looked more crestfallen than he realized at that, because Theo heaved a sigh and wilted in defeat. "Ask me," he amended his statement, "and I will do my best to answer you. But don't ask anyone else much, all right? It might bother them. Now, listen. The history of the coven...." Alistair, Number One. Pearle, Number Two. Owen, Number Three. Ishmael, Number Four. Anastasia, Number Five. These vampires in the house had known a life before the system, a time when they'd been allowed to drink freely, but over years they had curbed their appetites, the same as Theo was born and raised in the Undead to do. How eloquently he put it, August thought.

But what was the difference between "born" and "turned"? Hazel said vampires didn't procreate. Literature said they came back from the grave. Had Theo died then, or something? Had they all died?

"No," Theo said around a thoughtful hum, nodding vaguely. "No, that's... Well, that's part of what happens, I suppose. No, humans are turned into vampires—but there is only one way to do it, and it has to be done right."

August held his breath, staring at Theo. That closed the gap a little bit; that made sense, actually. In fact, it seemed a little sad, but August couldn't place why. He would have been more afraid if they had all been some secret, monstrous breed of their own.

"Vampires were powerful once," Theo said with a bitter little smile. "The blood inside us doesn't go anywhere, so we'll never *starve*, per se, but our strength is weakened if we don't feed regularly. Never mind we drink a lot less now in one feeding than we used to. Pearle tells me about the old times, when vampires weren't just underworld sideshows. Some vampires once had the power to *really* read a man's mind, to hypnotize, to travel at extraordinary speeds and with colossal strength. They had heightened sensory reception and the ability to harness preternatural energy into 'distance movement'—*telekinesis*.

And maybe we all still have those talents, but we feed only every other night now, and so little at that...."

August wasn't sure whether to feel fear or pity.

"We're travesties," Theo husked. "We're no better than ghosts, shadows of the vampires who used to be before the Great Reform. Oh, vampires are still powerful beings, August, don't get me wrong. Our charm and power of persuasion is inherent. We will always have speed and strength greater than a mortal's, and even if our Undead senses are impaired, enervated by a weaker flow of blood, they're still there. But we're shams now compared to what we used to be."

August swallowed over a knot in his throat, listening to all Theo's little clocks ticking out of time with each other.

"Please don't misunderstand me," Theo said through his teeth. "I'm not disloyal. I'm not. Sometimes I just wonder what it might have been like. I'm aware of the good of the system, but my Undead pride sometimes aches regardless."

"Why didn't you tell me until now?" August criticized. "Why did you wait for me to ask to explain these things? Do you know how awful it is to not know anything about all of you? It's lonely up there in the attic, you know."

"I know what it's like to be lonesome," Theo spat, seeming a little taken aback. "Trust me on that one, August. I know what it's like. I've been in the attic too."

What? Did that mean—?

Theo shook his head, softening a little. "Listen, I suppose sometimes we're afraid of being understood," he whispered, eyes flashing up to meet August's, raw and poignant. "We're too close to humanity for that."

Never mind the attic. He'd ask later. "What about stakes?" August pried. "What about sunlight? What about those things?"

"You're thinking about literature's vampires," Theo warned. He laughed. It surprised August, a sound totally contradictory to the grim elegance of his stare. "August," Theo whispered, and he spoke with the air of a conspiratorial child, "if you stake a vampire through the heart in reality, they will not die." How strange it was to hear those words in the same sentence. *Vampire. Reality.* "Sunlight, you ask? Have you ever been out too long on a summer day and gotten burned? It's something like that after the first few moments of exposure. It hurts! It stings. And if we stay in the sunlight, it just gets worse and worse. Eventually it debilitates us, perhaps even leads to combustion. I've only heard stories, though. I don't know why it's this way."

"You sleep in a bed," August pointed out, gesturing over his shoulder to the four-poster bed and knowing full well the things they'd done together in that bed skipped merrily between them, unspoken.

"We don't have to sleep in coffins," Theo said. "We're just nocturnal beings. As for stakes and holy water, I heard that there are a few apotropaics that actually work because they are ancient and charged with spiritual power. But if I remember correctly, those things have been lost. They consist of a flask of holy water, some old scrolls, alchemized chains. You have to understand, August, that vampires are not entities you can restrain by strong faith. We're physical beings too. All of the Undead are—except spirits of course, which are beings of energy, but that's obvious."

August was disgruntled. Ghosts he knew were a hot topic amongst spiritualist and occult societies, but what exactly did Theo mean by that? *All of the Undead.* What other fairy tale monsters were real if vampires were—more imperatively, if what Theo said was true, and August had no reason to doubt that, then what the hell was the difference between vampires and humans? Just their sharp little fangs and their strange means of survival, their freedom from death and a life of decay?

But these were *answers*.

And the answers invigorated him.

"Let's finish our game," Theo urged, pulling the games table back over without knocking down the pieces. He spoke like a tutor or a parent, trying to lighten their child's mood. His eyes darted up to glance at August through his lashes—clever, clever green eyes. "We've got a good one going here."

As usual when August was too distracted watching Theo play instead of actually playing himself, Theo won.

CHAPTER TEN

AUGUST WANTED more books.

He wanted to see the library. He was determined (and maybe a little emboldened by learning some of the rules). The bruised bite marks on his neck itched but they continued to heal somehow, he'd eaten breakfast, he'd finished all his tea, and he needed more books than those Theo had brought him.

Down the stairs in the borrowed smoking jacket, August drifted along past stern-faced busts and beautiful paintings, bundles of flowers, and that lonely, futile crucifix on the beaufet. There were candles lit in the east hall. Alphonse was, per usual, in the music room, staring at sheet music as if in a trance. Out the windows the sky was a velvety terrain of clouds and smoke.

The vampires had routines, he'd noticed. For the most part they moved about the house comfortably, sometimes having guests over who August heard from the attic. Now and again the house was noticeably empty, and August guessed those were the nights the vampires went out to enjoy London's nightlife. Every other night before feeding, the air was thick with tension as all awaited midnight in the Sanctuary.

August moved down into the vestibule, passing through warily to the library. *Never open a closed door*, Hazel had told him.

But he had already, so he did again.

The library was themed in dark colors, all black walnut and leather chairs and a broad, thick escritoire against one wall with gas lamp lit and surface cleared for anyone who might require it. A fire blazed in the hearth. A sizable globe lurked below the window.

It smelled like books and the sweet perfumes of ink, kindling, coke, and melting wax. August wandered around the room, its forest green wallpaper dancing with delicate, faded arabesques. He touched the spines of the books with reverent fingertips. There were classics and old English literature, treatises, essays, newspapers. Books of poetry, books of history, books August couldn't even discern the purpose of. They were just there and smelled delightful when he opened their pages and pressed them to his nose.

August pulled out a collection and sat down on the floor before the fire.

He wasn't sure how long he sat reading. The clock in the corner of the library chimed once at nine thirty and again at ten, so it must have been almost an hour before August was drawn back into reality by the sound of movement in the hall.

It was a door opening and closing. August looked up just in time to watch the Alpha strut by the open library, bringing the crisp scent of the night outside with him, smooth steps and modern waistcoat.

August froze. He stared, eyes wide, at the empty hall as he listened to Alistair enter the room next to the library, and August waited, heart pounding, for him to retrace his steps and look into the library with reprimanding eyes, but he didn't.

A door closed.

From the room next door there came the scrape of a chair moving and the rustle of fabric against fabric.

There was a door connecting the library to that room. August dropped the book from his lap and cautiously crossed the room to crouch down beside the door, ear pressed to the hinges, unreserved curiosity hot in his chest.

Ishmael's voice broke the silence. August jumped because he hadn't seen Ishmael pass by the library, which meant Ishmael had been in the room next to it for some time. Did he know August was just next door?

Ishmael's words were distant, but distinct enough. "How is James?"

The Alpha sounded mildly wearied by Ishmael, or perhaps by this familiar stranger James, or maybe just by the world in general. "I worry about him sometimes."

Footsteps across the room. "You don't think he'd really break the rules with full intention, do you?"

"No. He's too respectful for that. I fear he's growing tired of this long life."

"So his complaints were so urgent—?"

"Ishmael, are you really angry that he called without warning? Do you think that you have that right?"

"No. Not at all, Alistair."

"There's been another significantly sized revolt, he says. Vampires are going to be talking about this from here to Istanbul. The Lamb was particularly brutal this time."

The Lamb, mentioned again. There was a brief, tense silence. Then Ishmael, all his former moodiness momentarily absent, replaced by honest concern: "Where?"

"Ireland."

There was a foreboding weight to the pause there. August didn't understand. There were vampires in Ireland? Yes, Theo had said that. But—had the vampires risen in revolt, or the humans? What could vampires possibly be rebelling against?

Alistair spoke again. "James says that they'd decided to join the ranks of the Atoned. There's been a recent surge in that, have you noticed? But this group was especially defiant because of their heritage. Ireland is a land of great superstition, just like the East. You wouldn't understand what I speak of because yours is such purely English blood, and England has no fairy tales."

"I don't understand."

"England—"

"No, Alistair, I don't understand why they rebel!" For the first time, Ishmael sounded truly young and distressed. "What's the point in it? What did they expect? Ours isn't exactly a kingdom of fairness. The Lamb isn't going to argue with them until they find common ground. If they oppose him, why, they're offering their own lives! Oh, the Atoned, *really*? They may as well pin on a Hunter's regalia! Despicable, deplorable—"

The ominous obscurity of the discussion made August feel sick. It made no sense to him, and the frank way Ishmael ranted was not characteristic of him. It was alarming. August didn't want any opportunity to sympathize with him.

He gathered up the books and hurried out of the library. He didn't care about the rest of the conversation. He didn't want to hear it.

THE VAMPIRES fed. August's fingers twitched with the pain as sharp, elongated eyeteeth plunged into his throat. The pinch of the suckling mouths, the cool tongues and lips, the way it shook him from the inside out to feel the pull of blood from his body....

Something had changed about it.

Something changed about the way Alistair initiated the bewitchment, the way Pearle balanced it out with tenderness, the way Owen and Ishmael didn't care and drank from wherever they found fit, the way Anastasia brought forth the most primal instincts in August as a young man like an angel-faced enchantress, the way they passed him along from connection to connection—

But August knew more about them now. They didn't seem nefarious anymore, so much as they seemed full of sorrow, damned and conquered by nature. And every enlightened man knew how nature dictated all.

August shivered as he fell into Theo's embrace. He begged him. He, a respectable man from a respectable family he couldn't remember, *begged* the vampire to drink his blood. He pulled on the vampire's high collar and soft, dark hair, arched his back and pressed the vampire's nose into his bloody throat. And he heard—he heard a low sound, something like a stomach growling, a bestial gurgle, and August felt all the same ecstasy he had felt lying in Theo's bed on All Hallows Eve zero in to swell up in his chest again when Theo began to drink.

He forgot about the other vampires in the room. He forgot he needed to save his energy for the last two. All that mattered was that something had changed, and he loved the way it felt to balance the intrusive pain of the vampire's mouth with the singular bliss of squirming against Theo's chest. He was smitten. He was in love. All the desire crested again, stirring, throbbing, he was hard—

The candlelight danced and Theo delivered him to Number Seven. August groaned as Number Seven's mouth closed on the opened wounds on his neck, and a whisper in the back of his mind told him the vampire's name: *Laurel.* August rested on Laurel's shoulder and shuddered at the pass of blood. He watched in confusion, dizzied, as Ishmael settled cold, scrupulous eyes on Theo.

Theo returned the stare with a bit of red still beaded on his lower lip. He licked the last of August's blood away without breaking eyes with Ishmael. Laurel passed August to Alphonse, sweet, strange Alphonse.

Yes, something had changed in them all.

They gathered here in all their beautiful consumption-white glory, and August wanted more, something more. But the grief of not getting it faded as the Alpha helped him back up to the attic room; it faded as the feeding spell faded.

Hazel met them at the attic door, wet cloth in hand. She bowed her head to Alistair, who was pleasant and cordial with fresh blood in his system, and she guided August to the side of the bed where she cleaned his bloodied throat and wrist. He winced. He sucked in a hissing breath. He bit his lip. They were normal reactions to her gentle dabbing, the application of salves and bandages.

August thought about Ishmael sounding frantic in the room next to the library. He thought about Ishmael's sharp eyes on Theo and what they meant.

He fell asleep.

ALPHONSE PLAYED music again, but the door was closed. August supposed that was Alphonse's way of asking for privacy.

He caught his reflection in a hall mirror, momentarily stricken by the bags beneath his eyes and the way one side of his throat was more badly bruised than the other. The same livid bloom flowered on his right wrist. His hair was a mess. He knew it was strange to feel normal like this; surely he hadn't looked this way *before* the house of vampires. But he had no idea what normal had looked like then, just that this clearly wasn't it.

August decided another bath was in order.

He just sat in the water for a while, hunching forward against his knees. He washed his hair, sinking down under the water.

Ishmael was beside the porcelain tub.

August came back up with a gasp of air and wet hair plastered to his face. In a burst of panic he sputtered, recoiled, choked on some water and hurried for some decency, hands diving to cover himself under the water. Why did it matter? He hadn't thought to cover himself before Theo. But this was *Ishmael*.

The bath water calmed, rocking in gentle little waves. Soap floated where August had dropped it.

Ishmael stared at him. He stood with arms clasped behind his back silently, as if he were waiting for August to recover from his surprise. He was gleeful to have scared him, the unpleasant lackey; August was sure of it.

Ishmael's eyes were clear only in their sharpness. Above his plain waistcoat and full-sleeved shirt, he was actually rather youthful and handsome, looking as if he'd been hardly nineteen when he'd died—or, in Theo's words, "turned," been "born into the Undead." Before he became a vampire, as vampires' bodies never aged, did they? *Imagine that*…. His hair was clipped short and kept very neatly combed, a most peculiar color of faded blond that bordered on the edge of gray. What a shame the only ugly thing about him was his nature.

"It's not right, you know," Ishmael said in a slow, cool way. He smiled. August could see right through it. Ishmael was there on a personal mission.

His heart raced. August hadn't told Hazel he was taking a bath. He thought since things were changing—since the vampires were accustomed to his presence now, and he to theirs—he could bathe alone, but…. He swallowed around a lump in his throat. It just wasn't right, feeling so cowed by someone who looked so much younger than him. "Can't I take a bath?" he pressed. "It's just a bath—"

Ishmael cut through his feeble argument like a blade, head tipped to one side in a sham of innocence. "It's detrimental for a vampire to love a sacrifice more than he should."

A vampire to love a sacrifice….

There's a love between a vampire and its sacrifice, you know….

And the way Ishmael had sneered at Theo in the Sanctuary a few nights ago, and the way his eyes danced now as if he'd caught August in some disreputable, incriminating position—

"I don't know what you're talking about," August managed, clearing his throat.

Ishmael nodded as if he'd expected as much. The lying smile remained on his mouth. His eyes pierced right through August. They were different from Theo's eyes. They were violating and uncomfortable, seemed to promise nothing but intimidation.

"Do you know what you mean to us?" Ishmael asked.

August was rigid and cold. "I'm your sacrifice," he replied in an uneven whisper, gawking up at Ishmael from the bath.

Ishmael nodded again. "That's right, little lamb. You're just a source of blood for us, and we could find another man as beautiful and as smart and as *wonderful* as you. Oh yes, we could find another just as perfect in the blink of an eye."

"Are you trying to scare me?" August immediately regretted the question. He frowned, hoping it looked deferential or at least respectful. He just couldn't shake the feeling that this was a visit with secret motives.

Ishmael faltered, if only for a moment. He snorted, countering with unnecessary drama, "No. I just know you long for more insight into us, we the creatures who stole you away from the safe world you knew and feed on your very life to sustain our own."

Ishmael stooped down, crossing his arms on the edge of the bath. August leaned away, narrowing his eyes. He tried not to appear alarmed; he tried not to appear affected. He didn't want Ishmael to think he could frighten him so easily. But Ishmael only reminded him that no matter how much he learned, the vampires were above him here. The vampires were still closer to monsters than he was.

"Monsters," Ishmael echoed, as if tasting the word, and August's eyes widened. His discomfort was too palpable. Ishmael could probably read it all over him. He'd caught the word right from August's mind.

With that thought August gave up. He remembered again with shameful clarity that he was their slave, their servant, that he belonged to them, and that no manner of connection with them might change that. He met Ishmael's eyes helplessly, knowing Ishmael wished to say what he wanted and move on. He was a rotten child like that. August wanted him to leave him alone already.

"Yes, monsters," Ishmael mused in a tiny whisper. "That's what we are, isn't it? Monsters. We care only about your blood. We care only about ourselves. We are perfect actors, and we'll kill even our most intimate of friends and lovers if it means the unholy sustenance we need."

August was positive he saw a flash of Ishmael's fangs, another tactic to scare him as Ishmael stood and fixed him with a sharp, critical look. Every shadow on his face was too grim for his youthfulness. It was a jarring look. It was threatening.

Ishmael left the washroom, closing the door behind him.

August sat still in shock.

Water splashed as he clambered out of the tub, wrapping himself in a towel. He kept his eyes on the door, frantic, wondering whether Ishmael might come back to torture him some more. He dried off and closed Theo's smoking jacket around him.

Ishmael knew.

Ishmael knew what August and Theo had done.

He was taunting him with it; he was holding it over his head like blackmail, the dirty, spoiled fiend. And if Ishmael knew, surely the others knew also.

It wasn't against the rules, though. Theo had said that. So was Ishmael—August grimaced in disgust—was Ishmael *jealous*? God forbid Ishmael wanted him as Theo wanted him. Worse yet, did he want Theo as August wanted Theo?

He grabbed his clothes and ran back up to the attic room, shivering.

"DON'T SAY anything!" Hazel snapped.

"I'm sorry," August blurted anyway. "Please don't be angry with me. I didn't mean to get you in trouble."

Hazel held up her hand, eyes closed as she gathered patience. August watched her like a guilty child, brow dimpled and mouth drawn in a miserable frown. Hazel drew a short breath and fumed, "It's not that the vampires don't trust you. It's not even that the vampires don't trust themselves. It's just that, August, it's *my job* to take care of you, and if you're wandering about downstairs too often, bathing yourself, doing whatever it is you do without my knowing, I'm not doing my job and I'll be punished. Is that so hard to understand?"

"I'm sorry," August said again. "I didn't think about it that way."

"Well, now you know."

"So you don't think I'm actually in trouble?"

"I can't say *I'm* not a little frustrated with you, but no, Ishmael is the biggest apple-polisher I've ever seen in my life."

August's eyes veered up to Hazel. "Ishmael? Ishmael got you in trouble?"

"He told Alistair he saw you in the bath, that you were alone and he was worried about you." Hazel stressed the word "worried" like the lie it was. She snorted, a rather unladylike gesture that somehow worked perfectly on her pretty face. She crossed her arms and sagged down into the chair near the window, and the real frustration was obvious in her eyes. Guilt weighed on August, but it was prefaced by hatred.

"He's a liar," August muttered. "He wasn't *worried*. He wanted to scare me."

Hazel shot him a look.

August shrugged it off, waving his hand dismissively. "It's fine, Hazel. He didn't really scare me. You're right. He's the biggest apple-polisher in the world."

But it wasn't true; scheming seeds of contention or not, Ishmael's words haunted him. And August felt guiltily, quietly enraged about it.

We care only about your blood. We care only about ourselves. We are perfect actors, and we'll kill even our most intimate of friends and lovers if it means the sustenance we need....

HE THOUGHT about Theo.

Everything about Theo bordered on the line between man and vampire. His green eyes held the weight of eternity; his expressions pushed the boundaries of human capacity, emotions bleeding out like an empath's in ashen moments, handsome moments, moments that reminded August with brutal clarity Theo was indeed more than a fascinating gentleman. He exuded Undead charm and dark attraction like a sigh of cigarette smoke, and how was August to know whether Theo was lying to him or not? The vampire got what he wanted, didn't he?

Ah God, but he wanted to kiss Theo again. He wanted Theo's hands on him. He wanted to burrow into Theo's arms and stay there forever. He wanted Theo on top of him again, wandering hands prying and prodding and drawing pleasured shudders and moans out of him—

It's detrimental for a vampire to love a sacrifice more than he should.

August grabbed up the pen and paper from the table near his bed, getting his fingers inky, but that didn't matter. The words were buzzing in his mind. They begged to be let out. It wasn't a proper poem. The verses felt a little jumbled. It didn't have a clear pattern. But August scribbled the words out because they begged to be released, and he couldn't keep them inside when they crawled beneath his skin like that.

This unrelenting madness, bury me in the blackness.
The sky has never looked the same.
These eyes of mine see more than you know,
Your face says more than you'll ever show,
I scare myself more than I scare you;
Henceforth I ask: what else is insanity but love?

IN HIS dream the bath water was warm. It tingled on his skin. The whole washroom smelled like lilac and roses, and when August looked at his reflection in the rippling water, the bruises and bite marks had disappeared from the skin of his throat.

There might have been music playing—a gentle echo of Chopin, or perhaps Schubert. August washed. He hummed along to the music and ducked under the hot water, rinsing soap from his hair. It was really long now. He needed to trim it.

He came back up and shook water off before opening his eyes, and then he started to scream.

He screamed because blood poured from the scar on his left wrist like some deranged stigmata. The letters carved there were gory, oozing gashes, *l o n* gushing blood into the bathwater. August shouted. He wasn't sure what he said, just that he screamed. The blood moved slowly in the water, blooming out beneath it, and it looked beautiful, actually, the way it spread—like clouds—

August clutched at his wrist and the whole bath was full of blood. He clambered upward. He didn't want the blood on him, he didn't want it anywhere. It poured from his wrist and he didn't feel pain. The blood stuck to him. It stained his skin. It was everywhere—he didn't want it—

He *remembered*.

August Quincy Prescott. Three brothers, one sister, father, mother. Privileged. Wealthy middle class. A nice neighborhood and a childhood of trips to the zoo, to parks, to museums. The Prescotts called themselves a Christian family, although in an increasingly agnostic world, the only one who ever spoke of faith was Mrs. Prescott; the rest of the family suffered from a secret guilty absence of it. There was a little oval portrait of Her Majesty in the drawing room next to a picture of Christ. Mr. Prescott was accustomed to his children asking for money before kisses, rummaging through his pocketbook for them before going off to gamble at the races.

August studied what his mother and father found fit from the comfort of the upstairs playroom with a private tutor. He couldn't play piano; his violin sounded like an animal in misery; politics gave him a headache; his tongue tied knots over Latin when he tried to speak it aloud. But when it came to literature, August was an avid devotee. He didn't want to be a solicitor like his father, or his father's barrister like two of his brothers, or a doctor in Manchester like his oldest brother. He wanted to study the Classics. He wanted to write poetry. He wanted to travel the world and write what he saw.

Lucius Shelton read his poems.

Lucius Shelton said, "Forget law or medicine. You have a *talent*, August, and talents are what every conservative fears—"

Lucius Shelton was a handsome, charismatic bachelor fresh and popular in London's bustling Decadent scene of handsome, charismatic bachelors. Lucius was twenty-six; Lucius had deep brown hair waxed out of his face and dimples that softened his grave, manly beauty into something devious and tender. Lucius called himself an artistic revolutionary, and by that he meant he lived to shock the hypocritical masses. Lucius knew all the secrets of the world. Lucius had keys to all the secrets of the world. Lucius roamed the West End with his pack of handsome, charismatic bachelors, drinking and writing until sunrise, smoking opium-laced cigarettes, dining with Robbie Ross, flashing Parisian fashion and fur-lined coats and rebelling against the widespread obsession with self-righteous image and somber propriety. Lucius Shelton loved occult lectures and ghost-conjuring parties and raucous cabarets and *Faust up to Date* at the Gaiety.

Mr. Prescott despised Lucius Shelton. Mrs. Prescott refused to acknowledge his existence. The Prescotts' maid would poke her head into the breakfast room or the drawing room or August's bedroom and snap, "Your *friend* is here, and he's under the window, and he's calling for you, and I'm sure he's quite drunk and hasn't slept a wink." What she meant was "Do something about this *now*, please."

Lucius Shelton was a whirlwind of art and philosophy and daring experiences, and August was utterly swept away.

Lucius taught August to kiss. He taught August to love. He made no secret of his inclinations, and was even less subtle about what he wanted and when he wanted it. Against the front window in a bachelors' flat for all to see, sprawled half-dressed, flushed and gasping on a daybed in a lounge, sharing cigarettes and absinthe and body heat and ideas about love and prejudice that were safe in the moonlight, realm of both mystery and truth.

Mr. Prescott threw the daily newspaper across the breakfast table at August and roared, "I'm done! I'm done with it, son! Look at you, all rumpled and rough! You didn't even sleep last night, did you? You weren't even in your own bed last night, were you? What about *employment*? When will you choose a *profession*? You're completely unpresentable, all wrinkled and tousled, and it's that profligate Shelton's doing. I'm through with it, do you hear me? He's lazy. He's a spiritualist. He's intemperate, unvirtuous. He's a buggerer and I won't have you in that danger—"

August stormed out; he threw on his coat and left. He was burning with the injustice, bruised by frustration. He couldn't bear his father's misunderstanding and disconnect. He stormed straight to Chelsea, knocking in a frenzy on Lucius's door. But even in the midst of reckless, impatient kisses, stumbling through a messy Decadent's den, staggering past cluttered books and papers and grabbing at each other, clinging to each other, groping and clutching and groaning between the teeth as Lucius's knee went up between his legs against the wall near the stairs and the sound of their smacking mouths was loud in the morning quiet—even then August still defended his father against Lucius's biased reassurances.

"He's just afraid for me," August insisted.

"Afraid of what?"

"You, for Christ's sake, Lucius!" August shouted.

They made midmorning love, and just before August fell asleep in a borrowed shirt, Lucius Shelton criticized, "Your obsession with ethical understanding is the most unethical thing about you." He added with an insensitive curl of his lip, "You're such a contradiction of yourself: you're logical to a fault, you're sensible out of dangerous naiveté, and yet you are rebellious by nature and you thirst for the world while fearing its rejection...."

Lucius was so very, very good at forging weapons out of words.

They woke up around dinnertime and went out that night, still sore from sex and frustrated by the argument at breakfast. Swirl of gaslight, laughter, West End crowds, drinks like fire on the tongue and their little pack of bachelors out for all the Bohemian glories London's secret places had to offer. August thought when he'd found the bad-luck crooked sixpence on the corner that he should go home, but he didn't. He didn't, and the hook-nosed vampire came and snatched him away to the dungeon below the church, the dirt and chains and human sacrifices, took him away for an auction in the moonlight—

August jerked awake in the attic room of the vampire house, out of breath and cold with sweat.

He *remembered*.

Late-autumn afternoon sunlight spilled in through the curtainless windows, and August scrambled out of bed and snatched up his pen and paper. His hands shook. His breath came fast and emotional. He wrote before the words left him. He wrote down a poem he'd written before that Lucius had said was his favorite:

> *I would forever desire any level of hell, dancing beneath my feet,*
> *rather than the pale loveless hypocrisies above—*
> *And while the lilies are marred in the maw of the beast,*
> *the answer to the question is love.*

August climbed back into bed and cried.

Oh God, nothing was what it seemed.

It was a miserable, choking crying; he tried to swallow the tears but the anguish broke him to pieces. Who was this man he'd dreamed of? He remembered the Prescott family; he remembered Lucius. But who was this man, this naïve, privileged man who knew nothing of fear or despair or the meaning of anything at all?

Him. It was him. August Quincy Prescott. He couldn't deny it. It rattled him to the core, and he sobbed into the blankets like a child.

God, he had accepted this new life as sacrifice to vampires without a fight. He didn't recognize himself.

What did his mother and father think? Were they looking for him? Did they think he'd run off with Lucius? Were they glad he'd gone?

He cried to mourn that life, that August. That August was gone. Even if he had the chance after all of this, there was no way he could return to *that*. He wouldn't fit.

He liked himself better now.

He was so fundamentally different; he'd always been fundamentally different, but this place had carved away all the troublesome pressure of outside demands. He didn't want to see his family. He didn't even want to see Lucius. Lucius could sod off.

That was it. There was no remedying things.

He didn't want to go back.

August fell asleep with tears still drying in sticky tracks on his face, and when he awoke to Hazel lighting the lamp in the last feeble shadows of twilight, he had a horrible headache.

"Move," she sighed. "I need your dirty clothes and bedding for laundry."

PART TWO
THE LAMB

"And the wolf will dwell with the lamb, And the leopard will lie down with the kid,
And the calf and the young lion and the fatling together;
And a little boy will lead them."
      Isaiah 11:6

CHAPTER ELEVEN

THEO FOUND him in the hall.

August, meandering along in the borrowed smoking jacket, lingering at the banister of the stairwell listening to Anastasia argue with Alphonse about how he couldn't continue seeing this young lady from Knightsbridge because he'd ruin her life and she'd ruin his.

"How quaint," Theo commented, leaning in his bedroom doorway with arms crossed. August turned round, meeting his eyes over his shoulder. Theo smiled faintly, holding August's stare. He didn't like how dark and empty it was. "Like a regular old family, aren't we?" He meant the argument downstairs.

"Good morning," August replied.

"It's not morning." Theo frowned. There was nothing playful about it. He didn't like the distance in August's eyes, the way he wasn't smiling. "You were crying," Theo said, skipping idle pleasantries. "Why?"

August stared dumbly. He looked perplexed, as if he wanted to ask how Theo knew, but didn't want to know the answer.

Slowly August crossed the hallway.

Theo studied him quietly. He lifted a hand and brushed a thumb over August's chin, ran his knuckles up his cheek. Ah, his skin was so soft and warm. August closed his eyes, yielding to the touch.

"Why?" Theo prompted again when August opened his eyes.

"I had a bad dream," August deflected.

"I heard you crying," Theo whispered, pulling August into his room gently, guiding him with the fingers on his chin. August stopped once out of stubbornness, but he followed. Ah God, he followed.

"It woke me up," Theo murmured. "I heard you. I listened to it. Why did you cry?"

The silence buckled; the tension snapped. August shook off Theo's fingers and waltzed past him and into his room.

"There's only an hour to feeding," Theo husked over his shoulder, more to himself than to August. August didn't care. Theo watched him, the grace of his straight shoulders, the way he seemed very aware suddenly of his own sensuality. Ah, he was head over heels, Theo realized. He was starved for connection and affection. Theo wanted to give it to him.

"Love me," August suggested firmly from the foot of the bed.

Theo closed the bedroom door, hopelessly cultured, but then he turned to August and they were lost to the choppy waves of passion's impatience again.

Theo gathered August up against him with greedy arms around his waist, fisting his fingers in his nightshirt. August clutched him by the shoulders, the neck, the face, as if he aimed to memorize the feel of him, the taste of him, before letting his mouth fall open to welcome Theo's hungry, twisting tongue. He rocked his hips forward; Theo uttered a surprised little moan, ripe with desire, shivering with that guilty, inhuman *hunger*.

"I want you," August gasped on Theo's lower lip. The hunger came out in a low growl from the back of Theo's throat, a frail and grating groan through his teeth as he hoisted August up and onto his bed, following him down between his knees. "I want you!" August said a second time, more urgently, grappling for eye contact. But Theo was dropping kisses down August's throat and chest, ripping at the buttons of his shirt, seeking more skin to caress, to smell, to nuzzle, to sink his teeth into and drink the blood.

"Ah Christ, Theo, I want *all of you*, I want—"

A few of his clocks chimed for the time—eleven o'clock. The chaotic chorus slammed Theo back into focus. He bristled, eyes widening, struggling to reign back in his desire. He ran a tongue over his teeth to make sure his canines had not yet extended. Impatience crawled beneath his skin and the hunger twisted inside him. The temptation was so strong, so goddamn strong.

Temptation will weaken you.

You know what happens if rules are broken.

Damn the rules straight to hell, Theo just didn't want to give in to the beast he was.

Self-control in the face of infernal temptation was the only thing that kept him human, after all.

"Well, you'll have to wait," Theo hissed at August, flashing him a look without lifting his head.

August sat there, propped up on his elbows, breath coming in galvanized little hisses as he watched Theo hunched between his knees. August's fingers tightened in the bedding and his hips twitched.

Deeming the moment safe again, Theo demanded in a coarse voice, "Tell me about your bad dream."

It calmed him to listen to August talk—listening about the Prescotts, about the writing parties, about Lucius, about morals, about the hollow guilt of preferring himself now, indulging in this life now.

"You *indulge* in this?" Theo whispered, full of contempt and of bewilderment, and yet thankfully he felt remarkably more mellow than a quarter of an hour before. He lay on his side beside August, peering up at where August sat back against the headboard. "You indulge in this blasphemous existence?"

August seemed stunned too. Maybe he hadn't realized it, not in so many words, until he said it there in Theo's room. And in all truth, he appeared rather calm and resigned about the idea. Theo felt no underlying panic charging the air around him. What else was there to feel about the truth, after all?

"Well," August replied, flatly, "the things you do as vampires couldn't be evil if you didn't choose this damned existence. You didn't ask for a curse."

"Oh, August." Theo smiled at that, in pity, eyes narrowing even as they patiently roamed August's face. "Oh, my August...."

THEO. AUGUST would have Theo. He would have him as he'd had Lucius. He would have him and love him more than he'd loved Lucius.

Who was the real monster here: the vampire carrying on as unholy nature required, or the mortal man trembling in emboldened awe?

Maybe it was the way Theo stared at him as if he could read every dark, dirty secret of his soul whether August remembered or not. It made him feel vulnerable. It made him feel on display. He kind of liked that.

He didn't want to compare it to Lucius.

This was vastly different from what he'd had with Lucius.

Oh, in the Sanctuary the puncture of teeth into his throat and wrist was still a sharp, pinching ache, and August loathed it as he delighted in it. The pain of the sharp little fangs, the way his skin

was cold afterward and the pain was dull and heavy in his muscles—
delicious exhaustion.

They drank his blood to survive; he gave them that life. He was
their sacrifice.

Theo. He would have Theo. Theo gave this entire sinister existence
meaning.

And Ishmael stared because Ishmael knew. With a little shiver of
spite, August hoped Ishmael could taste it in his blood.

Back to the little attic room it was, and Hazel locked the door.

THE SNAP of the attic door's lock jerked August awake. He'd drifted
off into a little cat nap, fatigued from the trip to the Sanctuary, curled
up comfortably now in the borrowed smoking jacket and two blankets
with a hot water bottle at his feet. Under poultice and bandages, the
vampires' fresh bites throbbed dully. The tincture of laudanum didn't
help with the fogginess, though it blanketed him with a warm, numb,
happy feeling.

The attic door swung open, and the soft light of the candles
bounced merrily around Theo's shadow.

"Your skin...," August whispered, waving a little in greeting,
thinking back to the scribbled pencil translation in *Philologie*.
"'Peaches and cream, untouched by sun, pale from hunting love in the
shadows....' You translated that for me. I know you did. What does
that mean?"

"It means I want you," Theo purred.

He elbowed the door closed and crossed the bleak attic in four
even strides, climbing onto the bed with August. His long legs and
feline crawl, coupled with the clear gleam of purpose in his revitalized
eyes, was both ominous and thrilling. August sloppily kicked back the
blankets lest they get in the way of Theo's imminent embrace.

"Is this against the rules?" August gasped into his kiss, folding his
arms around Theo's shoulders. He was only asking out of honest
curiosity; there was no hesitance or dissuasion. What an irreverent man
he was.

"Ah, but I'm not feeding on you, now am I?" Theo hummed on his
lower lip, and August had to laugh at this clever reply, but then Theo dove
his hand down between his legs and the laugh became a wavering groan.

The little bed creaked beneath their rocking bodies. Nighttime wind drove hard against the chimney stacks and roof, scattered leaves down the shingles. The usual rain was not much more than a lazy drizzle of fat, cold drops, and in the dance and flicker of candlelight, this coming together was all well worth the wait.

Theo had August's sex in his hand, pumping, fondling, exploring. August bucked his hips into Theo's fingers. The arousal was nothing compared to the actual act, and the lust prickled head to toe like goose bumps.

Fresh after feeding, Theo was the handsome gentleman again, energized, rejuvenated, all soft flushed skin and warm lips, drunken eyes and teasing smirk. Muscles twitched under naked flesh as he stripped his upper half, and August dragged him closer, closer, by the smooth, hard shoulders. What a handsome, handsome man. He trailed his hands lower to Theo's taut middle, traced the fine trail of hair under his navel. Theo was stiff and warm at the front of his trousers. *Only with fresh blood....* His blood. It was his blood, fresh from his throat, that got Theo hard.

August shuddered with a deep, devious desire, drinking in the sight of Theo almost human again. He swallowed Theo's low, manly moans as they rolled off his tongue and into his kisses. August pulled and tugged and squeezed—*ah.* Just touching another man's sex was exhilarating in a dark, daunting way; it turned him on defenselessly, mercilessly. Funny how in bed one felt so dissolute and sinful, and yet it was the most liberating sensation in the world.

August remembered the careful art of penetrative sex.

It seemed second nature; rather, it made sense now that he'd remembered why so many things felt that way.

He was dizzy from the blood loss and the laudanum and the sensual stimulation, and his ears rang as he climbed to his hands and knees. Theo buried his nose in the nape of his neck, raining kisses on bandages and very mortal love bites on any open skin. "It's all right," he whispered there. "Let me...."

To which, with a tangle of fingers and the torturously close nudge of Theo's warm sex, August promptly hissed back, "I've done it before, I know how to do it best—"

What he meant was a little suspicion Theo had forgotten exactly how to make love as humans did—not the love part itself but the details.

August used his mouth, as Lucius had taught him. As Theo himself had done before, never mind with different motives. He was a little shy to be hunched between Theo's legs, a little troubled that Theo's hips didn't twitch as much as they maybe should have, but he was more galvanized to be the one delivering the pleasure. There was a special sort of thrill in that. He looked up, wondering if Theo understood.

Theo looked a bit awestruck, face pinched. He said miserably, "I almost forgot!" and it was the most innocent, endearing thing in the midst of the heated act that August wanted to laugh and then kiss him all over.

August didn't. He crumpled down to his elbows to drown a moan in his pillows because it wasn't the intrusion of sharp little fangs this time, no, this time the invasion was Theo's cock swollen with warm blood. Theo started steadily, but not entirely slowly, already penetrating deep, hard, bruising August's insides in the most delicious way. He even managed to prod that sweet sensitive secret place there in the center. August fumbled down between his own thighs, hungry for more, more. What was wrong with him, that this drove him to such depths of pleasure?

"Ohh, I adore you," Theo crooned, somewhere between a gasp and a growl, and he was right in August's ear, he had him tight in his arms, he was going to drive him mad with this bliss, this reckless sinful torturous bliss—

August came with a stuttering groan, body rocking, shivers rattling through him. The room spun. He was sticky with sweat. Theo kept on, harder, faster yet, until with a burst of heat and a rippling throb, he was over the edge and thrusting to the carnal rhythm of his own release.

Blood dried a faint, rust-colored smear on August's inner thigh; it bloomed slowly on the blankets.

Theo husked miserably, "It's not yours, darling. It's *mine*."

August groaned in dismay, flopping back on the pillows and still breathing hard from the exertion. His head throbbed. The bite marks on his throat pulsed. He wiped his dirty hand on the sheets.

Alas, not all the mechanics of the Undead could be romanticized—ejaculating the only real fluid in a vampire's body was one of these grotesque things, no viscous semen here but only thin, dark red blood already coagulating in the open air. It left Theo pale and drained as if he'd never fed. But he'd done it willingly. He'd weakened himself willingly, to love August.

August was appalled. He was mystified and morbidly fascinated. He understood that Theo was ashamed of this. He didn't want it to be that way.

He staggered out of bed and tugged at the sheets, ready to collapse into sleep but knowing this needed to be done first. "Come on, then," he snapped at the only vampire he trusted, "help me get these off the bed and ready for laundry so Hazel won't ask any questions." He stopped. He watched as Theo hurried to help him, frantic and guilty like a lover who'd spent the night instead of one of August's so-called *masters*. August smiled, still shaking from the sex.

"I adore you too," he whispered back finally.

Theo pretended not to have heard, but August saw the smile in his eyes.

CHAPTER TWELVE

THE GIRL vampire wore her blonde curls in intricate braids and ribbons, or with flower crowns woven above her ears. She didn't wear chemises. In certain gowns this was very obvious, a thin muslin neckline, here and there shifting to reveal little pink nipples and white skin. She didn't seem to like jewelry, but instead sometimes wore a strip of scalloped lace about her long neck. Standing at the end of the third floor hall close to her fainting room, she stared at August as he came down from the attic and she said:

"My name is Anastasia."

Her hair was damp from a bath, breaking in silvery-blonde ringlets and curls across her dainty shoulders.

August fidgeted in Theo's smoking jacket, raising his brows very slowly.

"Let's play!" she called, gesturing for him to follow her into her bedroom.

The room reeked of too many aged perfumes. She had her name embroidered on her pillows, painted on her looking glass, and pasted to her wall in colorful letters.

"I know you like books," Anastasia said. She moved past her bed, which was curtained in lavender and plum taffeta. August didn't answer. He wandered around her room as if it were Circe's mansion while Anastasia sat at her vanity like the witch-goddess herself, watching August through the reflection in the mirror. Her cabinets and drawers and other furniture were French and marvelous, elaborate gold and pale wood. Anastasia loved luxury, apparently. As if she were filling an emptiness with it. And like Theo, she had a secret collection of her own.

Music boxes.

All about the room were music boxes, of every different color, shape, and size. Some were closed so they wouldn't play; others were open, but not wound. The most beautiful of them all—smooth porcelain, ivory, and gold, studded with deliberately placed pebbles of turquoise—sat majestically atop a cedarwood *cassone*. The chest itself was covered in gold leaf and painted with languorous angels. Behind the tiny imperial-looking music box was an oval-shaped oil rendering of a striking young man, an Italian maybe, with small, gentle eyes and an even gentler mouth.

Anastasia was behind him suddenly. August jumped, eyes widening. He hadn't even heard her stand up.

He turned nervously but found no menace on the girl's face. She simply lingered behind him, peering down at the display on the cassone. There was a softness to her eyes August had never seen before. It unsettled him and saddened him all at once, as if it were reaching out to gather him into its depths.

"I loved that man," she sighed wistfully, gown dancing on her legs as she returned to the vanity. She sat down. She turned around, violently, and here she was the siren again, the ice back in her eyes, foreboding.

"Get away from those things now," she admonished, too sweet for her hateful scowl. "They're precious to me."

"Apologies, Mistress."

"Isn't that Theo's robe?" Anastasia hummed, carefully pinning her hair up off her neck.

August bristled. Suddenly he was suspicious that Anastasia only wanted to speak with him to play with his head, like Ishmael. She was watching him from the mirror, waiting for his answer.

"Yes," August finally replied. "It's cold in the attic."

Anastasia's hair was perfectly braided again. She simpered at him through her reflection in the mirror, steely eyes little crescent moons of full lashes.

"Come here," she hummed. Her voice was high and soft, not quite as ripe as a mother's but somehow very old in its timeless maturity. Somehow she intimidated him more than most of the males. In a different way than Alistair did, far different from Ishmael, but to a similar extent. August obeyed, moving closer.

Anastasia cupped his face in her cool hands, smiling at him. She craned in, smirking. She whispered along the corners of his mouth as her thumbs stroked hair away from his ears. "You're a respectable man, aren't you? You must be so ashamed to have fallen under Theo's spell.

He's our hopeless romantic, you know, but I assure you that's just the way vampires are—see? Like this."

Anastasia kissed his mouth, a whisper of dry lips. She was playing with him. She pouted.

She said, "August, our handsome little lamb, wouldn't you prefer me over those cruel men any day?"

August went stiff. *She knew.* Just like Ishmael, she knew. Or she suspected, and she was trying to milk a confession out of him. But why—because she wanted to get Theo in trouble? But as Theo had said, he hadn't broken the rules, per se. Unless.... What about what Ishmael had said—about a vampire loving a sacrifice more than it should—and whether they meant lust or love, it wasn't clear, but Theo was surely guilty of the one if not the other—but if that was the case, why hadn't Alistair been to the attic to punish August? Unless Theo was being punished, and didn't say?

"Relax, Antinous, I'm not threatening you, merely mocking your *very* Greek preferences," Anastasia muttered, throwing a pearl-studded comb at August. *Antinous.* He laughed, if only out of relief, brow knotting.

No, Anastasia was not like Ishmael, then; she was not clandestine and contentious. She was just different, very different from any other woman. That August could remember, anyway.

"Have you ever kissed a lady?" she pried, smirking at him with her pretty pink mouth.

"Once or twice." August cleared his throat, offering a bittersweet smile in hopes of seeming less awkward and defenseless. It was easy, chatting with her—teasing, exchanging witty lines and shy smiles. He liked it. He was not afraid. He was hopelessly infatuated with these creatures. He wanted to know everything about them, inside and out. Was there really anything else meant for him? Surely there was no getting out of this house alive. Surely this was it. This was all that was left for him. And the dangerously curious side of him was ready, receptive and waiting.

"But never more?" Anastasia asked.

"Never more."

"Well, what's it like?"

"What's what like?"

"Same-sex relations."

August looked at her dumbly, then in a flat, though also cheeky, way he murmured, "Oh, Anastasia, you're not telling me you've never in your long life kissed another woman?"

Anastasia threw a powder brush at him now, gasping dramatically. "How dare you comment on a lady's age!" She leaned forward as if she were sharing a secret, grinning at him. "Same-sex relations between *gentlemen*," she clarified.

August smiled quickly, avoiding her eyes. He didn't want any bit of an image of him and Theo drifting from his mind to hers, should she be sensitive somehow to it; maybe she'd already tasted it in his blood, but it still felt like privacy to fight for. Purposefully he threw to the front of his mind a cold, faraway memory of Lucius—Lucius, standing over him in the dark; Lucius, shirt undone and pulling off August's trousers; Lucius, sex flushed and hard and at attention. How did Anastasia like *that* for snooping around?

Speaking of Lucius, he would have been so very proud of August taking up cleverly worded arms in the war against society's prudish norms. August said, "I'm sure it's not much different from relations with the opposite sex, though maybe a little simpler and not so complicated by pretension and expectations. You just *love*."

Anastasia smiled at him.

It was warm.

Her eyes were distant. She nodded as if she understood this— love, whatever love was, love that was sometimes painful and love that was destructive, and love that was the slow eroding of the rational man's soul. Maybe she was thinking about her old lover, in the oil painting. Maybe she was ruminating on the debauched memory August had put up for her to steal. She stood, tea gown dusting about her ankles. Barefoot per usual she swept across the room to him.

"How right you are," she mused aloud, curling her fingers on his.

A sensual tension hung tacit in the air between them; no, it was the vampire's charm. That power of persuasion that crawled beneath his skin was something he could never brace himself for.

"But don't you want to kiss a woman sometimes too?" Anastasia coaxed. She leaned close and her loose curls tickled him. She kissed his ear, his cheek.

God, but closer he realized she was older than she first appeared. She could have been almost thirty when she became what she was, but there was still something soft and ageless about her. Feeling quite lulled for some reason, he tipped his head and let his eyes shut. She kissed his mouth and he thought Theo would be angry at him if he did not at least humor her, if he disrespected her. Maybe Theo would have even enjoyed watching. Tentatively he kissed back, breathing a little sigh against her lower lip. It was just a kiss; it meant nothing to him. And he had no real right to resist. She was his mistress. She lifted his hand and nipped at his fingertips, each, one by one—

Pearle, the vampire with the scarred face, appeared in the threshold soundlessly.

Anastasia jerked back and the vampire's spell was hacked away so roughly that it left August's ears ringing. He stood, stupefied, in the center of Anastasia's room as she swished away like nothing had happened. August stared.

"*Anastasia*," Pearle snapped from the doorway.

Anastasia uttered a scornful sniff, as if Pearle's reproof were a surprise. After a moment, with a little chill of clarity, August realized they were having a conversation with their eyes and nothing more.

"But you won't tell Alistair, will you, Pearle?" Anastasia spoke this reply aloud, voice tight and disparaging.

Pearle's brow knotted over stern eyes. Without looking away from her, he gestured for August.

"That's right, rescue the sacrifice," Anastasia hissed. "I just wanted a snack. It's not as if I were really going to drink his blood. I was just going to have his manhood as Theo did—"

Her voice stopped as soon as Pearle shut her bedroom door. August was tense. The snap of Anastasia's allure had left him a little dazed and hollow, stunned, as if she'd slapped him across the face. And now he was under Pearle's arm and his heart was in his throat. *As Theo did. His manhood. Just wanted a snack.* Was she lying? Had she been ready to nip at his fingertips for a bit of blood, while he had been stupidly hypnotized by her charm? It didn't seem very fair that he was in the wrong either way, whether he'd resisted her or given her what she'd wanted. That was the worst rule of all the house's rules—just as with Ishmael, blame always reverted to August, because he was at the bottom of the hierarchy here. He waited for Pearle to punish him, to threaten him—something, anything, some discipline he didn't know. He almost welcomed it.

But out in the hall, Pearle did nothing. He sighed, a long and encumbered sigh. He ran his fingers through his black hair and held August by the shoulder, walking him back toward the attic stairs. They passed Theo's room. Theo was there; he hadn't been earlier. He was lost in one of his fits of obsession, arranging and rearranging and rearranging again all the chairs in his room like a dangerous compulsion.

"She isn't exactly the most well-behaved," Pearle lamented about Anastasia. He could have been talking to himself. The door to the right of the attic landing opened. Hazel stopped short, rosewood tray in hand. She looked between Pearle and August, eyes wide. Pearle smiled cordially, but it didn't sway her. She knew better, it seemed.

"Just returning the lamb," Pearle murmured. "Seems that attic key doesn't work much anymore, does it?"

Hazel's mouth was bitten into a bitter line, wide eyes flashing. She gripped the rosewood dinner tray with hard fists. "Master Alistair assures me it works just fine," she replied thinly, "though it hasn't seemed necessary lately to lock anyone in or anyone else out. I always know when the sacrifice is out and about."

That was a lie for August's sake, he knew. He stood between them, trying very hard not to seem guilty when there didn't appear to be a clear place for guilt in the house. There was so much spite in this place, so many word games and so much deference; the division of interest didn't support the rules very well. There was more bickering and intimation than anything else—that was, that they showed him.

Pearle left him there with Hazel. Hazel looked to him pointedly, expecting an explanation or at least acknowledgment of her mercy.

August turned sharply and stalked back up to the attic room. Hazel followed him without a word.

THE NIGHTS were growing brisker and brisker. Soon August would wake to snow piling on the roof of the house, not the slash of London rain.

He remembered little leather journals full of poetry and Lucius reading them aloud with a bottle of cognac splashing in one hand and the book in the other, all their writer friends cheering drunken and lazy on comfortable love seats while August sat on the pianoforte behind Lucius, too lost in the haze of wine and brandy to feel embarrassed by Lucius's show.

August tried to write again, propped in the armchair near the attic window.

It didn't really work.

With a pinch deep in his chest, August wondered whether the Prescotts had held a funeral for him yet, or if they had tried to find him at all. He wondered what Lucius thought, what he felt, what had happened to him—

Resolutely he wanted to keep that life before as distant and distinct as he could from this life now. They were not the same. They did not relate. That other August was not him, and that other life was not his.

It wasn't worth it to wonder; it was far away and done.

August decided the Irish maid didn't like him because he reminded her too much of her own son.

He discovered, through whispers between the scullery maid and the cook, that her son had been a strong boy when the vampires began using him, but something happened along the way, and after three years, his constitution was just too drained.

"Come with me," Hazel said when she didn't bring breakfast one evening, and August stared at her in the candlelight, perplexed. "Come with me down to the kitchen, if you're so fond of walking around the house."

She wasn't mad at him, but she was still so endearingly vindictive. So August put on Theo's smoking jacket and went down with her, down the attic stairs and to that door to the right, into the servants' hall.

The few servants in the kitchen looked at August in curiosity, contempt, humble dismay at the pale young man with the bruised and bitten neck, the bags beneath his eyes and the head of uncombed blond hair.

Hazel hurried off to finish her other chores while the cook slid breakfast down in front of August. The scullery maid and the cook gossiped. If they wondered at all about August, they didn't pose any questions, but perhaps it was a defense mechanism here in this house to stay distanced from sympathy, pity, human connection. Or maybe they'd heard from Hazel or the vampires that August was a troublemaker. August didn't mind. His ham and eggs were perfectly cooked. He nursed a cup of hot Turkish coffee, listening to them talk—about the Irish maid who didn't like August very much, *that Vicky*, and about the affairs of London, of the world, which left August confounded because he could hardly remember the current events of before all this.

Hazel wasn't back yet.

August politely excused himself, wandering out and into the vestibule. He stood in the quiet, feeling it, basking in it, eyes roaming the old tapestries and art on the walls. Moonlight filtered in from the window above the door, pale with the glow of the candles in all the sconces. Sometimes the vestibule reminded August of a place for ghosts, not life—empty and eerie, like the fainting room upstairs.

He could hear voices in other rooms of the house, movement in all corners.

A sudden boldness struck August then. It might have been impatience, something a little more impetuous than curious. The house felt like a tomb. Even the maids were quiet, just flashes of dark wool and white lace here and there, drifting in and out of the halls like ghosts. The early winter wind was a force outside the windows, and the dim light in the vestibule caused shadows to dance in the corners. The doors to the hallway beyond were open, but nobody was in sight.

The drawing room was empty and the door ajar, and August couldn't help it.

He peeked through the threshold first, nervous. And for the first time perhaps ever, August entered the drawing room of his own volition.

The room was aglow. The scents of melting wax, fresh flowers, and polish were familiar and comfortable. There were no windows.

August stopped at the doors to the Sanctuary. They were made to blend into the wall, gilded white paneling with well-hidden hinges. The molding was smooth beneath his fingers. He pulled, and there was the subtle *click* of the latch, a gentle creak as he swung a door open and peeked into the darkness within. There were no windows here either. The candles were not lit. Shadows swallowed the room, all the antique furniture and the old empty sconces.

August left one of the secret doors open as he tiptoed into the Sanctuary, following the slant of light from the drawing room.

The Sanctuary was cold—ominous, hopeless.

There on that old couch was where the Alpha always started the feeding. And there, passed him along, over the velvet, the silk, the smell of incense, rot, and old upholstery, the seduction, the spell, the connection, and was that a stain on the cushions? Was it blood? Was that mark on the floor, on the rug, the same thing? August shivered, crouching down to examine the shadowy smudge. He scratched at it with his thumbnail, frowning. Was it another sacrifice's blood? Was it *his*?

There were footsteps. Sharp on floorboards, muted on carpet.

August jumped, eyes widening, as a shadow fell over the slant of light from the drawing room. The hair stood up on the back of his neck and he spun around just in time to see Ishmael's baleful eyes and gentle smirk as he swung the open door shut, sealing August alone in the darkness.

The click of the latch was deafening. August shot to his feet. He ran his hands over the doors, searching for a handle as panic infected him cold and white. His ears rang. He knew Ishmael was still on the other side of the door, listening to him, smiling to himself like a rotten child.

Darkness.

He was in complete darkness and he couldn't see, and Ishmael had closed him into the Sanctuary.

"What are you doing snooping around, little lamb?" Ishmael cooed from the drawing room. His voice was muffled, but held its usual intimidation.

August was frantic. His heart raced. His skin crawled. His stomach was in sick knots. "I'm sorry," he sputtered, clutching at the door. There were no grips, no knobs, no ways to open it from the inside. "I'm sorry, Master!" he amended, looking over his shoulder. He could see nothing. Quite suddenly he remembered what it was like to be small and terrified of the dark.

"Do you know what the Sanctuary is?"

August stared into the darkness as if he might be able to see Ishmael's voice. But he could not. It reached his ears cool and grim. "It's for the feeding hour," August said. "I'm sorry, sir, I won't snoop anymore, please just let me out and I'll—"

"Listen, *do you know what the Sanctuary stands for?*"

"No!" August fired back.

Ishmael divulged, "We serve the Lamb by following his rules. 'In sacrament and in honor, for salvation through sin, *in nomine Domini, mortui vivos docent.*' This Sanctuary is the place for feeding to keep the action *holy*, for lack of a better word. Pure, divine, untainted—"

The Lamb. August recognized the chant and the Latin. The vampires had recited it in the cemetery so many weeks ago. He covered his mouth to keep from groaning, fear stabbing deep into his bones. "I'm sorry," he said again. "I'm sorry, Ishmael, please let me out!"

"This Sanctuary is important to us," Ishmael reproved. "You wouldn't want anyone snooping around in your important things, would you?"

"No," August promised, but the vampires already trespassed; they trespassed on every part of him. What choice did he have? "Please, sir, I won't snoop again. I'll be sure to tell Hazel where I'm going and I—"

"Do you feel the significance in that room? Does it overwhelm you? Do you understand that you are but a tiny fly caught in our web? Do you feel the preternatural hum in that room that remains after so many unions are made among us all through your blood? In nomine Domini, mortui vivos docent. In the name of the Lord, the dead teach the living!"

The door opened suddenly and August staggered forward into the soft light of the drawing room. He choked on a breath, eyes wide, gawking up at Ishmael. Ishmael was across the room. How he'd opened the door and gotten there so quickly was disturbing to think about. He smiled a warm and tender smile, and if it had been on anyone else's face, August might have believed it. No, Ishmael's smile was a mockery. It was a threat.

"Have you ever heard the story of the boy who cried wolf?" Ishmael purred, and August didn't need to answer. The point had been made. Whether August was telling the truth or not, nobody would believe the sacrifice over the vampire should he go to them about Ishmael's taunts. Ishmael was well aware of that line of authority. And he meant to drive August mad with it.

August flew from the drawing room. He didn't even look to see if Ishmael was following him. Terrified, shaken, August pounded up into the attic and came to a stop in the threshold to find Theo there, holding his pillow while Hazel made his bed.

He gasped for breath, eyes wide. Theo had his pillow to his nose, breathing deep. They were midconversation as Hazel smoothed his sheets. And just as quickly as he registered these peculiar things to think about later, they both looked to him in concern.

"Ishmael," August blurted. "I was looking around and Ishmael scared me, and he said—that Latin that they said in the graveyard—and he thinks he can get away with it, but—"

"You look sick," Hazel said, hurrying across the room to him.

"I'm just winded," August insisted.

"Ishmael's like that," Theo snapped. He met August's eyes over Hazel's shoulder, uncomfortably. "Maybe you should stop walking around so much. He's bored and you're a perfect target for his foolish fun. Vampires like him, and Anastasia, Owen, Alistair.... They find amusement in being mysterious."

August gawked at Theo, betrayed. Was he defending Ishmael, now? Or was he just in one of his foul moods? August had no words. Neither did Theo, apparently. He just shrugged idly. August's jaw tightened. He ripped his gaze from Theo, shaking his head, looking elsewhere in perfect frustration

"So because I'm merely the tasty human, I should let any of you treat me however you please?" he grumbled. "That hardly seems fair."

"Go," Theo told Hazel suddenly.

Hazel obeyed without a moment's hesitation, laundry crumpled up in her arms.

Theo turned to August coldly. His eyes were sharp, resolute; his mouth was set in a resigned scowl. He was nothing but a vampire now, and for a moment—a brief, shivering moment—it was actually frightening. Bleak, unforgiving, ancient and unpredictable. *Vampire.*

He knew August was upset with his response to Ishmael's behavior. Good.

"Ask me," Theo gritted out, lip curling. "Ask me all the questions you are so dying to ask me, then."

That wasn't quite what August expected, but he snapped before he could check himself. "What, have you been reading my mind?"

Theo snorted. "I told you we are not mind-readers, just sensitive to strong thoughts, strong feelings—"

"And you use your own strong thoughts and feelings like some sort of witchcraft on mortals. You never warned me about that part."

"Ah, the lamb speaks his mind! On with it, then, darling, sing me the songs of injustice at the hands of immortals who cannot help their own nature—"

"Why are you speaking like that? All lofty and intellectual—"

"As if you aren't accustomed to it in the Romantic circles of Decadent writers. *Please*."

"You can't help your nature and I can't help mine!" August barked. "Do you really want to know what's on my mind, or shall I leave it for you to snoop through? Shall I leave you in ignorance, aching to weed through all my other thoughts and feelings until you stumble upon the truth? Wouldn't *I* know exactly how frustrating that is?"

"Ask your questions, then," Theo seethed, the tension in the attic room snapping and coiling like a whip; he was like a beast with hackles raised, ready to lunge. "Go on, ask your questions, demand your voice be heard by the arbitrary ruler!"

That was quite dramatic of him, but August played right into it. "Fine!" he roared, hotheaded. Worries that anyone else in the house might hear them shouting were far from his mind. Secrecy and fear were nothing compared to the stifled inquiry and burning need to be heard, to exist, to *matter*. What was this, a lovers' quarrel? God knew he'd had plenty.

"Fine," he hissed again. "Why am I allowed to walk around freely if I'm your slave?" It was far from the important question, but it felt good to ask.

Theo rolled his eyes. He paced the room. His presence was charged and volatile. It made August's ears ring. "Ha!" he spat, a spiteful laugh, coupled with a forced grin and narrowed eyes. He stopped pacing and the smile fell away. He just glared at August. It was almost a vicious pout. "You think we risk your escape? August, there is no escaping. We'd find you in an instant."

"So you'll taunt me?" August raged. "You'll wave freedom in my face to keep me complacent—"

"You've been broken by now!" Theo shook his head. "You're part of us. You're in the house, August. Your blood is in us."

"Stop saying 'us' and 'we' as if you're like the rest of them. You're not like the rest of them—"

"Ah, yes, and in your blood we can taste the rebellion, the hatred. But there's not enough of it in you to matter."

"Oh, I hate you right now!"

"Hate and love are two sides of the same feeling," Theo snapped effortlessly.

"Is that so?" August croaked, voice raw in his throat.

"Any more questions?" Theo said.

"Yes," August snarled. "Here's one—is it against the rules for a vampire to love a sacrifice? 'More than he should?' How much *should* a vampire love his sacrifice, eh, Theo? Is there any love in any of you at all, or is it all just petty little games and trickery, the predator stalking its prey? Am I an idiot for hoping there's at least one single delicate shred of human left in any of you? Or are you all monsters who would kill even their most intimate of friends and lovers?"

Ishmael's words tasted bad in his mouth, but he couldn't help it. He was a mess. He was distraught, and Theo was speechless. His mouth hung open but no words came forth. His face was a mask of fiery, vindictive resistance, but a sudden partiality softened the venom in his eyes. Something flashed through his mind, it seemed; he reconsidered. He faltered. He stood there torn up and astonished, defeated by August's brazen jab to the quick of things.

August was shaking. He flopped down angrily in the chair. It was leftover shock from Ishmael; it was new shock from this rash defiance. He didn't want conflict. He didn't want isolation. The defiance felt good. God, it felt good. But he was terrified suddenly he had done something irreparable, that he had crossed some line he had only until now been tiptoeing—

Theo was across the attic in a few short but powerful strides, almost before August could even brace himself. Theo caught his face in one hand, rough; his thumb bit into August's cheek as he held August in place by the chin for a hard, vigorous kiss.

August bristled, heart racing. Some sort of argument stuttered out on his lower lip, but it was meaningless. The aching need and fever-hot attraction burst open again within him like a wound, and he moaned, he yielded to the kiss, he kissed back with equal force, brow knotting.

In the corner a candlewick popped and the little flame shivered and danced.

Theo dropped down to his knees before the faded wingback armchair as if to prayer, ripping at the smoking jacket, at August's nightshirt, at the buttons down the front of his drawers. His deft fingers were cold; they shocked August's warm skin, sparked shivers of delight through his nerves. And before August could argue—before he could really decide what was going on—before he was stiff enough to truly care—Theo's mouth was on him again, wet, cool, tight, graze of human teeth, flicker of seemingly human tongue.

"*Oh...,*" August gasped, back arching from the chair, hips jumping forward. He slid lower in the seat, toes curling on the floor, knees twitching farther apart for Theo, and Theo's head bobbed between them as he gripped August's thigh with one hand and worked the other in perfect collusion with his devouring mouth, conspiring to drive August mad with carnal pleasure.

"*Ungh*—Theo—*Theo*—ahhh...."

Tears stung the backs of August's eyes, guilt hovering for having been so cruel with his words. He combed his fingers over and over through Theo's hair, squirming, thrusting deeper into his mouth, hissing between his teeth. He didn't deserve this. He'd doubted Theo— even for one weak instant, he had. *Is there any love in you at all, or... at least one single delicate shred of human left...?* He was awful, ungrateful, narrow-minded—

Theo's teeth grazed over the head of his sex, this time with the sharp shiver of a fang, and August choked on a breath, skin crawling. He rolled his eyes open and over to Theo.

There was no danger. Maybe it had been an accident. Maybe it had been on purpose. The dark starving shadows under Theo's eyes were almost inconceivable in the low light of the attic candles, this eternal twilight as the night poured in through the wide sealed windows.

Theo drew the pleasure right out of him, leaving him reeling, enervated, trembling with the thrill of release. His climactic groans shuddered around the attic room; August clapped both hands across his mouth to stifle himself, struggling not to arouse suspicion, but dear God, Theo swallowed everything again and August loved it, he absolutely loved it, it was so primal and shocking. It was also a mildly discouraging reminder that coming together like this with Theo was an event dependent on forces outside of his control. God, he wanted Theo inside him again. But without fresh blood, it wouldn't happen.

August panted, fever hot and shivering from the comedown, longing to curl into a ball but unable to with Theo still hunched before him. Blushing furiously, he mumbled, "You can't just mesmerize me with love to avoid telling me the truth."

Theo smiled up at him from between his knees, tongue darting out across his lower lip as if savoring the taste of August's sex. His eyes were dazed and glassy; all defensive immortal injustice had flown and left a softened, almost drunken look.

There's a love between a vampire and its sacrifice, you know....

"If you don't love me, don't tell me," August whispered faintly. "I want to believe that you do. Don't ruin that."

It's different from any love you've ever known....

Theo shook his head slowly, craning up and gathering August into another tender kiss. His mellow, bittersweet relief infected August with its warmth. Never mind the doubt; never mind how selfish and naïve it was to assume he was special in the eyes of a man—a *vampire*—who would live forever.

"I want you to believe it too," Theo husked against the corner of his mouth. The honesty stabbed August to the core. There was so much unspoken in that poignant confession. August clutched Theo closer by the pockets of his silk waistcoat. There was no cunning here, no lies, no manipulation. God, the need ached in the most beautiful, hopeful way. August wilted into Theo's grasp, and on a wavering, tired sigh, the fear resigned.

"I can visit you more often up here," Theo offered, turning away out of common decency as August redressed himself. "Ishmael only bothers you because you're out and about."

"I don't care," August murmured. He wanted to sleep. He was exhausted suddenly. "I don't mind. I like being out and about in the house."

But he did care.

And hopefully Theo knew he did.

CHAPTER THIRTEEN

ALPHONSE WANTED desperately to go to the Strand.

"I'm sorry for the interruption, sir," Hazel said from the door.

Alphonse and Anastasia stood at the landing of the attic stairs, and Hazel apologized bitterly in the attic, playing messenger for them. Anastasia and Alphonse refused to enter the realm of the sacrifice. They always did.

"That's fine, Witch Hazel," Theo mumbled, climbing off the foot of August's bed and moving their game of chess to the floor. He shrugged limply, fetching his frock coat from the wingback chair. "They've got the patience of children sometimes, I swear," he muttered with an exasperated sigh and a shake of his head.

August didn't ask where he was going. Theo tipped a nod at him and then at Hazel before slipping out down the stairs and disappearing into the house below.

FIRST THERE was something he needed to take care of.

How quickly Theo's mood soured as he descended from the attic. It was almost frightening, the way he could feel his nature change like the rolling skies of inclement weather. The smile faded from his face. He narrowed his eyes. He was a conductor rod of undiluted Undead rage. He moved swiftly past Alphonse and Anastasia, a man on a mission. Down the eastern hall he strutted, where the townhouse wrapped around the neglected garden out the window and down below. It was typical of this block's architecture, really. The fountain down there didn't even run anymore, tangled in vines and dead leaves—

There. Ishmael was outside in the garden.

Theo turned on his heel and stormed down and out through the kitchen doors. Servants scattered like mice at his fast, unthinking approach. The scullery maid dropped a tray of silver she was rouging at the slam of the garden door under Theo's palm.

"What the hell are you doing?" Theo seethed, voice ripping through clenched teeth as he stomped over uneven flagstones and fallen shrubbery to corner Ishmael against the unused fountain.

Moonlight spilled down into the garden, but it was in the wealth of shadows cast from the roof above that Ishmael turned to Theo, looking very surprised and inconvenienced and a little insulted.

"Pardon?" he said.

Theo grabbed Ishmael by the lapel of his coat, close enough to kiss him as he snarled, "What sorts of ideas are you putting in his head, eh?"

"*Oh*," Ishmael hummed, seemingly unruffled by Theo's fists in his coat. No, Theo could see it; he could see a sliver of unease in Ishmael's silvery eyes. Ishmael found glee in this, and Theo had never imagined he'd despise him any more than he already did. "The sacrifice, you mean?" Ishmael clarified. "Why, calm down, Theo, you'd think you were a rabid animal, not a gentleman—"

What a flawless jab right to Theo's insecurities. Theo released Ishmael from his hands with a strangled growl of frustration. It did nothing to help his cause. Ishmael adjusted his coat and cast Theo a moody glance through his lashes.

"I know you're playing games with him," Theo snapped. "Stop."

"*You're* playing games with him," Ishmael fired back. His face twisted and suddenly the innocent act was gone, tattered, thrown away, nothing left in its wake but the jagged angles of a pained scowl. "Seducing him, using him, you demon, you thing of the night—"

The sound as Theo's palm cracked across Ishmael's face echoed off the stone of the townhouse and its slanted gables. Smog and clouds choked the moonlight as they rolled by overhead. There was no starlight; what Ishmael's eyes glinted with was a very sharp, steely revenge as he took the slap and slowly turned his head back to meet Theo's stare directly. His mouth was in a firm line. His pale face was smooth, suspiciously smooth. His brows were even. But the hatred smoldered in his gaze.

Theo immediately regretted hitting him. Ishmael was his superior. Ishmael was older than him. Ishmael had known the time before the sacrifice system and Ishmael was a different type of vampire altogether because of that. Part of Theo didn't care at all about disrespect; he only regretted the slap because he was trying so hard, so very hard to keep control of himself, and he'd failed. No, perhaps he'd succeeded. His hands trembled in violent little fists. He could have done far worse to Ishmael. But he'd reeled himself back in after swinging only once.

Struggling to maintain a level voice, Theo said, "You're confusing August. You're scaring him, and torturing him like a bored little bully."

"He needs to understand his place," Ishmael replied coolly.

"*You* need to understand your place!" Theo snarled. "He knows his place. He's the goddamn sacrifice, and I won't have you feeding him lies for your own enjoyment."

"What lies? I've told him no lies. Remember what Alistair told you. He gave you conditions. Are you getting possessive over him? He's not just yours, you know."

A cold feeling washed through Theo. The spark of rage dulled down if only to be replaced by plummeting dismay. "Of course you listened in on our conversation, didn't you?" he said, more to himself than to Ishmael as it dawned on him. "Of course you did!"

"You've never been great with self-control," Ishmael chastised dispassionately.

"I cannot believe you...." Theo opened the hand with which he'd slapped Ishmael, and stared at the way his palm filled with moonlight. It didn't even tingle from the smack anymore.

"You'll break yourself," Ishmael said, as if it were a warning. Ishmael wasn't warning him. He was taunting him.

"I'm not you," Theo husked.

Ishmael scoffed. Theo couldn't tell whether he was angry he'd been caught in his schemes, or if he was genuinely upset. "He's not worth it, Theo!"

"Tell me honestly, then."

"I won't see you make the same mistakes as I did! It's bad for the coven, it's bad for you—"

Theo froze.

Dear God, Ishmael was *jealous*. He didn't want happiness to work for Theo because happiness hadn't worked for him. The selfishness of it was somehow still shocking to Theo. Ishmael had changed so much in the past half century—but so had Theo. He wasn't half the man Ishmael had made him think he was, and now he hardly knew Ishmael at all. Ishmael hated him for that.

He swallowed hard over a knot in his throat; it was brittle and bitter-tasting. He felt cold. Ishmael waited for him to look. He did not. But still Theo said, "I was a mistake to you, then?"

Ishmael's voice was fragile. "I didn't say that," he hissed.

"Yes, you did."

"I don't want to talk about it anymore."

"You don't want me to be happy because *you* couldn't make me happy. You don't want anyone else to make me happy. It's too much a threat to your fragile sense of self, isn't it?" Theo uttered a harsh laugh, two notes shy of a scoff. "My God, Ishmael!"

Ishmael had hung his head. He stared down at his feet, hunched into his coat as if he were cold. Theo gawked at him, conflicted. Part of him so wanted to rub this weakness in Ishmael's face. The other part of him wanted to flee before he let this revelation get under his skin.

"Sometimes a man does not get what he wants," Theo whispered before he even realized the words were there on his tongue. They tasted right. They were relieving. "Sometimes he does, but it does not last. This is just the way the world works, Ishmael. Centuries of life, and you still do not understand that? That's sad, so very sad...."

Ishmael's eyes shimmered with feeling, close to shattering into tears. Theo felt the bruise of guilt for it. But the words had felt so good. He lingered only a moment longer as Ishmael glowered at him without lifting his chin. Did the air nip at his face as it nipped at Theo's? It smelled like snow.

"Your games won't work, Ishmael," Theo said at last. "You may as well stop wasting your talents."

Theo turned and shoved his hands in his pockets. He accidentally stepped on a withered rose on his way back inside.

Maybe one day Ishmael would say, "You're right, Theo."

Maybe he would never say it.

Theo could not dwell on it either way. Alphonse and Anastasia waited to go to the Strand.

OUTSIDE THE house of vampires, it snowed.

August watched it from the wingback chair, warming his hands on the sides of his evening tea. In the dark, moonlight glittered like jewels in all the white.

August turned to Hazel as she gathered breakfast dishes together on the rosewood tray. He offered her a sip of tea. She politely declined.

"Why does Theo call you Witch Hazel?" August mused aloud.

Hazel stopped tidying. She didn't look at him. Finally she sat at the foot of his bed and shrugged, adjusting her pinafore. She met August's eyes then. "Laurel started it."

"Laurel?" August echoed skeptically. He was sure there was a slight blush on Hazel's face, a dusting of pink across the apples of her cheeks. She stared at him hard as if daring him to point it out. Laurel, Number Seven.

"Yes," Hazel confirmed. "*Laurel.*"

"Laurel doesn't seem like the joking kind. He's very... sullen."

"Perhaps to you," Hazel sniffed. Her pinched frown and raised brows said there was much more to the story—something significant between her and Laurel, surely.

August grinned conspiratorially at her from the chair. "Oh? But not to you, Hazel?"

"August, please."

"Maybe he's friendlier to you, then?"

"*August.*"

"Like a brother, perhaps? Or a beau? You'd think it'd be against the rules for a vampire to fraternize with one of his sworn-to-secrecy maids—"

"August!" Hazel cried, embarrassed, but despite her scandalized scowl and the spoon she threw at him from the tray, her eyes were dancing. "Well, aren't you suddenly talkative?"

"Hazel—" August laughed, picking up the spoon.

"You nosy, irreverent, stupid man!"

Her blushing guilt was endearing and innocent. She couldn't be mad at him, it seemed; she pouted, glared at him, but she was fighting a smile through his laughter. A maid consorting with a vampire as a sacrifice consorted with a master, how perfectly wicked and byzantine was that?

"So it's Laurel's pet name for you?" August surmised.

"Sometimes." Hazel heaved a defeated sigh. "Theo overheard it months ago and won't let me hear the end of it."

"'Witch Hazel' is a strange nickname, though. Doesn't witch hazel mean magic?"

"And who taught you the language of flowers?" Hazel hummed dryly.

August shrugged. "A friend, I guess. I don't really remember. She was at some of our writing parties."

The nighttime wind kicked up waves of snow from the rooftop. August glanced over at Hazel through his lashes, observing her in the candlelight. He felt a little guilty, as if he'd been neglecting her lately. She was his friend too, after all, and that called for more than whispers together as she brought food or came to tend to his bloodied throat and wrist.

"Hazel," August murmured. She perked up, deep gray eyes veering over to meet his again. "How did the vampires get this house?"

Hazel stared at him for a long moment; she was almost looking through him. August could trace the thoughts as they moved in her eyes, but he didn't know what they were. Finally she drew a breath and focused on him again. She shrugged. She said, "I'm not really sure, actually. They make a lot of friends, they have a lot of connections. But they've owned this property for a good seventy years now, I think."

Seventy years. "Where do they get the money?" August pried.

Hazel rolled her eyes. She reached up and tried to tuck loose curls back into their pins as she looked at him, so mature and patient. "Well," she supposed, "as I said, they make a lot of connections and a lot of friends. Maybe one of those connections was an old nobleman. Maybe there's some unknown Undead banking system. *I don't know.*"

August snorted.

"I'm sorry," Hazel insisted. "I'm not entirely sure of the answer to that question either. I've wondered too."

"You have?"

"Of course I have. But sometimes it's easier not to."

August frowned down at his tea. There was an awful mystery to it. Had they killed people for money? Had they stolen? Had they worked for some of their wealth, decades ago, as mortal men would have?

Hazel stood. She took up the tray of dirty dishes and left for the kitchen, nudging the attic door open with her hip. But she peeked back at him through the hinges, flashing a bright smile. She dropped the attic key into her pinafore pocket without locking the door.

AUGUST COULD tell that Theo was in a disagreeable mood.

It was as if he couldn't decide which temper to assume. He was uncouth like a grumpy child, then erratic and eccentric like the vampire he was, strung somewhere between elegance and apathy and surrendering to the obsession he had with his clocks and chairs and their arrangement in his room as a source of distraction.

August wondered whether his time out with Alphonse and Anastasia was what had put him so ill at ease.

It was raining over the snow. The dampness clung to buildings in the fog, and the drizzle turned to ice and slush on the pavement. Hazel agreed to accompany August to the washroom, not without a disdainful little scoff now that he was requesting her presence there and not refusing it. Maybe it was because she could see the disquiet in his eyes. Maybe it was because she was a maid and did what she was told. Either way August was happy she agreed.

In the washroom she drew his bath.

"The rain is really coming down!" Hazel cried, standing on tiptoe under a narrow leaded window to peek outside.

"I like it."

"Yes, it's nice."

"Is that water hot?"

"It's hot."

"My hair is so *long*," August bemoaned, staring at himself in the vanity mirror. He reached up, past the discolored skin of his neck and throat, raking his hand through unruly blond hair. "Would you trim it for me?" he asked, turning to Hazel.

Hazel stared at him, dull gray eyes and no response. Then she tucked dark hair behind one ear and slowly raised her brows with a tight little smile of acquiescence.

The water filled the bath and steam gathered in the dimly lit room as the wintry rain slashed against the house. Hazel fetched a pair of scissors from the vanity and stood behind August. She wasn't fazed by his nakedness, and whatever pointless compass of virtue he'd clung to before was gone by now, torn to shreds in the Sanctuary maybe or found to be ungrounded after remembering the world before—Lucius, his family, himself. But he was still self-conscious of his bruised skin. He felt too soft and frail for a man.

"Don't worry, I've cut hair before," Hazel promised.

"I trust you," August said.

ISHMAEL WAS a monster if any of them were.

Sometimes it seemed he tried very hard to be; other times it seemed to just be in his nature. His unsympathetic and hypercritical gray-green eyes, that bitter, inscrutable half smile, and all his outdated fashion, posture, gestures. Nothing seemed to interest him more than blood and mind games.

Ishmael was out to wrong August, and August didn't know what he'd done to deserve such treatment.

Ishmael appeared soundlessly in the threshold of the library, watching August curiously as he plucked through books to read for the evening.

"Good evening," Ishmael murmured, shadows moving in his eyes. He smiled. He wore a damask-covered waistcoat and velvet solitaire necktie, and August almost dropped the book he'd pulled from the shelf.

"Good evening," he returned below his breath, trying his damnedest to keep his hatred for Ishmael well-checked.

"I was wondering whether you might be available for a favor," Ishmael said. He circled the library opposite of August, skirting the desk and couches, smiling down at a granite bust as if it might smile back. His eyes cut over to meet August's again, imploring.

"What?" August asked quietly, voice clipped as he stooped to replace the book on the shelf.

Ishmael trailed a finger along the curved surface of the globe next to the bust. "It's really nothing very drastic," he said. "I just know that you've been in Anastasia's room recently, and she's rearranged it since I last visited her.... She borrowed one of my music boxes a while back, and I was hoping you might slip in and fetch it for me."

August's brow knotted over a distrusting frown.

Ishmael shrugged, looking at him again, at a loss. "It was special to me," he snapped. "She borrowed it and I would like it back. It's a little white one, with turquoise. You know how Anastasia can be."

Yes, August knew how she could be, but he also knew how Ishmael could be. But perhaps this was an opportunity to please the vampire, to give Ishmael reason to just let him be.

"Of course," August said curtly, then remembered his place. "Of course, Master."

Ishmael held his gaze a moment longer, then nodded and dismissed him with a gentle admonition. "Go along, August, before she abandons her fainting room and returns to her bed."

August hurried out of the library, heart jumping. Yes, maybe this favor would mollify Ishmael's antipathy. He just wanted to be left alone. How on earth did any of the others put up with Ishmael, anyway?

Somebody was in the music room, playing slow, gloomy Chopin on the pianoforte. August didn't stop to listen; he was on a mission. He checked over both shoulders to ensure the hall was empty, then peeked through the empty lock of Anastasia's door to see if the room was vacated, and when he found all these things satisfactory, he broke one of the first rules Hazel had divulged as he closed his fingers on the crystal handle and turned, opening the vampire's bedroom door.

He was greeted with that familiar scent of flowers and perfume, of beeswax and coke. In the corner, strewn delicately on a day bed upholstered in rich lilac velvet, as if laid out for a decision, were a few gowns of muslin, cashmere, satin—French dresses, dated folds and layers, embroidered with gold and silver ribbons, some encrusted with gems and others lined with thin rope.

August turned to the music boxes, searching for the one Ishmael had described.

So many different colors, shapes, sizes, some music boxes open, others closed, some wooden, some porcelain, some gold, some pink. And there on the cedarwood cassone was the ivory music box studded with turquoise.

August grabbed it. He slipped it in the large pocket of Theo's smoking jacket and trudged back out into the hall, closing Anastasia's bedroom door as silently as he could. He'd fetched the music box Ishmael wanted; Ishmael would stop bothering him now. He'd stop cornering him. He'd stop judging him. He'd stop threatening Theo, he'd stop scaring him, he'd stop all these petty foolish games and leave him alone—

August turned around and time seemed to come to a screeching halt.

Anastasia wavered at the corner of the hall like a ghost. August's heart leapt and then plummeted with a sickening lurch. Instinct sharpened to a point inside him.

Breathtaking and enchanting as always, Anastasia stood. Her hair burst in pale curls about her petite shoulders, perfectly blonde locks with a few braids and ribbons woven into them like drops of dew on a flower. Her tea gown fell in gauzy layers like spiderwebs down her frame and made her look almost like a Greek goddess, especially with the dreadful expression on her pretty porcelain face.

Or rather, the *expressionlessness* of her face, as her head was cocked to the left, and her arms were limp at her sides, and her eyes were wide and wild.

There were a few horrible, foreboding seconds of nervous breath as August met her frigid stare and knew exactly what had happened.

The music box wasn't Ishmael's.

Anastasia didn't even have to say a word. August's heart fell. His eyes widened. He reached into the pocket and snatched up the music box, holding it out in both hands. "I'm sorry," he blurted. "It was Ishmael—he tricked me—I think he persuaded me, as Theo said, how strong vampires can hypnotize and—"

A feral sound ripped from Anastasia's throat like something between a screech and a moan. August flinched back, ears ringing. He stared in perfect horror; such a noise should not have come from such a pretty lady, but Anastasia's face was contorted in infernal fury, and the lamplight glinted off her extended eyeteeth, two obvious little threats.

She shot forward in a sharp, determined stride, shoulders bunched up and the tendons in her neck standing out. Her lips were drawn back to show her fangs and her chin lowered like a lioness stalking her prey. Her gown danced about her slim legs.

"My music box!" she roared in a shrill voice. August stumbled on the stairs, frantic, looking over his shoulder at her as she followed him. "You went into my room, you took my music box, you are touching it and you are not worthy!"

August fell back against the wall and held the music box up like an offering to an incensed goddess. His mouth moved, but he couldn't figure out the right words. He pleaded with her to forgive him, he begged her to understand that it had been Ishmael's request, that

Ishmael had put him up to it. He promised that he loved her and that he hadn't meant to take her precious music box—

Anastasia smacked him. She slapped him across the face a few times with a hot *crack* of skin whipping skin. She shook him. She hit him some more. Her voice was a whirl above him, raising goose bumps on him head to toe.

"My love, Cosimo, oh God, Cosimo!" she wailed down at him, her fangs out and her face a maelstrom of feeling, all her emotion bleeding out from her and smothering August until he felt he couldn't breathe and the pain stung from her slaps, his eyes watered, the world was spinning. He dropped the music box as she shook him. It didn't break, but it popped open. Its delicate little melody began to play, filling the hall with a tinkling, lighthearted tune.

Anastasia burst into tears, still throttling him. Somehow it made her look suitably human again, disturbed and mad but now without her fangs.

"My precious music box that my Cosimo gave to me—don't you understand, you little worm? Cosimo gave that to me, he gave me that music box when we were young and in love and it was his promise to be mine forever, and when he died I kept him in that music box and you couldn't understand that, could you? No, you couldn't, oh my Cosimo, my love...."

In her violent distress, her fangs came out again. August watched them. It was fascinating just as it was shocking. His mouth fell open. He realized then, perhaps too late, that the music boxes were Anastasia's last bonds to humanity as time marched on, all following along behind this special music box from a lover who was connected to a piece of her heart. *Of course*. He was an idiot. He was such a damnable *fool*—

The Alpha appeared as if from nowhere at all and wrapped his arms around Anastasia's middle.

Anastasia stiffened. Her eyes bulged. Her fingers hooked into little white claws and she kicked and writhed like a child or a madman as Alistair yanked her away from August and carried her back a few feet. He set her down hard. The sound of his slap across her face echoed around the hall. It was different from Anastasia's blows, and August winced, chest aching. This wasn't entirely her fault, after all. He was mad at Ishmael. He was mad at himself. His entire face stung from her blows. She'd busted his lip; he could taste it. He touched his fingertips to it and stared at the little smudges of blood as if he'd never seen the color before.

Anastasia fell calm but not still. She was completely disheveled and her entire body trembled. She stared straight forward with wide, livid eyes, but her mouth was drawn in a tight line and her nostrils flared gently now and then as she tried to compose herself completely.

The Alpha spoke to her in susurrating whispers August could not hear; they were too quiet. There were brief pauses between words and phrases, long looks of various severity, and August understood Alistair was speaking to her with both his mouth *and* his mind. Just as Pearle had not so long ago, just as they all seemed to in the Sanctuary when August was dazed and groggy. "*You*," Alistair said coldly, turning to August, and August had never heard such distaste for him in the Alpha's voice. He swallowed hard.

Alistair gestured to the music box on the floor with a nod. The music box had fallen silent, needing to be wound again. August looked to it slowly, panic pulsing with every thud of his heart.

"Return what you've stolen," Alistair growled.

August's heart sank. He opened his mouth to remonstrate, but he didn't. His fingers shook as he stooped to pick up the fragile music box—but he stopped as he noticed the ashes that had spilled out of it when it hit the floor.

August went rigid. *When he died, I kept him in that music box....* He looked to Anastasia in a new kind of horror. Angry tears crept up, the sort of tears that would never come but just burn the backs of his eyes. He understood now. He wasn't sure what felt worse, the humiliation or the guilt, the horrible heavy feeling of having committed some deep and irreparable crime. He hadn't known, though! But he feared that was no excuse. He was the sacrifice; they were his masters. And Ishmael would make him pay if August blamed him. How could he have been so blind and callow, so eager to appease Ishmael?

August struggled to sweep up what he could of the ashes before the whole pile disappeared into the carpet, and as he brushed it all off back into the music box's center, he saw the tiny oval portrait on the inside of it. It was of the same man from the portrait by the Italian trunk.

August shut the music box with a crystalline *click* and held it out to Anastasia.

She snatched it back with feigned politeness—or at least as much true courtesy as she could muster. "Thank you," she hissed, but it was civil enough, and Alistair oversaw them like a father overseeing quarreling children.

With a shift of muslin and silk, Anastasia retreated to her room and slammed the door.

Alistair loomed in August's periphery.

August's heart hurt. It hurt far more than the bruises and scratches from Anastasia's abusive hands. The strength drained from his legs and he didn't care, he didn't care at all; he sagged down to sit below Alistair, fighting tears. He should never have longed for Ishmael's acceptance because he would never get it, and he would never *want* it. A thick, hot little hate sprung up in the pit of his chest, rooted to the image of Ishmael and everything he stood for.

Alistair's eyes pierced into him, right through his flesh and deep into his core as if he were evaluating every fiber of his being, every nuance of his thoughts and emotions.

"I would punish you properly," the Alpha fumed in the calmest, most regal way, and August finally braved his stare, meeting it miserably, "but I believe Anastasia has taken care of that for me."

"I apologize, Master," August said.

"You *apologize*?" Alistair echoed, raising his brows. The beginning of a laugh flickered across his face. He peered down at August critically, and August remembered what it was like to fear the vampires from the bottom of his heart.

Alistair hissed, "What gives you the notion that you can trespass in the privacy of our rooms without asking? What makes you think that you can touch our things? You come from a modern family and are so well-raised! I just don't understand what might have compelled you to invade privacy and take something belonging to someone else. Boy, you are the sacrifice. And you have gotten bold. You'd better think carefully about your existence. I could take away all of your rights. I could take away your *life* if I wanted to."

"Boy" stung August's pride a little; "boy" was either meant as an insult or to deepen the gulf between vampire and sacrifice. He was not a boy. He was a man. He was a man and he was terrified anew of these creatures who'd taken him prisoner. He felt violated. How dare he speak of August's other life as if it mattered anymore? But more than that—

More than that August was disappointed in himself.

Surely Alistair knew the truth about Ishmael's spite; why else was he so merciful with his warning? August opened his mouth to tell him everything, everything about Ishmael's hatred and cruel games. If Alistair liked August as much as he claimed to, surely he would be sympathetic to his frustration.

But no words came out. They all got stuck on the back of August's tongue as he remembered what Theo had said about Ishmael. Not even Theo had seemed willing to challenge the hierarchy of vampire over human—and that was what it was, August realized. Surely they all knew what went on. But they let it happen time and time again because he was just the mortal sacrifice. He was theirs. Ishmael was functionally untouchable because he was a vampire and he was one of August's masters. And how strange it was to suddenly be at the bottom of the social ladder.

But God, August wanted to understand them. *Vampires*. He wanted to be on their good side. He didn't want to be just another lowly sacrifice. He wanted to belong. He'd always only ever wanted to belong—and what did that say about his humanity?

Others were watching.

He was a spectacle, he realized. Pearle and Laurel were in the music room, Alphonse behind them. Servants peeked from their door near the attic steps, watching like careful little mice. Ishmael was on the stairs, face dimpled in distress as if this wasn't all his fault. This was so unjust and confusing; August was an example for the display of a vampire's volatility, and the whole house was audience.

"You were doing so well." Alistair shook his head, eyes narrowing. "I'm disappointed. Some lambs I've had to punish so many times, but you were doing so very well. *Behave*, August. Don't make me regret buying you."

"Yes, sir," August edged out, voice barely a whisper. He could only imagine what punishment Alistair meant. Beatings, perhaps. Or something more violating. Torture was probably too much and yet he could see it. That thought left him feeling rather disillusioned; what uncivilized behavior for creatures he otherwise found so pleasantly sophisticated.

"I don't want anything like this to happen again." Alistair turned to walk away, but paused. He cast August a bitter frown, saying curtly, "Have the maid get a cold rag for your face."

Just as suddenly as it had filled, the hall was empty.

The vampires drifted off. The servants hurried away. August stood alone and cold and dejected in the silence. The halls were empty and his blunder, his humiliation, his weakness were all palpable on the air. He was just a pathetic mortal man in a house of vampires. He was just the sacrifice, after all.

AUGUST HATED Ishmael with a passion, and he'd never felt such a thing before in his life.

For the rest of the night he didn't leave the attic room. After he sat with a cold rag on his face for a while, Hazel finally convinced him to read aloud to her. She did not ask about what happened; he did not explain. Theo was nowhere to be seen. Dawn approached.

When August awoke the next evening, he ate his breakfast in silence as Hazel lit the lamp and the candles. Someone was playing Chopin again in the music room. Hazel left to retrieve a new supply of bandages before the feeding hour arrived. And that heavy melody from the pianoforte begged August downstairs.

Resounding chords, passionate, with the awkward sound of a wrong note being hit here and there humming gracelessly behind the tune. Someone was punching the song out, slamming the keys, pounding the notes out raw and full of life.

August chased the sound. He left the breakfast tray on the bed and tiptoed down the stairs. He was curious and nervous to be back in the hall alone after what had occurred the night before, but he had the gnawing feeling there was more behind the curtain than was seen.

You're part of us now.

The playing suddenly stopped. It halted with a racket, a crushing dissonance of too many keys hit at once, the scrape of the piano bench, and then silence.

August stood at the music room door, left open a crack. His heart thundered. A maid passed at the other end of the hall and August swallowed, pressing back against the wall. He watched the bouncing lamplight for a moment or two, and then he ventured forth and took a peek.

Inside the music room with the flicker of candlelight and blazing hearth, the pianoforte had been abandoned. There was no sheet music. The Chopin had been played by memory, apparently.

Theo.

Theo stood at the window, hands clasped behind his back and hair slicked out of his face, shoulders straight as he peered out into the wintry night.

August didn't think twice. He slipped into the room, bare feet whispering on the floorboards.

Theo looked over his shoulder, eyes blank at first and then livening with recognition. "Good morning," he said, and he was reminiscent of the Theo August met two months before, the Theo who kept himself carefully subdued with an almost defeated kind of dignity. *Distanced.* He was distanced from August tonight.

"It's not morning," August parried meekly.

"Come here." Theo gestured. August obeyed. He crossed the music room slowly, hoping he didn't come across as glum as he felt.

"I'm sorry," he said first, standing beside Theo at the window. So *that* was what the world looked like beyond the roof and the chimney stacks.

"Haven't I told you to be careful?" Theo said. He didn't look at August, so August looked back out the window.

"You have," August mumbled guiltily.

"Vampires are capricious creatures," Theo said. It was strained, below his breath. "We are immortal but we are fragile. Time doesn't shelter us from everything, August. It doesn't harden us. It wears at us. We either survive it or we don't."

He meant Anastasia's instability, her unpredictability, her eccentricities, her obsessions. Indirectly he meant his own, and everyone else's, and August was silent.

"Did Alistair beat you?"

August shook his head. "No."

"So Anastasia gave you those bruises."

August refused to meet Theo's glance. "Has he beaten others, Theo?"

"Of course."

"Has he been punishing *you*? For...."

"For sleeping with you? No. Why?"

"It's not against the rules?"

Theo looked at him funny. "No. I've told you this. Only feeding on the sacrifice outside of the Sanctuary, outside of the feeding hour. Killing the sacrifice, hurting the sacrifice, turning the sacrifice without approval...."

Turning the sacrifice. August clung to that sliver of insight. Theo had said before that there was only one way to turn a human. He wanted to ask what it entailed—a coffin, maybe? Some magic ritual? That was all very macabre and uncomfortable in his head. It didn't feel like the right time to ask. He frowned up at Theo darkly. "Did you notice that I've trimmed my hair?"

Theo smiled. It was faint but it was there. "I noticed the night you clipped it, yes. It could still be combed, though."

August blushed, hanging his head. But he smiled a little. A silence fell between them, reprieve, reassurance, and then Theo drew a soft breath and moved over to sit on the piano bench. He leaned forward, elbows on his knees, fingers steepled at his mouth. His eyes were dark and endless with his thoughts, at the moment the only signals of his Undead nature. God but he was handsome.

"In this day and age, the word 'coven' sounds so archaic," Theo husked, and it summoned reverence from August. "But that's what we are. We are a family. We are a coven. I told you about this too, I'm sure of it—that we are allowed one sacrifice for every ten members—and August, that sacrifice right now is you."

"I'm the twenty-ninth," August murmured, remembering what the Irish maid had said to him.

Theo looked up, a little surprised. "Yes," he said. "That's what I was going to say next. You're the twenty-ninth. Do you understand what that means?"

"There were more before me." August shrugged. "You can all do as you please with me." For a moment, August was hung up on how easily that had come out. Weeks ago, it would have been far more horrifying to admit.

"Well, yes." Theo issued a little half smile. "More importantly what I'm getting at is this: a sacrifice is special to us. Once we have one, he or she is permanent until they die."

A chill pierced August. He stared at Theo indignantly. "You've killed them?" he demanded.

"No." Theo gave a weak scoff, with that same weak little smirk. "That's against the rules. Remember? Anyway I suppose what I'm trying to say is that we aren't new to the sacrifice system. This coven has been together for seventy-three years now, and in seven decades, we have had almost thirty lambs. You're not the first one to break a rule. There are always the shy ones, the difficult ones, the angry and the grieving ones. You may be important to us, you may be *special* according to the Lamb, but you are still just the sacrifice."

"I understand that," August fired back. A sharp frown creased his brow. He leaned back against the window, crossing his arms. He didn't think about the Lamb calling him special. He didn't need Theo reminding him he was virtually meaningless. He grumbled, "I've heard that enough. I've felt it enough. I am just the sacrifice. I understand that, Theo, so please—I'll behave. I promise."

Theo wasn't satisfied. He counted on his fingers as he spoke. "Our first lamb lasted for three years. Our second lasted three months, our third and fourth for a year each, our fifth for one month before he killed himself—"

August was aghast. He stared, mouth hanging open, as Theo brutally continued on with the begats and begottens. He listed each of the twenty-eight lambs before August, speaking of them like disposable toys that eventually broke—five of whom had killed themselves somewhere along the way, three of whom were born into the Undead and joined the coven: Alphonse, Laurel, *Theo.*

Theo had been a sacrifice too. He'd been in the attic before, as a human. He'd been in August's place.

August wanted to know what happened to the sacrifices who didn't kill themselves and didn't turn, but something instinctive told him that the mysterious Lamb was involved, that all-powerful enigma they all mentioned and revered. Theo's years as a vampire were few, then.

"It was an accident." Theo finally broke the heavy silence, casting a glance through his lashes that gave August shivers. He meant the music box incident. "They'll get over it."

"Everyone knows it wasn't an accident. Ishmael played me for the fool."

"Then don't be a fool."

"Easy for you to say. Why do you let him treat me this way? Does he always treat sacrifices this way? Did he treat you this way?"

"Well, he's not hurting you," Theo mumbled, and everything about him suggested he knew it was a pitiful argument. "I think Ishmael is jealous of you, to be honest."

"Why?" August snorted.

Theo seemed to have rehearsed this answer, or at least thought very long and hard on it. "Because you're not like the others. We all like you." He paused for a sympathetic smirk. "Don't let that go to your head." He trailed off again, squinting at August, studying him. He murmured, "Darling, all of your wallowing is unbecoming. Decide which you are—the rebellious sacrifice? The sad sacrifice? Or the accepting sacrifice?"

You're part of us now.

A catch jumped to August's throat. Clearly this was not the time to ask about Theo's years as a sacrifice. August shook his head, swallowing hard on a sudden crest of longing emotion. "I'm yours," he whispered instead.

Theo tried to laugh the idea off, looking away quickly, avoiding August's imploring frown. "Stop that."

"I am," August insisted. "I'm yours. You know that. I couldn't have a life outside this house again. There's this... this vast irremediable void between that and *me*—me, now. I know too much. I've seen too much. I've experienced too much. I'd be bored. I'd be disillusioned. I'm yours and that's all I'll ever be, body and soul."

"That's dangerous," Theo warned, but his voice was soft, vulnerable, yielding. He reached out; he took August's wrist and wound him closer, close enough to kiss. Soft, petal soft. August kissed him back tenderly. Ah, Theo's hands on him, one at the small of his back, cupping his face with the other—there was nothing more comforting. He understood attraction, the indiscriminate laws of love. And wouldn't any Romantic have sold his soul for an experience like this?

"Tell me what I'm not allowed to do," August whispered against Theo's mouth, tangling his hands in his hair as he shivered and leaned back so Theo could rain kisses down his neck and chest. "Am I allowed to love you?"

Theo fell still, ear pressed to August's heart. Without looking up, very quietly he said, "Yes." And it was as if he'd said "I love you too."

"You'll behave?" Theo asked. "And you'll beware of Ishmael now, as you promised before?"

"Yes," August pledged again. "I will."

CHAPTER FOURTEEN

NOVEMBER DREW to a close. The rain turned once more to snow.

Surprisingly enough Theo was right. Whatever went on unspoken, the tension from August's dispute with Anastasia faded within two nights. The vampires had disregarded the entire scandal.

"What's the worst a sacrifice ever behaved?" August asked Hazel, sitting on the floor by his bed and taking tea with her. The bruises and scratches from Anastasia's battery were fading.

"Well...." Hazel mused on this for a moment. "I'd have to say it was a boy named Charles. He attacked his keeper, Lydia, and they fell down the attic stairs. Lydia died. The vampires had to find a different sacrifice."

"Charles died too?" August demanded, already horrified to think a girl had died at the landing below the attic. Wonderful, he had ghosts to worry about now too, perhaps.

Hazel cast him a disdainful glance, cocking a brow. "They sent him back to the Lamb," she said, as if the answer were obvious. In that thin tone of voice, she might as well have said, "They killed him."

THE CALL of rooks just outside the southern window roused August earlier than usual. He forgot the windows were nailed shut. He tried to open one of them for the tempting evening breeze. It didn't work. So holding a blanket around his shoulders like a cape, August stood at the window and watched the rest of the pale dusk fade from the sky. The evening drizzle became sleet. He heard people for the first time, a quiet bustle somewhere out there. Over the roof he could see plane trees in the square.

He could imagine them: men and women bundled up for the winter cold, running errands, out for an evening stroll, hurrying from work to home or home to work. Nannies with children, men pausing to light pipes, ladies laughing as they rubbed their gloved hands together and hunched into their wool and fur for warmth. He didn't hate them for their freedom.

He pitied them for their ignorance, actually.

London became a reverie of grays and whites, slush at the sides of the streets, slick icy pavement under the bruised sky. Velvet ribbons, wreaths, bells, and holly came out for the Yuletide spirit. If August dragged the chair over to the southern window and stood on it like a stool, he could see a little bit of it all as the gas lamps were lit along the street. Soon there would be carolers. That was going to be *torture*.

"What are you doing?" Hazel snorted as she came in with his breakfast.

"Looking," August replied, still balancing with one leg up on a chair arm. "Come here."

Precariously Hazel wriggled up to join him. Standing side by side was too wobbly; she ducked under his elbows and stood between him and the window. "Oh!" she cried. "You're right, I can see so much! Look, they're scraping snow. Look, that girl just slipped on ice!"

They laughed together, breathing heavy sighs on the window to write messages and draw quick shapes and arabesques in the fog before it left the glass.

"Can I confess something?" Hazel whispered, her breath puffing out against the window. She wouldn't turn around to face him.

"What?" August grunted into her hair. He had never realized how much tinier she was than him; with her squished up against his chest, balancing on the edge of the chair, he had no choice.

"It's just that...." Hazel paused. She paused for a very long moment. If August leaned a little to the right, he could almost see her reflection in the bouncing candlelight. Her eyes were sharp, distant. Her mouth was bitten into a firm line.

"Sometimes," she whispered, as if she had no idea he could see her and all the agony on her face, "I consider becoming one of them. But they tell me that when they find a servant who does her job well, they don't want to look for a replacement."

August was speechless.

"I'm sorry," Hazel whispered, as if she'd committed some treason against him.

"Which one of them do you love?" August blurted.

Hazel scoffed. She feigned reproof. "What on earth gives you the idea that I love one of them?"

"It would be a good reason for you to want to become one of them. If you loved one, I suppose."

Yes, become *one of them*, become a vampire and no longer be sick, weak, lonely, or lost to the world. Inevitably one of these days, he would die. It was a new thought that plagued him sometimes, if he couldn't distract himself from it. He would die unrecognized by life because his existence was unknown outside this house. He didn't want to be meaningless. He didn't want to be forgotten. He didn't want to die. Surely Hazel felt the same way.

"Oh, right—" he whispered into her hair. "You love Laurel, don't you?"

"I do," Hazel whispered back, voice like shards of glass.

She turned, looking up at him over her shoulder quietly and unwaveringly. And then recognition bloomed in her eyes.

"Oh God," she breathed. "I can see it on your face. You want to be one of them too."

Bitterly August thought if it was that easy to read a person's mind, there was no reason to be surprised when the vampires did it. He blushed. He looked away. He didn't answer because he didn't know what to say. Hazel didn't seem angry. She didn't seem disappointed. She just seemed startled to have finally caught wind of his longing. He wouldn't deny it. He couldn't. He couldn't at all, and he knew that.

Just like Hazel, he wanted to be one of them.

IF HE could have stepped outside of himself and watched the activities in the Sanctuary, August would have been horrified. Maybe morbidly fascinated.

He would have seen the setting as it always was: dark, dark Sanctuary hidden in the drawing room, with an ancient ritualistic feel to its sparse, antiquated furnishing and crackling fire, as if the room had been carved out of some country castle, then attached to the house in Berkeley Square, London.

He would have seen eight vampires sprawled leisurely on the upholstered chairs and couches, languid like the men and women who met in opium dens and dreamed the night away together. But these men and women were hungry like lions and kept their sharp, inhuman eyes focused on their little lamb.

He would have seen an unkempt blond man in a meager nightshirt with bare feet and skin white except for the bruises and the bags beneath his brown eyes. The man was him, and maybe he looked tense and alert. Maybe he looked proud, convictions and morality distilled into nothing but instinct. He looked at the Alpha resolutely and he squirmed when the Alpha drank from him as if the Alpha were a long-awaited lover.

Maybe there was a similar sinister sensuality with all of them, a disenchanted devotion after the dreadful reality of their eyeteeth extending into fangs, their gaunt knuckles twitching, their mouths stretching wide, some preternatural stomach growling before they bit into him and drank his blood.

He would have seen the blond man, himself, bloodied and kissed and petted, passed along from vampire to vampire and meeting each with the same lazy consent of a practiced courtesan. He would have seen himself throwing his life into the jaws of each beast against whom he curled.

With Ishmael, of course, there was the hot spiritual inferno of hate. With Anastasia there was an intense innocence. He was spellbound and inundated. With Theo there was so much tension on so many levels, the ecstasy of making love without a climax, although all of it left him craving one.

He would have seen all of this, the cold shock of the intimacy and how easily he conceded to their rapacious touches. August would have seen himself enjoy it, though he never remembered looking so satisfied. He would have seen it with the prickling horror, the grotesquery of the reality. *They drank his blood.* He let them and he liked it. Yes, he would have seen it all.

But as it was, August was not outside of himself. He was the bloody blond man in the middle of the vampires, the human struggling for control over his passion and his distilled need as the vampires charmed him, lulled him with the graze of their fang teeth and their bewitching, dilated eyes, their breaths of bloodlust and their groping hands as Undead mouths raped aching veins for the sustenance required—the elixir of life, blood.

The loneliness, the irrationality, and the heavy, inexorable gloom no longer held sway over his heart. Gone were all these things, and morals, and fears, torn down by faith in an internal renaissance where what had once been evil now felt right.

Yes, August loved them for what they were.

And he was not afraid of admitting that to himself.

"WOULD ASKING a vampire to turn me be the same thing as making a deal with a devil, like Faust?" August asked one night in early December as he rubbed the sleepiness from his eyes. The sun would rise in a few hours. He seemed very tired. His fingers sagged down from his temple and he looked up, searching for Theo's eyes.

A cold wind swept through Theo's soul. The casual peace buckled, sharpening to a point between them.

No.

"I wonder, August," Theo hummed, snapping *Faust* closed without marking the page on which he left off, "why you compare vampires to demons?"

No, dear God, no—he's asking—

"I didn't say they're the same," August argued.

Theo's jaw tightened, his eyes cold and critical.

"You did not intend to, but that is what you did," he spat. He was suddenly horrified, and there were no words to define the bleak, hollow feel of it. He snatched his frock coat from the foot of August's bed. "It's a horrible idea, by the way—to even consider asking such a thing. You called it a curse twice. A *damned existence.* So why would you want it?"

August made no reply. Mentally Theo retreated. He took *Faust* and tucked it beneath his arm. He was done reading aloud for the night.

"I hope you think of more pleasant things when you lie down to sleep," Theo grumbled.

"Theo, where are you going?" August groaned. "Why are you leaving? I only asked a question—"

Theo gave him the cold shoulder. He was so angry. He needed to be away from him, or he'd regret it.

He did not want August even musing about becoming a vampire.

August was too precious; August was life and Theo was death, and Theo could never forgive himself if August gave up mortality to be by Theo's side. He did not want this. He was just lonely. Yes, that was it. August was just lonely.

Theo shrugged on his coat and left.

AUGUST WAS furious.

Theo's moods were fickle. In all his mysterious layers there were treacherous dark dispositions instinct told him to beware of. But August figured he still deserved explanations. He felt ashamed. He felt demeaned, as if his questions weren't worthy of answers.

He paced from window to window with anger hot and thick in his throat. He slid down into bed again, curling up tight in the quilts and pressing his nose into his pillow. He remembered walking in to find Theo smelling his pillow, once. Scowling, he threw it aside and covered himself completely in the blankets. He touched his fingers to his throat, still tender—always tender.

"God damn it," he whispered, and decided to just sleep.

AUGUST WAS in the forest.

It was the same dream as before and it was still mystifying. Cool carpet of grass and pine needles underfoot, humming breeze and filtered sunlight. He thought maybe the voice on the wind was whispering things about vampires and the Lamb.

There was that shadow in the trees he couldn't figure out, and there was the inevitable thunder. The fog rolled down in its misty tendrils, and then came the funeral procession and the wailing laments of the miserable strangers. Fingernails scraped at the casket from inside; the lid began to move.

Vampire.

It was a vampire inside.

The singers' sorrowful voices hit a new pitch, and August woke up.

Hazel was trying to be quiet. Breakfast sat neatly as always on the rosewood tray, laid courteously on the seat of the armchair until he awoke.

August rubbed the sleep from his eyes. He watched Hazel as she lit the candles. He cleared his throat and said, "I want to see the Lamb."

"*WHAT?*"

Theo's beautiful face was so innocently shocked it was almost comical. He stood, turned halfway from his bedroom window, fumbling with a polishing rag and one of his many pocket watches. He looked at August, stupefied. Then he looked to Hazel, eyes narrowing, as if her accompanying August to his room made her at fault.

"Take me to the Lamb," August said again, holding Theo's stare as boldly as he could.

Theo turned fully, leaning against the window as he cleaned the pocket watch. Apparently he'd reined in his surprise very quickly. In a much more calm and unfeeling way, he announced, "I'd pay a penny to see you at the show of Bethlem."

August reared back, insulted. Hazel even seemed offended on his behalf, eyes veering protectively from Theo to August and back.

"What the *hell* do you mean?" August hissed, suddenly keenly aware of how sick and bruised up he was with his tousled hair and striped nightshirt.

"I mean what I said," Theo said flatly, just polishing the watch; but his eyes were wide and wild. "I'd pay a penny to see you at Bethlem Royal because you must be *bloody mad!*"

He threw the pocket watch. Hazel and August dodged back, but Theo wasn't truly aiming for them. The pocket watch hit the floor hard enough to bounce, knocking a mechanism loose.

Hazel looked to August, almost begging him to reconsider his request. But August was unrelenting.

"Take me to the Lamb," he said again, low and even and steadfast, giving Theo the most damning stare he could muster. He wasn't really sure what he was asking for. But he wanted to know who the Lamb was. He wanted to know the source of all the rules, this king they all worshipped. He was tired of knowing *nothing*.

Lucius had said once, "Your hunger for knowledge is both your freedom and your downfall—"

No. No more Lucius; this was Theo before him, and Theo was very upset. Vampire Theo, not gentleman Theo. The age of his soul was obvious on his face.

Theo stood stiff and scowling. His shoulders heaved. But he was calming. He closed his eyes, fraught and reining in his distilled rage. The chorus of all the clocks in his room was overwhelming in the silence and Theo's struggle pained August. But there was a defiant little glee in it too; surely Theo had to have known this was coming. They'd argued the other night in the attic too, about Faust.

"Is it against the rules?" August pried gently.

Theo paced the room, opening and closing his fists. He crossed the floor and stooped to pick up his pocket watch; Hazel and August watched warily. Theo cast them hateful looks, as if he were ashamed and apologetic and their aversion only scathed him more. He was back to normal. Incensed but normal.

"No," Theo said in a ragged way, shaking his head. "It's not against the rules." He paused, not looking at either of them. His shoulders were hunched. He sighed, looking to his feet now. Finally he said, "We'll go."

August had enough sense in him not to celebrate until he was back out in the hall, dragging Hazel after him by the hand.

"You're awful," Hazel hissed, but he could tell she was excited for him. "You're a stubborn, rabble-rousing brat, and I can't believe he lets you treat him that way!"

"He loves me," August hummed triumphantly, winking at Hazel over his shoulder. "And so do you, admit it."

"HE WANTS to see the Lamb."

Alistair looked up from the chair in the corner of his apartments. Ishmael was there. His eyes sharpened as they settled on Theo. There was no shame to be found in him, even lounging as he was like a dog on the foot of the bed he shared with the Alpha.

Theo stood awkwardly in the open doorway, white-knuckling the edge of the door.

Alistair's brows rose in slow arcs; the light changed in his eyes. "What do you mean?"

Theo shrugged. He didn't have the patience for this. All right, that was a lie. He was afraid. He was afraid as he hadn't been in a very, very long time. He felt responsible somehow. He was unsure of the future for the first time in perhaps decades, and he didn't like it.

"August wants to see the Lamb," he repeated apologetically. "He's curious. He wants to know more about us."

"That's dangerous," Ishmael interjected with a dainty sniff.

Alistair held out a hand to quiet him, eyes unwavering on Theo. Theo waited for the inevitable annoyance, the inconvenienced sigh, the flash of Alpha anger at being undermined—but it didn't come. In fact he looked mildly entertained by this new development.

"It is not the first time a sacrifice has wanted to know more about us," Alistair mused aloud, perhaps in part to counter Ishmael's immediate protests. His slid his gaze over finally to meet Ishmael's sidelong. "The world is not the same as it was before," he murmured. It wasn't exactly sympathetic. "We are not the ancient monsters we used to be. You know, Ishmael. You couldn't count on one hand the number of spiritualist and occult societies in the city if you tried! What exactly is the danger of a sacrifice wanting to know about us? Why should we penalize that? Is knowledge not a natural right of all men?"

"He could know too much," Ishmael argued. "He could hurt us. He could tell others."

"Oh, pray tell, to whom would he reveal our secrets, Ishmael?"

"He could want to turn," Ishmael hissed, narrowed eyes flashing back to Theo as if to point a finger. What did he want, for August to hate Theo? He was far from succeeding if that was the case.

Alistair stood. He moved to the door, blocking Theo's view of Ishmael. His smile was accommodating, but his voice was clipped and cold. "Take him to the see the Lamb."

"Pardon, sir?" Theo tried not to seem suspicious. There was always something that made him uneasy when Alistair was like this, indiscriminate and somewhat uninterested.

Is it against the rules? August had said, veritably twisting Theo's arm with those beautiful eyes and a silent plea on his parted lips, a question on his open face. Goddamn, Theo could not resist him.

You know how Alistair feels about the Lamb, Ishmael had said not long ago.

Alistair nodded, smile fading. "I'm not about to humor him with a trip, so you might as well. Go on. You have my permission."

Alistair closed the door in Theo's face, and Theo knew Ishmael was probably in line for a very private talking-to for his uncalled-for input.

Heart pounding, Theo turned and made his way back around the hall. He wasn't sure why Alistair had been so supportive of August's request, but he wasn't going to question it either. Alistair always knew what was right. Theo was in no trouble. In fact it seemed Alistair was completely on his side. It wasn't even his request. He was relieved to not be under scrutiny, but he had to admit he shared worries with Ishmael on this one. Still, he could breathe easy.

And yet he couldn't help feeling as though he'd lost somehow.

ALPHONSE WAS perhaps too excited in his task.

Theo left August with him for a moment, during which August guessed Theo was talking to Alistair, and Alphonse sat August down on his bed and rummaged through the tall oak wardrobe in the corner in search of warm clothes.

They were going to see the Lamb. They were leaving the house.

He was leaving the house.

"I can't remember which of these are mine," Alphonse lamented, digging through the clothes.

Alphonse shared a room with Laurel. It was sparsely furnished (but perhaps it just felt empty because Theo's was full of random junk) and very mannish, plain, and dark. The curtains were drawn as if nobody cared to open them; that was probably very accurate. August thought maybe the beds were only made because the servants had fixed them. It still tickled him to no end that the vampires slept in beds.

With laughable ceremony Alphonse finally passed August proper clothes. August dressed obediently. Alphonse tucked a scarf into his collar like a cravat. He smoothed August's hair and found him a pair of shoes, and when Theo came back, Alphonse held his hands out before August as if displaying a work of art at which he'd slaved away for hours.

"Good enough," Theo grunted, shrugging.

"You're taking him to the Lamb?" Alphonse asked, totally distracted, his face wild but his eyes blank. "Did he break the rules?"

"No. He didn't. He's curious."

Alphonse nodded with seeming comprehension, lingering in the threshold of his bedroom and staring after them as they moved down into the vestibule. Theo snorted and tugged the scarf out of August's collar so it hung comfortably about his shoulders, shaking his head at Alphonse's inability to properly dress someone.

The other vampires knew where they were going.

How, August didn't know. But word traveled fast in this coven house. His skin crawled with their secret stares as he and Theo left. He wouldn't look over his shoulder to see who watched them as Theo retrieved outerwear from the coat closet. He didn't want to wonder what it meant that he was seeing the Lamb without breaking the rules— or, really, if he ever did break the rules.

Outside it was biting cold. But Theo wore a lighter coat, giving gloves to August and only settling for a thin scarf. August's breath fell in little clouds on the night; nothing of the sort came from Theo's mouth when he opened it.

They stood on the walk outside the townhouse, and in the dismal glow of streetlamps, for the first time, August saw it from the outside. Just another opulent townhouse in Berkeley Square: Georgian exterior, brick with pale stone corners and doorways, a Collyweston roof with familiar-looking chimney stacks and gables. And there, that was the southern window of the attic room, view partially obstructed by a portion of the roof. Ivy crawled on the brick in some places, like the old stoop with its modest shrubbery. It was humble and majestic in strange harmony.

It scared him a little. To be outside, to be walking around—it frightened him and it thrilled him and the cold damp air and the dusting of snow were like little miracles to him. He didn't want to be emotional. He was. He'd never imagined he'd get outside again. He wondered what would happen if he tried to escape another time— although he had absolutely no intentions of doing so.

They stood in silence as the wind ushered a deeper chill through the world and thin clouds passed in the dark sky overhead. Finally Theo gestured, palm open. "Shall we go, then, August?" he murmured.

THEY CUT directly through Berkeley Square, its park, and the London planes. Theo pointed out Gunter's and the reputedly most haunted house in London. He was quiet, speaking in short, plain sentences, keeping his voice clipped and his expression subdued. August didn't know where they were going, but he didn't question. He kept close to Theo's side as they left the Square and headed south on Berkeley Street.

Cabs and coaches rattled by. Voices rang out from open-doored restaurants and businesses. People bustled by on the well-lit sidewalks in their best winter clothes, and they paid no heed to the vampire and the sacrifice because they had no idea and maybe never would, and so many were caught up in their own business that they couldn't even care.

August remembered it all, the crepuscular life of London. The stomping horses, the old buildings spilling light out every threshold, so many voices and noises rising up to the night sky. They were in Westminster. They passed clubs and cafés, performance halls, prospering businesses.

It was an icy night and it was a relatively long walk. It was obvious from Theo's constant glances he was aware of August's fatigue. At a brisk clip it was twenty minutes to Trafalgar Square, passing Her Majesty's and the National Gallery. Theo didn't explain where he was going. He simply led the way, past the fountain to St. Martin-in-the-Fields.

That was their destination, August realized, and by the time they reached it, his body was numb from the cold and the walk. His knees shook. His cheeks stung from the chill, but a new vigor came rushing back with the warmth of urgency as he hurried after Theo through the double doors of the church. The Lamb. They were going to see the Lamb. He had so many questions to ask. He was *outside*.

Theo slipped through the shadows of the Corinthian columns, gesturing for August to stay close beneath all the gold and rich carvings, the balconies, the Classical pediment, the candles and the altar and the scents of wax, incense, and musty choir books.

Somehow Theo found the entrance to the crypts.

"Theo, what are you doing?" August choked out.

Theo looked at him wonderingly. "Going to see the Lamb," he answered. "That's what you wanted, is it not?"

"Yes, but—" August didn't know what to say. Heart racing, he followed Theo down into the catacombs beneath St. Martin's. It felt a little disrespectful. He had no idea what to expect next.

Theo navigated the dim corridors and chambers as if he'd traveled them many times before. And deep below St. Martin-in-the-Fields, having snuck into her crypts, Theo located a heavy marble sarcophagus he seemed to recognize immediately. August was a bundle of nerves. He didn't want to get caught. He didn't want to see a dead person. He was surrounded by inhabited coffins and the reeking shadows leapt. His heart thundered, and Theo grabbed hold of the stone coffin's lid and heaved it open.

Panic burst in August's veins. "Theo!" he hissed. His voice echoed. "Theo, what are you doing now?"

Theo ignored him. He opened the coffin fully and forced August to look with the firm but loving pressure of a hand on the back of his neck. The strong smell of dust and darkness and wet stone seeped from the mouth of the coffin. August's nose wrinkled in distaste.

But there was no bottom to the sarcophagus. It was a horizontal doorway opening on a set of stairs that led below the floor of the crypts, into blackness.

"Theo, I can't—" August sputtered, because he knew Theo meant to take him down there. Real panic seized him now, quickening his breath and his heart. "Maybe we should go back. Maybe this is an awful idea."

Theo snaked an arm around August's waist. August bristled, eyes darting from the open coffin doorway to Theo and back again. He swallowed, throat tight in fear.

"Quite beautifully typical, isn't it?" Theo chuckled dryly, climbing into the coffin. He walked down a few of the hidden steps until his head hardly protruded above the edge of the sarcophagus. He smiled bitterly, but his eyes were kind when he lifted them back to August. "It's the Lamb's humor. Come on, step in. See? I'm standing just fine. I'm leading the way. Hurry now before the guards notice. I told you before, vampires are not as strong as they used to be, so the charm will wear off quickly, and when they hear us, we're in for it—"

So Theo had somehow made them go unnoticed by the guards, some immortal trick, August supposed. For a moment he was frozen. He couldn't move. He could only stare, listening to his heart pound in his ears. But then a rat or another dreadful animal skittered somewhere in the corner, and August lurched forth, clamoring over and down the hidden stairs with Theo.

Theo placed his hands on August's sides to steady him. "Stay still," he said. He reached up, and the sound of stone scraping stone was horrible as Theo dragged the cover of the sarcophagus back into place. Surely he used a vampire's strength to do so, knuckles white and muscles tense. With each inch the stone moved, August's breath quickened. He was panicking. The dim reaches of light disappeared. How ironic that in his dreams there was something in a casket trying to get out—except here he was, being closed into one.

As the last sliver of light faded and the sarcophagus was shut again, they stood in complete darkness. Theo touched his shoulder and August jumped, swatting him away.

"It's just me," Theo promised.

The air was dank. Theo led the way slowly, cautiously, down stone steps only he could see with his inhuman eyes. August couldn't even see his own hand in front of his face.

At the end of the narrow and musty staircase, there was another door. Theo opened it on a corridor—but this one was wide and well-lit, with torches set up on the walls in antiquated rusty sconces. The ceiling was high. The stone floors were laced by a thin veneer of dirt, and August watched little clouds of dust form as he followed after Theo. It smelled old, like death and mold. It felt as if the air rotted in him with each breath. August coughed.

They were in a labyrinth of corridors below the city, he realized, not unlike the serpentine wonder of the new sewers.

It was cold, but not as bitter as it was aboveground. Instead the air was clammy and musty, the stone walls radiating a chill. August expected to see piles of bones gathering dust and cobwebs in the shadowy mortar corners. A rat scurried off at their approach, away from the glow of torchlight and back into darkness. Their footsteps echoed dully on the dirty ground, and every now and again a stone skipped or a drop of water plinked somewhere, and August couldn't help but get a shiver because this was all too surreal.

"Don't be afraid," Theo whispered, his voice cool and even. He sounded comforting, but his face was a mask of seeming indifference. August didn't answer.

The tunnel seemed to stretch forever in many directions. They traveled for another fifteen minutes below the sprawl of London. Theo seemed to know precisely where to go. They turned a number of specific corners. They avoided quite a few tall doors August didn't ask about. "We're almost there," Theo assured him.

Finally he came to a halt in front of a broad set of double doors, somewhere deep in the mazelike tunnels. August stopped short beside him, not allowing more than a hair's width of separation between them.

The doors stretched from stone floor to stone ceiling. They were sealed tight in the middle by tarnished golden knockers, rings through the little mouths of vicious-looking lion heads. Thick black walnut, dark and smooth and polished, and elaborately carved. The largest design was of the sephiroth—something that looked like a tree with lots of little circles attached to it, each one containing writing, words August couldn't read. Ribbons of wood framed the doors, little knots carved here and there. At the top corners sat two sconces in the shape of gargoyles, their wooden faces like chimeras of lions and angels. Black candles sat neatly above their heads, extinguished. Hanging on both sconces were prayer beads and little crucifixes with one too many bars.

August yanked the glove off his right hand. He reached out, gingerly pressing his fingertips to one of the beautifully crafted doors. The wood was cool and perfect. There was something fine and delicate set into the paneling of the doorframe, something that looked a little bit like words and quite a lot like inscrutable cursive. He squinted at it in the darkness.

It was in Latin, and then in something more like Greek—no, it was in every language of the world.

In the name of the Lord the dead teach the living.

It felt ritualistic and archaic and powerful, and it was so disturbing, so jarringly real. August had never felt more disconnected from the world he knew before than he did at that moment.

That was—he had never been more irresistibly enchanted than he was at that moment.

August dropped his glove. Theo picked it up for him, his mouth in a thin line and his eyes cold.

"I would like to think that look on your face is of respect and awe," Theo said. "But I sense your fear. Well, it was you who wanted to come here, so for the love of God, August, hide your fear. Be in awe. Love this. If only for this visit, love where you are."

August shot Theo a bitter look. The Lamb was their king, wasn't he? Why *wouldn't* he have a little fear? What could he possibly expect of the king of vampires? Beyond the double doors would there be blood, would there be torture, would there be an awful ghastly thing awaiting them with his fangs out, ready to rip August's fantasy of understanding to shreds?

Theo reached out and took hold of both golden knockers. They were so far apart that he had to stretch out his arms to reach both at once. He seemed to hesitate, if only for one moment, and August felt guilty, looking at him with his head hung and his shoulders bunched—but then Theo moved, knocking with all his might. The sound boomed around the tunnel.

There was an eerie silence. A mechanical groan began to rise and Theo stepped back beside August, clasping his arms behind his back. August looked between him and the moving doors; they swung slowly open as if alive. The movement stirred the dust on the floor and made the flames of the torches flicker.

The doors came to a stop and the dirt began to settle. Two men greeted them in the wide threshold, one much younger than the other. They were quite obviously guards, standing at attention grim faced and stiff. They were not human.

"What do you want?" the younger of the two hissed, sounding no older than Theo. His face was pinched and harsh. The man next to him, who was taller, sighed heavily and lifted his chin.

"State your name, coven, and number," the taller man amended. He sounded older, more responsible than the guard beside him, but he looked haggard and embittered.

August stared, eyes wide and mouth open. He was dumbfounded.

Fortunately Theo was not. He shifted, standing just slightly in front of August, a rather protective position. "Theodore Christle-Clarke, sirs. London coven, number six."

Christle-Clarke. Was it truly his real name, or just a fake one for a man who would live forever? August still blushed to know it, flustered and curious.

"London coven, number six, with sacrifice," the white-haired young man reported, seemingly to nobody in particular.

The older man spoke as if answering him: "Impromptu meeting of the tertiary category, for the sacrifice's sake."

The white-haired boy chuckled, a liquid sound. "It's been a while."

August looked around and tried to catch the more subtle implications of their words. Theo appeared to be doing the same. It was as if they'd plucked the information immediately from Theo and August's minds.

The men in the doorway stepped aside simultaneously, staring off at nothing and allowing them entrance. Theo bowed his head reverently as he passed them. August hurried to follow and emulated this gesture, still stunned into silence. The men had stronger presences than Theo and the rest of the vampires, which August hadn't thought possible. His ears rang as he passed them. There was an innate hierarchy at play here and he felt quite suddenly its vastness and significance.

The grand underground hall they entered then was even more inexplicable and mesmerizing.

The beautiful broad doors groaned shut and sealed themselves up again behind them. The two guards stood at attention to either side, silent and austere. Theo and August walked slowly through a wealth of candles and lamps.

August was distracted. He didn't know where to look first. Indeed, they were in a palace of sorts, suitable for a king, somewhere secret below London. He wanted to memorize it all. He wanted to tell Hazel everything when they returned to Berkeley Square. August instinctively clutched for Theo's coat, holding tight. He knew this place. He knew it from somewhere. That was impossible, wasn't it?

Vaguely the sound of a piano drifted into the throne room. That was it; they were in a throne room. The ceiling was covered in pastel frescoes, common scenes of angels that seemed to blend into the white plaster as if they weren't all the way there, a pearlescent pentimento. Some of the mountains of candles scattered about the chamber sat in the hollowed-out vertebrae of polished, lonesome spines. How utterly and perfectly grotesque.

Here and there on the walls, which looked like smooth, glassy white marble, were tapestries and old armor and gleaming ancient weaponry. Shields, broadswords, battle axes. From the ceiling hung glinting lamps—imported Murano, maybe. Two passageways led off out of the throne room. They didn't have doors, just gaped, leading deeper into this mystical place, old Moorish archways with serpents eating their own tails and roaring lions carved into the marble, vignettes situated in all the corners and eaves.

The sound of the piano was distant and slightly off-key. Whatever the piece happened to be, it seemed to come from every direction. It sounded familiar.

Theo pressed a hand to August's chest, stopping him. August obeyed, awestruck, as they came to a halt before a large throne. His eyes finally settled on it, the center of purpose in this underground palace, and once he looked he didn't understand why he hadn't looked there first.

A chill zipped down August's spine.

The Lamb was there, and the Lamb looked August's age or younger.

"Hello," the Lamb said. His voice was clear, precise.

This wasn't true. It simply couldn't be. That couldn't be the Lamb.

But there was intensity there, in the air in the throne room, almost iniquitous. There was a cold, obvious history in the Lamb's dark blue eyes. The gravitas radiating from him was strong, nothing less than immensely powerful and certainly vampiric. It was something holy and strikingly unholy. August gawked.

Memories rushed back, raw and hollow. Images and scenes and sensations, a vampire on top of a mausoleum throwing his hands in the air, his voice filling the cemetery with his honor of the hallowed—and the vampire crowd below him echoing the ungodly elegy.

To he who has been elected according to the choice of Christ, the Most Holy Lamb, blessed and sanctified by the blood of the Spirit—in sacrament and in honor, for salvation through sin, in the name of the Lord, the dead teach the living. In nomine Domini, mortui vivos docent!

August had expected something ultimately more ancient and grandiose, more irreligiously sacred, but this was still so macabre, too much to be real. He was dizzied by it, and the fear had gone numb by some supernatural glance. It was still there, though, buzzing beneath his skin like a fever. The obvious inhuman intensity of the pretty man on the throne was crushing, crippling. He was more unnatural than anything else, old eyes in a young face. He was immortal, and unlike with the house of vampires, unlike with Theo, it was *obvious*.

August felt a brief wave of despair, standing before the king of vampires as the only human in the room. He reached over and clutched for Theo's arm.

The throne itself was tall, spiked, and upholstered in fine Etruscan velvet. An animal fur hung over the back of it, snowy white shot through with flecks of gray. More pelts covered the dais in piles and lay beside the steps.

And the Lamb himself, a dark little god, was sprawled disinterestedly on his seat, cradled by lush pillows with his cheek propped in his palm.

Surely he had to have been around August's age when he became what he was—Undead, immortal, vampire. But that had clearly been a long, long time ago. A rich laurel of tousled chestnut hair framed the Lamb's even face. He blurred the lines of handsome and pretty into one simple, pouting loveliness. It was almost sinister, like the clever requiem of age in his eyes. Yes, the Lamb's eyes were deeper even than Theo's. They were endless. They seduced and pried at the same time, effortlessly. They carried the weight of a million heavy stares. There was a nagging pull of familiarity on August's mind that he couldn't particularly place or justify, and it made him a little paranoid.

In from one of the halls beyond the throne room drifted another young-looking, handsome vampire. He was finely dressed, flaxen hair slicked out of his angular face to show off his square, mannish jaw and high cheekbones, but there was an eerie passivity about him that made August uneasy. The collar of his shirt was unbuttoned to reveal two familiar-looking puncture wounds still clotting on his throat, up near the chin, under the jawline—and that's when chords of alarm rang through August's heart.

This bitten vampire took a seat off to the left of the throne. He was some kind of advisor, it seemed—or a plaything. August was chilled by this. Vampires could feed on other vampires? Theo had said it was the life in the blood they hungered for. Was there even anything in another vampire's blood for them to take, or was it about something else, like dominance?

This—this obviously irreverent, inhuman, incomparable, mythical sovereign frozen in time as a young man, with his knowing cobalt eyes and another of his kind still bleeding from playtime—this was the alleged ruler of the vampires. It felt both perfect and utterly unbelievable. This, this ageless fiend, was lord of *all vampires*?

Theo pulled out of August's hand, lowering into a sweeping bow. "Your Majesty," he said respectfully, his voice smooth and elegant again. August hurried to follow the example.

"All right, that's enough, get up," the Lamb mumbled. He waved them to stand. His voice was just as silky as his gaze.

"Thank you for having us on such short notice, my lord," Theo said. It was almost fawning, which was not like him at all.

"It's a slow night," the Lamb replied. His eyes flickered over them in quick, silent scrutiny. "London coven, Number Six, and the twenty-ninth sacrifice. There is nothing urgent involving your coven, I'm glad to hear."

"I just wanted to meet you," August said quietly, and Theo shot him a stabbing glance, jaw tightening and eyes fierce. August shrugged. Theo's disquiet tingled against him where their arms brushed together.

"Pardon him, my lord," Theo looked back to the Lamb again, "for speaking out of interest and without address."

The Lamb waved this off. "Number Six," he said flatly, looking to Theo. August followed his glance. Theo stood stiff and stoic, eyes wide. Every slight breath of subjugation that had ever seemed to grace him was magnified here and consumed him, leaving something that was not Theo but instead a servile young man with his mouth bitten into a tight line and concerned eyes turned upon his Undead monarch.

"Yes, my lord," Theo said.

The vampire advisor-pet sitting near the throne shifted, crossing one leg over the other, like his rumpled, telling appearance was not scandalous at all.

The Lamb swung his legs down and leaned forward on his knees. "Why did the Alpha not come?"

Theo was quiet. He looked frightened for a moment, brow knit together and mouth open as if he were lost on the threshold of speech, but wordless.

The Lamb shook his head. "I'm not angry. You'd be surprised how many unimportant visits I get from vampires accompanying their lambs."

The Lamb turned his attention then to August. He lifted a hand, motioning with one finger. August was confused. He looked to Theo for explanation, but Theo was equally if not more lost.

The Lamb gestured again, not impatiently.

Without a second thought, August was compelled forward. His footsteps echoed as he climbed the few steps to the throne, stomach turning in knots. He felt Theo's eyes. Theo said nothing. He did nothing. Theo *was* nothing when they were in this throne room.

"You wanted to 'meet' me, did you?" the Lamb asked.

"Yes, sir—"

"And your Alpha allowed this."

"I suppose, sir."

"You know I don't care enough to sit around and play nanny, answering all your questions."

August's stomach sank. A disheartened smile pinched his face, brow knotting, words dying at the tip of his tongue. His heart raced. This was a bad idea; they should have turned back at the church catacombs. Oh, he was an insufferable fool. Why had he ever entertained this as a good idea?

The Lamb snatched August's wrist. August stiffened, eyes widening. The Lamb's fingers were firm and relatively warm. He'd fed recently, then; there was warm blood pumping through his ancient veins. The Lamb enchanted him, left him breathless and fascinated. There he was, in the clutch of the vampire king, and he wasn't even afraid.

"Not afraid, hmm?" the Lamb hummed, as if August had spoken aloud.

Goose bumps prickled head to toe. August swallowed over a knot in his throat. The king of all vampires was much quicker at that thought-catching thing than August's vampires.

There was a gentle, wet sound as the Lamb opened his mouth and revealed his fangs—pearly, elongated incisor teeth. He touched his tongue to the tip of one, another sensual issue of cheek before they receded into his gums, shrinking to normal size again with a slick sound.

August reared back, mildly disturbed. But the Lamb held tight to him, dragged him with a rough jerk into a one-armed embrace and plunged his fang teeth into August's naked wrist before August could even see them shoot out sharp again.

The pierce of the Lamb's teeth through his skin was excruciating on the tender bruises and battered veins of his wrist, and then abruptly the drinking sensation soothed the hot pain with currents of luscious, pinching peace. The vampire's mouth moved as if leaving salacious kisses. August shuddered, moaned, longed to twist away, but he was caught in the Lamb's other arm.

It was an assertion of power, he realized. No, the Lamb wanted to break into his mind. *Taste it in the blood.* Maybe this was a formality in the vampire world, like bowing or accepting a calling card aboveground in the daylight. There was that same supernatural pull on his soul summoned forth by the transfer of blood, but this was stronger, this was infinitely stronger and more intimate, sweet and sensual and like the best-kept secret, a summer friendship, this bond, blood flowing from him into that old but beautiful throat—

The Lamb retreated, lips bloody. He tipped his head, licking the stains away, savoring August's taste, perhaps. August was sick with the stabbing pain in his wrist. He wriggled his fingers to keep them from tingling. There it was again, the gnawing, impatient feeling that he knew the Lamb somehow, that he'd seen him somewhere.

The Lamb smiled, more beguiling even than Ishmael. Not as sinister, but close. He asserted, "You make me think of Luka, of Felix. I love it. *I love it*."

"Is that what you mean when you say I'm special?" August asked, and he knew he was playing with fire now, but he really wasn't very good at thinking before speaking. He was mildly offended by the Lamb turning down his questions before he'd even asked them; he was determined to address at least one. *Luka. Felix.* Whoever they were.

The Lamb's face went cold and empty, in that strange, almost mad way all vampires seemed to have. For a moment he looked full of resentment, disgust, and disapproval, eyes veering all around August, viciously picking him apart. And then his face softened again, but his voice was jagged as he asked, "Who told you I said that?"

"The Alpha," August whispered back.

"Number One," Theo called from below the dais, as if he spoke through his teeth. "My lord, please forgive his disrespect, he's just a stupid man—"

The Lamb scowled at Theo around August's shoulder. "Shh," he said. "I'm speaking with your sacrifice."

He cut his eyes to August from below his lashes, a tiny suspicious smile tugging at his mouth in the heavy quietude. "Tell me," he whispered, and he looked young and carefree, but his voice was thick with ominous authority. "Tell me what your Alpha has said."

The Lamb's persuasion was subtle, almost unnoticeable, but August felt it, black magic in those dark blue eyes, whispering against his willpower to speak.

Still in the Lamb's marble grip, blood dripping down his palm to bead at the tip of his middle finger and then drop to the beautiful white floor with a fragile burst of red, August blurted, "My Alpha mentioned you, but not to me directly. I just overheard it and it wasn't enough to understand. Theo—"

The Lamb's eyes flickered over to meet Theo's when August addressed him by name. August went on, undeterred, undistracted.

"Theo told me that you were in charge and that you marked me. He said you are the king. I'm learning slowly, but I keep wondering exactly what you are. I just wanted to see you, to know this hallowed, mythical Lamb exists, this Lamb all my vampires speak of so worshipfully. That's all, sir."

The Lamb held August's stare for a long moment. Finally he issued a curt nod and slid a glance to his bloody vampire advisor. Something unspoken passed between them in the brief eye contact. The Lamb smirked.

"I can work with this," the Lamb said aloud to his advisor.

"What are you?" August gasped. Once again it fell from his lips before he could keep himself in check. He was hopeless; he was a fool.

With a deranged sort of calmness, the Lamb echoed, "What am I, indeed?" His voice was quiet, his eyes lucid and sharp. "What do you think, August? Am I a monster? Am I a god? Am I a devil? Am I living, am I dead—a child, a man—am I *mad*?"

August shook his head and shrugged at the same time, eyes wide. "You're a vampire," he answered, deeply vexed. He was dizzy from the dull throb in his wrist—but as after the feeding hour, the wound was already healing fast.

"We are not gods and we are not devils, but we are not human either." The Lamb shrugged in turn, impatiently. "It's as simple as that." He narrowed his eyes. Slowly he let go of August. He craned forward. His breath reeked of blood—so metallic and sour. "I know your desires," he whispered gaily. "You cannot hide them from me."

August didn't know what to say. He stared at the Lamb mutely. He didn't know what to think. The Lamb had surely raped his heart and soul while drinking his blood, divining everything. *Would asking a vampire to turn me be the same thing as making a deal with a devil? Oh God, you want to be one of them too....*

It struck him then. Familiar. The Lamb was familiar because he was the young man from Alistair's vision in the music room on All Hallows Eve. It was him. Dear God, it was him. And this room—he remembered coming to this throne room, weeks and weeks ago, after Alistair had bought him—

"Tell me more," August insisted sharply.

Theo made a frustrated noise behind him; the Lamb's hand twitched in the air, silencing him. August should have been more frightened. He should have been horrified of this vampire authority before him whose mind and soul were far older than his body, this ageless blood-drinking king. But he couldn't help it. He was spellbound.

"I have other engagements to attend to," the Lamb murmured, tossing some dark hair from his eyes, the inhuman little prince, and it was almost as if he had decided to be amenable merely to spite Theo's worried deference. "But before you go, I will tell you five things, and you must be content with them."

"Yes," August breathed eagerly.

"One," the Lamb said, "I am the master of all your masters. I am the Lamb. All vampires answer to me.

"Two, I am older than most of the vampires you know and I have been alive for a long time, but there are still others out there who have seen ages before mine.

"Three, the sacrificial lamb system that exists now between vampires and humans is my creation, and I maintain it. It is my duty to keep order between the humans and the vampires. This balance is necessary.

"Four, I approved of you and marked you, and designated you as the London coven's sacrifice. This means your life is in my hands.

"Five, I have killed, I still kill, and I *will* kill. I normally do not tolerate such unceremonious interaction as this with sacrifices. Be aware of that. You are special indeed."

The Lamb let go of August's wrist. August was stupefied.

"You want to know me," the Lamb hummed, infernally amused. It was almost spiteful—a giggle nearly. "But you're a *sacrifice*. Go on, your fledgling lover is itching to get out of here. Can you be content with what I've told you for now?"

August wavered, still astounded. He had no idea what to feel—shock, relief, confusion.

I approved of you and marked you, and designated you as the London coven's sacrifice.

You are special. Can you be content?

"I'll teach you everything one day," the Lamb whispered, staring August down, wide-eyed and conspiratorial. His lips barely moved around the words. "That's what you want, isn't it? It's fate's design, I think!"

This was the crux. This was the crux of it all, and what it all was, August didn't know. He just felt it.

They were dismissed.

Overcome, August stepped down from the throne. Theo grabbed him, arm around his waist. August felt a heat on them, the heat of eyes; he looked around to find the handsome vampire advisor perched neatly on the steps and staring at him very intently, eyes narrowed.

"Good night, lovebirds!" The Lamb chuckled—again it was almost sly enough to be a cackle—waving from his throne with all the smug innocence of a spoiled prince. It seemed to be his subterfuge of choice.

The guards opened the big doors. Theo and August left the Lamb's palace and were closed into the underground tunnels once again.

August could have sworn he saw other people out of the corner of his eye as they made their way back through the torch-lit corridors. Shadowy figures, turning corners in the winding stone tunnels. It might have been his imagination, but maybe the Lamb had other visitors. It didn't matter. He was exhausted and dazed, and Theo's side was comfortable to lean upon.

CHAPTER FIFTEEN

SLAP!

August reeled from Theo's smack, eyes shimmering in betrayal. Shocked and silenced, he watched Theo pace back and forth at the edge of Trafalgar Square, in the moonlight and the fog and the slush. His face burned and itched from Theo's hand. His eyes misted over and his throat tightened in wronged rage.

"What the *hell*—" August began, a heated hiss, but Theo moved fast to loom over him. For the first time in a long time, August was frightened of him. He flinched back, breath quickening in his panic. Theo was a vampire again and nothing else.

"You don't understand," Theo seethed through his teeth, eyes wide and wild. "You just don't understand *anything* about our society, August. You were disrespectful. You were blatantly disrespectful. You could have been killed! That was the king of vampires! He rules us all, and you just walked right up and started interrogating him! Do you have no common sense? Have I not explained enough to you?"

"You've hardly explained *anything* to me!" August retorted indignantly, and then he braced himself for another slap to the face. But Theo did not touch him a second time, as uncharacteristic as the first slap had been to start with.

Instead Theo uttered a growling sigh and started walking, back in the direction of Piccadilly Circus. It was late. Snow spun through the darkness again. The sun would rise in three hours, and August was freezing and exhausted and scared.

"You shamed me! You embarrassed me in front of the Lamb!" Theo spat over his shoulder.

"Is that why you're angry with me?" August snorted. He'd done nothing wrong. The Lamb had called him forth. He had obeyed. The Lamb had given him no choice but to walk up. The Lamb had sipped his blood. Was Theo jealous?

Theo didn't answer. He walked swiftly, shoulders rigid.

"Theo," August tried again, distraught. "What don't I understand? You're as cryptic as he was! I just wanted to see him for myself. I just wanted to ask him questions. Theo, I won't have you angry with me because you never told me there was a protocol to it all—"

In the snow and the darkness, Theo looked gaunt. He looked fretful and forlorn, and he cast August a severe glance over his shoulder as if he wanted to say something, but he didn't. He shook his head. His shoulders sagged. He surrendered. He slowed down to walk beside August again, like a dishonest man with his hands deep in his pockets and his movements stiff.

"First of all," Theo husked, "please don't call me by name when we're not alone. Call me Master, as you're supposed to. And for the love of God, August, don't act as though you love me."

August was aghast. "I don't act that way!" he cried, but he did. He was lying. He knew that he did. Avoiding Theo's pointed glance of accusation, he insisted, "Theo, you're all I have. Don't you understand *that*?"

"When we're not alone," Theo said again through his teeth, "when we are around others, especially superiors, you love me as a servant would love his master, not as August loves Theo. You're just a sacrifice, for Christ's sake!" Theo issued a rough shrug, scoffing a little into the night. His eyes were bright with some stifled pain. An embittered smile flashed across his face. "Listen, I talk as if they can't taste it in your blood. I talk as if the Lamb couldn't read your thoughts in your eyes. Damn it, August. Damn it all—"

"But it's not against the rules, is it?"

"You threw me to the dogs," Theo fumed, voice shaking. August just wanted his old tender elegance again, with his intelligent silences and wise glances. And all the things Theo had ever said and done, the eyes, the touches, the comfort. "You were out of line and you completely disregarded me."

"So you're angry because I called you by name. *Master*, I'm sorry. I don't think the Lamb took any disrespect, and I don't think he really cares that I called you by your name—"

Theo was appalled. "Look at you, you're in love with it all! You're proud of your insolence! You just love driving me mad, don't you? You crave rebellion, don't you? August, an intimate relationship between a vampire and a sacrifice is detrimental. In fact, sometimes shunned!"

"Well, you never told me that!" August stopped short, scowling at Theo from under a streetlamp. He was livid. He was so very tired of bearing the bruise of others' miscommunication, of somehow always being the problem, forever being lectured or critiqued. "No one tells me anything!"

Theo's face was all pinched up, voice raw and strained. "You are just the sacrifice," he edged out, as if he were trying to remind himself too. "I did a big favor in taking you to see the Lamb for something so trivial as curiosity. And yes, I have to admit he seems to have taken a liking to you for some reason—we all know this from when he marked you—but August, he's powerful. You don't have an inkling about him, and you're insisting you paid him no disrespect. You're smitten, aren't you?" Theo uttered a cold little laugh and resumed walking briskly. August hurried to follow. The jealousy in Theo's eyes was obvious. August remembered the night Theo had told him he was possessive of him. He wilted.

"That's the seduction of the Lamb, August," Theo went on raggedly, as they walked. "*That's* the way vampires used to be. That was the inherent pull of an old vampire, a vampire who drinks as much blood every night as he wants, because that's the privilege the Lamb has. You see? You don't know a single thing about him."

"Oh, you act like he's a monster, coldhearted and brutal."

Theo looked over his shoulder, mouth open to retort, but August shook his head vigorously to silence him.

"Don't say that he is!" he whispered sharply before Theo could talk. He was so angry now he couldn't even raise his voice. "I know that you will, Theo. You look as if you hate him. Why? Because of his archaic, arbitrary rule? *Tch*! Don't you think I sympathize, being your *slave*?"

Theo halted roughly. He stood with his back to a streetlamp. It warped him from gentleman to monster again in a matter of seconds, engulfing him in shadows.

"Do you want to know something, August?" Theo hissed. It was a conscious and dramatic outrage, hands flying for emphasis, eyes sparking and crazed. "That's exactly what you are: a slave. That's all that you are to me. We all love men—which isn't to be misconceived as an affinity, mind you, just that men's blood has a distinct vitality in it—and we especially prefer young men full of youth and passion. That vampire's desire of mine, my innate preternatural hunger for your virile vigor, your manly blood.... Maybe you misconstrued that as friendship or love. Does that scare you? The possibility of such a grievous error?"

"I don't believe it—I—"

"Does it scare you? It should!"

August winced back, scarf fluttering loose from his throat. Theo's crudity brought all the stab of betrayal and the ache of inhospitable disbelief. August was beyond furious. He ripped his eyes away to stare emptily at the slush and mud.

He didn't want to believe it. He wouldn't. He didn't understand why Theo had twisted the argument except maybe just to avoid a topic so touchy between them—but then he thought, with cold, confounding clarity, that perhaps Theo was angry because even *he* didn't understand some of what had happened, either.

Theo seemed lost in his own words for a moment or two. He threw his gaze elsewhere. It underlined August's suspicion, tacit between them like wrongdoings between old friends. But August could not forgive him yet. His head was still spinning. He still felt deeply wronged and so, so resentful of sensing something more going on than he knew. More to everything, to the house of vampires, to this kingdom to which it belonged, to his demanded visit to the Lamb, to the way the Lamb had treated him, and Theo was frantic with it, and August was confused.

"Seeing the Lamb makes me uneasy," Theo tried to apologize.

"If you were so uneasy, why did you take me to see him? Why didn't Alistair?"

"Alistair couldn't have cared less about your wondering," Theo countered. "I should never have taken you," he whispered fiercely. "I wish we'd never become friends, August."

Another aching stab to August's heart. "Why is that?" he spat. He refused to believe the words were sincere, but they still hurt.

"You should fear us." Theo was retreating. It was obvious in his eyes, in his gestures, in his presence. He retreated in on himself and closed everything off, and his face was blank as he implored August with a bitter, unpromising composure. "But you don't because of this unnatural *thing* between us. I have no authority over you. That's not the way it should be. Worse yet it makes me feel too human. That's not a good thing, August. Because what happens to me when you're gone?"

Theo didn't wait. He turned sharply and resumed walking—fast, purposeful.

August watched him.

He stood under the streetlamp and watched, brow knotted, lips parted for his worked-up breaths.

And it was strange, very strange, because that little speech hadn't hurt him at all. No, that hissing confession had been an invitation if anything. Theo might as well have just said, "I need you!" In fact he had, in different words. And August almost felt bad for having broken him down with affection; he almost felt guilt for having knocked Theo's comfortable routine horribly askew. Theo hadn't asked for that. But August also felt victorious because he had changed something in Theo, he had struck a nerve in Theo, and Theo was fighting it but he was powerless against it. That meant something, didn't it? He mattered to Theo.

That much was clear when Theo made it to the corner up ahead only to turn and saunter back for August, frowning so viciously it was almost a pout. His eyes were bright and glassy in the dark. He mumbled, "Are you coming or what?"

What happens to me when you're gone?

August had no intention of going anywhere but home with Theo.

THEY RETURNED to Berkeley Square together in the deepest dark before dawn. Theo accompanied him just to the third floor. August went to the attic by himself. He was numb from the cold and the exertion; he felt sick as Hazel helped him into bed. She replaced the hot water bottles at his feet.

The whole night hardly felt real. The only part that seemed tangible was his argument with Theo.

As for the Lamb, the entire visit felt like an illusion. All of it—the way he'd felt in the throne room, the Lamb's bewitching presence, the power and the mysticism—felt so dreamy. August could barely remember what he thought or felt standing before the Lamb, what was said. Alistair said the Lamb called him "special." The Lamb himself called him "special." The splendid Lamb, ancient but timeless, with those dark, dark eyes—

I know your desires.

I'll teach you everything one day. It's fate's design....

Yes.

Because August never stood a chance of hiding anything from the vampire sovereign, did he? The Lamb even told him so. The Lamb tasted his wishes, his heart, and his soul in the blood he sipped from his wrist, and August did not begrudge him it.

He didn't want to be a sacrifice.

He wanted to be *one of them.*

I WISH we'd never become friends.

What happens to me when you're gone?

Theo stared down at the Frodsham pocket watch in his lap, gold repousse case removed so he could get inside and fix the beetle and poker hands. The watch had stopped ticking long ago. Theo had the tools to fix the watch hands; he had his sleeves rolled up and his hair pulled out of his face. But he was too distracted to actually work.

All around him clocks and timepieces ticked and tocked. The fire under the mantle crackled.

Theo sat cross-legged on the center of his bed and stared.

If he closed his eyes, he could remember sunlight. The pale, bleached, and sullen slant of it through skylights and leaded windows, the way the attic floor creaked under bare feet and a wrinkled nightshirt tickled his back.

Theo could remember the bed being against the other attic wall. He remembered the washbasin being white porcelain with designs hand painted in blue. He remembered a maid, a keeper of the sacrifice, with copper red hair and a thin kiss of freckles, and then a maid with blonde curls, and then a maid with a mousy brown chignon who looked down her sharp nose at him with even sharper eyes.

Theo remembered walking that attic room upstairs as a mortal man.

He remembered celebrating birthdays and holidays up there, pinning blankets over the windows up there, waking up to the candles being lit and Ishmael at the attic door with wide eyes and a cautious mouth, as if he were afraid of seeming too excited or nervous Theo wouldn't be happy to see him. And Ishmael had laughed, and Ishmael had sung, and Ishmael had smiled, and Ishmael had dozed there in the attic room with him sometimes on nights there was no feeding, and Theo had stared down at him, shocked by how much he depended on him, curious about how love was different from dependence, running his fingers through Ishmael's pale ash-blond hair and musing on these things as if he had eternity to figure them out.

"But what happens to me when you no longer need me?" Ishmael had snapped one night, after years and years and years.

But what happens to me...?

Oh God, Ishmael was right.

Theo was using August.

Not for loneliness, though—no. Maybe Theo was using August to relive the past.

Was that so? Was it possible he did not want August to turn because Theo himself regretted turning? It wasn't even about protecting August, then. It was all about pleasing himself. Was he just that possessive? Had that much of his humanity rusted away already?

But Theo could not live a mortal life vicariously through him either. He had been in August's place before. He had been the sacrifice in the attic, begging to be turned because he had no longer belonged to the world of daylight and mortals. Had he gone back to that world, he wouldn't have fit in. He wouldn't have been pleased. He had been selfish. Immortality was what he wanted and he used Ishmael for it, played Ishmael's affection like a finely tuned violin, and—*Turn me, Ishmael. Please!*

He was in love.

Theo was in love like never before, the irrational, unconditional love that destroyed even the most logical and reasonable of souls. It would be his downfall. His selfishness was always his downfall. And he was selfish, so selfish.

What bitter irony that eternity made a man that much more afraid of loss than ever before!

Theo left his room. He wasn't quite sure where he intended to go; he could make his way up to the attic and apologize in kisses and tears to August. He could retreat to the music room, drown the swarming thoughts in song and wine. He could go out. He hadn't been out on his own in a long while. Solitude was soothing sometimes. Was it not?

He found himself at the open door of Alistair's office, staring just as blankly as before.

Alistair looked up from his desk, honey-colored hair falling loose at his temples as his eyes roamed Theo head to toe. "Well, you're in a mood now, aren't you?" he appraised, not entirely sympathetic.

Theo shrugged limply.

Alistair sighed. He lifted a letter from the papers on his desk, red wax seal broken. He held the letter up in two fingers and raised his brows. In the low dancing lamplight, he looked tired, so very tired.

"It's from the Lamb," Alistair said. "I need to show you."

Theo lifted his eyes and felt a strange, silvery anxiousness slip through his bones.

It was not quite as bad as he'd expected it to feel.

"YOU LOOK pale," Hazel said. She reached out and felt his face. August leaned away like a stubborn child, frowning.

He'd woken up in a sour mood, throat sore and head full of pressure, the telltale signs of a cold he wished he could ignore. "I'm fine," he grumbled. "Just let me go downstairs for a bit, and then I'll tell you about my visit to the Lamb. I promise."

Hazel shrugged, setting about to make his bed, lace cap crooked on her head. August straightened it for her.

He went downstairs slowly. The hall was empty but well lit.

There was the rustling sound of movement and a few light footsteps, and August knew who it was even before he turned around. In truth he didn't turn around immediately simply because he knew what he'd find—but finally he conceded, and in the lamplight of the hall, brown clashed with green as August looked over and met Theo's stare.

Theo was in his bedroom doorway, leaning there, arms crossed, flawlessly nonchalant. Messy dark hair, flashy waistcoat. August assumed an expression of indifference as if it were some kind of competition between them. The battle of wills lasted a long minute or so before Theo forfeited and broke the silence.

"Good morning," he said with all the mock politeness of a bitter lover.

"It's not morning," August returned flatly. The beginning of their conversation was also the end. August was stubborn on purpose. He wanted to teach Theo a lesson. He also sort of wanted proof Theo *did* need him. Not to mention he was still mildly upset by Theo's slap the night before. He wanted Theo to be tortured by it; he could tell by Theo picking at him that he already was.

August was sure he could hear carolers out in Berkeley Square. He turned away from Theo, trailing his fingers on the wall as he continued down the hall. Theo's bedroom door slammed; August heard him descend the stairs. He was probably going out, then, with his *friends*. Good. Maybe later he'd rearrange his room. Maybe he'd play chess with himself. Maybe he would simmer in his mistakes until he snapped and stopped trying to hide behind clever words and Undead convictions.

The air was thick with the tender feel of Christmas, and Laurel found August in the library.

August curled further into himself before the fire, looking up from his books unassertively to watch Laurel from the corner of his eye.

"Hello," Laurel greeted. He stayed in the doorway, inquisitive.

August stared, running his fingers over the edge of the book in his lap. "Hello," he returned, and guiltily he couldn't help but imagine Hazel doing something, anything, everything with the vampire in the doorway.

"You look absolutely miserable," Laurel said after a long moment, and with not much tact.

August had nothing with which to reply but a perplexed frown, brow dimpled in doubt.

Laurel smiled thinly. He wasn't unattractive, with all his stoic impassive charm. "It's obvious," he added further, his voice smooth and well-contained as it drifted into the library. "You could taste the tension in the air if you wanted to. I wonder how long you'll leave him to stew in it?"

Theo. He meant Theo. August was embarrassed, not because it was obvious but because he should have realized it would be obvious. Was Laurel trying to give him advice, he wondered? It was awkward. They knew. They all knew. They were completely aware of the precarious rift between him and Theo. They were kin and he was their human, and what were secrets to that dynamic, to the taste of his blood on their tongues? They knew. Maybe they also knew what had happened between him and the Lamb. Maybe they even knew what it meant, or why Theo was so aggrieved. But then again maybe they didn't know. They had their limitations too.

August waited for Laurel to leave the doorway, but he didn't. He stared, as empty eyed but obviously contemplative as Alphonse sometimes seemed to be. Finally he said, "If not for him, you know, we might all take advantage of you in one way or another. Remember that. Thank him for that."

August tensed, casting Laurel a dark glance. He shot back before he could bite his tongue, "Is the self-control of a vampire really so faulty?"

Laurel shrugged. "No. But you're ours to do with as we please, aren't you?"

"Except not, thanks to Theo, you're saying."

"Except not, thanks to Theo." Laurel paused; it didn't seem like a conscious drama. He shrugged again. "He claimed you, obviously, and we're territorial but not disrespectful creatures."

Laurel moved out of the doorway, leaving August to himself again.

He snapped his book shut, fingers cold. His mouth was dry; there was a lump in his throat. He wasn't quite sure why he felt so fired up, but he did. It wasn't guilt and it wasn't fear. It was just an awful, heavy feeling. He was still in Theo's smoking jacket. It smelled like him and he loved it—

The door from the library to the adjacent room was ajar, just a crack.

Had it been that way all along? Surely it had. There was no light in the room. It was empty and unused tonight.

August stood, staring at the door for a moment.

God, he was hopeless.

He crossed the library and opened the door very slowly, just a few more inches. He peeked in. It was the room in which Alistair and Ishmael had had their grave talk about the Lamb and some Irish revolt or another. *The Atoned*, they'd said. There was nothing but shadows in the room. And August didn't even try to fight the curiosity anymore.

He drifted in. It was like a second library, but much more put-together, organized. It was an office, he realized, running his fingers along the richly carved edges of an old writing desk. Moonlight poured in from the window over the shared garden behind the townhouse. There was a fountain out there, and little benches and tiny leafless trees.

On the desk was a book of financial records, some ink and a few folios. There was a fine letter stamped with red wax, seal broken. And the seal looked like a kneeling lamb. August poked at the corners of the paper unfolded from the envelope, wanting to snoop but not to leave obvious signs of it.

The writing was strangely straight up-and-down, bubbly but sharp in the loops of *G*s and *F*s and *L*s. It was beyond difficult to read, squinting through the moonlight.

Aleksandr, the Lamb, "Baron of Eden" … Has been approved … Number Six … XO XO … The Future Number Nine….

Future Number Nine?

No—it didn't mean—did it—mean *him*?

August leaned closer, pressing the letter flat with tented fingers. It was a letter from the Lamb and it mentioned a future Number Nine and it mentioned Theo, and it was so damn hard to read, but it said—

Will be searching for a thirtieth promptly; the future Number Nine has been approved should he turn; Keep a close eye on Number Six.

"August—"

"Ah! I'm just—I took a wrong door—" August jumped, rearing away from the writing desk so frantically that he knocked a paperweight over. Uttering a small sound of remorse, he hurried to replace it, glancing to the doorway of the office.

It was only Hazel.

She shook her head at him slowly; she knew he was lying. She gestured for him to follow her, rolling her eyes. "I cannot believe you," she whispered through her teeth. "What did I tell you about closed doors? Have you learned nothing from all your lovely adventures with Ishmael and Anastasia and…"

She wasn't truly mad. He sat with her in the vestibule as she worked, sweeping, dusting, polishing, changing out all the candles. He wanted to tell her about the letter on the desk but part of him was afraid of what she'd think.

The Alpha emerged from the entrance hall with his valet in black, shaking rain off his hat as the valet took his coat from him. Hazel bobbed her head. August stiffened.

"August," Alistair greeted with a short nod. He glanced at Hazel. "Dear," he greeted in turn, raising his brows.

Hazel didn't lift her eyes. "Master," she returned, dusting carefully.

The valet disappeared through the dining room.

The vestibule was silent—just the Alpha, the keeper of the sacrifice, and the sacrifice himself.

Alistair was staring. August stared back, terrified Alistair would read it all over him in a simple look that he'd been snooping in his den. Finally Alistair cleared his throat and said, "So you visited the Lamb."

Even the Alpha was sometimes soft and handsome in the lamplight, August had to admit. Everything looked healthier and warmer in the low bouncing light. And, heart pounding, he thought, *Dear God, don't let him hear a single stupid thought of mine—*

"I hope you enjoyed yourself," Alistair said.

"Why didn't *you* take me?" August asked demurely before he could decide whether it was a good question or not.

Something twitched in Alistair's expression; it was like All Hallows Eve all over again, and August supposed it had everything to do with that memory of the Lamb he'd shared with him then—the intrusive vision, the unspoken awkward pain, the strange shared memory of rejection and humiliation on a dance floor. He was like a jilted lover, for Christ's sake. It was almost pitiable.

Alistair clung to his composure, smiling his lie of a friendly smile. Squinting at August, evaluating him, he just *smiled*. He murmured flatly, "Theo was insistent."

"Thank you for letting him take me." August could feel Hazel's eyes burning into him, practically screaming, *Don't you dare start more trouble, you foolish man.*

"I don't advocate ignorance," Alistair replied.

"I don't want to be ignorant," August whispered.

"Are you satisfied, then? Did your trip to the Lamb fulfill your restive curiosity?"

"Partially."

Alistair raised his brows, smile tightening. Now it was almost a mockery, eyes narrowed. "Then I'm sure you'll be no thorn in our side for a while."

Ha! A thorn in *their* side while their teeth were quite literally thorns in his. August nodded quickly. He muttered, "No, sir."

The Alpha nodded in passing, touching a hand to August's shoulder as a father might. August held his breath. But Alistair just disappeared into the hall; the door to his office closed, or so August assumed.

All right, the letter. He had to tell Hazel. He couldn't keep it to himself anymore. He turned fast to her, leaning close and whispering almost against her ear, "You'll never guess what I saw."

Hazel's eyes jumped from August to the hall and back, wary. Finally she gave in, whispering back, "What?"

"There was a letter from the Lamb on his desk—"

"*August!*"

"Shh! And it said, 'Approved should he turn.' 'Should he turn,' Hazel—"

Hazel hit him hard with her polishing rag, eyes wide. She opened her mouth, but she had nothing to say. She was shaking. August couldn't tell if she was really furious with him or fearful for him—or fearful *of* him. She stared at him in quivering silence for far too long, mouth pressed in a thin line and brow slowly knotting. Did she feel betrayed? Was she jealous?

She whispered thickly, "Tell me about it. The Lamb."

August relaxed a little. He told her about walking all the way to Trafalgar Square, about the crypts beneath St. Martin's and crawling through the heavy stone sarcophagus to a hidden set of stairs.

"Through the coffin!" Hazel gasped, trying to stay quiet in the vestibule.

"Through the coffin," August confirmed, his eyes just as wide in recollection.

Through the coffin and underground, and through many winding old stone tunnels lit by torches to, finally, the beautiful double doors he tried desperately to explain in every detail to her. The walnut, the shine, the crucifixes, the gargoyles, and the ornate designs, the strange words and symbols. He pictured it all again in his head with a shiver and he told her: about the frescoes, the whiteness of the walls and floor, the bright light from strong lamps and so many candles, the feel of the sacred royalty of a darker world, the way that the Lamb was a young man and yet not a young man, the vampire advisor sacrifice, the fur and armor and weaponry, and the faint tinkling of a distant piano.

He neglected the part about the Lamb sinking his fangs into his wrist, the peculiar commingling of fear and delight that was so dizzying in that underground palace, with the vampire king who was more like an ominous prince. How was he supposed to explain that? How was he supposed to explain that something had happened that night that had driven a wedge between him and Theo, and he was scared it wouldn't go away?

Hazel huddled beside him in awe. She whispered, "How utterly terrible and remarkable."

August nodded.

He saw Theo again on his way back up to the attic.

"Haven't you anything to say to me?" Theo snapped from the stairs.

August cast him a frown. He was exhausted. He said, with weary surrender and not at all as if he meant it, "Yes, I do. You are one of my masters and I am just the sacrifice."

He waited for Theo to stop him. He waited for Theo to explain, to apologize, to pull him into his room as he'd done so many times before so they could talk in private, so they could embrace, kiss, love. August would explain he was still just being spiteful; Theo would explain vampires still had the emotional capacity to be afraid of being alone.

But Theo didn't. His upset was suffocating. August didn't know what to think.

Frowning coldly, August turned to go back to the attic. He heard Theo's door close before he'd even climbed the stairs halfway.

He was terrified this was more than just another quarrel.

CHAPTER SIXTEEN

AUGUST WROTE another short poem.

> *Of porcelain-faced beauties I know not*
> *But unbeknownst to gray eyes,*
> *With lace cap she is more perfection than the former lot.*
> *Careful like a sister, like a mother;*
> *Tender like a friend, like a lover;*
> *Of this I am certain, that the smile of witch hazel is like no other.*

It was a jumbled mess and besmirched by mediocrity, he thought. But Hazel gawked at him as if she might cry and August scrambled to mend things, not quite sure what he'd done.

"I'm sorry," he rushed, "what did I say? Because I said 'witch hazel?' Hazel, it's just a poem, it's just rubbish—"

"No," Hazel cut in, sharply. Surely she was going to berate him.

But she only leaned in to press a tiny kiss to his cheek, so harmless and full of love August was speechless for a moment.

"It's beautiful," Hazel said. "Thank you."

They played cards. He read to her from Dickens until his voice was scratchy and his throat raw. She brought him hot honey and lemon with supper.

He took a bath. It was strange, how three o'clock in the morning had become a familiar hour.

The smell of beeswax candles and the fresh soaps on the bronze rack beside the bath was comforting. The curtains were drawn and the lamps lit, and August relaxed. The hot water soothed his muscles. He soaked for a while, sitting with his feet propped on one edge of the tub and his back against the other, toes curled just below the faucet.

The water was almost too hot on the places where the vampires fed on him. The bruises and broken blood vessels healed but they didn't fade; the tampered flesh throbbed and tickled in the water, flakes of scab drifting away like little ships sailing for better land.

The sound of the washroom door's crystal knob turning caught August's attention. He bristled—but in truth he wasn't honestly frightened. Startled perhaps, but not alarmed. It wasn't that he'd become desensitized to the privilege of privacy. It was that, truthfully, after nights in the Sanctuary, shamelessness felt a lot more comfortable.

It was just Theo, though. He slipped in from the hall and closed the door quietly. The silence with which he met August's eyes was the same gliding hush of his movements, though the careful gentleness gave off a rather crestfallen air.

With a slosh of water, August sat up straight. The air was chilly on his wet skin. He cast the vampire a look through his lashes, mouth bitten into a decorous frown.

"Hello, Theo," he said.

"Good morning," Theo returned.

August wilted; all the tension drained out of him. He could feel Theo's apology humming in the quiet like the air before a storm.

"It's not morning," August whispered back. He almost didn't say it, but he would have regretted it had he not. His heart already hurt just looking at Theo and all his grimness. He wanted to bridge the gap between them before it widened any further.

Theo's face was a smooth mask of complacency, his eyes keen as ever but his emotions carefully kept within. It was as if he were trying to keep them veiled, or at least stifled, allowing only his vampire's presence to be palpable, and nothing else. August pushed a floating bar of soap away from his side with an idle knuckle.

There was a brief silence in which both waited for the other to talk again. They were gentlemen after all. August wondered, did the vampires look down on Theo for this? Did they laugh at the two of them? Was it entertainment in such a normally gloomy and reclusive household? Or was all the doom and gloom in August's imagination?

With a smooth stride, Theo crossed to the side of the claw-foot tub. August kept his eyes on him, patient and imploring—and a little nervous, longing for the silence to end but scared talking would cause another argument.

And then just like that, Theo's coldness evaporated. It took his hard critical look with it. His hands were cool and gentle as he crouched down in front of the bath and reached out, touching August's face. August relaxed into it, lowering his lashes. The touch was comforting. Theo drew him forth, pressing a chaste kiss to his temple before letting August turn with a squeak of naked skin to return the kiss on the mouth. There were no words; words would ruin the long-awaited arrival of a truce. The sad kisses were enough to pass the meaning back and forth on subtle breaths and shy nudges of tongue. August uttered a shy, shivering sigh; Theo lapped it off his lower lip, his fingers dainty and tender on August's jaw.

Was that lust or love in Theo's eyes, that raw honesty while the rest of him clung to a gentleman's composure? Was it desperation? Was it intentional, conscious forfeit, a vampire manipulating a vulnerable moment for his own interest? Or was he truly repentant for the way he'd acted, the things he'd said?

"I realize I'm a lot of headache," August surrendered first. "I'm sorry for the way I acted before the Lamb, Theo. Please forgive me."

Theo was wordless, curiously calm. He took his hands away from August's face and August shivered.

"August," Theo said softly, slowly. He seemed on the verge of a frown, looking at August but looking past him at the same time. August waited. But the words Theo had appeared to die away in the back of his throat. He smiled weakly as if dismissing them. August didn't push. He didn't ask. Theo's face was unyielding, but a little more human again. And it was easy, so easy, to forget the way his gentleman's mouth could stretch wide over inhuman fangs.

"Let's not talk about it anymore," August said.

"Agreed," Theo whispered.

Having Theo next to him had never been more gratifying. Theo fetched him a towel; August thanked him, stepping out of the bath. He didn't expect Theo to wind him in against his body in a covetous embrace, wet from the bath or not, but he didn't resist. He melted at the touch, let Theo tip his face up for more of those tender, hungry kisses. Strange how they were so impatient and impassioned at the same time, slow and deep and intoxicating. And he was wet and shivering, naked body pressed to Theo's fine clothed one, but he was forgetting the cold as a new heat infected him head to toe, flushing his cheeks, stirring his nerves, pooling in his gut like lust. It was a lazy, enchanted arousal as he cleaved undressed and unguarded to Theo. His back arched. He cocked back his head, swallowing the fragile apologetic breaths that dripped from Theo's tongue in the midst of the bruising, aching kisses.

"Are you hungry?" August gasped against the corner of Theo's mouth, fingers tangled in his wavy dark hair. Theo tightened his fingers on him under the towel, digging into the dimples at the dip of his tailbone. "Do you need a snack?"

Theo flashed him a glance that was almost offended. But then he smiled and it was the saddest, most sentimental seduction August had ever seen.

"Yes," Theo whispered back in defeat, tugging at the towel, slipping a hand up over August's hip and between his legs now. "Yes, I'm hungry for your love...."

On the floor of the washroom, he brought August down with pleasure, shuddering and moaning and throwing off the towel because now he was all hot and flustered. Theo used his hand, his mouth, and then his hand again, and let August cling to him, grope around, play with him as if he might actually get stiff with blood that wasn't fresh.

"Tomorrow," August whined through his teeth, eyes narrowed, "tomorrow night, after you feed, you better come up and see me—"

"I wouldn't dream of anything else," Theo whispered against his ear, with a new flick of the wrist and squeezing fingers. August bucked his hips, and in a deluge of shivers, he came.

Theo licked it from his knuckles.

Outside the house of vampires, the sleet fell; back up in the attic, Hazel brought August his dinner as Theo read from Goethe's *Faust* again, lounging in the wingback chair near the northern window, one leg crossed over the other in that elegantly improper way of his.

WHAT A life his had become.

Sometimes August and Hazel lingered together at the windows and tried to see down into Berkeley Square. Pearle donated some house shoes to go with Theo's smoking jacket so August's feet didn't get cold. Sometimes he wrote—trifling little pieces he loathed and loved at the same time. Sometimes he went to Theo's room, and they sat before the fire in different chairs, or played endless games of chess, or read any of the wondrous sweet-smelling books sitting amid the clocks.

The house of vampires was disturbingly like a big family, an apparatus that depended on routines like well-oiled cogs of clockwork, a curtain that opened nightly on immortals masquerading as humans. And it happened all over the world, August realized. The Oxfords or the Irish revolt, for instance. There were others and he was just one insignificant part of a sprawling underground system of dark Undead communities.

"Thank you for taking care of me," August whispered to Hazel as she wrapped the bandages on his throat after Alistair had led him back from the Sanctuary. She shot him a doubtful look. Her lace cap was crooked, as it so often was—just another one of her adorable details, like the flutter of her dark eyelashes, the loose dark hair curling at her ears, the slightly wrinkled corner of her collar, or the little stain on her pinafore and the way her shoelaces flopped when she walked.

"You're welcome," Hazel grumbled, trying not to seem touched.

"No, I mean it. Hazel, thank you for taking care of me when I'm sick, when I'm weak, when I'm lonely, when I'm a real bother—thank you for everything you do for me. If it weren't for you, I... I don't know. I might not be here."

Hazel narrowed her eyes at him, hard, but with such tenderness it chilled him. She was quiet for a moment, as if thinking back on every single evening from the night Alistair had brought him home from the Lamb's marking. Then silently she nodded, tucking a lock of hair behind her ear, and kissed his cheek.

The attic door opened. It was Theo, looking disheveled and hot with defenseless desire. August huddled down deeper into his blankets to hide the excited smirk after catching a glimpse of the need obvious at the front of Theo's trousers, probably throbbing with new blood by now. Fresh blood, his blood. He'd taken a little more than usual tonight. But August wasn't telling anyone.

"Good evening," Theo greeted thickly.

"Evening," Hazel and August chimed back.

"Am I interrupting something?"

"I was just telling Hazel how important she is to me," August explained.

"Yes, our Witch Hazel, she's so very important—"

Hazel uttered a disdainful sniff, gaze volleying between Theo and August's antsy, mischievous grinning.

"I'm just lucky they brought a man I can actually stand this time," she commented loftily on her way out, but August heard what she really meant:

I'm happy you're here too.

She closed the attic door behind her as she departed, and Theo practically pounced upon August like a kitten with a mouse. August laughed and writhed and wrestled, dizzy, but then Theo mounted him, and oh, oh, it was time to be serious, and the laughter dissolved into a slow, dreamy sigh of satisfaction.

IT BEGAN to snow again, in the earliest hours after midnight. August watched as it spit through the dark outside the attic's northern window, piling up on the rooftops and the world outside, and Theo's skin was cool and soft, white as lilies and just as silky where it brushed along August's.

He held him from behind, arms draped loosely about August's middle and face pressed into the nape of his neck. August didn't mind. He liked Theo's breath, tepid and slightly metallic-smelling, and the jut of his chin. He thought maybe he could feel the weak flutter of Theo's heart in the shell of his chest.

He wondered whether Theo was smelling his blood through his skin, or listening to his pulse. Was the amount of blood he drank on the designated nights enough to really satisfy him?

August looked over his shoulder, meeting Theo's eyes. He was so easily lost in their depths.

He remembered the fever breaking and the danger he'd flirted with by trying to escape, and the vampire with the garish waistcoat and the gentleman's poise, and the wild mane of hair, the vampire who had plucked him in from the chimney stack and with that simple act won August's trust over completely.

He remembered the first time he had run into Theo after that, the shyness that swelled in his chest with every touch from the green-eyed vampire in the Sanctuary, all the tentative blundering baby steps to friendship that first week or two after the sickness left and August was cognizant again. Theo and his messy bedroom, all the fractures and cracks in his graceful mask, the questions asked and the kind answers and the mysteries in his green eyes. Theo and his intensity, Theo and his sweet silences, Theo and his childlike temper, Theo plagued by hunger on All Hallows Eve, his guilt for being subject to such need, Theo's voice, clipped and emotional—*There's a love between a vampire and its sacrifice, you know. You call me your friend, but I am a monster.* And on the way back from St. James Park the night they went to see the Lamb: *That vampire's desire of mine, my innate preternatural hunger for your vigor and your blood, maybe you misconstrued that....*

It was admirable and a little endearing, the destructive way Theo insisted he was coldhearted when he so obviously was not. Immortals certainly weren't immune to things like love and hate, or happiness and grief, were they? They were just obstinate. Surely they were afraid of those things and the pain time might transmute them into.

August turned around and buried himself into Theo's chest. He didn't want to let go for fear of never having it again, this closeness, this comfort. He wanted to say it again. *Turn me, Theo.* He wanted to beg for it. He'd derogate himself like that. He'd fall down prostrate on the floor and plead, get on his knees and pray to his new gods as long as Theo never let him be alone.

When Theo did leave—which he inevitably had to, two tired, flustered men scrambling away from each other as Hazel came with supper and fresh bandages for August's throbbing neck—August felt a sudden resolve take root.

He ate supper with Hazel; they laughed and talked. Hazel snuffed out the candles and turned out the lamp, and as August burrowed down into his blankets, the sun rose slowly, gray dawn spilling into the attic room cold and silent.

Hazel was probably asleep downstairs with the other servants, and the vampires in their very human beds.

Sleep did not come as easily to August as it usually did.

Vampires.

Hazel had defended them in the beginning—sweet, angel-faced Hazel and her untainted understanding of the world. What had it come to now? What did he know about them, truly?

The vampires he knew were not entirely different from the creatures he'd read about in penny dreadfuls and other little novels, or heard about from Lucius's tentative dip into folklore and old legends. They were beautiful monsters; they were somewhere between living and dead; they were like the ghosts of Greek poetry, feasting on blood to replace something missing in their soul, entering some ritualistic rite as reparation for accepting whatever black magic it was to become what they were.

Vampires.

There was apparently a whole realm of them the selfish human world had hardly ever fathomed, an underground kingdom that spanned the entire expanse of the world, ruled by the curious Lamb in a palace below London.

They were refined and romantic. They were chilling and captivating, even the ones like Ishmael who were of questionable design, and there was also the curious childish way they all seemed unable to control their eccentricities. They didn't age. They were averse to sunlight. They slept during the day and repellants of fiction didn't seem to harm them—crosses and holy water, stakes and the like.

Their faces and eyes were what really gave away that they weren't exactly human, expressions and gestures that were too strong, too focused, too intense.

But the vampires around August seemed like a relatively peaceful bunch, abiding by the rules of their king to keep something of a balance between humans and their kind.

It was like what Hazel had said weeks ago about hypocrisies and a balance between living and Undead. Who indeed were the real monsters?

He wanted to be one.

From the bed August watched as morning broke and the sky lightened above the rooftops.

Yes, he wanted to become one of them.

He remembered, suddenly, the Lamb: "I know your desires. You cannot hide them from me. I'll teach you everything one day. Isn't that what you want?"

The brief flickering memory of the voice, the face, the mouth on his wrist, made August's heart jump and the blood rush to his face, the hair rising on his arms in a veneer of goose bumps.

Indisputably the Lamb knew it then, somehow tasting it in his soul that he wanted to be a vampire. He approved of it. He knew it before August knew it, and he obliged it. Surely that meant something. It certainly made August feel flattered and apprehensive, so apprehensive.

There was nothing in his life before that would make him prefer it over this.

He had changed somehow, and he didn't know when or where, but he wanted it—he *wanted it*—he didn't ever want to be cold and lonely again.

He wanted to be a vampire too.

CHAPTER SEVENTEEN

"TURN ME," August whispered.

Outside the attic window, the wind picked up, while inside the attic Theo looked at him so sharply from the chair under the southern window that August actually flinched back.

As if rippled by some wave of unseen Undead witchcraft, the flames on the candles flickered; the lamplight dimmed and then swelled. For an instant Theo's pupils dilated, became elliptical, and then just as quickly returned to normal as his entire face hardened. He stared at August in a calm sort of disbelief, as if he'd had to get a fast hold on his anger before even thinking about taking the breath to reply.

"Pardon?" Theo finally said then, sounding nearly mad in all his composure.

August's skin crawled, but he swallowed the alarm.

"Turn me, I said," he repeated.

Theo snapped to his feet swiftly and August rocked backward as if Theo had laid a hand on him, eyes widening.

"You demand it so casually," Theo scorned. August could hear the strain on his voice, such a lovely voice, so tight and flat as Theo kept a tight clutch on his self-control. "I don't want to fight with you again. I thought we'd finally found a comfortable place as lamb and master."

August was silent. His ears rang vaguely with Theo's volatility.

"*Turn* you," Theo echoed, spitting out the words with such disgust August could hardly believe he'd spoken them. His green eyes sparked with rage. His shoulders were rigid and his knuckles were white. His mouth cut into a bitter frown, and for a moment August wondered whether he'd seen a glimpse of his fangs, extended accidentally. There it was, the reality: a vampire across the room from him. Theo turned on his heel at the same time he sputtered out a hostile laugh. August's stomach knotted. Instinctively he pressed back into the corner by the northern window, eyes glued to Theo as he stalked about the attic.

Theo's hands twitched. His shoulders jerked. August was stricken with the sudden fear he'd start throwing things soon. He could hear the crash and shatter of the washbasin across the wall already, the smash of the lamp or the crush of a precious book. Heart thundering in his chest, he wondered whether it was just that he'd struck a nerve, or whether Theo's grasp on his inhuman temper was failing lately. All of Theo's layers of composure—the handsome gentleman, the assiduous young man, the curious, hopeless dark parts of his personality that were a bit obsessive and intimidating—all of those layers were quickly being stripped away, leaving nothing but a gaunt, pale vampire pacing the room with anger twitching in his fingertips.

"Turn you!" Theo roared, flinging his hands out. He laughed again and again, loud and mocking. And then, as if he were deeply injured by such a request, he said quietly for the last time, "You want me to turn you? How could you ever ask me such a thing?"

"I want to…." August swallowed, skin crawling. He refused to be intimidated. "I want to be with you."

Theo cut right through him with a cold, disdainful look.

"Oh, such a lonely man," he said in the same low breathless tone as before. "You'll be with me forever. Isn't that enough?" He stood next to the lamp. Its light danced on his face and intensified its shapes. It made him look rather sinister, even though he was disconsolate. And what a wonderful play on words and insecurities it was. *You'll be with me forever.* As if this were about lonesome love and not independence or meaning.

"No." August's eyes damned Theo for his cruelty. He fired back, "I know what you mean. I'll be with you for the rest of *my* forever. You'll never die, Theo, but I will. I don't want to die alone. I don't want *you* to be alone after I die. I want to be like you. I want to be something again. Not just a ghost in an attic. I want to sleep amongst the dead with you, so—please—Theo, turn me!"

Theo didn't hesitate. "You don't want this," he edged out, wavering between a laugh and contempt. His eyes were wide and bleak. August was caught off guard by such dark honesty. His heart ached; he couldn't tell if it was from fury or defeat.

"I do," he insisted.

"You love me that much, do you?"

"Don't mock me, Theo. My existence is more than that."

"You think so? Love is such a desperate, lonely emotion, though."

"Theo—"

"I don't want to lose you, innocent thing."

"Then why? Why won't you do it! Why won't you turn me?" August took a sharp breath, just as startled by the vicious sound of his voice as Theo was. The wildness left Theo's face. He stared at August with wide, empty eyes like a child, the tension and tumult within him so strong he seemed to tremble with it.

"Because," he said so simply. "Because then you won't be mine anymore, August. You won't be mine."

August stared dumbly, brow furrowed and lips parted. He scowled at Theo in such confusion he could hardly feel the fear any longer. It pained him to see Theo so distraught. "I'll always be yours, Theo," he said as honestly as he could. "I'll always be your friend, your sacrifice, your audience, your lover, your whatever you want me to be. I don't have any reason to be anything else."

"No," Theo said, inflexible and indignant. His shoulders relaxed, though, and he shook his head before staring at his feet and silently gathering all the layers of his gentleman's composure again. "Don't say anything else about it, August. Not right now. Just stop. I'm begging you. No."

August wilted, shocked. He felt denied. He felt rejected. He felt shut down, and unsatisfied because Theo's justification for his refusal was not what he'd expected, and he couldn't accept it. It was selfish. It was greedy. It was juvenile.

August considered reminding Theo snidely that, in truth, he wasn't the only vampire in the house he could ask to bestow upon him eternal life. But that would be vindictive and just as selfish. He couldn't threaten it, because he would never go through with it, and that just wasn't fair.

Theo snatched up his frock coat from the wingback chair below the window. He came to a stop beside August, hand on the attic door. He looked at him sadly, as if he didn't want to leave. Just as anguished, he spoke, low and soft:

"Tomorrow night, I am going out with Alphonse and Anastasia. Don't look for me."

He touched a knuckle to August's chin lovingly as he pulled the door open. August pulled back, avoiding Theo's eyes. He held the door as Theo descended the stairs, and he watched him disappear into the hall, feeling very cold.

It was not the same kind of quarrel as the one they'd just mended.

Unlike the row they had about the visit to the Lamb, this was definitely not the last time the bitter tension would arise between them, as comrades, as gentlemen, as sacrifice and vampire, as human and monster.

The Alpha came with his familiar smile of sinister warmth two hours later, and led August down to the Sanctuary like a paramour to privacy.

In the early morning hours, as fog rolled through London, August fell asleep to echoes in his head of the faint growls of imperceptible stomachs, an inhuman animalistic sound deep in the throats of some of the vampires, because they were hungry, they were always hungry, and he seemed to stir their appetite delightfully.

NEVER BEFORE had Theo lied to August.

Bending the truth or avoiding certain details was not lying; this however was an utter untruth.

Going out with Alphonse and Anastasia. Don't look for me.

Theo was out, but he was out with Ishmael.

They stopped at a dining house called Silvey's for some sweet red wine and then took to the streets, strolling together in a heavy but not entirely uncomfortable silence. The night was brilliantly lit, the air crisp and refreshing. They were anonymous together in the crowds.

"What did you want to speak with me about tonight?" Ishmael prompted, the swell of streetlamps bouncing behind his silhouette. A fog was creeping up on the bridges. Voices and laughter echoed around the popular squares. Ishmael looked so small and vulnerable in his overcoat; his shoulders were drawn up tight and his face pinched as if he were suspicious of Theo's company.

"The Lamb called him 'special,'" Theo murmured.

"Who?"

"You know who. August."

"I know." Ishmael wrinkled his nose. "Alistair said that after the Lamb marked him—"

"No, a second time." Theo shoved his hands deep in the pockets of his coat, though the chill he felt came from within. "The other night. When I took August to see him."

Ishmael was quiet for a long moment, watching strangers pass by under the streetlamps. A coffee stall near the bridge was attracting much business this early on in the night, from those on their way home and those on their way out. *Special.* The Lamb was not only unpredictable, but painfully secretive. There was something terrifying about that. But perhaps that was what made the Lamb the perfect king for their kind. Ishmael sighed tartly. He of course remembered the time before the current Lamb. Had it been any different then, or the same cryptic mysteries?

Ishmael murmured, "What does he mean, 'special'?"

"I wish I knew."

"He wants to turn, doesn't he?"

Theo flinched at the words being spoken aloud. He sighed through his teeth, avoiding Ishmael's prying eyes. "Yes."

"Well, that's wonderful! That's everything you've ever wanted!"

"Don't be that way, Ishmael."

"Is this why you wanted to speak with me?" Ishmael hissed again.

"No," Theo spat back. "No, this is my fault, it doesn't concern you at all…."

"Your fault? Not everything is about you, Theo."

"I—" The words died away at the back of Theo's tongue. He shook his head, storming away from Ishmael. But then he turned and strutted back, and it had been so long since he'd spoken so honestly to him, saying, "I don't want him to hate me as I've come to hate you!"

Ishmael's face stayed soft, his lips parted. But his eyes darkened. There was a retreating feeling about him, a shrinking back. The Undead light in his glare dulled and he looked very weak and mortal. But he lifted his chin regally.

He said in a low, flat way, yet not without feeling, "You don't want him to hate you as you hate me, hmm? Or maybe it's that you don't want to hate him as I hate you. Right? Either way, you don't want things to be different. Well, that's out of your control, Theo. Alistair told me about the letter. He's been approved. If August wants to turn, he can turn. So long as you don't lose control and do it without the rest of us."

"Oh, don't you dare shame me for the way I'm feeling—"

"I don't regret turning you," Ishmael said, widening his eyes coldly. "Do you hear me? Hate me all you want, I hate you too, but even if I had known it would be this way, I do not regret turning you."

A silence spun out between them. Theo's ears rang; his heart felt heavy and rotten as it thudded in his chest.

"Can we go back now?" Ishmael sighed impatiently. "I'm heading back now. Listen. He's in love with you obviously." He meant August. He brushed past Theo roughly, hitting his arm with his elbow. "Did you really believe you deserved his love without having to pay for it?"

Maybe it really was just that Theo didn't believe he deserved it at all.

IT DIDN'T occur to August to be nervous; he forgot about the way all the vampires seemed to communicate together in secrecy. He didn't think about the vampires knowing of his demands to Theo, so he wasn't apprehensive in the least going down into the hall while Theo and Alphonse and Anastasia were out, pretending to be human and enjoying London's luxuries.

Throat and wrist bandaged, August stood below the window in the western hall, looking out at a snow-covered Berkeley Square. Coaches rattled by on the slick gritty pavement, snow in dirty piles at the curbs, horses snorting out bursts of hot breath on the air.

The music room was empty. August stood in the doorway looking in at the lonesome piano and harp, the crackling fire.

House shoes flopping against his heels, August moved into the room, loving the way the shadows danced from all the many candles. Some of them needed to be replaced, little lumps of wax in delicate silver sconces and candelabra. He swept up some of the music sheets from the love seat and sat down at the piano. Chopin, a waltz in B minor.

The ability to read the notes came back to him easily, old lessons that stuck somehow from rainy afternoons in a drawing room, a childhood of tutors and practice. It had been so long since he had sat down at the keyboard. He was surprised he remembered how to play. What if he wasn't a sacrifice? What if this was his music room and he was a young, independent man of romantic intellect, and he would have Lucius and his writer friends over in the vestibule or the drawing room for writing parties, and they'd eat in the grand, neglected dining hall and gather in the library, and then he would invite his family and perhaps he'd make it somewhere, find a career, find a lover, find meaning...?

The piano keys were smooth beneath his fingers. August hummed with the chords and resounding notes. The more he played, the more came back to him. He could remember the music tutor prodding the middle of his back to keep him sitting tall. He could remember stretching his hands before playing and the music tutor being so aggravated he hadn't memorized the lesson from the week before—

Two hands reached around August's shoulders and spread over the keys. August recoiled, eyes widening. Yanked from his trance and painfully aware of the vampire presence suddenly behind him, he looked over his shoulder, stunned, to find Pearle, with his scarred face and his kind, murky eyes and the thin beard on his square jaw with shades of silver here and there.

Pearle's hands took control of the piece, playing the waltz flawlessly. He summoned forth all the melancholy with such impeccable precision that August just sat and watched his fingers move, graceful and lithe. Pearle swayed behind him with the melody.

With all the preternatural and unfair talent of a vampire, Pearle finished the page. The music stopped rather bluntly, incomplete and in shreds of sound that faded away in the soft hush of the room.

"You're fond of Chopin," Pearle said, halfway between a question and an assumption. August looked over his shoulder; Pearle was smiling, the gesture a little wizened by his scars.

"Yes," August whispered.

Pearle moved to the love seat across from the piano. He sat, one elbow propped up and one leg crossed over the other. He smiled tenderly, like a teacher or a friend. August offered a faint smile in return. He opened his mouth to thank Pearle again for the house shoes, but what came out was not gratitude. He felt the words shift in the pit of his chest, just below his throat, his thank-you plummeting suddenly and his voice spilling over impetuously:

"Where did you get your scars?"

Pearle's eyes were sad and a little glassy, but there was no menace—nothing dark or ghastly at all radiating from him.

"The sun," Pearle said, smiling still.

He held up a hand at August's dismay. For the first time, August noticed the very faint Scottish lilt to his words. "Many decades ago," Pearle elaborated gently, "on my first night of drinking blood, I was naïve and I was stubborn, and I did not listen to my kin. I slept in the open and I awoke midmorning with the sun scalding what skin it could touch, worried strangers screaming for me to wake because I was injured. My kin welcomed me back. I was lucky. I learned my lesson."

August stared, a little mystified, a little subdued. "Oh," he whispered, looking curiously at Pearle.

"You saw the Lamb," Pearle changed the subject, the end of his sentence upturned, almost a question. His endless brown eyes settled stealthily on August.

August leaned back, jumping when he accidentally propped his elbows on a few piano keys and sent a bellowing discordant echo around the music room. He moved to sit in a chair near the window, blushing in embarrassment. Pearle's eyes followed him.

"I did," August answered, clearing his throat.

Some pale skin creased into pleasant crow's feet at the corners of Pearle's eyes. "What did you think of him?" he asked with a childish kind of urgency, as if this were some debonair gossip.

August shrugged and shook his head. "He was not at all what I expected."

"Curious little thing, isn't he?"

"I suppose."

A maid came to replace the candles and both Pearle and August stopped talking, watching her coyly. Pearle flagged her down and asked her to bring August a cup of tea. August was flattered.

"What a horrible guise, don't you think?" Pearle murmured, for the first time looking rather saddened. "What is eternity when a man will never be treated as a man because he looks like a child? But that innocence, that simplicity of his, is the more sinister of his disguises."

August's brow furrowed quizzically. "What do you mean?"

Pearle still wore that disheartened smile. He stared at August as if deep in thought for a few moments, eyes speaking silent questions, a wordless probing.

The maid brought the tea and August thanked her shyly. Pearle waited for her to leave before speaking again.

"I remember a time," he said, with a faraway glint in his eye, "before the Great Reform and the current system, when coven sacrifices and coven rules did not exist as they do now. I remember the first Lamb, and I recall that he had four children—Charysse, Lawrence, Felix, and Sasha. He'd ruled for a long, long time—since the beginning of the kingdom, I think—and nobody ever expected that his youngest child would be capable of taking over the throne."

The first Lamb. His children were also vampires? Was there some sort of primogeniture to this dark sovereignty even without real progeny? No. That didn't seem right at all. Maybe Pearle meant something else when he said *children.* The tea warmed August's palms, and he took a few sips before seizing the brief pause, which Pearle had obviously been waiting for him to do:

"What do you mean?" August asked again. "Did the first Lamb resign, or die? And even if he did, why didn't his oldest succeed him? But wait, I thought that vampires couldn't die—?"

Pearle smiled beguilingly. "You ask the perfect questions, August. That can be a gift and a defeat. 'What happened to the royal coven before the youngest child took over?' That's what you're thinking. In 1816, the Year Without a Summer, there was the Great Reform. Bloody, tragic thing that it was, treason and murder. But it occurred and it is part of our history now, and because of it, the new Lamb reigns over a kingdom with structure and civil intentions."

Bloody, tragic thing… treason and murder….

Theo had mentioned the Great Reform before. It all held a weight now, a chilling weight, and it added another frightful detail to his already negative opinion of the vampire king.

Pearle drew a tired breath, looking away and idly combing his fingers through his hair. "The story of our current Lamb is so inspirational, I like to think," he grunted, Scottish murmur with a faint little nod of apology. "I love to tell it, but *that* is a story for another night. Do you understand what I mean?"

August was stupefied. He nodded at Pearle but he did not truly understand. He hardly thought treason and murder and bloodshed were inspirational. Which was it: had the new Lamb committed treason and murder? Or had the old Lamb killed everyone but him? And how, of course, was that possible? How did the Undead *die*, for Christ's sake?

"We're lucky to have Alistair as our Alpha," Pearle said, a little slow as he spoke his thoughts aloud. He had the spark of a proud partner in his eyes, and August thought if Alistair was the father, Pearle was the mother, and everyone else in the house was their children.

"I have to wonder," Pearle went on as August sipped his tea quietly, "what kind of coven leader the Lamb would be, with all his intricacies and idiosyncrasies? Alistair treats us quite nicely, to be honest."

"Ishmael maybe a little too nicely," August mumbled, and immediately regretted it. But Pearle looked at him with laughter in his eyes and a crooked little smile. He held out his hands as if to say, *What can be done about Ishmael?*

"There will always be those men who wish they had power," Pearle said quietly and evenly, and August smiled at him over his cup of tea. Pearle understood.

Pearle didn't watch him as he scampered back up to the attic room as the others did, and that was nice.

THREE NIGHTS before Christmas, August found the tree.

Someone had set it up in the middle of the vestibule, a tall dark spruce that filled the hall with its spicy perfume, fresh and crisp. Its green body was draped with glittering beads of silver, gold, pearl—tiny candles, expensive tinsel, paper flowers.

August came to a sharp halt at the top of the stairs, staring at the decorated tree long and hard as if it were a phantom that might dissipate at any moment. There was nobody around to witness it with him and nobody around to confess to setting it up, and August laughed and hurried down the steps into the vestibule and ran around the tree with a delighted grin on his face.

The tree looked a little out of place without any other Christmas decorations. No window ornaments, no mistletoe, no Christmas dolls. There were no gifts on the silk beneath the tree either.

August fell still.

It was sort of a sick shock he felt. He'd forgotten all about Christmas but here it was suddenly, appearing as if by magic, a sweet slap in the face to remind him of time as it passed without him.

Right, no cards, no gifts, no decorations, nothing but this tree standing in the middle of a cold vestibule, and August glared at it quietly for a long moment. He could feel the bitter frown on his face.

Theo found him. He stood at the top of the stairs, just off the upstairs hall, with his fingers resting on the thick balustrade and a look of heavy thought on his face.

August met his eyes, mouth bitten into a thin line. He couldn't explain the sudden bitter misery he felt. He was just distraught. He felt hopeless and lost and a little bit mocked. They were all childish things to feel, but he deserved to feel them, right?

"Why is this here?" August husked.

Theo smiled briefly. As he descended the stairs, the smile faded; he seemed to know exactly how August felt, whether it was out of sympathy or not. His hair was a wild mess tonight, his collar raised a little too high to be fashionable and his frock coat dancing about his legs. He looked at August with one of his usual piercing stares, curious and calm and secretive all at once.

"Why, it's Christmas soon," he explained.

"But it's a façade." August's brow furrowed on a dark, injured stare as Theo drew nearer. He gestured to the tree, frowning. "This feels like a joke."

"It's not." Theo frowned, hands in the pockets of his coat. He stood next to August and peered at the tree with hooded eyes. "But you're right, it certainly feels like one. No candles, no ribbons, no gifts. Why would we exchange gifts, though? What's the point?"

August was immensely distressed by this. It summoned forth a bottomless sadness, not for himself but for the vampires, who clung to human traditions by such a thin thread. Didn't it mean anything to them anymore, or did those values shift when one became something supernatural?

Theo stood guiltily at his side, as if it were his fault August ached for them.

August followed him back up to his room, weighed down by these worries. And then it hit him.

"I want a Christmas supper," he announced, studying Theo's giltwood clock while Theo sat before his fire with all the graceful weariness of an old nobleman.

"And you'll get one," Theo promised, raising his brows at August as if he were dumb. "You've gotten supper every night you've been here, haven't you?"

"Theo—" August heaved an exasperated sigh; sometimes Theo was so clever, and other times there was the most jarring disconnect. "I want Christmas supper, with bouillon and sweetbread, and goose or turkey, fruits and Roman punch and plum pudding."

Theo studied him hard, mouth pressed in a firm and contemplative line. Slowly he returned his gaze to the fire and reached out to take August's hand. He pulled him down into the chair next to him. August waited.

But Theo was silent.

The conversation ended rather bluntly there.

CHAPTER EIGHTEEN

THEO THREW an outfit from Alphonse's haphazard wardrobe down at the foot of August's bed.

"Merry Christmas," he said, smirking with all the handsome glory of his less manic and obsessive temperaments.

August looked up at him in doubt. "What?"

"It's midnight, it's Christmas now. Come on, get dressed."

"What's going on?"

"Come *on*, August—"

Theo waited with almost childlike impatience as August changed, nearly bursting at the seams with some great secret. Hazel waited with him, running her fingers idly through her hair. August squinted at his reflection in the southern window, trying to use the glass as a mirror: the outfit wasn't spectacular, but it made him feel far more normal than the plain nightclothes, and the collar hid some of his bruises and bite marks. Hazel crossed the attic to comb her fingers through his hair now instead, trying to tame the stubborn blond cowlicks near his temple and ears. She turned him around to face Theo like a matchmaker's presentation.

"All right, then," she sighed, "here's your fine gentleman, Theo."

"He is *fine*."

"The vampire's swooning!"

"Oh, hush up, you."

August cleared his throat, raising his brows. "Are you two through? Why am I dressed?"

Theo held a hand out, grinning that devious grin again. He was practically bouncing with excitement. "Come with me," he murmured.

"Let me get the smoking jacket, hold on, I'm cold—"

"We're not leaving the house."

"I don't care. I'm still cold."

"The desanguination," Hazel muttered below her breath, not exactly reprimanding Theo so much as reminding him. "Desanguination and anemia make a man cold."

"Huh," Theo grunted, musing on this as if it were the first time in all his years of vampirism he'd stopped to think about a sacrifice's mortal constitution.

Downstairs the usually neglected dining hall was ornamented with fresh wreaths of holly and mistletoe, and each of nine places was set with red velvet ribbons and delicate crystal finery. Garlands of flowers coiled around many sweet candles, decanters, and silver tiers; the fireplace was ablaze, the chandelier and candelabra spitting off light through the room. The Alpha had invited musicians, and they spoke to Alphonse as if they knew him personally, playing in the corner of the wide dining room as if it were any other usual engagement.

August was dumbstruck.

He whipped around to Theo, eyes wide and demanding. "You didn't have to—I didn't really mean it," he blurted.

Theo whispered back, "Yes, you did."

"You persuaded them to have Christmas dinner?"

"It didn't take all that much."

"You don't have to force tradition for me—"

"You're our sacrifice. If you're not happy, we're not happy."

August felt a little choked up. He was touched; he was deeply touched. He felt an utter fool hunched into Theo's smoking jacket, but at least he wasn't in his nightclothes. What had Theo said and done, he wondered? How had he convinced them? Or had August been too quick to judge the value they placed on tradition?

They were all gathered around the long table like a family—the vampires.

Perhaps it meant nothing. Perhaps it really held no significance. But as the sleepy valet led him to a chair across the long table from Alistair, August felt deliciously welcome.

He was utterly lost in the moment.

Music—such familiar, nostalgic pieces, and who were these men who would spend Christmas evening playing music for such a motley party as this? No guests but their household, seven quaint gentlemen, a sharp young woman, and a sickly blond bachelor in his Undead lover's smoking jacket. The air was rich with the scent of seasonal spices, cloves, poinsettia. Theo sat to August's right; Anastasia was to his left.

The cook and the head maid brought silver dishes into the dining room.

Rich bouillon steamed before him and August's mouth watered. Up and down the sides of the table, the vampires were served the same dish.

Most of them didn't eat.

The Alpha, Ishmael, and Laurel did, Alistair smiling at August from across the table as their voices rose in laughter and conversation, as if they were truly a party of friends gathered for the holiday. It seemed crass at first, a mockery, but as August ate, smiling shyly at the foot of the table with talk and music echoing around him, he began to relax. He hoped they didn't expect him to join in the chitchat. In truth he wasn't really paying attention, and he'd probably only say something like "How are you eating food right now? I thought you only ingested blood." His throat was tight with emotion. His smile was almost delirious with wonderment.

You're part of us.

Sweetbread, oysters, pastry, stewed fruits, cheese, celery, roast goose, and a boar's head with an apple in its mouth that seemed more lurid tablescape than meal—no Roman punch, but exquisitely aged wine August was thrilled to be drinking. God, he'd missed wine with dinner. Theo always shared his wine with August, but Hazel never brought any wine with August's meals.

When the plum pudding came, August was the only one eating. The vampires drank wine as they spoke, eyeing him as if he were to be the final delicacy of the night. It wasn't a feeding night, though. This was harmless.

Alistair, followed by Ishmael and Laurel, left the dining room momentarily as the servants came round to gather the dirty dishes and Alphonse's musician friends struck up a frivolous piece. Alistair's valet poured August champagne next.

Anastasia fixed her eyes on August with a dark curiosity, her mouth pursed in a thin line. Conversation had fallen to murmurs. There were no clocks in the dining room. August wondered what time it was. The wine tingled through his veins. He met Anastasia's eyes openly.

Anastasia was resplendent: red velvet gown of Empire silhouette, neck bare and skin pallid like a lily, with the faintest touch of color from the wine she drank. Ringlet curls bounced at her jaw, the rest of her soft locks swept away from her temple. She looked strangely soft tonight, usually adorned in a palette of colors paler than stunning crimson.

"Do you want to dance?" Anastasia ventured courteously, but the subtle pinch of her face was more demanding.

It was her apology, August realized, for what happened with the music box.

Face flushed from the wine and feeling full and comfortable, he smiled graciously in return and nodded.

It was awkward at first, shaky and uncertain as they struggled to find proper placement for hands and feet, but soon they were waltzing together near Alphonse's musician friends. Anastasia led; August laughed, uncaring. The Alpha, Ishmael, and Laurel returned together, Laurel dabbing at his mouth with a napkin.

Anastasia danced with a grace and authority, her steps strong, her hand guiding. It gave her a very androgynous flair, the charm of both sexes behind a petite pretty face and icy eyes.

They were not the hobgoblins, fairies, and spirits of his childhood Christmases before the fire, but it was the same sensation, the same creeping magic.

August loved it.

He was drunk on it, spellbound. He was comfortable; he was full; he was theirs, and it was an obvious and intrinsic weight to the evening, but he was content. It almost chilled him he could feel such desperate love for these creatures. Undead. Vampires.

Rain drizzled outside the house, freezing fast. Fog clung to the buildings. The vampires didn't tell stories or exchange gifts, but there were parlor games, raucous parlor games, the meal and the music and the laughter, and that was enough for August. Good tidings to all, he told them, good tidings, good cheer! Gaily they sang a carol together, led by the musicians. He was gloriously intoxicated by the end of the night, groggy and easily distracted, easily amused, but it was Christmas—it was Christmas, Christmas, Christmas, and August loved it.

He kissed Theo over and over when Theo helped him to bed in the wee hours of the morning. Hazel was there, turning back the covers and snuffing out the candles. Theo chuckled as if it tickled, his breath as heady with wine as August's, and returned the rushed kisses, chaste little presses of cool, wet mouth, and August let him bury his nose in his temple and smell his skin and hair, running his smooth hands along the slope of his back as he sat on the edge of his bed.

"Thank you, thank you," August whispered, clutching Theo's collar and speaking with his lips to Theo's soft cheek. Hazel left. "You did this for me. You did all of this for me."

"I did," Theo murmured, smiling at him with lashes lowered on eyes that spoke of something much more profound.

August fell asleep to Theo whispering sweet nothings on his ear, hands stroking, petting, coddling affectionately and protectively. He was there, and August felt comfortable, and a blanket of dreams fell swiftly and easily. Not dreams of sugar plums, not of jolly red-clad saints or carolers, but of a houseful of vampires with perceptive eyes and infectious smiles.

Theo left, of course, before dawn.

SOMEONE HAD put some of the poinsettias in the washroom, a little cluster of fragrant red near the stand of soaps.

August sat in the bath, distracted. His throat and wrist were as tender and sore as they ever were, wounds healing too quickly but always interrupted before the process could come to completion. They itched, a dull throb in his veins, but he'd learned to ignore it. Those places were for the vampires, and only them, and dear God, when had he come to trust them, these curious pallid beings who peered at him one moment like a precious younger brother, then held him flat the next to nip at his throat with their little pearly dagger teeth?

When had he accepted it, when had he begun to forgive them for the enervating, dreamlike evenings in the Sanctuary, sinister sensuous nights that were as spiritual as they were haunting?

August sat with his knees drawn to his chest, sticky as the skin dried where it broke the surface of the water. He clasped his fingers at his ankles and rested his head.

He remembered his father as a strong-jawed, weary-eyed man, stoic reserve and solemn middle-class pride. He remembered his mother as a tall, birdlike, prudent woman with dainty little hands and hair always swept perfectly off her neck. He remembered his oldest brother in flashes of tweed and broadcloth, and traveling cases full of books from Eton. His other brothers were loud and pushy, and he remembered overhearing them one night talking about who rightfully deserved their father's law firm when he died. He remembered Lucius—oh, Lucius—but now suddenly Lucius didn't feel like much more than a character from a book. None of them did. They didn't feel real; they didn't feel important.

There it was again, that bittersweet nostalgia—that mournful, wistful weight as faces and memories flickered by in the back of his mind from a catalog of recollections. They saddened him because they were cold in a new way—distant, unfamiliar, irrelevant. Memorylessness no more; the memories he'd been without didn't even feel like his own anymore.

And he didn't want them.

Now it was Berkeley Square, the house of vampires, the Lamb, a worldwide community of supernatural aristocracy, the twenty-ninth sacrifice and belonging to this coven of chilling humanlike men and women who were not dead and not living—

This was where he was meant to be.

It was fate's design.

His mother, his father, his brothers, Lucius—everything connected to the August from before was gone. In fact, that August had disappeared too.

This was him now, and he could either die lost to the world and forsaken from everything he knew—or he could be born again into the Undead as Theo had said before.

He could become a vampire.

August reached into the water and pulled the stopper from the drain. Hazel would be waiting in the attic to fetch him supper.

He was too tired tonight to think about how to bring it up to Theo again.

THE SERVANTS took down the tree in the vestibule. From the southern attic window, the streets were visible, obstructed by a thick fresh falling of snow. The windows were all icy and the end of the year encroached, and August saw for the first time what Anastasia did in the fainting room.

The fainting room, with all its sheet-covered furniture and dusty corners, was neglected by even the servants. It was a room fit for specters and nightmares, a creepy chamber of cold shadows and stale air. The door was open the night after Christmas; a delicate melody leaked out into the hall.

August stood at the corner where he'd seen Anastasia so many nights ago, eyes fixed on the cracked doorway. There were no lights on, there was no fire lit. It was dark in the fainting room, but the ghostlike sound trickled out, sharp and fragile like crystal or icicles.

He wasn't sure what compelled him to take a peek, to pause and listen—but perhaps it was the overpowering sadness that drifted out with the dainty little music, music box music, a tune that was familiar but one he couldn't place. It wrought out so much tristful emotion it was a little eerie.

Cosimo's music box.

That's what it was.

Anastasia's most prized belonging, the little white music box with the turquoise and gold, the imperial-looking craft she held so close to her heart.

To be safe and to cater to his conscience, trying to make up for peeking in the first place, August looked between the hinges, squinting into the fainting room as secretly as he could.

Without a doubt it was the tintinnabulation of the music box from Anastasia's room, the one from beneath the portrait, the one Ishmael had tricked him into stealing—the music box with Cosimo's ashes in it.

And there was a shadow on one of the seats, a couch that had been uncovered. The sheet was in a pile at its carved wooden feet. By chance the shadow shifted, the outline of a young woman, and August glimpsed the flash of hall light in a sharp blue eye, a brief glint in all the darkness of the cold fainting room. There was the sound of a breath being taken, painful and slight.

It was Anastasia of course.

There was no disputing it. She sat alone in the dark empty room with her treasured music box open before her, wound and wound so it would not stop playing. Was she weeping, or was that a trick of the shadows, a mere assumption? The abject emotion leaked out of the room like heat without the warmth, an unseen but very real force, a contagious touch of sorrow that August suffered the brunt of as he looked in through the hinges. Poor Anastasia, lonely, frigid Anastasia.

What is eternity when a man will never be treated as a man...?
Pearle had said. And it was like Theo's obsessive fits and Anastasia's
sharp goddess madness. Time took its toll, it seemed. And as Theo said
that one night, they either survived it or they didn't.

But it was selfish of Theo to appropriate such agony only to the
Undead; it was unfair. It was not just their pain. It was a human man's
pain too, the human condition, the sweet solace of suffering. It wasn't
unique to them. They just had longer to explore it.

Approved should he turn.

Theo had no right to deny him.

CHAPTER NINETEEN

THEO LIKED that August helped him rearrange all his chairs and clocks, scraping furniture across imported rugs and twisting timepiece keys to start the offbeat ticking again. But there was something August wanted out of it, apparently. After a moment, he stopped and cleared his throat and said:

"Turn me, Theo."

Theo bristled, and then promptly went on with what he'd previously been talking about as if August had never spoken a word.

August waited for Theo to look at him. When Theo didn't, he just as stubbornly said again, "I don't want to die, Theo. Turn me."

Theo snorted. "Well, aren't you selfish? Everyone dies, August. Even children accept that."

August was undeterred. He knocked a few meticulously arranged chess pieces over to get Theo's attention. Finally Theo looked up, and sharply.

"Turn me," August said a third time, very slowly. And the way he was staring at Theo from across the room was unnervingly resolute.

Dear God, it's really happening again.

Theo snapped. "Oh, you've fallen!" he hissed. "This darkness has seduced you! I'd hoped it wouldn't. I'd hoped we'd have to turn you over to the Lamb, but no—you're spellbound—"

August was apparently ready to argue this time. He stiffened, he steeled himself. He heard right through Theo's meaningless spite and fired back, "Turn me over to the Lamb, so the Lamb could kill me? Right? Ah, Theo, you saint, you gallant hero—*please!* Where else do vampires come from, hmm? Isn't every one of you 'born into the Undead'?"

Saint. Hero. There they were again, just as they'd come from the coven months ago after August's adventure on the roof, those words shaped like praise but utterly empty of it. They stung Theo, crucified him. He snarled defensively, "I regret ever telling you any bit of truth about us."

"I want meaning to my existence again, Theo!"

"What meaning is there here, in an existence like *this*?"

"I'm tired of just being the sacrifice. I want to be like you! I want to be something more—"

"But August, you won't be mine anymore!"

There it was, the same vicious circles of the same cruel argument, but neither of them had the answers to each other's questions. The demands of the heart were merciless.

Theo was outraged. Stiff and scowling, with fierce glances like murderous intent, he paced around his bedroom. He wandered between chairs and chess boards, his jaw tight and the vampire's anger burning in his veins like molten iron. Clocks ticked away out of sync. The dying fire popped.

Dear God, dear God, what do I say to him?

"It's not happening," Theo hissed, fingers fisting on nothing but air. He struggled to hold on to his equanimity. "Oh, would I be like Faust, is it the same thing, is it just as fantastic?" he mocked in a high voice that was supposed to mimic August's.

August's face pinched in offense, but he held strong. "I'm begging you, Theo! It's my only option. This is me now. This is what I want! There is no other life for me—"

"You don't understand what you ask!"

"Weren't you a sacrifice before you were turned?" August hissed.

Theo fell completely still. The rage drained from his face as the color did, leaving him blank eyed and pallid.

"Aha," August breathed, because he'd found a weak spot.

Theo had told him before, after all, when he explained the history of their sacrifices—Theo, Laurel, and Alphonse were all lambs before they joined the coven.

Yes, Theo too was turned from the human horizon to that of the Undead, so why couldn't August? It made sense of course. It was unfair. August was stubborn. Obviously he felt rejected and ignored. And why should Theo, of all of them, refuse? Who else was there for August to ask? Theo was the one from the very beginning, his sanctum, his friend, his partner—

The Lamb approved of August, anyway. Alistair had showed him the letter. It wasn't as if there were anything to gain from refusing August every time he asked. It was bound to happen. The Lamb endorsed it and it was going to happen, he knew it. But part of him wanted to hold on to how things were as long as he could. That way if they changed—if they changed and fate tragically ripped all this happiness out of him—he would at least have memories to savor.

Theo was at a loss for words. He felt young and lost, powerless. He turned his back to August and sat down heavily before the fire.

As always the argument ended curtly, without resolve and without comfort.

"I want to be one of you," August whispered before he left. He didn't seem any more satisfied or relieved than the last time they'd contended over the idea.

It was the strangest sensation to Theo, to feel his heart break at those words—and yet there didn't seem to be anything sad about the pain.

"HELLO."

August turned around, disgruntled, to see Ishmael standing at the end of the hall.

August tried not to look disgusted. Ishmael stood with his hands clasped behind his back in a plain gray waistcoat, his ashen hair waxed down—villainous, not quite, but venomous certainly.

"Good evening," August replied finally. His mouth was dry, his voice tired from the argument with Theo. "*Master*," he remembered to add.

Ishmael's eyes fixed on him, calculating casually as a little half smile plucked at the corners of his mouth, the mouth that so greedily closed around little wounds on August's throat and the blood therein, his blood, his life, such intimacy....

Reckless, Ishmael seemed—and even more so since Theo and August went to see the Lamb. Ishmael smiled further, as if trying to be friendly. "How is our little lamb doing?" he asked. The kindness was rotten.

August looked over his shoulder quickly, wishing another vampire—or a servant, anyone—was around to be a distraction, but there was no one. He was alone in the hall with Ishmael, and he was not in the mood for it.

"Very well, thank you, sir," August mumbled demurely, watching Ishmael through his lashes. He didn't respect Ishmael. He didn't really fear him anymore either. He just strongly disliked him.

"Well, you've been behaving," Ishmael muttered in disdain. "After that incident with Anastasia, I feared we'd have to send you to the Lamb." He shrugged idly, smiling. "I was afraid for a while that the *special sacrifice*, or so the Lamb called you, was actually defective. That would have been a disappointment. Yes?"

Defective. How insulting. Everything Ishmael said was some snotty, contentious twist of words, and wasn't that exhausting after a while? What had Theo said that one night, that some vampires found amusement in being mysterious?

August tightened his jaw; he cleared his throat. "The Lamb seemed happy to see me not too long ago," he remarked politely enough.

Something in Ishmael's expression twitched at that. He lifted a hand, examining the cuff of his coat to deflect from the crack in his façade. He knew what he was doing. He always did. He sighed curtly, eyes flickering up to meet August's again, cold. He spoke in the same sickeningly convivial manner, but his voice was starting to betray a gentle swell of aggravation. It was a little disconcerting, the way his youthful face could twist with such menace and spite.

"Yes, well, I wonder why the Lamb found you so *special*? There's not much about you that's any more invigorating than the other twenty-eight lambs we've had. You're not particularly handsome. You're not strong or heroic. You're not brave. You're not successful. You're a nosy, sickly little buggerer. You have no personality, you're a complete nuisance at times, and Anastasia can vouch for that, as can Theo. You're torturing him, you know. He hates himself because of you—"

"*Ishmael.*"

Both August and Ishmael turned abruptly. Alistair was at the corner of the hall, out of Ishmael's periphery. With a scornful pinch to his face, he looked Ishmael up and down.

Troublemaker's regret flooded Ishmael's face. August stepped back, bumping the corner of a sideboard. The vase atop it rattled gently.

Alistair frowned at Ishmael. He had a bottle of wine in one hand. His honey-gold hair was disheveled. His brow was low on sharp, inhuman eyes, and August thought about the night of the auction and the way Alistair had looked outside the Dashwood Mausoleum, and—

"'Not special,' you say," Alistair echoed sternly; it was almost a growl, lip curled. "Ishmael, if you can't taste the difference in his pranic energy, I believe I have reason to be concerned. It's not very often we find a sacrifice of such vitality. Are you questioning the Lamb's judgment? Dare I even ask whether you want to speak to our king himself, have him explain his decision making to you?"

Ishmael deferred to the Alpha like a guilty lover. "No, sir," he hissed, clearly humiliated.

Alistair gave a sound near to a chuckle, a scoff. "One might think you were jealous, Ishmael," he grunted. "I still wonder whether this has anything to do with your feud with Theo."

Ishmael was speechless, looking at the Alpha with stark, injured shock. Ishmael and Alistair seemed to exchange thoughts silently, in the curious wordless way vampires did. It was obvious on the air, a tension August could feel but not decipher. It felt private, an argument that belonged behind closed doors. Ishmael bowed his head suddenly, stood there a moment in the silence, and then disappeared around the corner without another remark.

Alistair turned a smile upon August, from up the hall. August stared back in uncertainty.

"Children," Alistair said with a tired dismissive air and a shake of the head.

August was stunned at first, then smiled tentatively, flattered by the Alpha's casual manner, the way he'd shut Ishmael down so effortlessly. *Children.* August laughed a little, fumbling with the sleeves of the smoking jacket. He remembered Theo telling him crudely, "Alistair couldn't have cared less about your wondering." But was Alistair really all that bad? Pearle said they were lucky to have him as their Alpha. Maybe this entire time August had misunderstood him out of trauma and fear. Maybe it had more to do with August wanting to be part of the family. Maybe it was just related to the wine bottle dangling from Alistair's fingers.

"Don't let him make you hate him," Alistair murmured wearily.

It was not the Alpha speaking to the sacrifice; it was not a vampire deigning to a human.

It was just Alistair speaking to August.

And with that he was gone again in the direction Ishmael went.

August had no idea what to think of it.

HAZEL DELIVERED the package to him, a small, light parcel with a neatly written *Happy Christmas* on the paper, even though December was two nights from over.

"Alistair wanted this brought to you," she said flatly, leaving the package at the foot of the bed and sweeping over to light the candles in the corner of the room. August crawled out of his blankets' little pocket of warmth.

"What is it?" he mumbled, looking at the parcel.

"I suppose it's a late gift." Hazel spoke softly, but here was an underlying timbre of weariness there. Maybe she and Laurel had had a disagreement, as he had with Theo.

If that was the case, Hazel hid it well. She stopped and propped her hands on her hips, peering at August from across the attic. The candlelight bounced, a warm glow on her pale face. "Sometimes if sacrifices are well-behaved, Alistair allows them certain privileges." She looked at him sternly, but a girlish grin spread suddenly on her face. "Open it," she urged, tipping her head. "Go on."

August sat quietly, listening to the wind outside the house. Was there an underlying message here, after Alistair found Ishmael taunting him?

The parcel was a little white bundle, packaged in paper and tied together with twine. August stared at it for a moment, distracted—by privileges, and arguments, and well-behaved lambs. Receiving a gift made him a little leery. Briefly it occurred to him the suspicion he felt was because the gift brought with it a sensation of being prepared for something important—but for what exactly?

August tugged at the knotted twine and gingerly unwrapped the parcel. Hazel was just as curious as him, looking over his shoulder.

Neatly folded within the paper, clean and freshly tailored, was a chic slate-blue waistcoat with shining buttons and matching trousers, and a fine linen shirt.

Hazel took a slow breath, admiring the clothing. "This is so fine!" she murmured.

August was flattered but confused. He let Hazel touch the new clothes, pulling them out of the parcel as he went to wash up in the corner. Clothes for him. But still—why?

"The color!" Hazel cooed, holding the waistcoat up by August's face. "It brings out your eyes, oh—wow!"

How nice it was to have clothes of his own. Clean, tailored, not bloodstained. Hazel watched him dress, the smile falling slowly from her face.

"You look handsome," she whispered.

"Are you lying?"

"No."

"What's wrong, then?"

"Nothing, August."

"You look as if you know something I don't."

"I know a lot of things you don't."

Hazel left. August's stomach growled. He raked his fingers through his hair a few more times, hoping he looked acceptable; he straightened his cuffs and the bottom of his waistcoat. He put on Theo's smoking jacket and slipped out of the attic and down the narrow stairs shyly. It felt so nice to be fully dressed again.

The house was quiet as it ever was, fog swirling outside as the lamplight spilled through the halls. He felt like a different person standing below *Bentheim Castle* now, in his new clothes, hands clasped behind his back. He felt empowered.

He drifted down into the vestibule. His footsteps echoed, and for a moment he almost believed he was the only one in the house—but as he turned down the stairs, he stopped short because Theo was on his way up the same flight, overcoat on one arm and cutting right to August's heart with his eyes. Curious and wondering eyes, probing and scanning; August blushed, straightening up a little more.

Theo smiled. He was nothing but a handsome gentleman tonight, his hair tamed for the time being and the usual spark of casual wit in his eyes.

"You look splendid," he said below his breath, though he seemed to be stripping August bare of the splendid clothes with his stare. "Did Witch Hazel tell you?"

"Tell me what?" August asked, brushing past. Theo moved to the side patiently, meeting him at the foot of the stairs.

"Alistair is letting me take you out to supper. I was just coming to get you," he explained.

August cut him a skeptical look. "Why?" he whispered, not wanting to disturb the hush in the house, not wanting anyone to find him and Theo talking together like schemers or paramours, a sigh and a breath separating them. If Alistair was allowing Theo to take him out.... He wasn't sure what it might mean. He wasn't sure he wanted to contemplate it. He was just shy and nervous, as if they were normal men, as if this were a normal courtship, as if the butterflies of flirting were new again.

Theo didn't answer. Maybe he didn't know the truth himself.

HE'D ASKED Alistair personally whether he could take August to dinner and speak with him. He wasn't sure whether he'd tell him the details about turning or not; Theo wasn't quite sure what he'd say at all, just that he wanted one last chance to have August the way he was now in case things changed, and irreparably.

Will be searching for a thirtieth promptly; the future Number Nine has been approved should he turn; keep a close eye on Number Six.

That's what the Lamb's letter had said. They did not trust Theo not to lose himself in the temptation. They didn't trust his instincts not to take advantage of his love.

But the Lamb had also approved of August becoming one of them.

They took a hansom cab to Simpson's-on-the-Strand. August seemed to know this chophouse too. But after months of almost nothing but the attic and the house, the sounds and the smells and the rattle of the cab and the prick of chilly air on his flushed skin were probably overwhelming. Theo jokingly made August go inside the restaurant first, then turn and invite him in after.

The place had gleaming paneled walls, a coffered ceiling, and tall fireplaces ablaze. The mahogany tables were set with fine crystal. Lustrous, the whole place seemed, but attainably so, and August wore a pinched look of self-doubt as if he worried he might forget certain etiquette or order wrongly. But the whole place had a comfortable atmosphere—men gathered about the mantles smoking cigars and playing chess, parties of bachelors perfectly unperturbed—and August finally seemed to relax after a while, sitting across from Theo in a corner of the dining room with his overcoat on the back of his chair.

Theo could see the questions written across August's soft, darkly curious face: Why? What did it all mean?

"Transubstantiation," August murmured, pointing to Theo's glass of wine. He was learning. He was testing himself.

Theo smiled dryly, voice low as he met August's eyes across the table. "Wine stays down when nothing else does. Thank God for the 'blood of Christ,' I suppose."

The smell of food and spirits filled the little restaurant, and the air was hot from all the fires. Somewhere in a far corner, musicians played a tranquil melody to accompany the dinner. The quiet waiters drifted to and fro; the place was full of the delicate dissonance of dishes and cutlery, the hum of voices and laughter and the conversations of the privileged and leisured, cigar smoke, soft music.

Reluctantly, Theo tried to get something down for sake of appearance. Nothing was worth tasting that was not wine or blood. Gritty meats, chalky soup. Even a few bites left an awful dry and sour feeling in his mouth. His palate had changed with the rest of him so long ago; his body just did not need this type of sustenance anymore. Maybe it would be better not to pick too much at the meal lest it be too gory when his body inevitably rejected it, dragging it back up his throat bloody and chewed but in the end utterly undigested.

August watched Theo as if words burned impatiently on his tongue. Finally he just spoke.

"Who turned you, Theo?" he prompted, low, although he didn't truly have to whisper for privacy in the loud dining room.

Theo felt his gaze sharpen, skeptical and vexed. A tense silence swallowed their table. All the other noise of the dining room faded away like a ringing in the ears.

Theo frowned, face pinching—he felt a little queasy, a little startled, but mostly frustrated. He threw his napkin down and folded his fingers against his mouth, squinting across the table at August.

"I absolutely hate that you're so obsessed with this idea of being turned," he mumbled glumly. Part of him still sort of meant it, but the words held no sway now. Perhaps they never had.

"I don't see what's so horrible about it," August parried below his breath.

"You're naïve." Theo said it as if it justified everything.

"I'm not!"

Theo opened his mouth to reply, but the waiter wheeled over a side of beef, interrupting them. The waiter paused as he had at first, glancing coyly at Theo with a mixture of curiosity and confusion in his eyes, an inquisitive familiarity, as if he suspected he recognized Theo as someone. Theo smiled at him as politely as he could. It was that preternatural intensity, the vampire's natural charm. Tonight, like some nights, Theo was very self-conscious about it.

The waiter carved them some meat and left them to their tense silence, surrounded by the smell of hot food. Theo leaned back and peered at August quietly. August couldn't eat with Theo staring.

August heaved a sigh. He said once more, "I want to mean something again." He cut his eyes up to meet Theo's and another hush settled between them for a long moment.

Did Theo look sick to August, even in the soft light of the restaurant? Pale, vampire pale, and a little hollow? But for the most part still handsome, Theo hoped. He was vain, but not so vain he'd lie to himself.

Theo gulped some wine. If only it had the same effect on him as it had had once before, he could be a regular drunk.

Any chance glance sent in the direction of their table made August stiffen—Theo glimpsed it each time—horrified somebody might be able to see past Theo's gentleman's pretense. But it was an absurd and inconclusive fear, something childish and frantic, and in Simpson's they hardly stood out at all.

"Ishmael," Theo said after the long silence. He looked up at August, brows gathered together dismally.

"What?" August breathed, astonished. But he knew what Theo was talking about.

"Ishmael turned me." Theo took more wine but left his meat untouched. His heart was pounding. Why did he feel as if he'd betrayed August somehow?

"Ishmael!" August snorted. Theo tensed; he caught the sharp little pang of jealousy that shot out of August, a jump of the heart, a rise in body temperature, a tightening of the frown. Fury, possessiveness, injustice. Ah, it only made the vampire's sensitivity more ruthless to know a man's blood so intimately. And what black magic it was.

"You didn't know him before," Theo insisted flatly, glancing around the dining room. Nobody cared about their conversation. He tried to maintain the sadness that left him feeling bruised and guilty; he didn't want it to bother August.

It was just that he'd come to terms with all of this. After talking with Ishmael, after talking with Alistair, after seeing the fire in

August's eyes when he spoke of becoming part of the coven—Theo had come to terms with it.

"You didn't know him before," Theo said again. "When I was the sacrifice, Ishmael was different. People change, immortal or not. It's the way of life. You adapt to your surroundings, you change to survive."

People change. Yes, because much as so many of them tried to insist otherwise, immortality did not immediately negate humanity. Vampires had once been people; where, really, was the line drawn between myth and man?

"Did he turn you against your will?" August snapped. "Is that why you don't like me asking—?"

"No." Theo smiled faintly, amused by August's vigilance. Hopefully he looked more like his handsome, classy self now, nonetheless gaunt and wearied. "I was the eighth lamb for the London coven. I was eighteen when they took me, and at that time it was just Alistair, Pearle, Owen, Ishmael, and Anastasia. I still don't quite know why, but Ishmael took an immediate liking to me. Ishmael used to be... how else can I put it but 'young' and 'carefree'? Yes, Ishmael used to be young and carefree, and for nine years he was my teacher, my friend, my exemplar. He wasn't afraid to break any of the rules because he was Alistair's little chum. Obviously still is. *That* hasn't changed.

"But Ishmael has always been tormented by this inner strife, this internal struggle between shame and indulgence, something I don't really understand. I never have, but maybe it has something to do with God and sin. When I asked to be turned the first time, he was viciously offended because he knew I'd asked out of greed, not love. I just wanted to live forever. I admit that. When I asked to be turned the second time, he was abruptly emotional, tearful even, and wept to me that he'd been afraid after the first time that I'd never ask again—"

Theo broke off, staring at the food he left untouched. Thought consumed him, left him blind to the world around him and content with such. Theo took a breath to realign himself with reality again before speaking. He shrugged limply. He smiled.

"That was in 1831," he divulged.

August seemed stricken.

He sat back in the chair and stared at his hands, overcome by the images that sprang to mind at Theo's words. Theo caught some of them.

August imagined him, wild hair and catlike eyes, as a human, as a child, as an adolescent, as a prisoner of the same vampires he was a prisoner of now. *Greed, not love.* Ishmael *young* and *carefree*, Ishmael and Theo together, sacrifice and vampire, pupil and mentor. Ishmael crying as he turned Theo. All the possibilities of what might have gone on between them in nine years, and nine years Theo had been with them before he was turned, nine years, which would have made him twenty-seven when he finally asked to turn, and all of this fifty-odd years ago.

Yes, that was so.

August looked fraught with questions suddenly. Theo could feel them—the shapes of them, really. Like light flashing off a mirror. What was the coven like then, in 1831? What were the vampires like? The world? Theo as a lamb, Theo's family, had he missed them, had he been lonely, had they looked for him?

Cold with all the revelations, it seemed, August turned to his food. He ate a little. Theo waited for him to ask any of those questions.

He didn't. Instead he murmured, "I wish you would tell me more one day."

Theo relaxed, realizing bashfully that he'd been waiting for August to decide for him whether or not he was going on. "One day," he complied, looking at August from across the table forlornly. "I don't like to remember it," he explained, voice low and scratchy. And it was the truth. He didn't like remembering his relationship with Ishmael. There was no sense in dwelling in the past.

There was no sense in it, and so he could not hold August's wishes over his head any longer. It was wrong of him.

The waiter came by to remove their dishes, allowing only a little surprise on his face at the uneaten food before Theo.

Theo drank his wine. Raucous laughter burst across the dining room from around the fire, where a group of gentlemen still puffed on their pipes and cigars.

"I'm not you," August said slowly, taking a sip of his own drink. He looked sinfully satisfied by Theo's gaze as it fell on him again, familiar heat of an inhuman stare.

Theo grunted in response. It might have been defiant. He tossed back more wine and refilled his port glass from the bottle on the table.

August looked up at him, trying to appear stern, but Theo could see the imploring despair creasing his brow. Theo didn't move. He didn't speak. He stared back at August from across the table. He felt hollowed out by the words. *I'm not you.* He knew exactly where this was going. And he had no right to deny it.

"I know why you refuse me," August said quietly. "You say you wanted to be turned because you were greedy, because you wanted to live forever—but you're not greedy, Theo. You're not selfish. You know that as well as I do. And that's why you refuse to turn me. But I'm the sacrifice now! The Lamb told me I was marked so that, should it come to such, I could join the ranks of your coven. You have to accept that. You have to trust that I can handle it."

He paused, breath wavering on his lips, grimacing as Theo's eyes burned into him.

"Theo, my life *before* is over. You... your kind ripped me from a warmth and comfort I never knew—no, no, I love you all, I do, I really do—and honestly, Theo, honestly, I just want to be like you. I admire you. I'm befuddled by you. I'm terrified of you. I'm fascinated by you. I want to be what you are. Life—death—whatever world lies between—it's not worth it anymore, and I want to be like you!"

August caught his breath, resolute.

And ah, God, Theo fell in love with him all over again.

Those straight shoulders, that elegant resolve, those deep eyes— so full of compassion, of courage, of curiosity and zeal.

He saw himself in August. No place amongst the living, but far from dead. And Theo was still terrified August would leave him once it was over, once he joined the coven. He was afraid of the same gap opening between them that had opened between him and Ishmael. He was afraid one of them would change, that August would find other things to occupy his time once he'd never run out of it, that he wouldn't *need* Theo the way he needed him now.

But what happens to me once you're gone?

He'd meant when August died; it had been a selfish plea for pity. But it meant more now. What happened when August didn't need Theo the way he needed him now? Even after all the cruel, misleading things Theo had said trying to dissuade August, to protect him from—from what? From the choices of his own soul?

At that moment in the dining room, sitting across from August, Theo could never know whether those fears would be realized. Maybe they would. Maybe they would not.

And that aching hope felt very human to him.

Human.

Theo smiled faintly.

August relaxed, returning the little smile.

It was the least he could do to comfort Theo as their hansom cab waited at the slushy curb with a tender hand on his shoulder and a grimace on his face, while Theo hunched over in an alley and vomited the tiny bit of food he'd eaten at Simpson's, his Undead body finally rejecting it. At least he'd kept it down long enough to get out of the restaurant.

"WELL, THE little bird was freed from its cage, was it?" Pearle said softly, and if he had been anyone else, it might have been derisive. August jumped, having not seen him come into the hall. Pearle smiled at him cordially from the corner near the stairs, a newspaper tucked under his arm.

August blushed, returning the smile. He was still in his new clothes. Overcoats replaced in the closet, Theo had gone to speak to Alistair. August could have been imagining it, but there was what looked like a hint of sorrow in Theo's clear green eyes. It made August fearful—but of what, he didn't know, and just as quickly the fear had withered away when Theo pressed an offhanded kiss to his temple. They parted ways in the vestibule.

"I've been out once before," August explained to Pearle. But the words were unnecessary; they were all quite aware of his visit to the Lamb. And apart from that, there was some other meaning to Pearle's words. Some omen, some significance. August didn't know what it was.

Pearle's eyes scanned him. "Yes...," he murmured, crossing the hall with a little crackle of the newspaper in the crook of his arm. He smiled down at August, crow's feet and scars at the corners of his eyes. In that faint velvety accent of his, he said, "That's true, isn't it? You look suave, by the by. A regular bachelor, our handsome lamb is."

August smiled coyly, glancing away. He saw the date on the newspaper in Pearle's arm: Tuesday, December thirty-first. So it was Old Year's Night.

There was a sudden heat on him, the imposing heat of angry eyes. It raised the hair on the back of his neck. August dreaded looking; he was too tired and contented by his date with Theo to play these games. Pearle disappeared into his bedroom and August turned, meeting the gaze of Ishmael. Of course.

"Good evening," Ishmael said, hair neatly combed above his ears and head tipped gently to the side.

"Hello," August replied. He hardly got the word out before Ishmael spoke again, curt and even. But there was no fallacy in his voice tonight. In fact he sounded as if he were trying to make honest conversation but had no idea where to begin.

"I'm sorry there's no celebration to bring in the New Year," he said slowly. "You'll learn that *time* can be very elusive. We lose track of it...."

"It's fine." August shook his head. He shrugged. He looked to the attic stairs; he looked back to Ishmael. He said with a boldness that didn't necessarily feel newfound so much as it felt remembered, "I know you turned Theo."

The most amazing thing happened then—Ishmael's face went entirely blank. No snide contempt, no wicked mischief, no malice or menace. For a moment he looked vulnerable and defenseless, and it matched his youthful stature. But then a guarded shadow fell over him, and it was a little petulant.

"You know nothing," he fired back. Maybe it was meant to be threatening, but it just sounded wounded and defensive. "You know nothing—what did he tell you? Hmm? What was it? What fanciful tale did our quaint little romantic spin?"

"You try so hard to scare me," August whispered. "But you just make me sad sometimes."

There was a hush in the hall between them, embittered and pivotal. They were at a stalemate of sorts, and August didn't fully understand it. Eventually Ishmael broke his eyes away and turned, drifting downstairs.

He left, and August hurried up into the attic room again.

ALISTAIR PUT the Lamb's letter to the fire once the decision was made, as was protocol for the safekeeping of the underworld's secret laws and operations.

He stood with a creak of his desk chair, smoothing down his damasked waistcoat, tucking golden-blond hair behind his ears. In his office he said to Theo, "You believe it's time, then?"

Theo nodded, arms crossed. He didn't want to look Alistair in the eye; he wanted to stay in the shadows of the office forever. But part of him was very excited.

"Definitely," he whispered.

Alistair nodded again. "Then our coven will welcome a new brother tomorrow night."

CHAPTER TWENTY

WHAT WAS being born into the Undead?

Was it some sort of spiritual alchemy, or something purely physiological, some ancient witchcraft?

It happened so suddenly August did not expect it, and ritualistic as it was, it did not change his mind.

Theo came to the attic as August undressed, fine slate-blue waistcoat folded at the foot of his bed.

He looked up, exhausted but happy as he moved into a smile—but the expression was interrupted by the look in Theo's eyes. Nameless, dark, and profound. August's heart fell.

He drew a breath to speak, worried Theo was bothered by their conversation at Simpson's, wondering quickly in the back of his mind what to do or say to mollify it. But before August could even open his mouth Theo offered a smile, suddenly looking perfectly human and soft. Kindhearted Theo, his hero, his master, his friend. There was a weight on the quiet. It breathed down the back of August's neck.

Theo said, "The Lamb sent word roughly a fortnight ago that, should the moment come, you were to be turned."

August's heart jumped. He wanted to say "I know." He didn't. His stomach knotted. Cold—he felt cold but not afraid. He'd seen the letter, yes. He hadn't read the whole thing but he'd seen enough. For a moment August gawked dumbly at Theo, torn between confessing as much and keeping it to himself—for Theo's sake, the latter seemed best. Maybe Theo had already tasted as much in his blood, anyway. Yes, he felt cold, but not out of fear. It couldn't be this easy, could it? Not after all of Theo's opposition. And why didn't Alistair bring him this news?

Theo smiled faintly, a pathetic shadow of his usual dancing expression. "You look shocked."

"No, I just...." August shook his head. The words were lost to him.

"You're frightened."

"No—well, yes, I don't know what's going to happen, but—"

"You want it. I know you do. We all know you do." Theo's smile was still there, but his eyes were clouded. It alarmed August more than the announcement did, this ominous chill on the air. "We've tasted it in your blood, after all," Theo confirmed, brow knotting; he spoke low and deliberately, carefully pronouncing each word smoothly and whisper soft. Was this really the same man who so easily relapsed to monstrous?

Theo continued, "The Lamb sent word in the beginning that, even should you never ask, even should you refuse, we are to make you one of us. He never specified why, but he wants you to be one of us, August. He approves of it, most importantly."

August's eyes widened. He dropped his braces to the bed and a chill rattled through him. His breath quickened, nervously. *Should you refuse....* How jarring to think his own fate was so outside his control. Had he been daft to ever trust them in the first place? No. He believed in them. The world of mortal men and spiritual ignorance held no draw for him now. *He wants you to be one of us.* He felt betrayed suddenly, offended Theo had ever denied him if that was the truth. Unless Theo hadn't known.... And yet he also felt strangely comforted by this information.

As if on cue, the crystal knob of the attic door turned and the hinges creaked. Hazel slipped into the room, eyes on her hands and what she carried, face pale and lace cap perfectly straight. Theo retreated to the corner near the southern window, standing by the candles and staring out into the night with his hands clasped behind his back.

A lamb prepared for slaughter, ha!

This was a ceremony. There were no more words suddenly, just rite and silence. August didn't need further explanation. He knew what was happening.

They were going to turn him—*now*. Tonight.

And maybe Theo had known all night; maybe Theo had known for longer than that, that this was the night they would welcome him into their world. August looked to Theo, breath catching in his throat. Theo did not look back.

Hazel sponged him with the warm water she'd brought, using the soap he liked. She combed through his hair. She did all these things with bleak eyes and absolute solemnity, like preparing a loved one for burial. August waited to meet her eyes, glassy as they were with a layer of tears ready to shatter down her cheeks, but she refused. Her hands shook.

Desperately he reached out and pulled Hazel close, feeling her body press against his. He clutched onto her, face buried in her shoulder. She smelled like tea and beeswax. She was stiff and compliant at the same time. Did she feel abandoned by him? Forsaken? Discarded? Did she loathe him for leaving her in the human realm when she wanted to be one of them too?

Hazel drew a breath; her chest swelled against August's. She leaned back and gave him a long look, lashes lowered on her glassy eyes. She didn't try to smile. August appreciated that more than false happiness.

Theo oversaw them with an air of reluctant authority. Did he hate this? Was he still against it, this admission of August into their ranks, this unnatural graduation from human to vampire? No. Theo gathered him close, clasped his face in his hands, kissed his forehead, his nose, his mouth. August felt cold and stiff with wide-eyed instinct.

They left Hazel in the attic, her back turned on them.

Theo led him down through the house toward the Sanctuary. With each step they took, Theo seemed more and more torn between ritual and emotion, and by the time they passed *Bentheim Castle*, he broke. He looked to August with excited eyes, his pale face quite alive with enthusiasm. It was not at all what August expected; he'd been waiting for more of that strained regret, the volatility that had met all of his talk of turning before. But Theo was clearly over his initial fear.

"You see, Theo?" August whispered, all worked up with the most beautiful, hopeful terror. "Be happy. I'm going to live forever."

"You speak as if *I'm* the one who needs *you*," Theo whispered back.

August's heart thundered. It felt as though they approached an execution.

In the Sanctuary, sprawled as casually as ever amongst the stately old furnishings of velvet and leather and silk, submerged in the dusty, daunting feel of the room, the vampires waited. Little flames danced and shivered from thick red candles. *Ritual.* The excitement fled, leaving nothing but the chilling aspect of it all, the dreadful, ghastly truth of the matter.

They were going to turn him into one of them.

How did it happen? How did it work? Would it hurt? Would he even feel it? What if he didn't want it, but it was too late? No, it was already too late. It was too late the evening the creatures snatched him from Lucius's side; it was too late when Alistair bought him, when the Lamb marked him and took a curious liking to him. No, August would rather be dead than live any other way—

They stared at him in the eerie hush—from the Alpha to Alphonse, eight pairs of inhuman eyes piercing, prying, luring. Somebody touched his arm and August jumped. But it was just Theo, pulling him gently into the middle of the Sanctuary, into the middle of the circle in which the vampires had gathered. A little haphazard but a circle all the same, standing nearby or seated on the old furniture, watching.

On the fur rug, Theo embraced him. An overwhelming sense of peace washed through August—comfort, warmth, numbness—a very familiar feeling. They knew he was beginning to panic, all the old fear resurfacing. But they placated him with their powerful eyes, blanketed his emotions and qualms with a layer of preternaturally imbued *peace*. God but he both hated and loved that they could do that.

Slowly Theo peeled the shirt off August's shoulders, leaving him half-naked and confused. It was sensual, in a brisk and startling way. In a *vampire* way, August thought. His skin crawled. He curled his toes in the rug.

How many of them had been turned in this same place, this same orgiastic fashion? How meaningful and ancient, how disturbingly sacred, this room and all it stood for. Was it really Theo who would do it? How did it happen?

Alistair took hold of August's wrist and pried his hand away from Theo. There was a little fear then, a shiver of it down August's spine, but it was an old fear, a fickle fear he'd learned to ignore in the face of faith and fascination.

One by one, excepting Theo, they drank from his wrist in the same familiar order.

They swallowed loudly. August forgot about being cold. He forgot about being confused. He bit back startled moans and grunts at the jagged pain, the way the ache throbbed and burned and itched inside his veins as he felt their lips and their tongues, pulling the blood out of him. They took much more than they ever had in the feeding hour, and August was lightheaded and sick to his stomach already. His arm went numb as he held it out stiff and their sharp little fangs broke into his bloody wrist like into the skin of an apple and oh *fuck*, what if it was all a lie, what if they were going to kill him, what if he'd fallen for some sort of trick—

The room spun.

The first seven had taken their fill. Alistair, Owen, Pearle, Ishmael, Anastasia, Laurel, Alphonse. And then there was Theo, blessed Theo, and August welcomed him with desperate open arms, burying into his neck as the room tipped and swayed. But it didn't really; he was dizzy and breathless, and the shadows danced around the Sanctuary, little flames popping on old, old wicks. Theo's hold was protective. There was a primal fear in him, but oh, August wanted this. He wanted it.

There was a moment of shuddering tension—hope, dread, hesitation. August's fingernails scraped the fine silk of Theo's waistcoat. Without a doubt it was the singular moment that the forsaking of a human life was firmly and vitally decided, and August closed his eyes tight and said good-bye deep, very deep down in his soul, silent farewells to everything he'd once known: humanity, morality, salvation, freedom, *sunlight*.

The moment rolled onward, unfolding—and then the floor creaked as Theo shifted forward, which was loud in the brutal silence, and Theo's extended fang teeth cut through the sore, livid skin at the nape of August's neck. They penetrated through and hit an abused artery, tapping into the blood flow.

The pain was excruciating for a hissing breath or two. August stiffened. His heart leapt and then plummeted. He groaned, voice rattling out of him frantic and horrified.

Theo pulled away and the sensation of his fangs leaving August's throat was *awful*. He licked his lips and whispered against August's ear, "Remember one thing, and one thing only: when you taste blood, you *drink*."

"*Yes*," August moaned. The moment was supposed to be intimate, but it was not private; seven others watched. August hated it. He was helpless to it. But he was going to change, he was going to be one of them, and that was all he wanted, nothing else about the world pulled at his soul like this—

Upstairs in Theo's room, myriad little clocks struck the midnight hour.

Theo latched onto August's neck. His tongue moved, and then the real drinking began, harsh and strong. It pulled all the pleasure and all the pain into one perplexing swell, and there—the cusp of the connection between them—the powerful hum of their souls finding the same tune in the transfer of blood sang through him. It buzzed into every fiber of his being and warmed him up from the inside out. The feel of Theo drinking made his hips twitch, so lecherous and animalistic in ghastly concurrence.

It was the same, really, the passion and the commingling of hearts that seemed to beat at the same pace then, the sacrifice feeding the vampire, life force passing over to be transmuted within an Undead core. It was the same at first, the pull of blood and the cresting spiritual bond, August victim to the spell and the chill and the way Theo moved against him as he swallowed, but then with one innocent current of delight shuddering through him, the whole thing took a quick turn for the terrible.

August felt death the moment it sparked at the tips of his toes.

That was what it was; he had no doubt about it. Instinctively he knew. He could feel it. It impinged on the black magic of the vampire's feast.

Death.

Something deep inside him felt violated. The ties of his soul to his body were fraying and death crept upward into him, flowered up from his toes to his ankles to his knees. It was a curious prickling sensation, something almost like the way it felt when a limb fell numb. It snaked up his spine and branched out into every weakening nerve and cell. It tingled all over, crawled beneath his skin like something—ironically—alive.

Death.

Strange how one never really realized how very close and familiar death was until it was sinking into one's very bones.

August gasped for a breath, curled up on the floor of the Sanctuary. When had he fallen down? He was groggy; he was delirious. He felt on the verge of sleep. He could hear the pulse of his heart, an echo in his ears slowing down tranquil and untroubled. He felt weak—so weak—so deliciously fatigued and ready to close his eyes and drift off for the night.

The stench of blood bloomed up thicker than usual in the Sanctuary. August's lashes fluttered shut. Hazel would take care of it.

Hazel would bandage him up. Hazel would sponge him and light the candles and bring him food—

Something wet touched his mouth. Ah, it was sweet and heady like wine. And his mouth was so dry.

Drink, Theo had said. *Drink.*

August was too tired. He didn't want to drink. He'd drink when he awoke. He couldn't move, anyway. He couldn't even open his eyes. He could hardly breathe. He felt numb. No, he felt like a doll made of sticks and every breath threatened to snap him to pieces. His ears were ringing, ringing, ringing—

"Drink, for Christ's sake, August, drink!"

It was like being half-asleep and half-dreaming, so very aware of everything but unable to do a thing. August took a moment to summon all the conscious strength left in him and opened his mouth as wide as he could. The wine felt good on his lips, cold, wet. Woke him up a little. Something quivered in his chest, something like a hunger pang. The silence rang in his ears, sharp and grating. He tried to open his mouth farther, and the wine trickled in between his teeth and down his throat. Some of it ran down his chin. It was lukewarm and pungent. He was *thirsty*—

He drank. He swallowed. It hit that pang in his chest and bloomed out hot and comforting and he moaned.

With a sudden burst of control over his dying limbs, August reached out blindly and felt Theo kneeling before him. He clung to the wine, drinking, drinking. He opened his eyes. His vision cleared.

Blood.

It was not wine; it was *blood*, and it was Theo's blood, and August was choking on it like a man who'd finally found water in the desert. It was smeared across his face. It dripped down his chin, down his chest.

And he wanted *more*.

August cleaved to Theo, wound his arms and legs around him, clung tight and closed his mouth around the open wound in Theo's wrist. Almost immediately the strength returned to him, washing through in waves, starting somewhere in his bones and spreading out through him like a shiver. Ah, it was ecstasy; it was erotic; it was purifying and carnal.

From somewhere overhead in the dark reverie came Theo's voice, Theo, his Theo: "I saw it, August. I saw your soul. It looked like the wave of heat above a flame, hanging over your body. It looked like a mirage. Drink, August. Christ, drink, and you'll be one of us—"

August wanted to vomit but he wanted to drink too. The concept repulsed him. *Blood.* He was gulping blood. But the taste and the consistency, ah, thick, sweet blood, heady in his throat, pulsing down through him with each beat of his heart. What was that slurping, suckling, gnawing—were those sounds coming from him?

The blood brought the whole feverish world back into focus and yet it confused him in a different way. Suddenly August understood what it meant to taste something in the blood. He could taste death and life. His death, Theo's strange Undead life. It was hot and holy as it rolled through his body—sweet, sparking on his tongue, refreshing but also heavy. He felt sick with it. He felt sick without it. His heart kicked in his chest and he thought, oh God, had it not been beating before?

There was a cosmic continuity there, here, all around him, the luscious warmth of the soul, the feeling he was worth something and part of something much bigger. There was something more here. He was part of its ethereal fabric. Except no, there was only this, and for one single second they were all connected. And then it was just blood, thick, crimson velvet on his tongue. He felt the power, the transfer of energy, the purity and the volatility and the fact that this was true, this was real, this was changing his very core, awakening and capturing and tethering back his soul—

For one brutally lucid moment, August saw himself as Theo saw him. No, he tasted it in Theo's blood, like the vision Alistair had given him of the Lamb on the dance floor, as the vampires had ever tasted anything about him in his sacrifice.

He saw himself, with the dark-red stain of blood across his mouth. He saw himself, blond man with wide, feral brown eyes and dark, light-deprived skin around them. He saw how beautiful he was to a vampire, and he saw how ill he was as a human. This was it, then. He was one of them, ushered back from the brink of natural death and handed across the horizon to the world of the Undead.

And then all that wonderful understanding was lost in the chaos of *really* being born into their ranks.

Theo jerked his hand away. August held tightly to it, gnashing his teeth as he tried to get his mouth around the bloody fount again. He could feel the blood caking on his face. He found Theo's wrist again and swallowed the moment blood touched the roof of his mouth.

There were murmurs from the others around him—chilling whispers that reminded him the rest of the coven was still present and holding audience to his agony, his induction, his renaissance.

Something shifted in him. August felt the full brunt of it all. He was not their lamb anymore.

He was their young one.

He was their Omega.

He was one of their coven, one of their kin. There was a shuddering, irreverent *delight* in this, and there was nothing guilty about it.

Theo called out, struggling. August didn't know what he said. Sound itself rang in his ears; he couldn't hear anything at all. His teeth hit something hard. Bone, maybe. Theo pulled away from his hungry mouth so hard it lifted him off the floor. August groaned, he whined, and then someone grabbed him around the waist and yanked him from Theo. He let go of Theo's arm and hit the floor hard again, trembling as natural and supernatural collided within him.

Dazed, he looked around at the others. His captors, his masters, his brethren, his coven. Alistair, eyes wide with depraved satisfaction; Ishmael beside him, looking loath to watch; Owen with his arms crossed, standing in the dance of flame from one of the crimson candles, his eyes glinting in all the shadows of his bearded face; Pearle with his arm around Alphonse and Alphonse looking just short of horror-struck; Anastasia in the far corner, Laurel just a bit closer, both appraising passively; and Theo, oh, Theo, standing with his back to the fire, staring at August, eyes shot through with shards of cold shock. His mouth was red and his cheeks were flushed, and it was obvious he was a little intoxicated from the profuse blood he'd been allowed tonight. He gawked at August as if at something he'd never seen before—and then a keen smile suddenly animated his face, as if to say *Success!*

The ritual was far from over.

A sick shiver rattled up August's spine and became a wet cough, and then a choke, and finally a retch. Unaware suddenly of everything around him, dazed and feverish, August lurched to the side and promptly vomited all the human contents of his stomach. Superfluous, unneeded blood splattered with bile and undigested food on the rug.

August heaved, gagged, growled. His body spasmed hard but there was nothing left to regurgitate.

August didn't like this. He felt so sick. He crawled for Theo, desperate and scared. What were these new sounds, the ragged groans and the wet choking? *Theo.* He wanted Theo to hold him, stroke his sweaty hair, pet his twitching back. The change had full control over him now. He couldn't crawl anymore. He fell to the floor on his side and Theo stood only a few feet away, watching. The others, where were the others now? They were simple shadows against the walls, in the corners of the sanctuary. Gargoyles, dark phantom masses in his peripheral vision, waiting and watching, whispering.

"How long will it take now?"

"Yes, what the Lamb wants…."

"Poor soul—"

"Well, if he was to die, he would have died by now."

"Are you sure?"

"Christ, it's been years since we've seen a show like this!"

On the floor pain burst in all August's nerves. He cried out. He writhed. His muscles twitched. His back arched, curled, and arched again; his toes and fingers wriggled and jerked. He squirmed between the fetal position and attempts at moving, searching for relief but finding nothing but more agony. He groaned and his voice cracked. His insides were knotting, atrophying, dying beneath his skin. He cried and the tears mixed with blood and snot and spit.

He threw himself to and fro, fingers clawing at the fur rug. His fingernails scraped the floorboards where he reached out. Pain, so much *pain* in every fiber of his being, unfathomable pain, pain as he'd never felt before, pulsing behind his eyes, in his ears, in his head. He begged for something—but what? He just knew that he spoke, voice vibrating in his chest, scratching his throat, but he didn't know what he said. Maybe he was screaming. But everything around him was muffled, like the world from underwater. He could not form a coherent thought. Where was he? Why was he alone? When would this end?

August hit his head against the floor. He curled in on himself and wept harder, dry hitching sobs, choking on his breath and shreds of words.

There was a stench in the room, the rancid rot of old blood and death. An awful chill penetrated to his marrow. God, but was there even a word for pain like this? *Suffering*. This was what hell would feel like: unmitigated *suffering*.

The vampire blood suffused through his faculties quickly. His whole body was reconstructing itself from the inside out. The hunger implanted itself in his being, an irrevocable change. The vampire blood rewrote everything inside him, everything primal and innate, changing his entire being. Refining his core, anchoring his soul, converting his entire *living* system to that of the Undead. Human muscles hardened. Human functions receded. Tissue and sinew were transformed. Supernatural gifts burst in the seams of his brain. Screaming human cells turned to vampire cells; overwhelmed human senses turned to vampire senses.

August's humanity withered and died.

"*Ma—*" he howled a few times through clenched teeth. He wound his arms tightly around himself. He shrieked, "*Mamma!* Mamma! Mamma—"

"August...." Theo beckoned from somewhere in the pain.

"Mamma, where are you? *Where are you?*" The words poured out and August didn't know why. His mother and father were not there. They wouldn't be. He wouldn't see them again. Why did he call for them?

"August," Theo said again, more deliberately.

August let out a wretched scream, low and from deep within, one final cry for help before he fell flat to the floor again. The strength left him in one gust of breath. The pain faded like urine from strained insides in the cold, in the morning. Where it went he didn't know.

But he fell still.

The tears dried on his face with the snot and the blood, and August could do nothing but breathe. He felt so many eyes on him, felt them like hands touching him, but his own eyes were heavy. He wanted to sleep, with a feverish urgency.

He felt bruised and tender all over. His insides pinched and ached. Hands truly touched him now, gentle pressure scooping at his limbs and back. They were lifting him off the floor. August closed his eyes, moaning. Moving hurt him deep inside. His head rolled back, limp.

Finally, finally, with a swift blanket of numbness, unconsciousness fell.

CHAPTER TWENTY-ONE

AUGUST WAS in the forest again.

He didn't know what forest, but he was deep in it, turning circles in the filtered light. Pine needles were a cool green carpet underfoot between his naked toes, fresh on his bare skin like mint on the tongue. The breeze combed its fingers through his hair and swirled whisper-soft kisses on his face, threaded through his fingers as he held his hands out like a child and turned round and round.

August stepped carefully over fairy circles, aware somewhere in the back of his mind he was making wish after wish, but he couldn't hold on to them long enough to know what it was he wished for. There was an echo on the wind, a humming voice, a singing voice, a low and bubbling hymn that swam through the clearing and tickled his ears. It made his hair stand on end, his heart pound, his blood rush.

Someone approached outside the clearing. August didn't know who it was. With the easy subtlety of dreams, the scene changed.

Thunder growled somewhere above the trees. A shadow fell, swallowing up all the green and leaving nothing but fog, creeping misty tendrils. August looked around. It sent fog rippling away from his elbows and knees. The carpet of pine needles and grass turned to the cold hard-packed dirt of a land too bitter for crops. August searched for the line of trees, for the place where he saw the shadow, but it was all gone. Thunder clapped and August realized with a flinch of surprise that he stood in the middle of a funeral.

August watched as the grieving strangers passed him, rendered speechless and disoriented. The people moved with sluggish purpose, some watching their feet and some looking up into the thundering sky, but all of them singing, singing. They ran into him, jostled him. The people were shadows. He could make out their presence and numinous outlines, but the fog was still too deep; they stumbled along.

And then there was the casket.

The shadow people laid the flower-covered casket at his feet like a sacrifice to a god. The wails of the funeral procession echoed. There were no lyrics, just ghostly hums of voices, stretched-out whispers tickling his ears and running down his spine like a cold sweat. The casket overflowed with hawthorn and wild roses, rosary beads fixed among the blossoms, the velvet, the moldering lace. August's breath tasted like the fog, like death and rain. He knew—he always knew—exactly what hid beneath the ornamentations, and when the lid of the casket began to move and the doleful singing wavered on the air above the scratching of nails and the grind of wood upon wood, August's ears began to ring and he watched in horror as the corpse began to rise from the casket—

The dream didn't end.

The coffin's cover hit the earth with a shallow *thud*, kicking up pebbles and dirt. The sorrowful wails of the funeral procession shifted, becoming something altogether more fierce and ghastly, sounds of hysteria and agony clinging to a melody. The sound grated on August's ears. His eyes widened.

Perfectly visible, lying in the satin and piles of flowers, was a young man. For one flickering, cold second, it was himself—and then it was someone else, and August did not recognize him with his eyes, but something deep inside of him gave a sickening lurch. Chestnut locks, skin the same soft texture and milky hue of the pale lilies around him.

The strange, unknown men and women howled with their song of death and mourning. Black clothes, black earth, fog. The young man seemed familiar, but why? His identity was on the tip of August's tongue. He was in dated but resplendent fashion, a foreign fashion, hands folded peacefully on his chest. Sparkling in the half-saturated light of the nightmarish scene was a delicate little chain around his neck, its fragile silver cross lay on the boy's knuckles. It was a strange cross. It wasn't a crucifix. It was Eastern—

The Lamb.

The Lamb's eyes opened, and August couldn't move.

Slowly, slowly the Lamb smiled, revealing tiny white fangs terrifying in juxtaposition with his normal teeth. The coffin creaked. A gust of bleak wind rattled through them all. The Lamb began to climb up out of the coffin.

August wanted to scream. Maybe he was already. His heart thundered. His knees shook. He was cold with alarm. If he was making any sound at all, the men and women around him drowned him out.

The Lamb smiled at him with wide, tender eyes, and then he took a step forward and was somebody new. As translucent and erratic as a mirage, just another part of the phantom world of August's sleeping mind.

Dream or not August was crippled with fear. Standing before him now was somebody who looked like him: same stubborn blond hair carefully combed and curling daintily at his neck, same wide eyes, but they were ice blue; his nose was softer, rounder, his cheeks and jaw were squarer, his brow was a different shape with the subtle artistry of kith and kin and family heredity. Was it himself, older? Or was it someone who simply looked like him? This young man was taller; he was stronger and thicker than August with tan muscle; his baby face was what made him soft and pretty.

The stranger shapeshifted again as he moved forward. Suddenly it was the Lamb before him once more. A sable-collared cloak fell from his shoulders to reveal his slight frame, this time in royal Russian grandeur: blue velvet and cream-colored taffeta, elaborate silver, split waistcoat, matching breeches and pearls and shining gems.

The Lamb's face seemed too young and untainted to evince its true wizened mystery. But it was the Lamb, no doubt, and August lifted his hand but didn't remember telling it to move. He watched as both their hands met in the air between them, fingertips brushing, then palms, fingers lacing.

The Lamb's mouth unhinged and he dove for August's neck. In a split second, he was no longer the Lamb but Theo, tall Theo hunched over August's shoulder. August cried out. He felt the pull of blood as Theo drank from him, felt it with all the realness, sensations gathered from memory. Heart thudding rapidly, life swirled in the connection between them. But August felt it from a distance, detached and numb. He relaxed in Theo's arms, arching his back, offering more, more—

And then he fell. Theo's arms slipped away and the air tickled August's skin as he fell down into the satin-lined casket out from which the dream people had crawled in the first place. The cries of the men and women were deafening now, no longer atrocious but a chorus of miserable funereal voices coming together in perfect harmony for this elegy August did not know.

August stared up at Theo, standing above him with the tendrils of the fog pale and cold around him. It was the vampire Theo, white and gaunt, eyes sharp and unsympathetic, crazed, inhuman, fangs out, and the blood a burst of violent red all over the lower half of his face.

The men and women began to lower the coffin into the ground. They poured flowers down over him. August couldn't move. Panic was raw in every nerve but he couldn't move. He could only stare and breathe, gawk up at Theo as Theo watched them lower him into the earth. He felt betrayed. He was going to be buried alive. He wasn't dead, please, he wasn't dead. Or was this what death felt like? No control over his body? Could his soul crawl forth, or was it stuck behind his eyes forever?

Suddenly it was black, all black.

There was nothing.

All right, there was silence, and the slow, slow beating of his heart. It was there but not there. The ghost of a heart.

August opened his eyes.

A sharp pain in his head greeted him, a stab of sensory overload that made everything tingle briefly—like rising too quickly after a night of drinking. And then just as suddenly, the pain faded. August stared up at the coffered ceiling of the Sanctuary with easy fascination. Had it always been that color? He was ravenous. It shook deep in his very core, a hunger that twisted in the pit of his chest. He remembered absently he'd missed supper. Hazel might be worried. The ceiling was captivating. He could see the wear and tear on the wood and plaster. He could see the cobwebs in the far corner. He could hear fire popping on wicks, he could smell melting wax and old metal and the residual stench of gore, and he really needed to eat something before he got irritable—

August sat up. He was not alone in the Sanctuary. He looked over to his right; the Alpha and Theo were the only ones still in the secret room with him. Theo stood like a guard at the doors. Alistair sat on one of the old stiff-backed chairs, one leg crossed over the other and cheek propped on his hand.

"Good morning," Alistair greeted.

"It's not morning," August cut back.

He kept getting distracted by the way he could see the sheen of the Alpha's hair, the lines of his face, the wrinkle in his collar. And Theo behind him in the same extraordinary detail. Where were the shadows? This room had been darker before. Was he a vampire? August didn't know. Theo's eyes pierced into him with a covetous gleam, not very secret in the usual mask of nonchalance he wore outside private moments, allowing through silent, well-composed intrigue as if he couldn't believe what had happened or what he thought of it all yet.

There was a little quiver of adoration and loyalty in the pit of August's chest—Theo made him. *Theo made him.* Theo turned him.

"Actually it *is*." Alistair nodded, eyes hooded. "It is just after six in the morning, the first of January in the year 1889."

August recoiled in brief, instinctive horror he couldn't place immediately as any familiar fear. Then he relaxed, brow knotting. "But don't you need to sleep?"

"We all need to sleep," Alistair said. Behind him at the door, Theo was stony faced, but his eyes were filled with longing. Alistair smiled again, gently this time. He gestured casually. "But you see, we had to wait until your death was over. We couldn't just leave you here, after all."

August looked around. He was in a polished casket, sitting before the unlit fireplace in the Sanctuary. He was dressed in the clothes he'd been given earlier in the night, the blood gone from his throat. Stunned, August looked at his wrist and found the scars from the vampires' mouths nearly faded already. He looked around more, inspecting everything. When had they gotten this coffin? From where?

"How do you feel?" Alistair asked, fingers laced in his lap.

August looked at him, face blank and eyes wide in frenzied curiosity. "I feel fine," he breathed, wondering whether he was supposed to feel something else.

"You'll find that your senses have sharpened." Alistair settled farther into his chair. Theo was motionless. August was almost distracted by him, the strange, livid longing with which he stared. Alistair's voice carried on: "You might be able to see things more clearly, especially so in darkness when you wouldn't have been able to before; you might be able to hear things more clearly, to smell things more clearly, to understand, sense, and manipulate feelings. These things are a vampire's nature. Now truly, August, how do you feel?"

"I'm hungry," August whispered, feeling rather shy about it. But the hunger cramped in his chest. It was something he couldn't explain, something sudden and innate. He was cold with it. He was desperate with it. He didn't truly feel it so much as he knew it, maybe something like a drunkard itching for the succoring kiss of liquor.

Alistair laughed. The sound tickled August's ears, giving him chills. Theo perked up and issued a quick, impassive smile.

"Of course you are," Alistair purred, one of the moments where the formerly sadistic look in his eyes seemed but the shadow of a suspicion. "Come, then. Get up. You may have a little bit of the Baron's Remedy, but that's it for the night. Then we rest for the day. Let's hurry, sirs. We have less than an hour before dawn."

THE SKY was lightening, but the curtains were drawn on all the windows.

Alistair entrusted August to Theo's guidance after giving him what they called the Baron's Remedy, cool rationed blood that had been stored somehow like wine. The flavor was bitter and strong on his tongue. It rolled into the hunger and soothed it immediately, warmed him from the inside out. He could feel it pulsing through him. It made him drowsy. He no longer felt horror at the idea of drinking blood. It felt natural now, the fear of it irrational and paltry, and it was an urge as instinctive to him as to breathe.

Fate's design.

His ears rang. August wanted more, but he was only allowed one glass of the Remedy.

Theo guided him along to his bedroom. August was full of amazement. He took one of Theo's hands and followed, feeling Theo's fingers with all the new precision of his senses. Oh, smooth, cool, perfect. They fit with his as if they were made for only that. And the sounds of all the little clocks, and the light gleaming on each chess piece, the smell of the dying fire and the flickering candles—

August was utterly transfixed by the candles, staring into them, watching the glistening beads of wax slowly, slowly roll down the candles' sides. But Theo pulled him away from all the scattered details of his room before he could become too engrossed, gently tugging him by the waist, folding down against him until his nose nudged just behind his ear.

"Please come to bed now," Theo breathed down his neck. "You can explore later. I promise."

Obediently August lay down to sleep. Not in a coffin and not in a grave, but in a comfortable, sturdy oak bed with high headboard and hand-carved posts, beckoning pillows and bedding. The blankets were bliss on his body, like summer rain. Theo's body was cool consolation beside him, his skin like silk, and August realized then as his limbs relaxed that he was immensely exhausted.

Many had already awoken for the day as the sun emerged from the horizon over cold London, and August fell asleep.

THE CURTAINS were tied open in Theo's room, letting in the early evening shadow when August stirred.

When he opened his eyes, he didn't feel totally different. But it was true. He was different. Undead. *Immortal.*

He understood it as if the change had always been there; it was innate knowledge now, instinct, common sense.

He would drink blood for sustenance. He would avoid the sun. He would be able to communicate wordlessly if he thought strongly enough.

Farewell death, disease, finality.

These things were clear and cold in August's mind, beneath his skin. His heart beat slowly as his breaths came. He looked up at the ceiling in Theo's room, and he realized Theo was already awake and dressed, sitting in front of the fire with a book.

For a moment August pretended he forgot what had happened; he waved at Theo from his bed and Theo waved back. Everything, he saw everything, so spectacularly clear—Theo's loose, wavy hair, his widow's peak and narrow nose, elegant brow, strong shoulders under the velvet lapels of an old frock coat, pinstriped trousers on legs kicked up on a footstool.

August saw his own reflection in the looking glass near the mantle, and the make-believe drained away quickly. Everything had happened so fast. Was there really a change in him? Yes, there was. It was there, subtly, in his face and his appearance. He was not human anymore. It was as if he'd emerged from a chrysalis or shed his skin; the same young blond man, but somehow more beautiful. Pale, so pale, the soft brown of his eyes so arresting in his lily white face. He watched his reflection as he touched his cheeks absently. Why, he couldn't be a vampire, he was just a dead man—

"Good morning," he said to Theo.

Theo smiled faintly. "It's not morning," he murmured obligingly. "You'd better get dressed. In a few hours is the banquet for your induction."

August dressed. He wandered around Theo's room examining all the creases on the books, the light glinting off the chess pieces, pressing his ear to timepieces and taking note of the way they each ticked. Theo followed along patiently. He seemed totally aware of a fledgling's nascent rapture with the world as it came to them fresh and detailed.

August listened. He breathed just to feel the new ease and grace of it. He felt the hunger again. The sensation came rapidly and briefly, like a muscle cramp or the pinch of rupture, clammy like panic or a strong impulse—but the whole spasm faded quickly into a sore stomach. August breathed through it, brow knotted.

There would be a banquet, after all, Theo had said.

A banquet, for him? For his *induction*. A banquet indeed.

Alphonse's musician friends returned, oblivious perhaps, foolish, or wickedly aware.

They stood before the fireplace in the dining room with their strings, and the music they played tickled August's ears just as all the sights tickled his eyes, the smells tickled his nose, the touches tickled his nerves. Hardwood wainscoting, carefully painted wallpaper, modest chandelier, the gleaming urns atop the mantle and the timepiece with the golden face. The atmosphere had all the comfortable grandeur of a private party—the casual music, the popping fire, the lack of true formalities as they gathered around the long dining table. Perfectly gothic, the setting was, as this was a life that embraced death wholly more than life before ever had.

The banquet, Theo had said, *for your induction.*

Fat, dripping candles sat in old hollowed-out skulls along the dining room table, but they did not scare August. They were almost nostalgic to something deep inside him, stirring his soul with their majestic chill.

August sat at the foot of the table as he had on Christmas, hands folded in his lap. Everything was bright and sharp, and so fresh to his mind. He liked this daze. His new senses overwhelmed him one moment and mesmerized him the next. It was hard to concentrate—and blanketed in such wonderment, he felt a little awkward, a bit stupefied by everything, but restive with the urge to explore. It was an exhilarating state of existence, lusciously bewildered, feeling so awake and full of life instead of the sick exhaustion of the past long few months.

Up and down the walnut table with him they'd gathered, the entire coven, and August shuddered with the significance again as he had in that pivotal, primal moment of turning in the Sanctuary.

The hierarchy was obvious. In the same order August had been aware of since the start, they sat—Alistair, the Alpha, at the head of the table, hair tied back and smiling the cordial smile that distracted from the naturally sadistic gleam in his eyes; Pearle, Owen, reproachful Ishmael, and Anastasia down his right-hand side; Theo, Laurel, and Alphonse on his left. And August was their dim-witted fledgling.

The doors to the kitchen flew open; servants filed in with dishes. With them came the exquisite smell of blood. The hunger twisted viciously inside him, like something alive.

Alistair stood and peered down the length of the table regally, the servants halting in a line behind him as he gestured to the musicians to quiet, and seized the silence that filled the dining room upon his command.

Alistair smiled thinly. "My brothers and sister," he announced in that alluring baritone of his, "I would have you all remember the reason we've been granted this repast tonight. Chosen and approved of by the Lamb, our twenty-ninth sacrifice has been welcomed into our coven as kin. This banquet is in honor of our ninth member and present Omega, the young Mr. August Prescott. Welcome, August."

Alistair smiled down the table at August, lifting his glass although the wine had not yet been poured. Like members of a dinner party and not of this ceremonial rite, the other seven vampires lifted their empty glasses in the toast.

From August's left Anastasia's stare pierced into him, as if she found him wholly more attractive now that he was Undead. To his right Theo sat with all his usual decorum, but his chin was high and his eyes were bright. With relief maybe? Pride? August smiled between the two of them, blushing at the murmurs of welcome that rippled through them all, some casual and some formal. Surely they weren't all as pleased by his initiation as Theo was.

Alistair gestured for August to stand.

August obeyed. Their eyes were heavy on him. He held the Alpha's stare, feeling a flattered blush creep up into his face.

Alistair made the sign of the cross upside down. August shivered with the memory, but followed suit.

"For the life of the flesh is in the blood: and I have given it to you upon the altar to make an atonement for your souls, for it is the blood that maketh an atonement for the soul!" Alistair's eyes sparked, glimmering not really with something peaceful and warm, but with unholy veneration. August bristled. Alistair went on, although he was certainly aware of the brief pinched look on August's face. "The speaking of that verse is your redemption, August. Do not speak it lightly. We are not *entirely* godless creatures, after all."

August was stunned for a moment. The words struck something deep in his heart, some secret place where the memories and the sensations of being human were still utterly familiar—and Alistair so swiftly and astutely pierced into it with those words, intentionally stirring the corners of faith and religion August had buried there.

Something naïve fluttered in his throat—oh, his nervous heart?—something totally weak and fragile and emotional, the echo of a spiritual love and the trust in it. It was as hard to see and easy to feel as a spider's web. August thought it was very human. Was it wrong to think in terms of vampire versus human? Or would there be a time when he stopped feeling so mortal? And then abruptly, with that same nostalgic, sorrowful flutter in his throat, August remembered the way he'd felt in the Sanctuary before. So aware of a higher power, so aware he was below it, and it occurred to him finally that vampires, being Undead, revered the Lord because they were allowed this diabolical grace, this realm between living and deceased. Or was that, perhaps, wishful thinking? Oh, like the vampire atop the Dashwood Mausoleum—*To he who has been elected according to the choice of Christ, the Most Holy Lamb, blessed and sanctified by the blood of the Spirit—in sacrament and in honor, for salvation through sin!* It was true, wasn't it? The covenant was really that simple.

The thoughts fell silent as August's conviction settled. He smiled humbly beneath the force of all their clear critical stares. Did they know his relief? Did they know he understood that this was fate's design?

Certainly they did. His voice was smooth in the dining room, above the sound of the fire and the silent hum of discomfiture coming from the line of servants who belonged to this cult of vampires.

"For the life of the flesh is in the blood: and I have given it to you upon the altar to make an atonement for your souls, for it is the blood that maketh an atonement for the soul," August recited. He moved his hand to make the sign of the cross, inverted. He felt a strange sense of comfort and release, of sacrament and brotherhood. The Alpha's eyes danced.

And to everyone's relief, Alistair said, with rather playful blasphemy, "Amen. All right! Let us feast!"

August sat down, pleasantly overcome. The hunger came again, with a vengeance, and August understood what it must have been like for the others while he was an oblivious human sacrifice.

The servants circled around the walnut table. Sound burst in the dining room as candlelight flickered above the skulls with the vibrations. Voices, a gentle chaos as the music began again before the fire. The casual feel of it was still a little foreign to August, but he would adjust to it. He was a member of their elegant immortal party now, which made him shy in a second and totally different way.

The first course was set down before him. August looked at it, and for a brief shocking instant, there was a ruddy pool of blood, coagulating already in the thin china. But no, not blood—potage, soup, and it smelled so fine.

A little rational voice in the back of his mind tittered and giggled and said, *You know what you saw first is the truth, but you'd rather charm yourself to cover it up? How terribly delightful!*

The servants poured wine. The taste of it was bitter at first, burning his tongue, but it hit his gut and exploded in sweet warmth. August's skin crawled with it. The smells were divine.

Four courses of blood and raw meat, carefully carved organs and the scarlet liquor of life they contained, and August was not aghast in the least. The hunger took over, casting out all qualms and shock. The taste was sweet and thick. It made August's heart pound. The feeling swelled in his stomach and branched out into every inch of his being, distilling itself with the blood already inside him. His muscles tingled. He buzzed, indulgent. It was the same decadent pacification and inebriation that the Baron's Remedy had given him early in the morning, but somehow better. August was dizzy with it. It warmed him from inside like fire; it satisfied something deep within; it temporarily satiated the miserable aching hunger. August felt his fangs slip out a few times accidentally. He laughed about it, embarrassed, with Theo next to him, as red-lipped as he.

The musicians played Schubert, and the vampires were rowdy and red faced.

Anastasia started the dancing with Alistair, little satin-slippered feet showing now and again as her gown swirled about her legs. There was the hint of a smile on Alistair's face and a slightly human glitter to his eyes. Yes, all of them—looking a little more mortal after gorging themselves on the gory celebration they were blessed with. The adjustment period to come would be dreadful after such a banquet.

Around the open area of the dining room, Alistair and Anastasia turned and dipped, their careful, elegant steps slightly off-kilter as the abundance of blood swam through their systems. But it was sophisticated in its own way, and when their steps ended together, Owen swooped in and took Anastasia by the waist, a silent request for a dance or two of his own.

Clapping, laughter—like drunken friends but somehow more graceful. Anastasia tripped once and Theo caught her, spun her out, spun her back in, and gave her a kiss on the mouth as the music crescendoed.

The others hollered about this, heckles and laughter, their mirth hardly reminiscent of grim, ghastly vampires as August waltzed with Anastasia next. Anastasia's warm hand was on his shoulder and in his own; she grinned at him, not unladylike, Caesar leaves and pearls like a crown on her temple. *Imagine being the only female in the coven.* Anastasia's eyes glinted as she stooped down and pressed kisses to both sides of his mouth. *Unfair,* August thought, but it was jumbled in the rush and the intoxication, the dumbfounding inundation of fresh blood in him. He kissed her back on the mouth as Theo had, feeling her velvety lips and savoring the aftertaste of blood and tepid skin.

The sense of subservience, the inferiority he'd felt as their sacrifice, reformed into the distribution of authority. The eerie way their presences had infiltrated a room when he was human now became something of a hum in the back of his mind, just a simple knowledge of potency, that they were there, and an occasional shiver when a powerful glance was sent his direction or a thought got out of hand and phantom-touched everything around it like heat. Their communion in the dining room caressed August's senses like a sound that had no sound. It was simply there, and he felt it.

Anastasia laughed, the laugh of a woman free of all chains in the world, a powerful and independent woman. She spun August out of her grasp and he stumbled back a few steps, bumping into Laurel. Laurel, auburn hair and hooded, contented eyes, stared down at August as if uncertain of how he'd fallen into his arms. But then he smiled, and Laurel smiling was a breathtaking rarity, and August understood a little how Hazel could love him.

"You'd better go see her tonight," August reprimanded. "You'd better go see her because she's probably very lonely and sad…."

Owen tapped his foot to the music and the Alpha rested his head on his fingers, smiling a smile quite unlike all the other secretive ones he'd ever worn. Ishmael, savagely stubborn, stood with his arms crossed in the corner farthest from all the activity, as if averse to anything that might make him seem less monstrous.

Pearle took his turn with Anastasia, as disheveled as she was now from the dancing. They urged the musicians to pick a faster tempo because nobody was in the mood for something drab and dreary.

And this was when they were at their simplest, August thought. This was when all the layers of ugliness were stripped away, allowing frivolity and warmth and careless romps, kisses and caressing hands between them all because as vampires, sensuality was their nature. And he had come so far, hadn't he?

He was not human anymore either, and the Lamb would have never allowed him to remain mortal, and August wanted to know why. He would ask; he knew he would. But right now he wanted to explore the world anew again and nothing else.

"You wear your heart on your sleeve," Theo said, coming closer to August's left and putting an arm around his waist. August knew what he meant; he wasn't very good at keeping his thoughts to himself yet. He looked up at Theo, catching for the first time the very subtle elliptical shape to his pupils. So subtle it was nearly imperceptible—what had seemed an illusion before was actually quite consistent.

August took a deep breath, savoring the way it felt in his chest. "Then I must look exceedingly happy."

"You do."

Behind the shouts and laughter as Anastasia and Alphonse attempted the Barynya dance at Owen's instruction, August could hear the little pocket watch ticking away daintily in Theo's waistcoat. Alistair joined them and performed some Cossack knee bends so flawlessly Alphonse promptly gave up, while Anastasia hoisted up her gown and emulated the moves with the talent and grace of a vampire, and a wholly indecent showing of her thin legs. Pearle and Alphonse roared with applause.

"I'm surprised you're not terrified," Theo said plainly.

August looked at him, perplexed. "Of what?"

Theo shrugged as if to say, *You know what I mean.* He flicked his eyes over to meet August's, green irises alive with his thoughts and mouth perked in an uncertain smile. "Of being what you now are," he replied slowly below his breath. His eyes searched for a moment before finally focusing on August's, subdued and grim but evocative. "A leech, a parasite, a monster, a vampire. That's what you are now, August."

August knotted his brow. He didn't quite know what to say at first, feeling a little patronized. "I know what I am now," he insisted gently, peering up at Theo—elegant, dark-eyed Theo. "I am totally aware of it."

"The charm," Theo sighed. "It's always so invigorating at first. But one night soon, you're going to wake up and be appalled at yourself."

August felt his sharp frown. "I know this isn't a dream, Theo," he edged out, slow and deliberate. "I know this is not something that will just go away. I understand that this is eternity now. Please don't think I simply wanted an escape. I wanted to be this. I *want* to be this."

Theo was quiet for a moment, with a very subtle crease in his brow and his mouth open as if he meant to speak but didn't know what to say, his eyes simultaneously incensed and inquisitive. He looked at August wordlessly for a moment, something moving in his gaze that he hid from August's now-keener senses; he took a short breath, and then his flushed features softened a little, almost into a smile.

"I'll have to get used to your graduation to Omega," Theo murmured, a look of thought on his face as the others went on wild and unrefined as any self-respecting men and women ever had been behind closed doors. Anastasia showing too much skin; Pearle kissing her over and over; Ishmael at the table like a grumpy child; Alphonse doubled over in laughter; the musicians and the servants involved but uninvolved.

"So will I," August confessed.

Theo sought out his eyes again, digging his fingers gently into August's arm to get his attention back. He said, "I can see the change in you. Oh, can I see it, and it's thrilling and it's alarming all at once. I'm sorry, August, but it's just so startling still. Yet I love it. I adore it. Don't think that I loathe it, please don't. It's simply so different to look at you and know you're a vampire now—the change is there, distinctly, but so discreet—and I like it, August. I do."

Suddenly the look of brooding thought left Theo's face. He smiled. It was very well a smirk, lashes lowered on a real gentleman's sort of lust.

"I approve," he whispered. It was the good old banter, the seductive wit August so loved.

He blushed hotly below Theo's eyes, feeling the desire creep up through every inch of him from a shivering knot of it at the base of his spine. He was flustered suddenly to think Theo's blood was in him. It was Theo's blood that had tethered him to the earth as an immortal. It was Theo, his maker and his savior, and that was refreshing and salacious in so many profound ways—ways of the soul, ways of the body, ways of the heart.

Out like bumbling thieves together, leading each other along, through the vestibule and around the antiquated furnishings, up the dark staircase. They left the party.

In Theo's bedroom with clocks and chairs and chess pieces, there was the fragrance of blood and old books under the usual, comfortable scents of sweet wax and a dying fire.

Theo moved his hands down August's back, rocking their hips together in a groping embrace. August clung, rolling his head to one shoulder. The sensory delight was like the first orgasm all over again.

"You will never age, you will never be sick, you will never die," Theo murmured as August explored every inch of him with new, curious fingers. Stripped him of his waistcoat, plucked at his buttons, kissed the pale flesh over his quiet heart. "Oh, you will feel hunger such as you think you can't control—but you will learn to. And this is your life now...."

"Come on, come on, I want you!" August groaned back.

"Welcome to the parade of sacrament and blood," Theo whispered against the corner of his mouth, and ravenous for love, August kissed him hard, biting, bruising, moaning, begging for the tangle of their bodies as one and the same.

Hot and alive from the bloody banquet, they collided in a feverish, reckless passion, ripping at clothing, exploring each other's bodies with new careful hands, and Theo schooled August in the pleasures of sex for a vampire.

"It's really all the same, I promise," Theo coaxed, not that August needed any coaxing. He was full of blood and full of lust and hopefully this wouldn't happen every time—this reckless need for physical pleasure that blossomed up in him the instant fresh blood hit his belly—but tonight it was perfect.

"I think," Theo added, as if he couldn't actually remember whether it was the same or not. "It's just that having just fed, your body will actually wake up, so to speak, to the deed...."

Oh, August loved it when Theo talked, but right now he just wanted him to hush up and kiss him hard. And it was true—it was really all the same, in essence, but wanton pleasures like the way sighs and gasps tasted on his tongue now, the new intensity of the way Theo trailed his fingertips up his arm, every little detail from the graze of Theo's fanged teeth on his naked chest to the tickle of Theo's eyelashes... These things were all utterly precious and dazzling to his senses. The hair on his arms stood on end. He could smell the blood in Theo. He could feel its swollen heat inside him, deep. Because Theo was inside him, like he'd been inside him before. August could feel the swollen heat of the blood inside *himself* and it was torturous. He couldn't keep his eyeteeth from elongating; they just kept slipping in and out on their own. Theo laughed at him, kindly. August's hips twitched and his sex throbbed impatiently.

It was like being drunk, every sensation at once heightened and yet purified, and there was some new twist in the nature of the act that made it seem carnal and deliciously powerful in a way August had never felt before. *Urges.* Everything was an *urge*, an obsession, a drive. It was like feeding. Well, he hadn't *fed* on someone yet—except for

Theo, in the Sanctuary—but he knew it was the same dizzy bliss. The relief, the satisfaction, the need. He just knew it.

FLAMES DANCED in all the little baroque sticks as Theo dozed in his bed of dark blankets, sleeping naked, and August stood at the window and peeked around the thick curtains. With his new eyes he could see the faint map of stars beyond the layer of London smog.

Welcome to the parade of sacrament and blood, Theo had said earlier.

August looked drowsily over his shoulder at Theo, who was sprawled like a languorous king in his sheets and coverlets. He'd shown August the secret of guzzling wine after a bloody climax so as not to feel too weakened by the loss of sustenance—and *that* had been both shocking and fascinating, the gush of red between Theo's fingers as Theo's hand moved swift and skilled between August's legs.

Ah, he wanted it again; he wanted Theo's kisses raining down on his naked skin, the roll of his body.

But this wouldn't be the last time, of course. This was, actually, something like the first time all over again.

August turned, crouching next to the fire to feel it on his open palms. He wandered around the room, pulling out a book here and there to look through, finding with childish joy he could read languages he hadn't been able to before. How was that even possible? How had he ever been satisfied by mortality if this was what immortality meant?

At a quarter to seven, Theo held up the timepiece closest to his bed to remind August sunrise was near. Seventeen other clocks around the room ticked and tocked. August smiled shyly and scampered around the room, blowing out all the candles and crawling into the big oak bed as the darkness fell. Getting comfortable, he felt around for Theo, although he didn't truly have to. The sliver of light below the curtains began to pale just a bit, but the vampires were asleep before daybreak.

CHAPTER TWENTY-TWO

SOMEHOW ISHMAEL was still a constant beacon of undisguised loathing.

Once or twice August turned a corner in the house and saw him at the other end of the hall—through a doorway—across the room—and August jumped at first, because he was not astute enough to track their presences yet, and Ishmael glared at him coldly before turning and leaving, dismissing the entire moment.

It didn't feel as if too much had changed, actually. It was as if they'd always known he'd become one of them, and the shifts in the coven's attitudes toward him were not very drastic.

"I do believe at times I miss the taste of your blood, my man," Alistair told him one night after rationed Baron's Remedy, and August blushed.

Alistair patted August's shoulder and motioned for him to come into the library to sit, and before the fire there, he taught August the Rules of the Coven, many of which August had heard months before from Theo's mouth. Did he swear to honor them, Alistair wondered? He did, August promised; oh, of course he did. Swearing as much required a blood oath—a cutting of the finger and stamping a bloody fingerprint to a page that seemed to contain the fingerprint of each coven member, some sort of recordkeeping or like a personal wax seal—which seemed sort of silly and underwhelming for all the mystery of this new Undead world. Yet at the same time, when the blood beaded at the tip of his finger after Alistair cut it, an unfamiliar almost primitive panic surged in August. Instinct screamed, *Don't lose a drop of blood!* But it was just a drop, or two.

"Pardon me, sir, but...." August frowned at Alistair, not disrespectfully. "Why tell me the rules now when I know half of them already?"

Alistair nodded wearily like just such a question was what he expected of August. "It's part of your 'contract'—yes, I suppose that word suffices—part of your entry into the coven. Knowing the rules doesn't mean you'll follow them. Swearing an oath to follow them means I have every right to turn you in to the Lamb should you willingly break them." He nodded again, as though just remembering something. "The Lamb will visit soon anyway, to mark you as Number Nine."

The Lamb, coming to visit the Berkeley Square house! August was sort of excited about that. Nervous—but thrilled, nonetheless. He tried not to question just exactly why.

He went up to the attic, the taste of the Baron's Remedy still strong in his mouth. The house was strangely silent save for the constant movement of the maids, and August heard every creak of the floorboards as he drifted up to the door so familiar to him, with its crystal knob and his distorted reflection in it—

The door was open a few inches. August opened it, listening to the hinges whine, feeling cold because the last time he'd been in the attic was when Theo came to take him down to the Sanctuary on the eve of the new year.

There was the attic. Dusty windows, plain bed, a new Argand lamp swelling with light—the armchair, the stack of books, the smoking jacket, and the chamber pot—

And Hazel making the bed up, the books and the robe next to the door as if she were about to remove them from the room. At August's approach her movements slowed. She looked up. But not at August.

She looked straight ahead, at the southern window, her thin white fingers splayed on the coverlets she smoothed down, her lace cap crooked, her skirts swishing against her calves. In all the black, her face was like the sad little flame of a candle, her gray eyes striking.

Her beauty was nostalgic to August. It made his heart swell and then ache, terribly, guiltily. He stood in the doorway, in the waistcoat she'd helped him unwrap nights before. He stared at her, unable to do much else.

Slowly, gravely, Hazel moved her eyes over to meet August's. Bittersweet—that was how the breath tasted that wavered on August's lips as he looked at her. He wanted to say, "I love you, Hazel, thank you for everything, I didn't leave you, I promise, I'm still here." Or anything else of the sort. But he said nothing.

Looking at her now, August could see every crack he'd never been able to catch before in her mask of smiles. He could see the weariness in her, the loneliness, the struggle. She was beautiful and tragic. *Witch Hazel*. Such a horrible nickname.

The silence spun out. Hazel stared at him mutely. August felt more deplorable the longer the quiet stretched. He needed a purpose to be there or he might break.

She hated him. He could tell. She felt betrayed, she hated him—no, he knew better than that. She was lower than him now. That was all.

Swallowing around a catch in his throat, August stooped down and gathered the books and smoking jacket from where they'd been placed near the door. Without looking back, he trudged downstairs again. With each step his heart ached. He heard the movement behind him as Hazel resumed her chores.

August returned the books to their rightful places: some to the room he shared with Theo, some to the library downstairs. He put the smoking jacket in Theo's wardrobe. He stood in the hall and stared at *Bentheim Castle*. He heard tears somewhere. They were Hazel's. August stalked downstairs to join Pearle and Owen in the drawing room so he couldn't hear them any longer.

THE HUNGER was awful. The closest pain August could compare it to was the old feeling of a stomach cramp, an agonizing, burning twist that felt empty and queasy at the same time, so overwhelming at times August broke out into a cold sweat. The adjustment period between sacrifices was excruciating, the Baron's Remedy every third night not nearly satisfying, and he developed a taste for wine that almost rivaled Theo's.

Time was hard to keep hold of for August.

Sometimes it was there; sometimes it was gone in the blink of an eye. It was strange not to need to relieve himself or to be bound by any other human necessities. Suddenly he had a keen sense of everything, and it was still a little startling at times.

Theo was near to him almost always, protective or maybe still astounded. It was almost as if he were afraid of August being on his own, or he felt responsible for August's comfort. August didn't mind. He didn't like the shadow of fear in Theo's eyes whenever he looked at him when they rose in the evening, but he did think the concern was quaint and endearing. August explored the house over again, examining all the wood panels and wainscoting, the velvet and hand-painted wallpapers, the old furnishings, the paintings, the cobwebs, the candles, the curtains—everything and anything he studied scrupulously. Now and then he just sat and listened to the world.

He played chess with Theo. He stowed his poetry in Theo's sideboard. He played piano with Alphonse. He went with Alistair to a tailor's on Fleet Street (perhaps the only one open past midnight) and Alistair ordered him some new suits. But at the end of the night, August just wanted to sit before the fire in one of his many upholstered chairs and talk and talk like old men. This pleased Theo endlessly, although Theo tried not to show it—smiling faintly, green eyes clear and thoughtful.

"You know, August," Theo said, high-collared waistcoat and feet kicked up on the chair in front of him, "you are not imprisoned here. You no longer require supervision. If you want to go outside, *you can go outside.*"

"I just went shopping with Alistair," August explained. But going outside for leisure was a tempting idea, August wouldn't deny that.

Tempting, but still daunting. He was uncertain. The house was all he knew. He thought once or twice about seeing people he recognized—his family, his friends, Lucius—but he knew such a thing could, would, and should not happen.

So August drifted around the house, busying himself while others were gone, wandering around when they were not, drinking wine and old blood and wishing for the taste of something better, something he hardly knew yet.

Sure enough, lo and behold, after quite a few tries without approval, a brown-haired boy of about eighteen was brought back as the new sacrifice, unconscious in Alistair's arms when he returned with snow in his hair from Trafalgar Square and its entrance to the tunnels to the Lamb's throne room.

August realized that when he'd seen Hazel in the attic room, she'd been preparing it for their new lamb.

He was both fascinated and dismayed by this, watching from the drawing-room door as Ishmael returned the coats to the closet and the Alpha took the seemingly lifeless boy upstairs to the attic.

Bloodied wrist, bloodied neck, knobby knees, and sun-kissed skin.

The hunger shuddered through August at the sight, gut knotting. He wanted to smell the young man's skin, to taste it, to break the sweet flesh and pull the blood from his throat and any other tender spots—

Behind him Pearle called, "It's nothing to watch, August, it's not a show; did we all watch when you were brought?"

Ishmael smirked from the coat closet, casting August a hideously contemptuous glance. "Don't worry," he whispered, fangs out, "you'll be well-acquainted with our thirtieth sacrifice soon enough."

It was near the end of January, the night after the new sacrifice was brought and the house full of vampires fraught with anticipation, that Theo finally coaxed August out for some fun.

"Say," Theo said, winding one of his clocks to the correct hour. "What do you think we should do this evening? A walk, just you and me?"

August smiled because there was the Theo he recognized; finally not the carefully calculated Theo of ritual and routine, but the relaxed, elegant green-eyed gentleman whose charm August had never been able to resist. The casual, handsome young man whose wit was irrefutable, and whose laugh was infectious, and whose softness was respectable, and whose sharp Undead eyes could still paralyze August now and then, love-struck and flustered.

They went out relatively early in comparison to other crepuscular excursions, strolling through Berkeley Square as the last of evening settled and the winter caged the world in a perpetual chill.

August stopped short across the street from an undertaker's shop. Mourners were leaving; there must have been funeral preparations to tend to.

Theo came up beside him, hands behind his back and a grim look of understanding on his face.

August felt the cold of the night very clearly suddenly, watching the small crowd pass before visibility was completely destroyed. There was still a gray tinge to the air, the sun gone but darkness not yet fully blanketing the world. August had become attuned to this hour.

He was struck then by a rather numbing thought. Not entirely distressing but not really comforting either. Just a little glimmer of truth, blooming in his mind:

There would be no interment for him, no cortege, no flowers, no jet black ornaments and mourning crowd while he lay never to awake again.

Perhaps his parents had held a wake for him, if they'd stopped looking for him, if they'd looked for him at all. For all he knew, they probably thought he'd run off with Lucius. Perhaps he'd missed his own funeral.

And he would not have a real one. Death's imminence was a human thing, and he was not human anymore. He was a *vampire*. Death was simply one of the prismatic colors bursting around him and dazzling his mind as he started this new way of living.

No, he was not going to die. He'd evaded destruction two or three times now. He would never die. For him now that was simply—to use the Lamb's endearing phrase—fate's design.

August looked up over his shoulder at Theo. Theo returned the stare silently, subdued green eyes and a handsome mask of politeness. But he understood. He understood precisely. And he would be there to listen if August needed to say it aloud to set the idea free.

August smiled faintly, calmed by these tacit niceties.

This was only the beginning.

EPILOGUE:
PRELUDE TO TRAGEDY

SHE WAS beautiful.

She had skin like porcelain, milky white and smooth as velvet. Her hair was long and dark, wispy strands and layers and curls. In the thin chemise, she looked delicate like a bird.

"You are in *so much trouble*" was the first thing Theo said, eyes wide.

"I cannot believe you!" was the second thing he hissed, all cold, undiluted vampire rage.

"How could I have allowed this to happen?" was his third lamentation, voice fraying and breaking into a raspy moan.

She was still breathing, which was good. But the blood staining her marred throat, flowering along the muslin of her chemise, was worrisome, and the fact that she had not been marked by the Lamb was concerning.

And August was covered in this deep scarlet blood of hers, which was the most alarming detail of all.

"I'm sorry—" August gasped, feeling like the very picture of utter misery.

Theo shook his head. He paced. He ran his fingers through his hair. He stopped and turned and looked at August as if he didn't recognize him, and he said:

"We'll have to make Alistair believe she's meant to be the new sacrifice. You can help me with that, right?"

August swallowed hard around the knot of panic in his throat.

August looked at her, unconscious, and back to Theo.

August nodded.

J. I. RADKE goes by a variety of handles and pseudonyms, most commonly "themissinglenk" and/or "white silver and mercury."

Once upon a time he wanted to be a marine biologist because of sharks. That lasted a year or so. A Seattlite at heart, Radke is currently studying English/History, Classics, and Russian Studies at USF in Tampa.

Radke writes ghost stories, romance novels, transgressive fiction, and fanfic that's sometimes all of that in one. He loves passionate speeches and tangent-studded discussions, strong coffee, rainy days, swimming in coves with bioluminescent algae, sushi and pad Thai and pizza. He specializes in Victorian-era English and Russian history, and loves folklore, classical music, parapsychology, Greek mythology, and true crime/forensics shows—to keep things brief.

E-mail: radkejisaac@yahoo.com

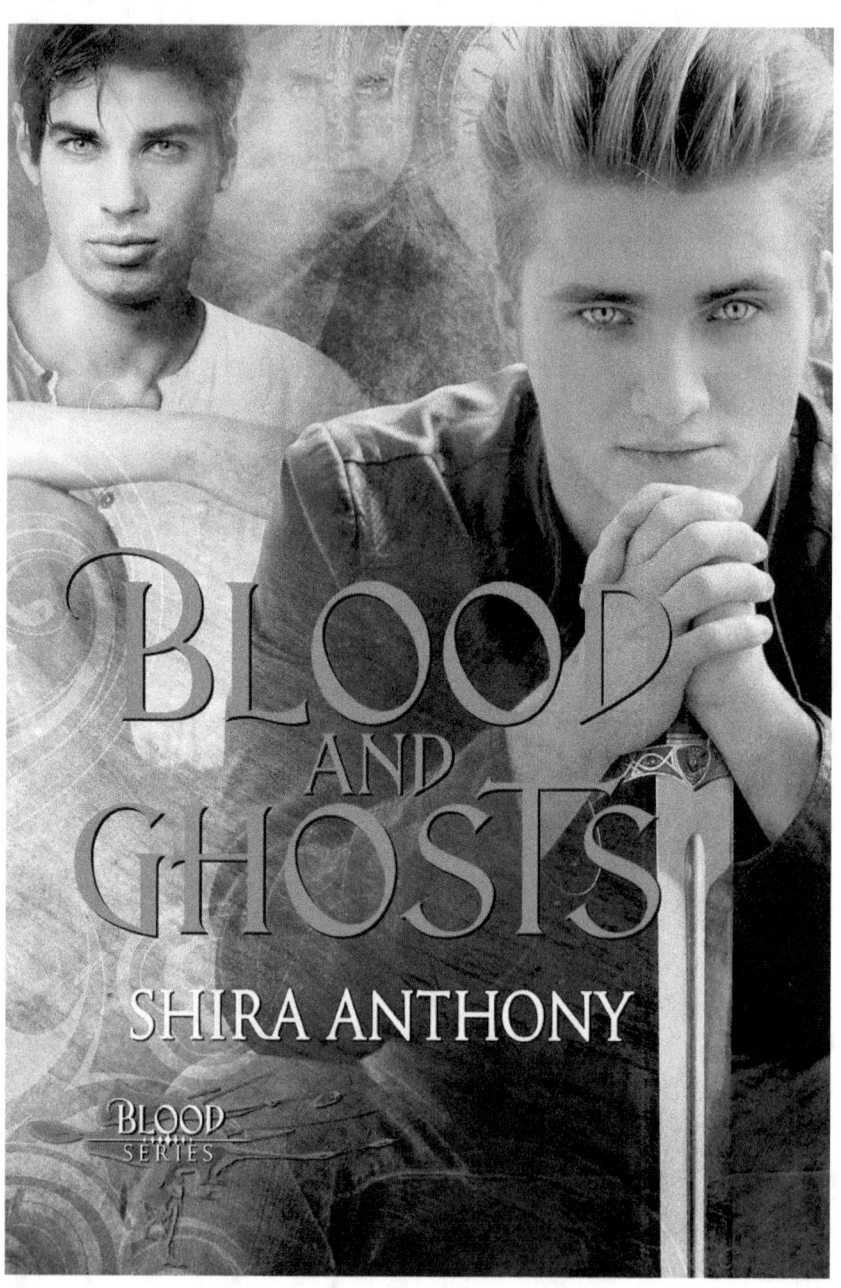

BLOOD
AND
GHOSTS

SHIRA ANTHONY

BLOOD
SERIES

www.dreamspinnerpress.com

JACOB Z. FLORES

SPELL BOUND

THE WARLOCK BROTHERS OF HAVENBRIDGE: BOOK ONE

www.dreamspinnerpress.com

THEY COME BY NIGHT

TINNEAN

www.dreamspinnerpress.com